Praise for

SUMMER'S NEVER OVER

"Eerie and propulsive. A fantastic debut that will have you racing toward its final pages."

—Jessica Goodman, *New York Times* bestselling author of *The Counselors*

"Darby Bozeman has the perfect beach read in this sinister summer camp thriller, where the paradisical woods of Dread's Cove hide not only hot bodies and cold waters but dark secrets. Like the best campfire s'mores: layered, singed by flame around the edges, a little dark, a little sweet, and a whole lot addictive."

—Ashley Winstead, *USA Today* bestselling author of *This Book Will Bury Me*

"Pulled me under like a riptide, each twist sharper and each revelation more satisfying than the last. A shimmering debut about the love that won't let you go, the friendships that change you, and the long-buried secrets that threaten to ignite it all."

—Kelsey Cox, bestselling author of *Party of Liars*

"A book that feels like August sun on your skin and spooky nights by a crackling fire, *Summer's Never Over* lives up to its nostalgic title. A must read for anyone chasing that high of a sparkling summer on the lake—or the spine-tingling chill that awakens after sundown."

—Ande Pliego, *USA Today* bestselling author of *You Are Fatally Invited*

"The perfect book to curl up with after a long day spent in the sun, when all you want to do is hide under the covers with a page-turning mystery. The atmospheric summer camp setting is a dreamy backdrop."

—Olivia Muenter, *USA Today* bestselling author of *Such a Bad Influence*

"A mesmerizing story about friendship and secrets that will keep you riveted until the very last page. Reading this book is like returning to summer camp, full of new best friends and whispered confidences. . . . Bozeman's writing succeeds on both a level of incredible tension and lyrical prose, making it sure to be your next unputdownable thriller."

—Jessica Payne, author of *Somebody Worth Killing*

"An addicting mix of family secrets, sweltering summer love, and the ever-twisting strands of female friendship. . . . Darby Bozeman skillfully weaves heart-panging romance with a gripping murder mystery."

—Catherine Walsh, author of *Holiday Romance*

"Simmering with suspense and summer camp nostalgia. Packed with emotional tension and haunting imagery."

—Miranda Smith, author of *Smile for the Cameras*

"Has everything you want in a summer thriller: a tight-knit summer camp setting, long-buried secrets, sizzling romance, and tension that crackles from every page. As intoxicating as the intense, all-consuming female friendships at its center."

—Olivia Worley, author of *So Happy Together*

SUMMER'S NEVER OVER

DARBY BOZEMAN

Berkley
New York

BERKLEY
An imprint of Penguin Random House LLC
1745 Broadway, New York, NY 10019
penguinrandomhouse.com

Book design by Alison Cnockaert

Library of Congress Cataloging-in-Publication Data

Names: Bozeman, Darby author
Title: Summer's never over / Darby Bozeman.
Description: First edition. | New York: Berkley, 2026.
Identifiers: LCCN 2025037531 (print) | LCCN 2025037532 (ebook) |
ISBN 9780593953532 trade paperback | ISBN 9780593953549 ebook
Subjects: LCSH: Camps | Grief | Friendship | LCGFT: Thrillers (Fiction) | Novels
Classification: LCC PS3602.O986 S86 2026 (print) |
LCC PS3602.O986 (ebook) | DDC 813/.6–dc23/eng/20260205
LC record available at https://lccn.loc.gov/2025037531
LC ebook record available at https://lccn.loc.gov/2025037532

First Edition: June 2026

Printed in the United States of America
1st Printing

The authorized representative in the EU for product safety and compliance is Penguin Random House Ireland, Morrison Chambers, 32 Nassau Street, Dublin D02 YH68, Ireland, https://eu-contact.penguin.ie.

For my dad and my father-in-law—the Davids. Rest easy.

SUMMER'S NEVER OVER

PROLOGUE

While the woods burn around her, she runs.

She flies down the trail, afraid to slow for even a moment. Distant screams carry through the wind, the voices of her friends muddled and distorted. She hopes they are running, too.

The campers are gone—buses took them home just this morning. But the staff is still here. People she cares about. And somewhere in her stomach, there is a single cord of guilt that snakes out behind her, toward them.

She knows she shouldn't be heading north, where the lakeshore grows rocky and too high to jump from. If she's not fast, she'll find herself trapped out here. She'll find herself dead. All of it will have been for nothing.

The fire licks at the trees behind her, and she keeps running, because she knows there is no time to waste. No time at all.

Had it really been only minutes ago that everyone had been at the beach together? Sad, yes, but safe. Knocking together Solo cups of cheap wine, drinking to the dregs of summer, saying their goodbyes a week too early. Whispering stories about the Phantom, who'd been slinking through the shadows for months. Sowing doubt and distrust and a festering, contagious fear.

A monster from that old campfire story, the kids all claimed. A monster who was waiting in the trees, scarier than any nightmare. It's not true, but it doesn't matter anymore. The damage has been done.

Everything is her fault, of course. She has been stupid. Reckless. If only she'd told someone what she'd found, if only she'd–

No. She does not have the luxury of guilt right now. The fire rages and crackles in the trees behind her, but the trail in front of her is, for the moment, clear. That must be a sign from the universe that she has to keep going.

Her muscles burn as she propels herself forward, one quick stride turning into another. Lightning bursts up ahead, and, moments later, an explosion of thunder thrums through her very heart.

The sky is on fire. Everything is on fire now.

Still, her feet move. Between the trees ahead of her, the lake sneaks into view again. But, wait–it should be on her left, not her right–

She's completely turned around; the woods feel like another planet, a place she doesn't know at all. She has to stop for a moment, just to get her bearings. Has she gone the wrong way, or is the darkness playing tricks on her? In the depths of her brain, she gropes for the memory of what to do next, but it's growing hazier by the second, jumbled around from the smoke and the heat and all that awful wine she'd slugged at the beach.

She can do this. It's not over yet. For ten more seconds, she will allow herself to catch her breath. She rests her forehead on the tree in front of her, bark snagging her hair, and starts to count down. *Ten, nine, eight–*

That's when the branch snaps behind her.

CHAPTER ONE

NOW

When I found out my mom was dead, I was scrubbing vomit off the floor of the bar bathroom. It was just before midnight, and I'd been at Dogwood House for close to seven hours. I was caked in sweat and chunky glitter, and I bore the battle scars of three beers that had been spilled on me by a bachelor party who hadn't even tipped.

My phone vibrated on the sink, and I shook my head and ignored it. Rig. As if I'd had a change of heart, in the middle of the night. But he called me again, and again, then finally texted the words he knew would get my attention: It's your mom.

I called him back, and he upended my whole life in a few words. It was sudden cardiac arrest, on a late-night walk around the lake. Her cousin—my Aunt Val—had been the one to find her. She'd been only fifty-one. Way too young to die. Healthy and strong, on the brink of the most important summer of her life.

And now, she was gone. Without any warning or preparation.

I shrieked so loudly that people started pounding on the door, threatening to break it down if I didn't open it. I just slid slowly to the floor, feeling the earth shift entirely beneath me.

"No, that can't be right, when the ambulance gets there, they'll–"

"She's gone, ladybug," Rig said, gently cutting me off. "They're already here." His voice cracked, and I closed my eyes, struck dumb by the raw shock of pain.

Rig's voice had always been comforting, and I was briefly disoriented by the wave of nostalgia that came over me. But listening to him now, as he told me that she'd been dead before she hit the ground, was the least comforted I'd ever felt. And the most alone.

The tears were flowing freely down my face, into my mouth and onto my shoes. My mother was not– She could not be– No. She'd texted me just last week, hadn't she? A picture of the new mess hall, which I hadn't responded to.

"This isn't real. Say it isn't real. Please."

"I'm sorry. I'm so, so sorry."

"What do I do?" I whispered, though I already knew. Of course I knew.

Rig sighed, the sound terrible and heavy on the other end of the line. "You come home."

I could picture him with shocking clarity, knowing he was sitting hunched over on his heinous plaid couch, the same one Chelsea and I had fallen asleep on hundreds of times as kids; somehow, it had been left untouched by the fire. He'd be running his hands through his hair, helpless, wondering how he was going to run Dread's Cove without my mom. They'd been doing it together for almost thirty years. He'd be looking out the window at the full moon, bright and ominous, seeing the sky lit up with the stars I never saw the full scope of here in Atlanta.

"Do you need me to come get you? I'll drive down there right now. Or I can send Wes."

There was a buzzing in my ears as he spoke, a numbness in

my fingers that was slowly crawling its way up my arms, over my shoulders, down my spine.

"No, it's okay." I swallowed the boulder-size lump in my throat, drummed my chewed-up fingers on the cool tile floor. "I can do it. I'll drive myself." Even though the thought of being back there—of seeing camp for the first time in five years, seeing it without her, and without Steph—was enough to steal all the breath from my lungs. Enough to consume me, yank me beneath the surface, down into the depths.

"I know what happened that summer was hard on you," Rig said, like he was reading my mind. "You've got a lot of bad memories here. But you've got good ones, too. This is where you belong. With your family."

The banging on the door was getting more insistent. I hauled myself up off the floor and opened it to a line that was ten people deep; the purple-haired woman at the front looked murderous. But when she saw my face—my bloodshot eyes, mascara and snot-smeared cheeks—she put her hands up in surrender. I barreled past her, down the dark hallway, and out into the night.

On the other side of the alley, at the front entrance of Dogwood House, a group of a dozen college girls were cackling and snapping photos of one another. I watched them for a long moment, slack-jawed, because I couldn't reconcile the fact that the world was still moving, that people were still laughing and happy, and my mother was no longer alive.

I pressed the phone closer to my ear and squeezed my eyes shut. "I'll be there," I said. "I'll be there soon. Give me a few days to get my—to get it together."

"Thank you." There was so much exhaustion in his voice. So much despair. "I know that the timing—I know that this is horrible.

All of it. But the last thing your mom would want would be for us to postpone anything. She and Chels have been working on next weekend for months, and—well, getting the Cove reopened is all she's wanted for years. I guess what I'm saying is, we're gonna need you, kid. I'm gonna need you."

I sucked in a breath, overcome with a guilt so strong that it almost knocked me over.

I had sworn up and down that I would never, ever return—that summer had taken far too much from me. But I'd taken things, too. Things I thought I'd never be able to give back.

Things I was so tired of carrying.

CHAPTER TWO

NOW

I didn't realize how suffocating it would be, to see her face everywhere.

I kept my head down as I weaved my way through the mess hall, and by the time I made it outside and onto the deck overlooking the lake, I was practically gasping for air.

My mother's photos were hanging on every surface—childhood moments on the tire swing, my grandfather hugging her beneath the hand-carved *Dread's Cove* sign, and even a few snaps of her ill-fated wedding to my dad. In all of them, she seemed caught in a laugh; the same way she'd been her whole life.

But I'd felt her eyes watching me since I'd gotten in last night. She was blaming me for waiting so long to return. For not being here when she'd died.

Welcome Back Weekend was supposed to be *fun*, allegedly, even with my mother's funeral now happening tomorrow. While I knew this was how she'd want to be remembered, I couldn't find any sort of peace. Instead, all I felt was grief and shame. And a sense of foreboding that I couldn't shake, living on my skin like a parasite.

Thankfully, there was no one else outside, and I hoped the oppressive heat would be a deterrent for anyone considering following me. As I looked out over the water, I took a sip of wine that was so big I almost choked. The off-brand Riesling was cheap, too sweet, and not at all cold enough, but I was preparing for four straight days of schmoozing and being schmoozed, so I was already on my second glass.

The sky was cotton-candy pink, right before sunset. As a kid, this was always my favorite time of day. I'd stand on this very same porch and watch the sun dip behind the mountains. Standing here tonight felt like stepping into a time machine, if only for a few moments.

Behind me, I heard the squeak of the screen door. I tensed, afraid it was another reporter, foaming at the mouth for an interview I would have to not-so-politely decline. But it was only Wes again, coming to check on me for the third time in the last hour.

"How you holding up?"

I shrugged, resigned, knowing he'd stand next to me, regardless of whether I told him I was fine. I'd already tried.

"I'd be better if Chelsea hadn't skimped on the good wine." I swished some around in my mouth and grimaced, mostly to be dramatic.

In another life, a different summer, Wes would have laughed at this. Bumped his hip into mine, pulled me close. Instead: "Go easy on her, okay? She hasn't exactly been having a good time."

My skin burned like he'd slapped me, though I guess I deserved it. Not that Chelsea had yet given me an opportunity to go easy on her; she'd been ignoring me since I'd arrived.

"Dinner's starting soon," he said after a beat of silence. I could feel him studying me. "Do you want me to get you another drink, and then you can come inside? You don't have to sit up at the front table. You can hang with me and Rig in the back. Lay low for a bit."

He was trying—far harder than I deserved from him—so I made myself look him in the eye. He stood almost two heads taller than me, like he had since his growth spurt when we were twelve. In the years I'd been away, he'd let his dark blond hair grow long, almost to his shoulders. Tonight, he wore a button-down, something I'd seen only a handful of times before. But his hair was loose and tangled, like he'd just gotten out of the water and couldn't be bothered to do anything about it.

It's you and me, we used to say to each other, back when we were together. But that wasn't true anymore. It hadn't been in a long, long time. I'd made sure of it.

"Greer?" he asked.

I flinched, realizing I'd been staring. God, it was weird, being back here. In so many ways, Dread's Cove really was stuck in a time machine—the shape of the lake, the mountains beyond, the sunset, and the squeaky doors—and all of us were, too. I didn't know what to make of it, standing halfway between the past and now.

"I'm honestly surprised you're letting anyone else in the kitchen tonight," I said, a smile that was only a little bit forced stretching across my face. If he was willing to try, then I could, too.

Wes huffed a surprised laugh at my teasing, but I could see he was pleased. "You know I allow myself one night off per summer." For a fleeting second, his grin turned bashful. "Your first official day back in five years seemed like the best excuse for it."

My fingers tightened around my wineglass, though I hoped he didn't notice. *I'm sorry*, I thought about saying. *I missed you. I hate me, too.* But I settled on: "I'll see you inside in a second, okay?"

He lingered for a long moment as I looked back out across the water. The years of silence and distance had made things strained between us, and I wondered what he knew about who I'd become. How different I was, how the past had molded me into something practically unrecognizable. I felt all of his questions, unspoken–thousands of them, built on almost two decades of friendship that had been snuffed out, practically overnight.

I wondered if he could really want that friendship back. I wondered if I was capable of giving it to him.

I was still wondering when I heard the door again, and I was back to being alone.

My solitude was short-lived. Two women I didn't know stumbled out a minute or so later; they both had telltale press badges hanging around their necks. Reporters. I wanted to run away and hide myself, though it didn't seem like they were looking for me. They stood at the other end of the deck nursing sweaty wineglasses, their heads pushed together conspiratorially.

"What's the deal with the daughter?" the one on the left asked before open-throating what was left of her drink. "A little snooty, right? So your grandfather was a senator in the seventies, give me a break."

"Well, apparently, she was friends with *the dead girl*," the other one said. "They shared a cabin."

My whole body tensed.

"Honestly, I wouldn't have wanted to come back, either. That summer was a fiasco, from start to finish," the first woman said.

"I can't imagine actually letting your child come here, after what happened. That psycho running around in the woods, luring campers away? I know everyone loved Anita, but she was clearly inept–" Just as she said the words, we locked eyes. She snapped her mouth shut almost comically fast.

I raised a hand in a two-fingered wave, not having the gall to say something mean. Though if they didn't go inside soon, I knew it was more than possible that I would retch into the lake. Or push one of them in.

They disappeared at lightning speed, mumbling something about *refills* and *our condolences.* I said nothing as I watched them go, just dug my nails so hard into the wooden railing that I thought they might get stuck that way.

I made myself take a few deep breaths, then went to find Wes and Rig inside. Tucked back by the kitchen, I might be able to avoid prying eyes, at least until my heart rate settled.

I kept a bland smile on my face and dropped down between them, letting my head fall against Rig's shoulder. He put an arm around me immediately, and I felt fractionally better.

"How you holding up?" he asked, patting me gently on the back. I bit back the urge to make a joke about how similar he and Wes had always been. Not that either of them ever took it as an offense; two men, with a twenty-five-year age difference, living the same life on the same timeline.

"I'm ready for this to be over." It was going to be a long four days. But eventually, the reporters would be gone, the memorial would be over, and I would be so distracted by my endless to-do list, by the piles of paperwork and conversations with lawyers, that I wouldn't be able to wallow in this ferocious sadness. One hour at a time. I could manage that. Then, when everyone was gone, I could figure out what the hell I was going to do with Dread's Cove and the rest of my life.

If I was going to stay or go.

Rig squeezed me tighter to him, and tears stung the backs of my eyes. *Do not cry,* I told myself. I knew the rest of the staff, and especially our donors, were politely unsure about my return. Those bitchy reporters had been right: I hadn't been back in years. In every photo that had been posted of the reconstruction over the past half decade, every social media post, I'd been absent. People had noticed.

And now that the circumstances had abruptly changed–the circumstances being that my mother's heart had stopped, and I was now solely responsible for one hundred acres of land in North Georgia–the media was champing at the bit, wondering what the famous Anita Olsen's prodigal daughter was going to do next.

"Where's Aunt Val?" I asked, desperate for a more innocuous topic.

I didn't like the way he was looking at me, searching my face for any sign that I might be about to shatter. Val had been running herself ragged all day–stepping in to help Chelsea in my mother's stead–and we'd barely had time to hug each other.

Rig scrunched his eyebrows together, scratched at his salt-and-pepper stubble. He looked more weathered than I remembered. "You know it's impossible to keep track of that woman," he said, half chastising, half amused.

A genuine smile tugged at my lips. They'd gotten married the summer before the fire, in a small ceremony down by the lake, and the memory was still one of my very favorites.

"I'm glad you're back, ladybug," he said, his voice gruff and serious again. "Val is, too. And Chels . . ."

I couldn't help the laugh I snorted as he trailed off, harsh as it sounded.

"She'll come around," he promised, squeezing my shoulder. "She might not say it, but she's happier than any of us to see you."

Bullshit, I thought. But before I had the chance to disagree with him, the lights changed, the room quieted, and Chelsea floated her way onto the stage.

The dress she wore was white and gauzy, and her hair was in her signature braids that she'd tried and failed to teach me how to do more than once when we were kids. Even I could admit that she looked the part. She seemed strong and confident and so reminiscent of my mother that my chest tightened. It was physically painful to remember how close we'd been, for so long. My oldest and greatest friend. My sister, really. But just like Wes, she felt more like a stranger to me now. And unlike Wes, she wanted absolutely fuck all to do with me this weekend.

Seeing her up there without my mom was terrible enough that my eyes finally betrayed me, and one lone tear snaked its way down my face. I brushed it away. I could not let myself break. Not yet.

Chelsea thanked everyone for our endless support of Dread's Cove as we ushered in a new generation of world changers, a new generation of kids who would get to experience the best summer camp in the world. She beamed and applauded us, saying that we were the ones who had made this weekend possible, that we were the ones who were allowing something beautiful to grow from such tragedy. How lucky these children were, thanks to the generous donations from all of us in this room tonight.

How lucky they were, at long last, to see this place restored to its former glory.

Though I clapped along with everyone else, I disagreed. Instead, I wondered if the kids were lucky at all.

If, like we were, they'd just be lucky to make it out of this summer alive.

CHAPTER THREE

NOW

All that wine I'd forced down almost made a reappearance when the screen behind Chelsea changed to a photo of my mother and me.

In it, she was standing on the dock, the lake behind her winking in the late-afternoon sun. A flame azalea was tucked behind her ear, and her cheeks were bright with color and warmth. I was just a baby, toothless and grinning.

It was jarring, how much I had grown to look like her, though there had been no brightness in my face for a long time. We had the same sun-streaked, dark blond hair that we kept at our shoulders; the same round brown eyes and the same dark freckles dusting our cheeks and chests.

It made me feel both terribly close to her and unbearably alone.

I screwed my eyes shut when the screen changed again to a picture I hadn't been expecting. One that was somehow worse.

This photo was not of my mother but of Stephanie Bennett. *The dead girl*, I thought before I could stop myself, the woman's cruel words from earlier making my teeth ache.

She was standing in front of Black Bass, the cabin the four of us had shared as counselors that summer–Steph, Chelsea, Margo, and me–arms thrown in the air, her smile effortless and face-splitting. A pair of my sunglasses perched on her head. Everything came rushing back, in a way that almost knocked me out of my chair. The memories were vivid, gut-churning, and it was all happening again.

She was burning alive again.

I wanted to jump out of my skin, flee the premises, flee the state. As Chelsea spoke, tears dripped down my face. So much for holding it together.

Having to face my mother's memorial tomorrow was going to be hard enough. But watching a slideshow of more photos of that summer was going to fully break me in half.

Only when I rubbed my fist to my eye did I turn my head and see her, sitting at one of the press tables. I wasn't sure how I'd missed that violent red lip. Her once waist-long hair was chopped into a stick-straight bob that now fell just above her shoulders, making her somehow prettier and more severe. I couldn't read her name tag from here, but it didn't matter–I already knew what it said: *Margo Pierce,* The Atlanta Times.

Even if she hadn't been clearly identified as a reporter, you could tell by looking at her that she didn't belong. It was in the way she was sitting, maybe; back ramrod straight, chin lifted so that she was perpetually looking down at you, hand gripped around her champagne flute like she might be about to use it as a weapon.

Or maybe it was in the way that her lips were pursed, in near-permanent disapproval, like she couldn't believe she'd somehow ended up here, of all the places in the world. Like she'd been kidnapped, forced against her will to drive the winding mountain pass into the dense forest, down the curvy, three-mile road that spit you out onto the shores of Lady's Lake.

Part of me wanted to stand and go to her, figure out what the hell she was doing here, but I couldn't cause a scene. Mostly I just didn't want to talk to her. I was embarrassed, even years later, that she'd never answered any of my texts or calls.

Chelsea was still speaking, the whole room hanging on her every earnest word. She was doing her gracious hostess duty of scanning the crowd, a pageant-worthy smile spread wide across her face. I wondered, with a stab of guilt, if there was anyone in the crowd who'd simply assumed *she* was Anita's daughter.

Could she have invited Margo here? It seemed impossible, knowing what they thought about each other. Knowing how broken we'd all left things.

But somehow, here Margo was, sitting at a table at the welcome dinner. There was no question that it was her, and yet my brain was having such a hard time computing it that I thought there was a distinct chance that the wine and the heat and the stress of it all had somehow collided to conjure this single, shocking hallucination.

"At Dread's Cove, we think of Stephanie Bennett fondly," came Chelsea's voice, cutting through the roaring of blood in my ears. "And although her life ended far earlier than it should have, I know, without a shadow of a doubt, that she's smiling down on all of us. That she, like Anita, would be nothing but proud to see this place finally open its doors again."

It made me nauseous, hearing her speak about Steph that way. I remembered all the things she'd said about Steph—and about me—the night she'd died.

"And that's what this weekend is all about. An opportunity for us to celebrate the resilience of Dread's Cove. I can't begin to tell you how grateful we are to see so many of you back here in the mess hall tonight. There was a time when we didn't think this would be possible."

I scanned the room, desperate to lock eyes with someone, to point out Margo and make sure I wasn't imagining things. Someone else had to see her, to confirm her existence.

My gaze snagged on Trevor Townsend, and my heart bumped painfully up against my rib cage. I could see only the back of his head, but I knew instinctively that it was him. I would be able to find him in any room, in any universe, try as I might to avoid him entirely. My hands flexed, some long-dormant part of me aching to run my hands through his hair–like Wes, he'd grown it out, and it was longer than I'd ever seen it. It was such an unwelcome, distracting urge that I cracked my neck looking away, desperate to banish any more thoughts of him.

But God, I still missed him so much that I wanted to throw myself into the lake. I wanted to kiss him. I wanted to hold him and punch him and make him cry like he'd made me cry.

The sound of a chair scraping backward caught my attention, but I didn't need to look to know it was Margo. Fleeing outside, likely overwhelmed by the influx of memories. She must have had nightmares about that night, too, though I'd never been able to ask her.

I fought the urge to go after her. I didn't even know what I would say. Worse, I didn't know what she would.

No, my official stance on Margo Pierce for the rest of this weekend would be to stay out of her way and hope she stayed out of mine. Hope that whatever story she was planning to write for the *Times* was simple, straightforward, and didn't call us all *FUCKING MURDERERS*, like she had the morning after the fire.

It's not that I hadn't fantasized about seeing her again. I had. I knew we were both living in the city, and not surprisingly, she was far more successful than me. Not writing novels yet, like she used to talk about, but interviewing all of Atlanta's best and brightest for the *Times*.

Sometimes, I'd imagine running into her while walking the Beltline, or standing in line at a coffee shop. Or maybe she'd even come into Dogwood House and ask me to make her a drink before we both recognized each other.

We'd pause, then smile, embrace. I'd say I was sorry, and so would she. We'd pledge to start fresh and move forward. To be the friends we might have been, if the circumstances had been different.

We'd forget everything that happened that summer. Everything we became. All the wonderful and wicked ways we were willing to change and bend and break for Steph Bennett.

And the ways we were both still haunted by her, even now.

CHAPTER FOUR

THEN

Fifty-Two Days Before the Fire

I found my mother in her office, head in her hands.

We were only a few days away from the first day of camp. Usually around this time, she was brimming with a nervous, excited energy. I almost never saw her looking so defeated.

"Mom?" I asked, my heart rate accelerating painfully. "What happened? Is Dad–"

"No, no, nothing like that," she said quickly, shaking her head before I could really panic. "I'm sorry. Everything's fine. But there's a bit of a situation. I just got off the phone with Taylor. She and Madison have mono, of all things. They're both out for the summer. Which means I've got no counselor for Smallmouth." She rubbed the bridge of her nose, as if she were warding off a migraine.

I tried not to grimace, but it was hard. She was right; this would be a problem. I sat down in front of her desk and reached out to squeeze her hand.

"We'll figure this out," I promised. "We've had last-minute changes before. We can do it." She gave me a weak smile.

"All right, so. How many girls in that cabin?"

"Twenty-six, as of yesterday."

"Shit," I let slip, before I could stop myself. Because there were another twenty-six in Brook Trout that Chelsea and I were already responsible for. Which meant that, if we didn't find anyone, we would each be fully responsible for a group of almost thirty middle school girls for the next eight weeks.

I grabbed the laptop in front of her and spun it around, going into problem-solver mode. "Have you checked the floating application pool yet?"

She shook her head.

Typically, we finalized our hiring for each summer in February, and people began applying long before. We made a big deal of closing applications in the winter so that people would get them in early, but we did have an *Open Application* link available all the time, in case of emergencies like this.

To my surprise, there were two unseen applications, from a couple of days ago, sent at the same time. It must have been a pair of friends. Their names: Stephanie Bennett and Margo Pierce.

"These two look good," I said. "Journalism majors at the University of Georgia, just graduated last week. Both have 4.0s, in Kappa, and love kids, apparently."

I skimmed through both of their applications, trying to understand their last-minute interest in Dread's Cove. Margo was preparing for an extended Euro trip at the end of the summer. And Stephanie—she listed her nickname of choice as Steph—explained that, while she didn't have a job lined up for the fall just yet, she was exploring her options. She'd always wanted to go to summer camp, she wrote, and it seemed like this was her perfect chance.

"Any red flags?" my mom asked when I'd been silent for several minutes.

I shook my head. "Not that I can see."

"Great. They're hired."

"You don't want to interview them first? Not even—I don't know—give them a call? Make sure they aren't serial killers?"

She gave me a look. "The kids get here Monday. If they've got reliable transportation to get here before then, they're hired."

"Shouldn't we at least run a background check?"

"We'll get Sheriff Ramon to run a light one. I'm not that worried about a few sorority girls from Atlanta." She smiled, and she looked almost back to herself. "Thank you, Steph and Margo. Our lifesavers."

By the time I'd left her office that night, she'd already had me send emails offering them the jobs, requesting their presence by Monday morning at the very latest.

I had a hard time believing they'd be able to make the turnaround that quickly, but the next day at lunch, they'd both already responded and accepted.

Just like that, Chelsea and I had two new roommates for the rest of the summer. We had no idea what we were in for.

When Steph and Margo arrived at Dread's Cove, we heard them before we saw them. There was a laugh that was more like a squawk that made both me and Chelsea jump.

Steph barreled through the door of Black Bass first—I recognized her from the Instagram stalking I'd done the night before. She wore a red tennis dress, and her sneakers were a blinding, scuffless white.

"Steph Bennett," she announced, doing a pirouette. She surprised me with how loud her voice was; it echoed around the small cabin.

"I'm Greer, and this is Chelsea," I said, pointing behind me. Steph squealed, as if learning our names was the best news she'd ever heard. Before I knew it, she was hugging me, our faces smashed so close together that her earring crashed into mine, and I worried they'd get caught on each other. I'd never met someone with such a disregard for personal space, except maybe Val. I couldn't help it, though—I found myself oddly charmed by her friendliness.

"This is my first time at a summer camp, can you believe that? My aunt and uncle never let me go when I was a kid. So overprotective. Oh my God, it's so cute and, like, quaint, though, isn't it? Have you met any guys yet?"

Behind her, Margo Pierce seemed to be deciding whether the floor was clean enough for her to set her bag down. She frowned before finally letting the leather duffel drop at her feet.

I looked back at Steph, who was smiling at me expectantly, tan arms crossed over her chest. "Oh, yeah, we know all of them already. Chelsea and I grew up here, actually."

Her mouth popped open into a delicate *o*. "Wait, seriously? That's so cool. How exactly does one grow up at a summer camp?"

I knew Chelsea was going to tell my secret, so I spoke quickly, trying to cut it off at the head. For one more minute, I wanted to be normal. "And you're Margo, right?"

Margo was now standing with her arms crossed, assessing us with a faint grimace on her face. Like Steph, she was dressed like some kind of off-duty model, though her color of choice seemed to be black.

I was struck by a wave of shyness, wondering what I must have looked like to her: old T-shirt, dirty shorts, hair wet and tangled from an early-morning swim in the lake. After a brief, awkward pause, she stuck out her hand.

It felt dumb and oddly formal, but she clearly wasn't a hugger. Her fingernails were gold and shaped like talons, and they dug uncomfortably into my skin. But then her smile went from displeased to almost mischievous, and I found myself standing up straighter, wondering what she might say.

"Do you have a nickname, or is it just Greer?"

"Margo's the queen of nicknames," Steph gushed as she plopped her bag down on the bed beneath Chelsea's. For a second, we locked eyes—we'd already planned on sharing and letting the two of them be on the other side of the room.

But I didn't acknowledge it, and neither did she, and the moment passed. Which was totally cool and fine. I was going to share a bunk bed with Margo Pierce, who was both beautiful and slightly terrifying, who maybe hated me on sight but maybe also wanted to give me a nickname.

"No, it's just Greer," I answered, feeling even more self-conscious. "But you can call me whatever."

She put her hands on her hips and looked at me for a long moment, while behind us, Steph was talking Chelsea into a hug. "*Bunk buddies!*" I heard her say, which brought an unexpected laugh from Chelsea.

"Greer," Margo said again, slowly, trying it out. She tapped a finger on her chin like she was solving a riddle. "That's a tough one. I'll have to come back to you."

As they unpacked their suitcases, I tried not to be too nosy, but it was hard. Steph moved like a hurricane. She was a swirl of colors, exclamations, curses, belly laughs. Within minutes of arriving, her bed looked like she'd lived here for years; it was already covered in clothes, bottles of perfume, bikinis, and four different makeup bags, all half spilled out onto the sheets.

Margo was almost an entire contradiction. Unimpressed with Chelsea's handiwork, she'd actually unmade her bed and *remade it*, with hospital corners and all. When I peered at her from the bathroom, she was putting a silk pillowcase on her camp-issued pillow, a divot forming between her eyebrows as she tried to smooth out invisible wrinkles with her hands.

They could have been related, save for a few defining features. Where Margo's eyes were so brown they were almost black, Steph's were a shocking blue, brighter than even Chelsea's. They were both toned and tall, with glowy skin and the kind of fluffy eyelashes that were either the result of good makeup or good genetics, though you couldn't be sure.

"Are those magazines?" I asked, eyeing the sizable stack that Steph had just put together beside her bed. It seemed to be the only thing she'd taken care in organizing so far. She must have had twenty-five or more.

Margo snorted as she sprayed something that smelled like lavender on my bed and hers. "Please, don't get her started. I can't hear this asinine TED Talk again." She dipped her chin toward the floor on our side of the room, where she had her own neat stack of paperbacks. "She likes to claim that they're the same as books, that people don't respect magazines the way they used to, and that it's a fatal flaw with humanity. Did I get it right, S?"

Steph crossed her arms and jutted out a hip, but her eyes were sparkling. Both my head and Chelsea's were ping-ponging back and forth between them.

"Tell me, babe, what *are* magazines if not *literal books*? Are they not *a bunch of paper and words, sewn together*? What else would I call them, you elitist?"

Margo rolled her eyes and turned back to her duffel, though she was smiling. I was already getting the sense that this was normal; they sparred and quipped and laughed and never, ever got bored of each other. Watching them interact was like watching the best kind of bingeable TV show–absolutely addicting.

"Is this the rest of them?" Steph asked a few minutes later.

I was unpacking my toiletries in the bathroom, and I poked my head out to see her pointing at the framed photo beside my bed. Me and Chelsea and the rest of last year's college crew, crammed together for a picture on the last day of summer.

"Yep, you'll meet them all tonight."

"So there are boys," Steph said. "Oh, he's adorable." She was pointing at Wes, who was standing shirtless, his arm wrapped tightly around me. His wavy hair was sun-bleached and messy, his chest bare. I was pressed so closely to him that it looked like we were one person, rather than two.

"Is he your boyfriend? He's so hot. They all are. Damn, you guys have it right. Maybe I should live at a summer camp."

I felt oddly vindicated that she thought Wes was hot, though I wasn't exactly sure why. "That's Wes. He's actually my ex-boyfriend," I explained, hoping to sound casual and breezy. "We broke up in December."

I avoided Chelsea's eye, though I could feel her pointed stare on my face. She still wasn't happy with me.

"What about him?" Margo asked. She was pointing to the boy on the other end, the tallest one with a shock of dark hair and a smile that was more like a dare. He was the only person in the photo not looking at the camera; instead, his gaze was on the lake behind us.

I coughed, only somewhat idiotically. "That's Trevor. Lifeguard the past few years, but he'll be waterfront manager this summer."

She gave me a small, dangerous smile. "Let me guess, he's your *current* boyfriend?"

"No," I said, but the word was too quick, the sound too high-pitched. I wanted to explain—*we're just friends*; *he's way out of my league*; *it's not even an option*—but it was too late.

"I wouldn't go there. Trevor's kind of a mess. He's nothing like Wes," Chelsea said from the top bunk, and the three of us turned toward her in unison. Her face turned pink, like she hadn't been expecting the full weight of our combined attention.

"What kind of mess? Besides a hot one," Steph asked with a Cheshire cat grin as she threw her arm around Margo's shoulders.

"He is *not* a mess," I huffed, because I couldn't help myself.

Outside the window, a bird chirped.

"Carolina chickadee. And don't listen to Greer," Chelsea said. She sighed and rearranged herself so that her feet were dangling off the side of the bed. "She has a soft spot for him. She likes to stare at his abs."

"Excuse me, I do *not*—"

"I'm not saying he's a bad guy," Chelsea said, cutting me off. "But he's just kind of adrift, you know? He graduated from UGA two years ago, but he's got no plans at all for a life, or a career. This is what he does. He wastes nine months in some dead-end job in Atlanta, then comes to Dread's to tan by the lake for a few months. Rinse, repeat."

We could all hear the disdain, stark and clear in her voice.

She might as well have called Trevor a hopeless, bumbling loser, which was completely unfair. I loved Chelsea, but she wasn't exactly afraid of jumping to conclusions.

"All right, so Tall Trevor—who *definitely* doesn't have nice abs—is on probation until we feel him out, then. What about this one? Please tell me he's single." This was Steph again, blessedly redirecting the conversation into safer territory.

She pointed at Garrett, the second tallest. I knew that he was objectively handsome, had a nice, white smile, but I still made a face. "He's my cousin."

Her eyebrows shot up. "That's kind of fun. Anyone else from your family work here?"

This time, Chelsea beat me to it. "Her mom's Anita Olsen. They own the whole camp."

I wanted to stare daggers at her, but Steph would see.

Chelsea knew that I got weird talking about my family, especially with strangers. Dread's Cove was famous in Georgia, and across most of the Southeast. My grandfather Dread Olsen purchased an abandoned POW camp from the state after World War II, and he'd turned it into a summer camp. He was a character, later in life becoming a senator, and his contributions to Georgia's environmental policies over the years had made him a quasi celebrity. Before he died, he passed the reins down to his only daughter—my mother, Anita.

When my grandfather got sick and she took over as a fresh-faced college grad, she became a bit of a celebrity in her own right. She overhauled all the old buildings and keyed in on our marketing efforts. In a matter of years, Dread's Cove became not just a summer camp but *the* summer camp of the South. It quickly became a rite of passage for kids to spend their summers here, deep in the mountains, and the waitlist became years long.

My mom had breathed new life into this place, and it was her greatest achievement. One day, it would all belong to me.

It was a duty I took very seriously, even if it was sometimes overwhelming. I also hated the strange sort of fame that came with being associated with my family and the Cove.

It made me feel cheap somehow, like I wasn't a real person. My last name was merely an emblem of the family I had done nothing to earn.

Chelsea saw this all very differently. Although she wasn't an Olsen, her dad was now married to one, and she'd lived here her entire life. Because Chelsea had an annoying amount of pride in her own heritage, she never understood why I was so hesitant to tell everyone I met about my family. So although she knew I hated it, she felt the need to call me out every chance she got.

As if I could ever forget exactly who I was and what was expected of me.

"Shut up," Steph said, looking between the two of us, like she was checking to see if we were messing with her.

"Yeah, um, that's true. My mom is Anita."

Steph put a hand over her heart and blinked at me. "Wait, seriously? That's . . ." She trailed off, like this reveal had made her speechless—which seemed like a hard thing to do. "M, did you hear that? Isn't that amazing?"

"Absolutely wild." Margo didn't turn around from her suitcase, but she answered in a singsong voice that was either mocking in a nice way or mocking in a mean way. I couldn't tell which. But then she stood and spun around, then looked at me like she'd never seen anyone more interesting. She was starting to give me whiplash. "So, what's the dress code for this party tonight, Little G?"

"Oh, Little G is *good*!" Steph beamed at both of us, before winking at Chelsea. "You're next, don't worry."

I smiled like I was pleased, though the name felt like it might have been an insult. I couldn't quite put my finger on why.

"Hear me out: What if we went *all out* and did matching?" Steph said from her bed, clapping her hands together. "We could wear pink!"

"Not a chance. You know how I feel about pink, Stephanie Bennett."

"She only says my full name when she's serious," she explained, putting her hands on her hips. "And that's only because you know I look way better than you in it."

At that, prim and slightly stuffy Margo grabbed her pillow from her bed and whacked Steph over the head with it. Within seconds, they were both laughing, and I found myself smiling, too.

As I watched the two of them just be together, I couldn't help but think about my friendship with Chelsea. She was in almost every one of my best memories. When we were kids, the adults would call us the *twins*. She was sixteen months older than me, and we looked nothing alike, but we were each other's shadows. There was never one of us without the other.

But she'd been shocked when I'd told her I wanted to leave for a few years and go to college, live on campus. She'd opted to get her degree remotely so that she could stay at Dread's Cove full-time and had just assumed I'd do the same. That had been one of the only times that we'd ever genuinely argued. She'd warmed up to the idea after a while, told me she trusted my judgment, even if she didn't understand. And it had prickled at me, in the back of my mind—for years now—if she'd really meant it.

For the most part, it was easy with Chelsea, but it wasn't always fun. Margo and Steph, though—they had fun. You could tell, by the way they smiled. Like they were sharing a secret.

It didn't take long for me to decide that I wanted to know the secret, too.

I wanted it more than I wanted anything.

CHAPTER FIVE

NOW

I was practically asleep standing up by the time I got back to my mom's cabin. My feet were wrecked from the stupid wedges I'd been bold enough to wear, and I could feel the blisters growing hot on my heels, even just from the short walk.

The sky was black, the stars mostly hidden now by clouds, giving me the itchy, claustrophobic feeling that I was trapped inside a room with no exit. Wes had offered to walk me back, but Chelsea had insisted he help clean up, and I didn't feel like giving her another reason to be pissed at me. So I'd smiled at them both—even as she refused to meet my eye—and said I'd see them for breakfast.

I'd wanted to ask her. The question had been on the tip of my tongue—*Did you see Margo?* I'd almost grabbed her arm, pulled her back, forced her to look me in the face and listen. Just to make sure that I hadn't lost my mind.

When I put my hand on the doorknob, I stilled. I hadn't locked it, for reasons I was unsure of now. I swore I could hear someone inside, rustling around. I pressed my ear to the door and listened.

Then, I heard it: the sure sound of a cabinet clanking shut.

My heart thumped painfully against my rib cage. Someone was going through my mom's cabin. One of the snaky reporters, no doubt, trying to dig up some dirt on Anita and her troubled daughter.

Or it might have been one of the old campers, feeling sad and nostalgic. Equally creepy, maybe slightly less exploitative. I wasn't prepared to see anyone else losing it. I could hardly stay standing myself. There was a gaping black hole threatening to suck me inside at any given moment.

Or maybe, a more sinister voice whispered in my ear, *maybe it's something worse.* Someone with far darker plans. I couldn't help but think of that summer, and the Phantom. All the unexplained break-ins, the vandalism, the dark figure skulking through the trees—how scared everyone had been—but I made myself push the thought down.

The Phantom was gone. I was sure of it.

Despite my better judgment, the cheap wine swirling around in my stomach won out, and I pushed the door open. It was dim, only the light of the moon shining in through the high kitchen window.

And a silhouette, in the shape of a person, just beneath it. The scream that ripped through my throat was met with a laugh that made my ears ring.

"Miss me?" came a lilting voice that I hadn't heard in years.

Perched on my mother's kitchen counter, as comfortable as if she owned the place, was Margo Pierce. In each hand, she held a glass of whiskey, like we were on a game show, and I'd just won the grand prize.

"What the *fuck*?" I put a steadying hand on my chest, willing myself to breathe.

"Nice to see you, too, Little G."

It had been five years since we'd seen each other, since she'd called me that stupid nickname, but she looked the same, even up close like this. Perfect, poreless skin from the SPF she slathered on. Eyes that could cut glass.

I tripped over my feet while turning on a lamp; she'd been sitting in near darkness, presumably to scare the ever-loving shit out of me. It had worked.

"Very funny," I said, gesturing around, not sure at what. This had to be a trick, some kind of setup. But I didn't know why. "What the hell are you doing in here?"

"Sit, sit," she said mildly, rather than answering, before shoving a glass into my hand and guiding me toward my own couch. I didn't know what else to do, so I sat down and gaped at her.

"What is this?"

"This is whatever shitty whiskey I found in the cabinet. Don't blame me for your bad taste." With her pinky up, she took a delicate sip, then made a face like she was drinking gasoline. "God, this is so bad."

"No, I mean, what is *this*? What do you want?"

"I'm writing a story about the ongoing legacy of Dread's Cove, same as every other writer here." With her free hand, she jiggled the press badge around her neck, as if that was somehow an explanation in and of itself. "Though, between you and me, I would have preferred to be here without an assignment. But I wasn't lucky enough to get one of those fancy VIP invitations. You really hurt my feelings, keeping me off the list."

"Chelsea organized this. Take it up with her." I could hear my voice shaking; I was trying and failing to keep my cool.

She knew it, too. I could see it building—the gleam in her eye, the excitement. This is where she'd always thrived: exploiting other people's insecurities.

"How did you even know this was happening?"

"Oh, stop it," she said. She pinched me on the arm, hard enough to hurt. "The whole goddamn state has been salivating over this for months. Everyone loves a redemption arc. Come on. You know I hate it when you pretend you don't know how rich and famous you are."

Fine, I'd walked myself into that. "But this is—"

"This is every bored adult's wet dream, isn't it? Cosplaying like they're a kid again, at summer camp? Please, be sure to give Baby my sincere congratulations on a fantastic idea. Didn't know she had it in her."

And then, for the briefest moment, her expression changed into something more somber. "I am sorry about your mom, by the way. For the record, I always liked her."

I couldn't process or accept her unexpected condolences. For a moment, I could only stare.

"But you hate this place, and . . ." I trailed off, unable to finish that thought. We both knew what I meant. *And you hate me.*

"I do," she agreed, which didn't help. It only made me picture exactly why that was true, with a disturbing clarity. It played out across my mind, uninvited as always: the morning after the fire.

The way that Margo had lost her mind, had threatened to sue all of us, kill all of us, for not looking hard enough, in the dark and in the smoke—for letting her best friend burn alive. I'd been speechless—utterly terrified, by the wildness in her eyes. Between the two of them, I'd gotten so used to Steph being the live wire, the impulsive one. She was the one you had to keep a close eye on so she didn't slip through your fingers.

Margo was more collected. She thought things through and kept things close. So close that you never really could be sure what she was thinking, or what she wanted.

Until she snapped.

I'd never seen anything scarier than Margo that final morning. The things she'd said, voice hoarse from her screams, when the flames had finally burned out and her best friend was lost forever to the woods. She'd left a few hours later with the first responders, soot in her hair and smeared across her face, without saying another word to any of us.

I thought of the embarrassingly long texts I'd sent her in the months that followed, begging her to talk to me. All the calls that went right to voicemail.

But now, she was back, sitting next to me, drinking my whiskey, and offering me words of comfort on the eve of my mother's funeral. My mouth was dry, and I tried to swallow. "So then why–"

"You don't look bad, by the way." She gave me a performative once-over, raising her eyebrows in some kind of half-assed approval I was supposed to be grateful for. "I always knew you'd look better with some layers in your hair. As usual, I was right. Though, remember, Botox is your friend."

She winked, her sincerity from a moment ago already gone. But I knew her game. She was trying to throw me off, disorient me. I wasn't going to let it work.

"Is it yours?" I shot back, more quickly than she was used to. "Because you're looking a bit puffy."

For a long moment, we considered each other. She ran an idle finger around the rim of her glass and cracked her neck, like she was squaring up for a fight.

"Didn't see you all cozied up to Lifeguard Ken tonight. What's the story there?"

"Hey, weren't you going to be an author?" I asked, ignoring her dig at Trevor, even as my stomach clenched. "How come you haven't published anything? Just writing about other people's successful careers, right? Not your own."

"Touché," she said, raising her glass to mine before taking an alarmingly large sip of her drink. She made a face as it went down, then topped off her glass from the bottle she'd brought to the coffee table. I opened my mouth to ask again, to demand answers, but she beat me to it.

"It was sort of a coincidence, if you must know. I wasn't assigned to the story originally. But my boss saw the press release last week, about your mom, while we were having coffee. She knew that I'd been best friends with her, *that girl who died in the Dread's Cove fire*, so she asked me about it.

"I told her that Steph and I had spent the summer working here together, that I'd been here the night that . . . when it happened." She scrunched her nose and looked away from me, and for a wild moment, I wondered if she might be trying not to cry.

"Anyway," she continued, swirling what was left of her drink. "She thought that my personal connection to Steph and Dread's Cove would really add some color to the story. I agreed to come out here, take that filthy bus through the mountains, and cover this whole fucked-up funeral-slash-party weekend. So I could tell this story from the heart, as someone who knew Steph. But, more important"—she paused, giving me a thin, lethal smile—"tell yours."

And here it was. The real reason she'd returned, the reason she had broken into my cabin and was trying to get me to share a drink and relive the past with her. She wanted my interview, the one I'd staunchly said no to, from every angle, from every asker. I should have seen it coming, the second I'd seen her disapproving frown in the mess hall.

It was so fucking Margo, to assume that she'd be the exception. That because of our history, and what little time we'd spent together, she'd be able to convince me. To guilt me into saying yes.

The thing is, I did feel guilty. About too many things to count. But I was also selfish. I was also scared.

"No." I said the word flatly but with finality. "I'm not doing an interview. But I really do hope you have a nice weekend." I stood, stretched my arms over my head in an overdone show of exhaustion. "I'm pretty tired. You can let yourself out."

Margo didn't stand or give any indication that she was close to leaving. On the contrary, she grabbed the bottle of whiskey and topped herself off before nestling back into her corner of the couch. "Well, I was thinking I'd stay with you instead. I'm supposed to be sleeping in a cabin, if you can believe that." She said *cabin* the same way one might say *garbage dump* or *vat of toxic waste.*

I sighed, felt the beginnings of a headache prickle at the base of my skull. "This is also a cabin, if you hadn't noticed. We actually exclusively have cabins here, at summer camp."

She waved a hand at me in bemused annoyance, like I was being intentionally obtuse. "Yes, fine, but this cabin has air-conditioning, Wi-Fi, a wine cellar, and showers with serviceable water pressure. Let's not act like sleeping in an open-air bunk bed is the same thing."

My heart rate spiked painfully at the mention of the wine cellar, but I pushed that dormant fear away. Now wasn't the time.

I opened my mouth to argue with her, but nothing came out. Because really, what was I going to do, force her to leave? Get into a fistfight? Throw her shit out the front door, spill her suitcase on the porch? She was already here. And all the things I'd been trying to avoid—speaking to her, looking her in the eye—well, we'd already ripped that bandage right off. It was done, and I was alive.

Welcome Back Weekend would only last a few days. I'd smile in public and cry in the shower and drink copiously, and then it would be over, and she'd be gone. I didn't know what exactly she thought she'd get out of me, if she really thought she'd convince me to go on the record with her, but it didn't matter, in the end.

Although I lived alone in Atlanta, my apartment was on the second floor. I could hear my upstairs and downstairs neighbors at almost all hours of the night, which had become a comforting sort of white noise over the past few years. I'd barely slept at all last night. It had been far too quiet.

At the very least, having a roommate for the next few days might give me a little peace of mind.

"Fine," I said at last, and the corner of her mouth twitched, almost imperceptibly. "You can stay in the guest room. But I'm not doing an interview. I'm serious."

Val had called me last week and said that several of the attending journalists had reached out to her, trying to nail down a time to talk to me, one-on-one. Part of the original thinking behind this weekend–as much as Chelsea wanted to claim it was only about *celebrating the children*–was to get our foot back in the door with the press.

But I didn't want to talk about my mom while someone shoved a recorder in my face. I didn't want to relive the night of the fire, dredge up the old rumors about the Phantom, or tell stories about Steph. I didn't want to pose for a photo; I didn't want to talk about my plans for Dread's Cove. I'd barely been able to handle the idea of spending a long weekend here. I had no idea what was next. I wasn't the girl I used to be, with a vision and a timeline. Now, I took it a day at a time.

"Thank you. Whatever you say, *boss lady*. I should really start calling you Big G now, shouldn't I?"

She was humoring me. But I would let her, because the whiskey and the wine were making my eyelids droop, it was warm in here, and it felt nice to sit on my mother's couch and pretend that everything was fine.

Nothing had felt close to fine in so long. And over the past two weeks, every part of my life had become damn near intolerable.

Tomorrow, I would mourn my mother. I would stand at the edge of the dock as cameras flashed at my back, and I would weep for all the years I'd spent away from her. For a little while longer–even a few minutes, if that's all I could have–I wanted to keep those feelings at bay.

There was a voice in the back of my mind, warning me that it was too easy, saying yes to Margo. Reminding me that she couldn't possibly have come here just to make her peace or write some feel-good story. She was smart, and secretive, and I'd be right to be nervous around her. To watch my back.

But if I squinted, with the lights dim like this, it almost felt like it was five years ago and Steph was sitting beside her. Like the whole summer was still stretched out before us, and the rest of our lives were just getting started. Anything was possible. Steph was alive, and my mom was, too. The world hadn't ended yet.

For now, that was enough.

CHAPTER SIX

THEN

Fifty Days Before the Fire

I've always believed that everything looks better in the summer.

Something about the heat gives the world a stillness and a calm that it doesn't usually have.

As we walked to the mess hall that night, the four of us dressed to the nines in varying shades of pink, I was hopeful. Excited. Steph and Margo were here, and I was certain that everything was about to change. I felt it, pulsing beneath my skin—a deep sort of knowing that I couldn't explain.

We called tonight's party the Night Before, and it was a big event, as far as summer camp dinners went. As the name suggests, it was always the last night before the campers arrived. The staff would get all dressed up, and the cooks would make us an elaborate, three-course dinner. Some of our alums and donors would come, too, and my mom pulled out all the stops. It was as close to fancy as we ever got at the Cove.

Steph had let me borrow (practically forced over my head) a hot-pink dress that was gorgeous but entirely unlike me. She'd even sat me down on her bed and applied blush to the apples of my cheeks, promising that the colors matched perfectly.

Though she'd only arrived this afternoon, I was already learning that she was impossible to say no to.

The counselors, lifeguards, and other college-aged staff always sat together at a few long tables in the very back. Wes preferred the one right by the kitchen doors so that he could pop back in at a moment's notice. Now that his parents—the longtime head chefs—had retired down to Destin, he was the longest tenured member of the kitchen staff, albeit the youngest. He basically ran the whole show back there. Even still, my mom had been adamant that he get the Night Before off like the rest of us. He was just a little bit obsessive about making sure things were going smoothly without him.

I took a seat, then felt a brief surge of dopamine when Steph dropped down next to me. She immediately started asking for the names of everyone at the table, greeting them all with the gusto of a seasoned politician. Within seconds, she was holding court, polling the rest of the college staff on their favorite camp desserts and the best places to connect to Wi-Fi.

"Well, look who it is," someone drawled in my ear, and my attention snapped to Trevor, who was pulling out the chair beside me.

His dark brown hair was wet, sticking up in all directions, and he smelled like mint and salt water. "I was hoping I'd snag a seat next to you."

I felt my internal temperature rise. Trevor had started coming to Dread's Cove three years ago, the summer after my freshman year of college and the summer after his junior year. He'd hung out with an older group back then, though he was the only one of them who'd returned this year. I'd never *stared at his abs*, as Chelsea had claimed, but I did think he was one of the cutest guys I'd ever seen. Not that I would have done anything about it, of course, because I'd always been dating Wes.

There'd been one moment, though, between us. At the end of last summer. The kids had gone home that morning, and the rest of the summer staff, including me, were preparing to head out the next day. Back to school, back to our off-season lives.

The day was brutally hot, and I'd snuck out to the lake for a post-lunch swim–slightly frowned upon, considering how much work had to be done that afternoon. I'd asked Wes if he wanted to join me, but he'd only shook his head, disappointed at the thought of shirking responsibility.

Trevor, on the other hand, had clearly had the same thought as me, and we'd both laughed when we saw each other on the dock. "Our little secret?" he'd said, and then he'd winked, and it was like I'd been electrocuted.

He'd smiled, grabbing my hand and pulling me with him. Then he'd jumped in, put his elbows on the edge of the dock, and said "I'm waiting" in a voice far too close to velvet. As hot as it was that afternoon, I'd shivered.

And even though Wes was still my boyfriend, I wasn't thinking of him at all.

I was only thinking of the feeling of Trevor's fingers interlaced with mine.

I blinked, stretched a smile across my face, hoping he couldn't tell that I was playing that memory back now, as I had far more times than I would have liked to admit over the past year. "It's good to see you."

I didn't miss the way his bright green eyes coasted over me, into the lower-than-usual dip in my dress.

"Well, I think congratulations are in order. How's it feel to be a graduate?" he asked.

"Amazing. I'm glad to be back for the summer."

"For the summer, or forever?"

I opened my mouth, then closed it. The word *forever* had been on my lips, poised to agree with him, but I couldn't bring myself to say it. Maybe it was the way he was looking at me, with so much naked interest. Like he would be hanging on every word I said. I wanted to give him something good to hang on to. Something exciting, in the way that he was exciting.

So, I surprised us both: "For now."

Trevor's eyebrows shot up. "Whoa, really? Not trying to follow in your mom's footsteps? I thought that had been the plan since, like, conception?"

I couldn't see her, but I could sense Steph beside me, listening, even as she talked to Garrett. It made me feel bold, powerful. I wasn't used to feeling that way. "Forever is a long time."

"So, what are you going to do instead, little rebel?" he pressed, his mouth lifting in a smirk. I didn't have a good answer to this, of course. The plans for my life had long been set in stone.

My business degree had been to take over the operations. My years of being a counselor with all age groups had given me the training I needed to handle every type of child. My love for this place, my mother, and my family had made it the easiest thing in the world to be excited about.

And yet, over the past year, I'd been second-guessing all of it. I hadn't told anyone, and I hadn't planned to. Until now, it seemed, with the heat of Trevor's arm just barely pressed against my shoulders. I shrugged, going for coy. "You'll have to wait and see. I'm still considering my options."

It felt like the cool, unbothered thing to say, though I was neither of those things. I was a girl with a plan. It was written into my DNA. I tried not to think about what my mother, or Chelsea, or Wes would do if they'd heard me talking like this.

Trevor, however, seemed to like this answer, because he raised his water glass to clink with mine. "Here's to not being tied down." Then he winked at me, that same way he had once before, and my stomach dipped in a way that I knew would become a problem.

After dinner, I wandered outside. Wes and some of the other guys were nursing beers at the end of the dock, and I raised a hand to wave. He caught my eye and grinned.

An arm looped through mine. I turned, expecting Chelsea but instead seeing Steph. Her cheeks were flushed from the heat and the freely flowing wine.

"All right, spill it," she said, nudging her head in Wes's direction. "Is this the summer you win him back? Should we make a game plan? We could probably use the lifeguard to make him jealous. He seems to like you just fine."

"Oh, God, no," I said. "You have a lot of catching up to do."

"All right, then, tell me everything," she crooned. We sat down on the edge of the dock, dangling our toes in the water.

"We've been friends since we were kids," I began. "We started dating when were fifteen, and it was just–simple, you know? Easy. But I don't know. Not to sound like a cliché, but there was something missing."

We'd always had a great time together. He'd take me out on the lake on his days off, and we'd sit around and plan our fantasy renovations for the Cove, when we both inevitably took over as coheads of camp—like my mom and Rig. Only we'd be married, have a family of our own. We'd bring a blanket and leftover desserts that he'd snuck from the kitchen, and he'd kiss me as the sun went down, telling me how lucky we were to get to spend our lives here.

It's you and me, he'd say. *Forever.*

I'd rest my head on his shoulder and say it back.

In a lot of ways, the two of us made sense. We both liked things that were simple, without nuance. We were risk averse. Wes had been the one who'd helped me decide to go to University of North Georgia—it was close by. I could come back on the weekends, whenever I wanted. It was a big school, but not too big. The safest choice. He always helped me make the safe choice, and I was grateful.

But as my senior year began, something shifted in me. I started avoiding his texts, putting off calling him back. I told myself that I was busy, that I needed to focus on school. The fall came and went, and I realized that I was dreading going home. I was dreading seeing him.

That's when I knew I had to end it.

It wasn't that I didn't care about him. I just couldn't shake the feeling of two green eyes resting on me on that final day of summer. How alive I had felt that afternoon with Trevor. I'd never once felt that way when Wes had looked at me.

When I came home for winter break, I'd asked him to talk down by the water. I told him it was over, and he'd been floored. I'd left out Trevor, of course, knowing there was nothing that would do but hurt him. Nothing had happened between us, but I'd wanted it to. That felt like reason enough.

Wes told me that he didn't understand. He told me he loved me, that he'd been planning on proposing next summer. He hadn't cried or yelled, but his whole body was trembling. And then he'd left me standing alone, with a sunken stomach and a guilty conscience.

I'd resented him, just a bit, for not having seen it coming. For not noticing the ways I'd been pulling away over those final few months. As I looked at him now, dimpled and sun-kissed and so familiar, I wasn't sure if that had been fair.

But it didn't change anything.

"Did you love him?" Steph asked, dragging her toes along the surface of the water.

"I wanted to," I admitted, before I could stop myself. I was still watching Wes. "But no. I don't think so. Not in the way he loved me, at least."

Steph was quiet for a moment, and I found myself getting nervous that I'd said the wrong thing. That I'd given too much of myself away, before knowing what she'd do with it. We'd just met today, and, already, I was talking to her like we'd known each other for years. I was telling her secrets that I'd barely been able to admit to Chelsea, or even myself.

She slid an inch closer so that our legs were touching. "You know, it's okay to want something bigger. And there are big things in your future. I can sense it."

At the time, *bigger* wasn't the word I would have used. Just *different*. I thought about Trevor's words in my ear, his arm resting easily on the back of my chair. How good he'd smelled. That he'd seemed as happy to see me as I was to see him. *Here's to not being tied down.*

Bigger was a scary word. One I didn't know if I was ready for yet. But Steph dropped her head against my shoulder, and I felt our friendship take root, then and there. If she was bigger, then yes. Bigger was what I wanted, after all.

As the sun dipped below the horizon, we got tipsy and sleepy, sprawled out on the dock. Margo and Chelsea found us outside, a pilfered bottle of champagne from behind the bar with them—Chelsea was grinning at Margo like they'd just pulled off the world's most elaborate heist, though not an hour ago my mom had told me that we'd way overordered.

I didn't say anything; I liked seeing this side of Chelsea. I liked that Margo and Steph seemed to be having a similar effect on her—making her a little bit bolder. Bold would be good for her.

Before too long, the party wrapped up. We had a noise curfew out here in the woods, and though it wasn't strictly enforced—Sheriff Ramon was nursing a beer inside, last I checked—my mom was a stickler for the rules. We heard the noises of car doors closing from a distance, the final noises of the party drifting into the night.

The boys had inched closer and closer to us with each throw of the football, until Trevor practically stepped in Margo's lap. She took it in stride, wrapping her hand around his ankle in a vise grip that caused him to almost fall into the lake.

My eyelids were growing heavy from the heat and the exhaustion. I was about to ask if they were ready to call it a night when Steph cleared her throat. "I have the best idea," she said, and we all turned to look at her. Like the moon was a spotlight shining solely on her, she pulled her dress over her head, leaving her standing in a thin, cotton bra and matching underwear.

"I knew you were going to say skinny-dipping, I *knew it.*" Margo smirked before ripping her own dress over her head.

Trevor and Garrett were hooting and laughing and cheering them on, while Wes was squinting up at the moon as if it were far more interesting than the two practically naked girls on the dock. Steph and Margo grasped hands, about to jump, before Steph turned back to me and Chelsea. "Come on, y'all, no excuses! Strip."

Chelsea and I looked at each other. Her eyes were wide and unsure, and I felt the smallest pang of guilt.

"You don't have to," I promised, and I meant it. But I was already pulling my own dress up, over my head.

Wes and Trevor were both watching me with such an intensity that I wanted to jump out of my skin. Wes, ever the gentleman, looked away so fast he might have sprained his neck, but Trevor's eyes rested on mine for a long beat. That perfect moment last summer, repeating itself with everyone around.

I was invincible, weightless. I wondered if, when I stepped off the dock, I'd land in the water or if I'd start floating away.

Garrett had already jumped into the lake and was hollering about how cold it was.

"You're a wimp," Trevor said, before diving in after him.

I reached for Steph's hand, and she squeezed mine once, twice, as if she were saying, *I knew you could do it.*

Steph started her countdown, but Margo clicked her tongue to stop her. "Your turn, Chelsea. It's a requirement. If you want to be in our cabin, you have to jump, too."

At the time, it felt like an invitation. Later, I wondered if it may have been a taunt.

But it had the desired effect–I don't know what was in the air that night, but, to my absolute jaw-dropping shock, Chelsea Riggins stepped out of her pink sundress and reached out a trembling hand. From somewhere in the water, there was a wolf whistle. She gave me a guilty smile, and I squeezed her hand the same way Steph had squeezed mine.

"On the count of three," Steph said, and I braced myself for the cold. "One, two, *three*."

I didn't even close my eyes as I stepped off the edge. I wanted to see it all.

It was magical, out there beneath the stars, and it was then that the rest of the summer seemed to crystalize around us. We all stayed in the lake for at least an hour, our fingers and toes pruning, and I smiled until my cheeks ached.

That was the night I fell in love with Steph Bennett and Margo Pierce. I fell in love with all the possibilities, endlessly stretching out before me. The way that the world felt so much bigger with them around.

I sensed Chelsea's gaze burning a hole in me, every time I put my head to Steph's in a laugh, or returned one of Margo's smirks, but we both knew that even she wasn't immune. She'd jumped in, too, after all.

Everything that's happened since can be traced back to what I decided that night, out there in the water: That I would do anything, anything at all, to be like them. To keep being seen by them. To be in on the secret.

That I'd sell my soul for it.

CHAPTER SEVEN

NOW

Eventually, the bottle of allegedly shitty whiskey was nearly empty, and Margo stood and stretched her arms over her head. It was hard to tell exactly how drunk she was—but if my own swimming head was any indication, she was well past tipsy.

I stifled a yawn, already imagining how good it would feel to turn on the fan, open the windows, and fall into a deep, hopefully dreamless sleep. "The bed in there should be made, but—"

"Is it still there?" Margo's hair was matted from where she'd been leaning back on the couch, her earrings askew, and she looked like some kind of mad scientist who'd just had an experiment go wrong.

I blinked at her, trying to make sense of the question. "Is what?"

"Black Bass," she snapped, like I was being stupid on purpose. She took a small step back, her ankle rolling, then caught herself on the side of the couch. "Is it still there?"

"Yeah." I said the word slowly, stretching it out into two syllables. "It's one of the only buildings that didn't burn down."

"Have you gone yet?" She no longer seemed drunk at all.

I was quiet.

"I just need to see it," she said, clearly sensing my hesitancy.

"Please," she added like an afterthought. "I've been thinking about it ever since I decided to come back. I can't stop imagining her in that bunk bed, laughing and reading a fucking magazine, and–"

Her voice broke and, for the second time tonight, I found my resolve wavering.

The truth was that I needed to see it, too. That bone-deep desire both made sense and didn't. It's not like Black Bass was the last place either of us had seen her alive. She'd been at the beach that last night, we'd both spoken to her, just minutes before–

I clenched my jaw hard enough to hurt and forced the thought away.

I needed to see the cabin because, in my darkest moments, I'd found myself questioning everything. If any of it had been real. If the Steph who'd whispered with me in the dark that summer had ever really been the friend I thought she'd been. The friend who I had been so desperately needing her to be, even when things started to fall apart.

"Let's go," I said, pausing before grabbing the near-empty bottle of whiskey on the table. Liquid courage, and all that.

"Brave little heiress, aren't you?" she said, but her smirk was playful now that I'd agreed.

I unscrewed the top and took a sip that was much too big.

Shoving my feet into a pair of sneakers, I tilted my chin at the front door, encouraging her to go first. "Come on, before I change my mind."

Camp was still and silent as we weaved our way through the

edge of the woods, toward Counselor Row. At Dread's Cove, all the twelve-and-up campers slept in cabins without a counselor—we all bunked together in our own cluster of cabins. Ours were nicer than those for campers, but not by much. Nothing like the gorgeous homes in Staff Village. But while the campers slept basically outside, just with a roof over them, we at least had walls and our own plumbing.

Those last few sips of whiskey seemed to hit me all at once, and I stumbled over a root, almost eating shit on the trail. Margo helped me up with one hand and clapped the other over her mouth to suppress her snort of laughter. It didn't work very well.

"Be quiet," I chastised, holding a finger to my lips like she was a petulant child. She mirrored my movement, giving an obnoxious "*Shhhhh*" that was so loud I cringed and staggered back a step.

"You're going to wake up the whole camp."

"Oh, boo, you're no fun at all. Glad to know some things never change."

"Really?" I said, barely quieter than she was. "That was your biggest problem with me, back then? That I wasn't fun—"

I stopped talking abruptly at the sound of twigs snapping behind us. We both froze.

"Who the fuck is there?" she said, her pitch a little too high.

Another twig snapped, closer this time, and I fumbled with my flashlight. I'd kept it off so far on purpose; the light of the moon and my own muscle memory were typically enough to guide me, and I hadn't wanted anyone to see us prowling around. The last thing I needed was a photo of me roaming the woods, Bigfoot-style, holding a bottle of whiskey by the neck. The headlines wrote themselves.

But if there was someone following us, I needed to know. Right now. It took me an agonizing few seconds, but finally, I turned on the ancient flashlight my mom always kept by the front door.

I shone it on the path behind us, and into the surrounding trees, but there was nothing and no one. "An animal," I said, not sure if I believed my own assessment. I had that strange, intuitive sense that someone had just been there, watching us from the darkness.

"Didn't sound like an animal," Margo breathed before grabbing my arm and pulling me along. "Guess the Phantom's back to his old tricks, huh?"

I sucked in a breath, forced my legs to keep moving. Her arm was still locked with mine, tight enough that it might cut off my circulation. "Don't say that. It's not funny."

Margo snorted, unimpressed, then took a long sip. She smacked her lips before speaking, her eyes still darting between me and the trees on either side of us. "Cool it with the pearl-clutching, please. You and your mom were always the first to say the Phantom was just a story."

"It was. It is. I just don't think this weekend feels like the right time to bring it up. It feels . . . wrong."

We both fell silent as we continued walking, and I wondered what Margo was thinking. Before I got up the courage to ask, the trail spit us out in front of Black Bass. My pulse quickened at the memories it triggered—by the sound of Margo's quiet gasp, I was sure she was remembering it all, too.

There was no one staying in it this weekend; a pipe had burst in the bathroom a few days ago, Rig had told me, and he didn't have time to get it fixed before the weekend began. It was at the far end of Counselor Row, cut off from the rest by a large oak tree–that was why Chelsea and I always preferred it. It gave us more privacy than any of the others.

Tonight, though, all that privacy felt ominous. Like we were the only people at camp, the only people for a hundred miles.

I was suddenly very glad that Margo was with me. That she, of all people, had her arm tangled around mine. The irony wasn't lost on me.

"Shall we?" I said, going for levity, even as I eyed the carved sign above the door with a gnawing sense of unease.

We both hesitated at the threshold, not wanting to be the one to break the seal. When it was clear that she was waiting on me, I squeezed my eyes shut and grabbed the handle, flinging it open without looking.

The smell hit me first. That same pine smell of my childhood, concentrated. It looked different but wholly the same, like so much of Dread's Cove.

I was struck with the type of nostalgia that almost bowls you over. For the first time since I'd been back, I realized that I had missed this place, more than I was willing to say.

Cautiously, Margo and I stepped inside. I could tell she was holding her breath. Waiting for a ghost. I was, too.

"God damn," she whispered behind me. "I can't believe we actually slept here."

Both of our eyes were immediately drawn to the back left corner. Steph's bed. My legs moved of their own accord, and then I was sitting down on the thin mattress.

I knew Margo had to be reliving it, same as me–the lifetime of moments we'd spent here.

Though it wasn't really a lifetime at all, I had to tell myself repeatedly. It was less than two months.

Beneath my feet, a floorboard creaked. I looked down and noticed a small gap between two boards, just slightly bigger than the space between the others. Barely noticeable. I pushed on it with the tip of my foot, trying to see if it was a fluke, or something intentional.

It shifted again.

"Margo," I said, and she was by me in an instant, crossing the room as though she hadn't been scared of it a moment ago.

"What?" She followed the glow of the flashlight to the board on the floor, watched the way my foot made it move. She bent down, put her manicured hand in the seam where the two boards met, and lifted. It came up easily.

In all the years that Black Bass had sat empty, no one had noticed a loose floorboard. No one had noticed a hollow space, beside Steph's bed. Which meant that no one had found the single old photo hidden there.

Margo snapped it up. I stood, tried to grab it from her, but she was too quick. She held a finger up to me in warning, like a librarian.

I studied it over her shoulder. It was a picture of a young family, clearly taken at Dread's Cove, maybe sometime in the nineties. There were three of them: mom, dad, and baby. The parents both had big, toothy smiles, and the little girl couldn't have been more than a few months old. She had dark, thick hair that stuck out at all angles and bright blue eyes. They were lovely, though they were strangers to me.

I did recognize the cabin they stood in front of–it was in the Staff Village, right next to Rig and Val's. Or it used to be, before the fire. They'd all been rebuilt now. I felt a weird sort of dissonance, recognizing the place, but not knowing any of their faces.

"Some family that used to work here, I guess." I snatched it from her and turned away before she could take it back. "I don't recognize them. Do you think Steph put this here?"

Margo had gone strangely still. "Does it say their names?"

"Nope," I said. I squinted my eyes, wondering if that would give me more of a sense of recognition, but there was nothing. I turned it over, but there was just a drawing of some weird symbol that I'd never seen. A few odd lines and a circle. The longer I looked at it, the more confusing it was. "What do you–"

"I think that's a picture of Steph." She swallowed. "And her parents."

I held the flashlight upright like a torch, and the light cast shadows on Margo's face. "Steph's family never lived at Dread's Cove," I said slowly.

Margo was still frozen. Then her jaw trembled, and she blinked up at me, like she was coming out of a trance. The seconds stretched out, and I realized she was deciding whether to tell me something.

"What is it?" I whispered.

She blew out a breath, glancing over at the bunk bed we'd shared. "Yes. They did. Steph's parents met here. I didn't know she'd lived here, though, too. She didn't tell me that part."

I gaped at her. "Wait, start over. What?"

She lifted her shoulders in a shrug, eyes going back to the photo. "When Steph was a kid, her dad refused to talk about her mom. But he let it slip once, I guess, when he was doped up on morphine right before he died, that they'd met and fallen in love here. It's the reason I let her talk me into coming here that summer, of all places. She was looking for some closure."

"No, but–she would have told me." Even as I said the words, I didn't know how true they were. Because I knew there was so much Steph had kept at arm's length. She'd let me in just enough, made me feel just special enough, that I hadn't wanted to push her.

Even when I caught her in bald-faced lies, she wanted me to play dumb. So I did.

Margo was frowning, studying the photo like it was a jigsaw puzzle she was a piece away from solving. "I'm telling you. That's her dad. Franklin. He died when Steph was in high school, but I recognize him from the pictures I've seen. He's got those stupid glasses on, and he's way younger obviously, but I'm sure of it. And look at this woman. You're telling me she doesn't remind you of Steph?"

The woman had a wide, open smile, and warm eyes that crinkled. It wasn't their features; she had pale blond hair, milky white skin, and freckles. But there was something about her expression that was hauntingly familiar. The corner of her mouth was caught between a smile and a smirk.

So very Stephanie.

The back of my neck prickled, and I sensed more than one ghost around me. "Do you know anything about Steph's mom?" As much time as we'd spent together that summer, we'd barely ever broached the topic. The one time I'd asked, she'd been quick to shut the conversation down, and I'd been too scared to try again.

Margo pursed her lips. "Just that she left when Steph was a baby. Her dad refused to talk about her. He was pretty troubled, from what she told me. She moved in with her aunt and uncle when she was a kid. They adopted her, raised her. But they knew almost nothing about her mom, either. That was why she wanted to come here so badly that summer. Dread's Cove was the only thing she had to go on."

I shook my head, bewildered, doing quick math in my head. My birthday was in April, and hers was in August of the same year. "This means that Steph lived here at the same time I did. We would have been babies together." It was weird, almost unbelievable, and yet–as strange as it sounded, the photo gave me a charge of guilty excitement. There was something, after all this time, tying us together.

There was nothing random about Steph coming to Dread's Cove that summer.

Because this had once been her home, too.

"Okay, so you guys came here so she could try to learn more about her mom. Did she find anything?"

Margo shook her head, the movement sharp. "Not that she ever told me. But things got a little weird between us." She pursed her lips. "I'm sure you remember that."

Of course I did.

"I wanted to help her, but–" Her eyes widened, and I saw it on her face, clear as day: a new idea, taking shape. My heart bumped up against my chest, and I was already afraid of whatever she might be about to say.

"This is it," she said, running a finger across the photo. "This is the story. We'll figure out what Steph couldn't. We'll find her mom for her."

A spike of unease shot up my spine. "Margo, come on, that's–"

"Think about it," she said. "I read all your texts, listened to all your messages, all right? I know how guilty you felt about what happened. I'm guessing that hasn't gone away. You told me that you'd do whatever it took to make this right. Well, what if it's this? What if telling the story Steph never got to can make it right?" She swallowed, and I could tell she was trying to hold back the true breadth of her emotions. "We didn't save her then. But maybe we can help her now."

I couldn't speak. I could only stare.

"Don't you understand what I'm saying? We're not going to tell your story, Greer. We're going to tell hers."

A vulnerable Margo Pierce was not something I'd often seen. But now, as she stood in front of me, I could feel the desperation. It was rolling off her in waves, palpable. Permeating into my own skin, coursing through my bloodstream, stronger than any alcohol.

"Think about it this way. It won't just be for Steph. You said yourself that you don't want some big interview. And I have to concur–you're not exactly up to providing award-winning work at the moment, sweetheart. But finding the long-lost mom of Stephanie Bennett? Talk about karma. Talk about getting Dread's Cove on the map again. *That's* your front-page story. That's the kind of story that your mother would have wanted. So are you in or are you out?"

I bit my lip and considered this absurd proposal. I thought back on that feeling of foreboding I'd had earlier on the couch. The sense that she must be up to something. That I shouldn't trust her. There were so many ways this could go wrong.

Obviously–*obviously*–this wasn't a good idea. More likely, it was a terrible idea. Reckless, even. Because I knew exactly who Margo Pierce was. Or, rather, I knew who she wasn't.

I knew she wasn't my friend. I knew she never had been. I knew she held grudges.

But if she was determined to look into this–and I could tell by the hard set of her jaw that she was–it was probably wise to keep an eye on her. God knows someone needed to.

It was more than that, though. For years now, I'd been drowning. The guilt was a gaping, bottomless chasm, threatening to pull me in and never let me resurface.

I didn't know if I could face another minute, another second, feeling so fucking useless. So fucking small. I hadn't earned the title of my mother's daughter in so, so long. She had been a problem solver; she had been a fiercely loyal friend.

If there were any good parts of me left, I owed them to her. I was certain that if she were in my position right now, she would say yes. Damn the consequences.

Anita Olsen would have done anything for the people she loved. Through it all, I had loved Steph.

So, yes, maybe it was reckless. But it also might have been the best chance I had to make it up to both of them. To feel worthy, for the first time in so long, of anything at all.

"Let's do it," I breathed, eyes resting on the little Steph in the photo. "Let's find her."

When we got back to the cabin–the bottle of whiskey completely empty now–Margo staggered down the hallway, holding her hands out against the walls as if needing them to stay vertical.

I waited for the sure sound of the guest room mattress squeaking, the light of the lamp spilling underneath the door. Then, I grabbed a glass from the cabinet and stuck it under the faucet. I could already feel the beginning of a hangover crawling up my scalp. Water helped, sort of. I drained the glass, then filled it up again.

That's when I noticed the single match sitting on the counter.

I stilled, stared at it like it might be about to bite me. Finally, I picked it up, took my time inspecting it. It was truly just a match. Used. Someone had lit it, then left it here.

But the cabin had been clean when I got here yesterday. And these counters had been bare when I'd brewed coffee this morning. I was positive.

"Margo," I called down the hallway, a clear waver in my voice. A few beats of silence, then her door creaked open.

"What is it?"

"Did you light a match earlier?"

She yawned, long and exasperated. "Why are you asking me stupid questions right now? No, I didn't light any matches." Then the door snapped shut again, and I was fully alone.

There was a strange ringing in my ears. A quickening of my pulse.

Outside, I'd told Margo not to talk about it—about that *thing* we'd dealt with that summer. But as I stood in my quiet kitchen, wondering if someone had entered my cabin while I was gone, had left this behind as some kind of message—it was all I could think about. A figure sneaking in, disappearing without a sound. Evaporating into the darkness.

Just like the Phantom had.

CHAPTER EIGHT

THEN

Forty-Eight Days Before the Fire

The first full day of camp was always the longest, but it was also the most fun.

We had our work cut out for us this year. When Chelsea and I got to Brook Trout to pick them all up for our first morning on the lake, getting them out of bed took ages. I was blown away by the sheer number of things they'd all packed, the potions they absolutely *needed* to apply to their perfect, thirteen-year-old skin. One girl said she'd brought twenty-three pairs of shorts, and another one-upped her with twenty-six. Then I swore I heard one of them ask if anyone had seen her *retinol*.

On the first bunk bed closest to the door, I noticed a tiny blond girl wearing a blue shirt with a kitten on it that made a weird sort of sadness bloom in my chest; the rest of these girls were dressed in crop tops and Lululemon shorts. The ones who were awake were in front of the shared mirror, pushing each other out of the way to apply lip gloss and blush.

I hoped this summer wouldn't be hard on her, though I had a sneaking suspicion it might be.

"What's your name?" I asked, overselling my cheery smile.

"Kendall Everton," she told me, her tone oddly formal. "My parents said I had to come here and make friends. The problem is that I don't actually like water. Or trees. Or anything outside."

I tried to channel my inner teacher and gave her a nod of abundant understanding. "I totally get it, Kendall. The first time I went into the lake, I was really scared, too. But no one's going to force you to do anything you don't want to do, you know? Camp is supposed to be fun." Though I wasn't sure how she'd be able to avoid the outdoors, but, well. Baby steps.

"If you say so," she said with a sigh.

"All right, girls!" Chelsea called from the back of the cabin, clapping twice. "We're heading out in five minutes!"

This announcement inspired a series of groans and shrieks and the frantic ripping of bedsheets.

Kendall was ready to go, and she sat primly on the edge of her bed like a little doll, legs crossed and chin resting delicately in her hands. I sat down next to her while we waited.

"Will we ever get to sleep in?" a tall, gangly girl with a dark brown ponytail I was pretty sure was named McKenzie asked from her bunk.

"No sleeping in at summer camp!" Chelsea called back, practically indignant. "Two minutes! This is your two-minute warning, girls!"

I repressed the strong urge to roll my eyes, wanting to keep a united front. I loved Chelsea, but she could get a little intense as a counselor. Her wallflower tendencies were superseded by her love of giving directions. She was a micromanager to her core. I, on the other hand, was often chastised for letting the kids just *be.* More than once over the past few summers, my mom had to pull me aside and remind me that I was in charge. That I was allowed to be strict, say no to them. That I wasn't here to be their friend.

I would always apologize, promise to do better, but secretly, I disagreed. When I looked at Kendall, I didn't see someone looking for another mom. I saw a shy girl looking for a friend. I didn't want her to fall through the cracks.

"And, time!" Chelsea shouted, though she may have fudged the numbers a bit.

The girls filtered out, Chelsea in the front, holding a clipboard and shouting today's agenda. I waited to be the last person out, not surprised to find Kendall hanging back.

"You ready?" I asked, bumping my hip into hers, which was sort of challenging because she was so short.

She gave me a quick tilt of the head and the faintest hint of a smile.

We met Steph, Margo, and the girls of Smallmouth down at the lake. Trevor stood in front of the dock house, shirtless and smiling. I definitely didn't notice how good he looked in aviator sunglasses.

He raised his hand in a wave, and I was grateful for the blistering heat, because otherwise, it would have been clear that his attention was having a physical effect on me.

"Morning, girlies," came Steph's voice, and it was almost funny how magnetic she was. All the girls in my cabin sized her up immediately–smooth hair, perfectly pink lips, and oversize cat-eye sunglasses.

I could tell that her magnetism wasn't limited only to the Brook Trout girls. There were two girls from her own cabin with their arms already looped through hers, like a mini entourage.

They were both wearing matching smiles that took up their full faces, and the other girls were eyeing them with obvious envy.

Margo was warding off a burgeoning entourage of her own. She was surrounded by four girls who–I was guessing not by accident–had all styled their hair in tight buns on the top of their head, just like hers. They were circling her like she was chum in their tank.

"What was college like? Did you just, like, go to parties all the time?"

"Sometimes," Margo said coolly, her gaze fixed somewhere on the lake. "But mostly I studied. I'm applying to graduate school next year. And I'm planning to write a novel."

"But, like, what are boys like in college?"

Margo clicked her tongue. "Don't worry, they're all still losers. Stay far away, as long as you can."

"You don't have a boyfriend?" one of them asked, putting a hand on her hip.

"All right, all right, y'all ready to get started?" Trevor called. Because he was actually speaking now, and he of course needed my undivided attention, it made all the sense in the world that I look at him. At his face and definitely not his abs.

Unfortunately, the girls of Smallmouth and Brook Trout were not so inclined to play it cool. "What about him, though, Margo?" one of them whisper-yelled. Her name was Jade, and she'd been an awkward, quiet girl with her nose constantly in a Percy Jackson book last year. Now, apparently, she had a thing for college boys.

"What *about* him?" Margo said, feigning confusion, though I didn't miss the knowing look she gave me over the top of Jade's head.

I ignored it and shushed the rest of the girls so Trevor could start his spiel on lake safety.

For the next few hours, the girls tired themselves out, while Steph, Margo, Chelsea, and I watched from the shore, drinking copious amounts of water so we didn't pass out from the relentless midmorning heat. It was more chaotic than I'd expected, even after my stint as a counselor last year for the nines.

"So, tell me more about Trevor," Margo said when the others went to refill our water bottles.

"What do you mean?" I asked, not casual at all. "You don't like him, do you?"

She shook her head, the ghost of a smirk on her face. "Nope."

"Then why are you asking?"

"No reason," she said, examining her cuticles. "Except that you're obsessed with him."

When I didn't say anything, she gave me a sidelong look, her mouth slowly curving into a knowing smile.

"I am not *obsessed* with him. Chelsea was being dramatic. He's cute, obviously. I . . . like to look at him, I guess. That's all."

"Whatever you say, Little G."

"Margo, please," I chided, not wanting to do this with her. Not when he was standing thirty feet away from us, making sure Jade and McKenzie didn't fall off their paddleboards.

"You don't have to explain it to me. I can see the appeal," she said, fully smirking now. "If you're into the Lifeguard Ken thing. I'm all for a himbo, trust me. But, you know," she said, leaning close. "He's gotta be on something to have all those muscles. I bet his dick is tiny."

My cheeks heated. I did not want to think about anything tiny of Trevor's.

I picked at my nails, wildly uncomfortable with the direction this conversation was taking. "I'm not concerned about . . . that," I said. "We're just friends."

A moment later, he sauntered by us and down the dock, whistle swinging around his neck. He didn't stop or say a word, but he did look at both of us, his eyes full of light and mischief, and then he smiled. At me.

I had to work hard to keep from cringing.

"Just friends, you say," Margo cooed in my ear, just quiet enough that he couldn't hear. "You're such a little liar."

"Greer."

Many hours later, I blinked into the darkness, trying to figure out what was going on. I'd been sound asleep, and now, I wasn't. Because someone had said my name.

After a moment, I realized where I was. My cheek was crammed against the wall beside Steph's bed. Our backs were pressed against each other, and I could feel hers rising and falling as she slept. Someone else was snoring softly–Chelsea, I was pretty sure. But it might have been Margo. It might have been both of them.

We were all asleep in Black Bass, and it was the middle of the night. So who had said my name? Was I hallucinating?

"Greer, do you copy?"

Understanding hit me like a surge of caffeine, and I sat bolt upright. It was my mom, calling me on the walkie-talkie plugged into its charger beside my bed. I groped around for my phone, trying to check the time, but I couldn't find it anywhere.

"I need you, Greer. Please, do you copy?"

Now that I was slightly less disoriented, I could hear the urgency in her voice.

"Fuck," I said, louder than I meant to, and Steph's head whipped toward me.

Her eyes were still closed. She had all the sheets pulled up around her, like she was in some sort of cocoon.

"Was that a ghost?" I couldn't tell if she was joking, half asleep, or both.

"Shh, I'm sorry," I whispered, climbing over her as gently as I could. "Go back to sleep." I slunk across the room, trying to keep the floorboards from squeaking, and immediately cranked the volume down on my walkie before slipping outside.

Judging by the darkness, I figured it must have been around 2:00 a.m. We were still a long way from sunrise. The witching hour, my mother liked to call it—when it feels like the whole world is asleep.

"Mom, it's me," I said. "What's up?"

A few moments of static, then: "Hi, sweetheart. Everything's fine, but we need you at Brook Trout. Right now, please."

"What happened?" I said, already taking off down the path.

"Just come, Greer."

"Be there in three," I promised. I was wearing flimsy sleep shorts and a tank top, but the air was still warm and humid. As I walked, I ran my hands down the sides of my face, thinking back on last night and how I'd ended up in Steph's bed rather than my own.

After we'd done lights-out at Brook Trout and Smallmouth, we'd all met back at the cabin just after ten. It had been a long day, and Margo and Chelsea had both been out cold before I'd even turned off the overhead light. But as I'd made my way to my bed, Steph and I had locked eyes from across the room. Her face was lit up from the light of her laptop.

"Please tell me you're not tired." She'd patted the spot next to her in bed, a hopeful smile on her face.

I'd hesitated, but only for a second. "Nope, not tired," I'd whispered, crossing the room to sit beside her.

"I like to be on the outside," she'd explained, and I'd done a sort of awkward crab walk over her to get to the far side of the bed. We'd both had to clap our hands over our mouths to muffle our laughter.

She'd pulled up a show on her laptop—"*What do you mean you haven't seen* Fleabag, *Little G?*"—and we'd proceeded to watch three episodes.

I was fairly sure I'd pay for the lack of sleep tomorrow, but in the moment, I hadn't cared at all.

As I approached Brook Trout, I could just make out two figures sitting on the front steps, illuminated by the full moon and the dim front lights. One was definitely my mother. The other, I was pretty sure, was—

"Is that Miss Greer?" It was Kendall. She didn't sound thirteen right now—no, she sounded like a toddler, desperate and afraid of the dark.

"Don't worry, it's just me," I said, jogging the rest of the way to them. As I got closer, I could see that Kendall's face was blotchy, tear-stricken. At her request, Chelsea had done her hair in two French braids last night, but they were matted now and coming undone. Her pajama shirt had a cartoon of three smiling girls holding hands around a big heart, the phrase *Girl Power!* emblazoned in pink.

My mother had a protective arm wrapped tightly around her. "She requested you specifically."

I dropped to my knees and grabbed Kendall's limp hands from her lap. "It's okay," I said, hoping I sounded comforting. "Tell me what happened. You're safe, everything's fine. I'm right here."

She blinked, her chin trembling slightly. "I woke up because I really had to go to the bathroom. I tried to get Harper to go with me, but she didn't want to. So I just went by myself, because it's not that far."

My mom brushed a loose, tear-soaked tendril of hair from Kendall's face, and tucked it gently behind her ear.

"She thought she saw someone in the woods," she explained to me, though her eyes stayed on Kendall. "She screamed, and I was close by, just finishing my night rounds, so I came running."

Kendall looked up at me from beneath her eyelashes, brow furrowed. "I *did* see someone. When I came out of the bathroom, it was standing there. Watching me."

My scalp prickled at the way she said *it*. "What was watching you?"

"A monster," she whispered.

"What do you mean? What kind of monster?"

She gave me a guilty sort of look that I wasn't expecting. "What did he–it–look like?" I asked. "It's okay, you can tell us. You won't get in trouble."

She glanced at my mom, who gave her a small nod of encouragement. "Well, last night after lights-out, um, McKenzie wanted to tell ghost stories. I know they're not allowed," she said in a rush. "And I *told* them we'd get in trouble, but nobody was listening to me. So she said to shut up and then told us this story that her older brother, Jacob, told her."

Neither my mom nor I spoke, but I knew we were both thinking the same thing. When Jacob Green had been a camper here, there were only two things he cared about: beating other kids at basketball in the rec center and scaring the shit out of every camper who was younger than him, ghost story rules be damned.

"What was the story?" I asked, though I had a bad feeling that I already knew.

She sniffled, rubbed her nose on the back of her hand. "Well, a long time ago, there were two girls who came to Dread's Cove. At night, they would sneak out of their cabin after the other girls went to sleep to explore the woods. They went farther and farther out every single night, until they made it to the very edges of camp, past where anyone was allowed to go."

Her voice grew quieter. "That's where they found the secret graves of all the prisoners who died here. They were all in a row, their bodies buried next to each other. The girls could feel the spirits there, and that they were angry. One of them got scared and said they should turn back. She said it was a bad idea to disturb them. But the other girl wanted to stay.

"They got down in the dirt and started digging up one of the graves. And they were right. There was a body there. It had been there for so long that there was only a skeleton left. They each took a bone with them, like a souvenir. Then, they went back to their cabin, and they woke everyone up to show off what they'd found."

She looked between me and my mom, her pupils blown wide. "The next morning, there was a message written on their cabin in blood. It said, *YOU WILL PAY.*"

My teeth clenched the way they always did when I heard that phrase. No matter how the story changed—sometimes it was two boys, or two counselors; sometimes the bones were in the middle of the lake, or buried in the Barn—they always found those same three words.

I knew what came next. The story always ended the same way.

"A day later, they were both gone. They'd disappeared out of their beds. The bones they'd stolen were gone, too. The prisoner came to take back what was theirs. And to punish them."

Kendall took a deep breath, like the adrenaline had finally slowed down, and she looked thoroughly exhausted. "McKenzie says that the monster is still out there in the woods. Whatever thing they woke up is just biding their time. And they'll only be happy when every camper is gone for good. When *everyone* here is gone for good."

My mother kept her features smooth and expressionless, but I could tell she was frustrated. She'd forbidden telling ghost stories years ago, because it always led to something like this. Especially when this story started to make the rounds.

"That's what I saw. A monster. It came up from the grave, and it's wandering around in the woods, looking for its next victim. To punish us." Her throat moved as she swallowed. "I know what I saw. The Phantom of Dread's Cove."

I knew it wasn't real, and even so, I shivered. I would have to have a serious talk with McKenzie tomorrow—absolutely no more late-night ghost stories. "That sounds really scary, Kendall. But you don't need to worry."

"You don't believe me?" Her lip trembled, and she was on the edge of tears once more.

Just as I opened my mouth to speak, my mom caught my eye, and I hesitated. I knew we were both thinking the same thing. We didn't want her to grow more agitated by telling her she was wrong. But we also didn't want her to believe there *was* someone—or something—out there, stalking through the trees in the middle of the night.

"I think your eyes were playing tricks on you," I said at last, and my mom gave a subtle nod of approval. "A good night's sleep will make you feel a million times better." I squeezed her hand once, then twice. "I promise, there's nothing out there. The Phantom isn't real."

CHAPTER NINE

NOW

I knew that it was just a ghost story. There was no monster.

But there were a hundred people here this weekend. And as Margo had proved, it wasn't hard to break into this place.

That thought alone made me stand up straighter. The walls were paper-thin. I could hear the creak of the guest room bathroom door, the sound of Margo turning on the sink and loudly completing her skin care routine that was surely eighteen steps long. If there were someone here, I would be able to hear them. And anyway, who breaks into your house, lights a single match, and hides under your bed to . . . what? Kill you?

As ridiculous as the thought sounded in my head, it still made my chest tighten. I thought again of being out in those woods, fumbling with the flashlight. Leaves crunching and branches snapping. That deep-seated feeling that someone was just out of sight, watching.

I strained my brain, trying to remember what I'd done last night when I'd gotten in. It was all such a blur—being back in my childhood home for the first time in five years, waiting for my mom to appear at any moment. Having to remind myself that she wouldn't.

Had I lit a candle last night? I didn't think so, but I must have. There was nothing else that made sense. Besides, the cabin smelled faintly of warm cookies, my mom's favorite scent that she always kept stockpiled.

I checked, rechecked, and triple-checked my bathroom and closet, just to be sure, and locked the door to my room. I knew I could have walkied Rig, but it felt so childish. What would I even say? I found a used match on the counter? No, I was being paranoid. Everything was fine, and I was completely safe here.

But I couldn't get it out of my head, as I lay in bed and waited for sleep.

I couldn't help but feel like it meant something. That it meant fire.

I woke up early on the day of my mother's funeral, around sunrise, jittery and wired. Light was just barely peeking through the curtains, spilling onto my pillow.

As the coffee brewed, I eyed the staircase, and a strange sort of boldness took hold of me. I wanted to go upstairs, finally. I wanted to see my mother's room. I needed to.

But when I finally stepped inside, I almost turned around.

Our cabin wasn't tiny, exactly, but it was cozy. That's what my mom had always said, at least. It had been a gift from Grandpa Dread, when my mom and dad had moved to camp after they graduated college. They were young and in love, freshly engaged, and my grandpa had built this place for them as a wedding present.

Their marriage hadn't lasted long, but my mother and I had lived here my entire life. It had always been a safe space for me. It had always been my home. And I'd spent a thousand hours in this room—sneaking up here to sleep with my mom when a thunderstorm shook the ground, begging her to read me one more story even as my eyes drooped with sleep.

Rig and Val had been kind, hiring cleaners to come in and pack up the place. They knew I couldn't bear it, and neither could they. The window was open, the curtains billowing in the soft breeze, and I took a deep, shuddering breath.

The furniture was the same as it had always been, of course: the old four-poster bed she'd inherited from her grandparents, and the twin side tables beside them. There was a gnawing pain in my chest as I saw how sterile the room was now, without all her color and light. I didn't see the little pocket Bible that she always kept on her bedside table, and the lack of it made the room feel completely wrong. I made a mental note to ask Rig if he knew where it was.

I opened every dresser drawer, a wave of anxiety creeping up my back. They were all empty. The room looked blank, unlived in, and it made me feel strangely detached. Like I wasn't really here. Like she'd never really been here at all.

But in the left bedside table, the bottom drawer caught on something; I heard a screech, like something was stuck in the mechanism. I reached my hand in as far as it could go, groping around in the dark. Finally, I found it.

In my hand was a dainty gold necklace that had been damaged somewhere along the way. It had three small, glittering charms—an *N*, an *I*, and an *E*. My breath caught.

My mother was Anita professionally, but to her closest friends, she'd always been Annie.

The chain looked old, and slightly rusted at the clasp. I wondered just how long she'd been missing it.

I'd never seen it before, though that wasn't exactly surprising. My mom had loved jewelry—the good stuff, the cheap stuff, and everything in between. Most of it was locked away in a safe-deposit box that Val had set up for me, on the other side of the pass in Lavender. I couldn't handle going through all of it myself, so I'd let her deal with it. Now, though, in her sterile room, I regretted that choice.

Not only were a couple of the gold letters missing, but the chain was tangled, and I took my time unraveling it, not wanting to make it worse. After a few minutes, it was all straightened out. In a moment of crippling sadness that almost knocked the wind out of me, I stood in front of the small mirror and clasped it around my neck.

I put my hand to the remaining charms, feeling the small grooves in the metal, comforted by the sharp edges.

This was real. My mom was real. I was real. She was with me, even in some small way. Looking after me.

I'm safe here, I told myself over and over, forcing myself to stop thinking about that damn match on the counter.

When Margo and I got to the mess hall for breakfast a few hours later, it was crawling with strangers. It set my teeth on edge.

Logically, I understood why we'd invited reporters here. It was all part of Chelsea's master plan, to make Welcome Back Weekend the hottest ticket of the summer, to get the whole state talking, and to get every kid in the Southeast foaming at the mouth to spend their summer at the remote paradise that was Dread's Cove.

While I wondered how many of them were planning to make fun of me in their articles—a washed-up bartender, nepo baby with no experience, the sole heir to an infamous, possibly haunted summer camp—I did hope that, for my mother's sake, they would see whatever beauty was left here. Even if they had to squeeze it to its breaking point.

Before the summer of the fire, Dread's Cove had never experienced such a swift fall from grace. My mother was called every name in the book; our family was dragged through hell and back, accused of gross negligence at best, black magic and cult rituals at worst.

Everything we did was questioned in the aftermath—all our safety protocols and emergency evacuation plans. Our vetting process for staff members. Our training procedures for counselors. No one was satisfied with the simplest answer: that the fire had been an act of God. A brutal, yet entirely natural and non-preventable tragedy.

No, for many people, that was too easy. They wanted a witch hunt. They wanted a culprit.

It wasn't just because of the fire itself, or Steph's death. It was everything that led up to it, too, the treasure map that landed with a big black X on that awful, awful night. The break-ins and vandalism. The boys who went missing in the woods. That final message, left in bloodred paint on the mess hall, laced with rage and warning.

It didn't matter that my mom did damage control in the months after, agreeing to interview after interview. It was a wildfire, she said—and it had absolutely nothing to do with the faceless criminal who'd been terrorizing Dread's Cove for two months. There had been lightning that night on the other side of

Lady's Lake. It had been a dry summer, one of the driest on record.

But there were still rumors, of course. People came out of the woodwork to claim that there hadn't been lightning near the lake that night; that she was lying to save face. That it hadn't been an accident.

My family owned hundreds of acres, and technically speaking, the fire had burned across private property. Which meant that police findings had never been made public. And though no one could prove my mother wrong, that it was simply a terrible, natural accident, it was never clear if she was right, either. If the fire had been the final act of the Dread's Cove Phantom, after a summer of little horrors.

Or if she was hiding something. If we all were.

And now those very same reporters who'd called my mother a liar, who'd printed stories accusing her of gross negligence, of being a dumb heiress who had no business being responsible for children, were all here this weekend, pretending to mourn her.

I was scanning the room for a somewhat private table (of which there were none) when Chelsea grabbed my wrist, spinning me around so that our faces were inches apart.

"Are you trying to sabotage me?" she hissed through bared teeth.

I could see the wild expanse of new freckles across her nose, a testament to her hours spent in the sun over the past few months as she oversaw the final days of construction.

I also saw the exhaustion, up close like this. The bags under her eyes were poorly disguised by the wrong shade of concealer.

"No, of course not." I kept my voice quiet, intimately aware of the strangers and friends watching us closely. Margo had made a beeline for the espresso station, stating that the coffee I'd made had tasted like dirt water.

"Then why is *she* here?" Chelsea said, keeping her tone low but dangerous. She was watching Margo with a sort of vitriol I'd rarely seen before. She'd always been anxious, sure, the first person to call out a worst-case scenario. But that had been from a place of worry or fear. This felt more like rage, and I didn't know what to make of it. Though, I supposed, I didn't know her all that well anymore. I'd spoken to her about as much over the past half decade as I had Margo; which is to say, almost not at all.

Ignoring Chelsea hadn't been personal. It's just that I couldn't handle coming back as they rebuilt–though my mom asked, then begged as the years stretched on. Chelsea had understood my intentions much faster–what my silence meant–and she was far less kind than my mom, or Wes. Six months after the fire, she sent me her final text: You're a coward. I'd deleted it and blocked her number, proving her right.

"I was going to ask you the same question," I said under my breath, fake smile bright on my face. "She's here with *The Atlanta Times*."

Chelsea blinked rapidly, mouth going slack, like she'd had her factory settings rebooted. "She's here as a fucking reporter? Are you kidding me? How did that happen?"

Now was not the time to acknowledge that this may have been the first time on record that Chelsea had ever said the word *fuck*, so I resisted the temptation. "Don't look at me. I wasn't in charge of the press invites."

"You weren't in charge of anything, if I remember correctly." Her nostrils flared, and I knew this was no longer about Margo. This was all of her resentment toward me, built up over the past five years and maybe even longer, finally bubbling over in real time. Margo's arrival in the mess hall this morning was merely the catalyst. An easy reason for her to finally open the floodgates.

The tension stretched taut between us. "Chels, I didn't know she was coming. She scared the shit out of me–snuck into my mom's cabin during dinner last night."

She stuck a finger in my face, as if I'd just admitted to Margo having pointed a loaded gun at me. "That's a crime. Breaking and entering. I don't care if she has to *walk* back to Atlanta, she's out of here–" She tried to push past me, presumably to head straight for Margo, and I could only imagine the scene that might be about to unfold. This weekend–the one that she and my mom had worked themselves to the bone to make perfect–would be tainted with scandal before it even started.

I grabbed her arm, but I wasn't about to tell her what we'd found last night, or that I'd agreed to help Margo. I didn't think that would go over particularly well.

"Take a breath," I said instead, and Chelsea stilled, like I knew she would–not because she wanted to listen to me, but because I'd said it the way my mom would have. "Margo Pierce is writing a story about Dread's Cove for *The Atlanta Times*, okay? Now is not the time to piss her off. You know she plays to win. You're just going to have to smile and nod at her for the next few days. This is happening. There's no stopping it."

I chanced a look at Margo, who was sniffing the carafe of oat milk before daintily pouring the world's smallest splash into her mug. Before she took her first sip, I watched as she closed her eyes for a beat too long, like she was centering herself. It tugged at something in my chest. I wouldn't say it to Chelsea, but there was another reason that I wanted to help her, that I'd only just started to realize: I pitied her.

The fire had taken Dread's Cove from my family, from Chelsea and all of us who had grown up here. And that had been a tragedy.

But Margo had suffered, too. She hadn't shared much that summer about her family life, but I knew she had a single mother who she wasn't close to. Steph had been her life raft. Her found family. Now, she had no one.

I'd thought about Steph, and the fire that burned her alive, every day since it happened. During the year I'd been dating Trevor, and things had been good, my fixation on Steph had been what pushed him away, in the end. Even now, thoughts of that night kept me from sleeping; it would play out across my closed eyes, a terrible movie that I couldn't turn off.

So although she'd never let me ask her about it, I knew it must have been worse for Margo.

Chelsea crossed her arms and sighed, the sound more like a growl. "Don't let her ruin this for us. We can't trust her. I know she's up to something."

My shoulders tensed at her use of *us* and *we*. She'd been outright ignoring me the past two days, but now that Margo was here, we were back to being aligned.

But the truth was that, if she'd had her way, I wouldn't have been on the invite list, either. No, I'd be back in Atlanta, under permanent exile, while they reopened the camp without me. She could fill my mother's shoes, in the way I'd always been expected to, and they could all have their perfect happily ever after. No traitors allowed.

"Listen, I haven't exactly given you a warm welcome," Chelsea began.

I gave her a look.

"Anita was like a mom to me. I'm still–" She stopped and scrunched her nose, her classic tell that she was trying to keep back tears. "None of this is easy. For any of us. I get that, and I'm sorry. But think this through, before you let her get close to you again. There is a lot riding on this weekend. We don't want any . . . complications."

She was attempting diplomacy, but there was no question of what she meant. Me, turning into a complication. Me, allowing Margo to dredge up the past when everyone was trying to move forward. Me, making rash and stupid decisions, making things harder on all of them. Just like I'd done five years ago.

After the fire, I'd left them all behind, built a completely new life on *maybe* and *not sure yet* and *I'm too busy to talk about this right now.* I'd cut almost everyone off, except my mom.

I only gave her scraps, even though I could feel how much it hurt her. I wouldn't talk to her on the phone; I'd only answer every third or fourth text, but she kept trying.

But it was too hard. I knew what they all thought–that I was throwing my life away, the plans I had and the people who cared about me, all because I was fixated on the death of a girl I hardly knew.

"I've got it under control," I said, and swept past her.

I thought she might stop me, but she didn't. As I made my way across the crowded mess hall to Margo, I put on a vacant smile, waving blandly to the reporters and the alums I'd yet to greet. I almost tripped over my own feet when I saw little Kendall

Everton, all grown up, flirting with a group of old campers who must have been college-aged now, like her.

She blinked several times, like she was trying to place me, then looked pointedly away. My back stiffened as another wave of shame rolled through me. But I kept walking.

I made myself smile broadly, ignoring the whispers that I could hear at my back. I pretended I didn't hear the guy next to her say, "It's fucking crazy that she's the one in charge."

CHAPTER TEN

THEN

Forty-Three Days Before the Fire

Even after what happened with Kendall, it had been a near-perfect first week. No serious injuries, no teenagers caught making out in the Barn. After our annual camp-wide capture the flag game this afternoon, everyone was tired from the heat and had crashed early.

I was tired, too, but I'd stopped by my mother's cabin around ten o'clock for a celebratory cup of chamomile tea, as was our tradition. We were sitting out on her back patio, looking out over the water, watching the fireflies wink in the dim moonlight.

My mom took a long sip from her favorite mug, the one with a rainbow trout jumping in a stream. "So, how are Steph and Margo adjusting? I feel like I've barely spent any time with them."

"Well, the girls love them. Which makes sense, because Steph is hilarious. And so much fun. One of the Smallmouth girls, Celia, told me that every night, Steph has them vote on three Taylor Swift songs, and they have a mini dance party before bed. And then Margo is–well, it's hard to describe Margo. She's sort of mean, but in a cool way?"

My mom's mouth quirked up. "Does she join in on these dance parties?"

"She must. Steph doesn't really take no for an answer."

After I talked about both of them for five minutes straight without stopping or taking a breath, my mom leaned back in her chair, looking smug and satisfied. "Who would have thought that mono would actually be a blessing in disguise? You seem pretty smitten."

We both laughed, the sound echoing through the trees. She was right—I was smitten. Especially with Steph.

We had the bottom bunks and were usually the last two awake. We'd done the same thing every night for the past week. After Margo and Chelsea had started snoring, I'd sneak over to her bed, like we had that first night. We'd share headphones and watch something on her laptop—we'd finished *Fleabag* last night, and had already decided our next project would be all the *Twilight* movies.

I loved being a counselor, but I'd never been so excited for curfew. This summer, it meant I had uninterrupted hours with Steph Bennett.

It had only been a few days, but—as ridiculous as it sounded—I couldn't believe I'd spent my whole life not being friends with her.

Because it wasn't only that she was interesting. She made me feel interesting, too. She made me feel like someone worth staying up late for.

"This summer just feels special," I said in closing, as I fiddled with my tea bag.

I glanced back at my mom, expecting to see her smirking still, but a wistful kind of cloud had passed in front of her face. "I'm glad to hear it. This place is magic like that, I think–always bringing us the people we need the most."

I was about to ask my mom what she was talking about–if she was okay–when one of the counselors came around back. It was clear from the way he was wringing his hands that he hadn't come by for a simple social call.

"Logan," my mom said, jumping into her role seamlessly. "What's the matter?"

He scratched at the patchy stubble on his chin. "I was finishing up my rounds and passed the office. The front window is completely busted out, ma'am. Someone, well–someone broke in, I think."

I gasped, before I could stop myself. "Are you serious?"

He rolled back on his heels and looked out at the water as if our rapt attention was making him uncomfortable. "Or maybe it was an animal. I don't know, ma'am."

"Thank you." My mom's tone wasn't unkind, but it lacked her usual warmth. She set her mug down on the table with a soft clank, then flexed her hand before tucking a loose strand of hair behind her ear. "Please head back to your cabin. We'll take it from here."

After Logan was out of earshot, she let out a single, whispered "*Shit.*"

"Should we . . . ," I began, and we locked eyes. Hers were round and bright, but there was a tension between her eyebrows that I rarely saw. She usually reserved that sort of frustration for the annual budget meeting, or the few times per summer when she had to seriously reprimand a camper.

My mom called for Rig on her walkie-talkie–said we had a *Code Yellow*, which was our shorthand for potentially dangerous situations—and we waited in stilted silence for a long few minutes before he met us at the head of the path.

"Someone broke into the office," she told him before he had a chance to ask, and Rig frowned, his mustache drooping.

"Who?" A look that I couldn't decipher passed between them. After a moment, Rig gave us both a stiff nod and patted the revolver in his holster. "Let's go check it out."

I opened my mouth to protest—a gun? I didn't argue, though, worried that they'd tell me to head back to Black Bass.

Silently, we made the short trek to the office. All I could think about was what Kendall had said the other night. That she had seen someone—a monster—stalking through the woods. My mom and I had been so quick to dismiss it as the result of telling stories, a figment of her imagination.

But now . . . I didn't know what to think.

The office was the first building you saw when you entered camp property, just in front of the rec center. Right now, it was shrouded in heavy darkness. My mother shone her flashlight, and just as Logan had described, the front window was smashed through.

"Some kind of prank," my mother suggested with forced lightness, breaking the tense silence that had been building between the three of us.

She took out her master key and let us inside, and thankfully, Rig didn't take out his gun. It was immediately clear that there was no one inside. The office was a small space, with only three cramped rooms and a locked closet where we kept all the camp archives. There was a large rock and shards of glass in front of the window, and my mother held her arm out in front of me to keep me from walking through the mess.

I heard nothing but the soft hum of the cicadas, and the dull sound of my heart thumping in my rib cage.

Crime wasn't exactly a common occurrence around here. Yes, we kept a lot of the buildings locked, but that was more for safety reasons than the actual fear of someone trying to steal or vandalize. I could tell by the way my mom was fiddling with the pendant around her neck that she was more uncomfortable than she wanted to let on. I didn't ask, but I wondered if she was thinking about what Kendall had said, too.

The door to her office had been forced open, the papers and frames on her desk thrown around haphazardly. Eeriest of all, the screen of her computer was awake—someone had been here, only a few minutes ago, trying to log in.

To do . . . what?

I was hit by a wave of nausea. Though it was my mother's office that had been broken into, I felt strangely violated.

I couldn't pinpoint exactly why I was so afraid, but I was. Maybe it was because of how isolated we were out here. That had always made Dread's Cove feel like a refuge from the rest of the world. I'd never thought much about how dangerous that remoteness could be—what might happen if someone took advantage of it.

We were three miles from Lavender, the small town where many of the staff lived during the off-season. Even so, you could count the number of stoplights on one hand; it wasn't exactly a mecca of civilization. Sheriff Ramon had jurisdiction over the whole county, which meant his office was at least an hour's drive on a good day. It would be even harder to rouse him in the middle of the night.

If something terrible really did happen—if we were in danger—how long would it take for someone to get here?

What would happen while we waited?

"You don't think this was whatever Kendall saw, do you?" I asked, my voice high-pitched and strained. "Was he . . . real?"

"There's no monster in the woods, ladybug," Rig said, with an easy kindness that bordered on condescending.

"Then who did this?"

They were both quiet for a moment.

"Rig, will you walk Greer back to Black Bass?" my mom asked, leaning down to examine the broken glass on the floor.

I didn't like being excused and ordered around like a child, but I didn't argue; I wanted to get out of there as soon as possible.

I kept close to Rig's side as we walked, feeling a strange sense of relief that he had that gun, after all. I'd never once felt nervous walking through Dread's Cove before—how many times had I wandered these paths alone, even as a child, popping between my mom's place and Chelsea's, or Wes's?

I thought of the girls in our own cabin. I thought of the younger campers, heading to the bathroom in the middle of the night. I thought of someone following them through the darkness.

Everything suddenly felt a little more dangerous. Even the moonlight felt ominous, rather than welcoming.

"Who do you think did it?" I asked Rig when we got to Black Bass, my hand hovering over the doorknob.

A muscle in his jaw ticked. "Like your mom said, probably just some kids playing a joke." He glanced at the door, the tightness in his eyes betraying his worry. "Tell the girls to be careful, all right? Don't walk around by yourselves, especially at night. Just until we nip this in the bud."

I gave him a wooden nod. "I'll tell them."

He squeezed my shoulder. I didn't miss the way he patted the gun on his hip, once, then twice, before disappearing into the woods, back in the direction we'd come.

My roommates were all asleep, but I was so rattled that I woke them. We sat in a circle on the floor while I told them the whole story. Chelsea's face was white when I finished. "But you're sure they didn't take anything?"

"Not that we can tell. It was weird, though. There's nothing worth stealing in there."

"Does your mom have any idea who it was?" Steph was quieter, more somber than usual. She sat with her head resting on Margo's shoulder, legs crisscrossed so that she appeared folded into herself. "The same guy Kendall saw?"

"Kendall didn't see anything." I said the words as confidently as I could muster, but I didn't know if I believed it.

"We're just supposed to be careful. It was probably some kids being stupid. We'll tighten up the curfew requirements. I doubt it will happen again."

I was wrong.

CHAPTER ELEVEN

NOW

Margo had taken a seat in the back of the mess hall at the last empty table. She gripped her mug in both hands, back facing the corner, as if she didn't want anyone to be able to sneak up on her.

"Are you going to eat anything?" she asked, eyeing my empty hands.

I shook my head, not trusting myself to say anything.

"Welcome, welcome!" came Chelsea's voice from the stage. Gone was her anger from a few moments ago. Now, she was all smiles, the perfect emulation of my mother, yet again.

She waited a short beat for the voices in the room to die down. "Good morning, y'all. We've got a packed agenda for today, so make sure you eat up. This morning will be guided tours of the new facilities, and this afternoon we will be honoring Anita Olsen with a memorial service on the pavilion."

I squeezed my eyes shut, feeling the weight of more than one glance in my direction.

"Why is Baby running the show?" Margo leaned over to ask me. She was attempting to peel an orange with her pointy acrylics. She sucked the juice from one of her nails, then glanced at me expectantly when I didn't answer. "Aren't you the big boss now?"

"It's complicated."

"How so?"

I sighed, rubbed a hand to my temple. "I guess I technically own the property now, yeah."

Margo's lip twitched. "Still playing coy about being a millionaire, are we?"

Heat rose in my cheeks. "I'm not playing coy, I just . . ." I trailed off. Not wanting to say the truth, because it was ugly.

I just don't feel like I deserve it.

I just don't think anyone believes I can do it.

I just don't want it at all.

"You just what?" Her voice was more serious now. When I didn't say anything right away, she cocked her head to the side. "Tell me this: How long are you planning to stick around?"

"I haven't gotten that far yet," I said, my gaze on the ceiling. "It would be . . . a lot, you know? Running a summer camp. I don't know if . . . I don't know."

When I finally met Margo's eye, she wasn't looking at me with pity but something close. "So you're punishing yourself." I had no idea what to say. My silence was answer enough.

Chelsea finished her announcements and flounced off the stage, and after a beat, the room grew loud again. She gave us a wide berth, and I watched her make her way to a table on the far side of the room.

She dropped down next to Rig, and my stomach hollowed out. Because on the other side of him was Trevor, coffee mug halfway to his lips when he saw me.

For a long moment, neither of us moved. Then he lifted his

free hand in a slow, lazy wave, his smile only a little unsure, and like a middle schooler, I glanced away without acknowledging him.

"Lifeguard Ken is looking at you," Margo deadpanned from next to me. "I swear he's gotten cuter."

"Stop it. Please."

Her lip twitched. "He's coming over here."

"I'm serious, just—" I started, but abruptly cut myself off when I saw that Trevor was, in fact, weaving his way through the crowd.

"Shit." I thought Margo might have at least a shred of decency—that she might excuse herself and let me flounder alone—but no. Instead, she leaned back and let her eyes drift between Trevor and me hungrily, as if her favorite show was about to start after a multi-season hiatus.

My spine stiffened when he dropped down on the bench next to me. "Been looking for you all morning," he said, reaching out to pat me on the shoulder. I tensed, and I wondered if he noticed. He glanced at Margo, eyes dimming only slightly as he took her in. "Margo. Good to see you."

She only waggled her fingers at him before violently digging another talon into her orange. Though she was attempting to look uninterested, I knew she'd be hanging on every word.

"I've been busy," I said, sitting on my hands so I wouldn't fidget. "Did you need something? More towels?"

His expression grew somber, and he scooted closer. "No, I don't need anything. I haven't had a chance to talk to you yet, and I wanted to see how you were doing." He gestured at the room behind us; the squealing former campers, the camera-clad reporters. "This has got to be a bit overwhelming, yeah?"

"I'm fine," I said, absolutely not fine at all.

It had been four years since I'd last seen him. We'd been together for just shy of a year at that point, and we'd been getting ready to move. For months, we'd talked through tons of ideas–Missoula, Portland, San Diego, Amsterdam. Anywhere. We'd finally decided on Boulder.

We had it all planned out. Both of our leases were ending around the same time, and we'd road trip, make a whole summer vacation out of it. Trevor had already gotten a job leading fly-fishing trips, and my résumé was in the final rounds of consideration for a coveted position at a buzzy new cocktail bar.

We were going to live together, in a tiny apartment we couldn't really afford, and ride bikes on the weekends, and float the river in the summer.

And in the span of one night, everything had fallen apart. Shattered like glass. He'd left, and I'd stayed. I hadn't seen or heard from him since.

Now, here he was–after so much silence, so much bone-shaking sadness–sidling up to me in the mess hall like we were in an alternate timeline. One where the camp hadn't burned down, no one had died, and he still loved me enough to stick around.

I couldn't do this. Not today. Not with Margo Pierce watching. "You know what, I've actually got to–do something for Rig. I just remembered."

I bolted from the table before he had a chance to stop me, though I was almost sure he called my name. Margo trailed close behind me, her black sandals nipping at my ankles. When we got outside, the tears were already blurring my vision, and I pressed my back against the wall to keep myself upright.

He still smelled the same. I hated myself for noticing.

"Just breathe, Little G." Her words were neither soft nor kind, but she was the one who'd followed me out, who was making sure I wasn't slipping into a panic attack. So I followed her direction for a few long moments before feeling steady enough to push myself off the wall.

"You want to tell me what happened between you two?"

"We broke up," I said, a quaver in my voice that I couldn't hide. "We were together for a while after the fire, but . . . it didn't work out. Doesn't matter. I'm totally fine, I just wasn't expecting to see him this weekend. He caught me off guard. But I'm over it. Seriously."

"Same old Greer," she sighed, even as she grabbed my wrist and pulled me gently forward. "Always pretending."

I forced my feet to move off the porch and squinted into the midmorning sun. "I'm not pretending," I said, though we both knew I was. Then, and now.

CHAPTER TWELVE

THEN

Forty-One Days Before the Fire

My mother was shaken up after the office break-in, though she tried her best to hide it. Especially since we'd enacted a much stricter curfew system. We'd doubled up on night rounds as well, meaning there would now be at least four counselors awake and on duty until midnight.

We were under explicit instruction to not gossip with the campers about what had happened, but that didn't stop the news from spreading like wildfire; it was hard, after all, to completely hide the evidence of a trashed building. It didn't help that more than one camper had noticed Sheriff Ramon's patrol car when he'd stopped by the next day to check things out.

In another unfortunate turn of events, Chelsea had twisted her ankle slipping on the dock, which took her out of commission for a few days. She hadn't broken it, thankfully, but it was bad enough that hiking was entirely out of the question.

That was a problem, because today was the overnight trip to Lady's Lurch for Brook Trout, and it was well known as being the best hike of the summer. I couldn't exactly lead the group all on my own, but both the girls and their parents would riot if we canceled.

So there were a few things stacked against us. But I quickly found a silver lining–my mom asked Trevor to be Chelsea's stand-in.

It was his night off, but Anita Olsen was passionate, persistent, and difficult to say no to. So he didn't.

I was more excited than I wanted to let on. Every time I looked at him, the butterflies started to swarm. It seemed serendipitous, that we could spend a little bit of time together, away from everyone else.

The path to Lady's Lurch was well marked and mostly flat, a simple and beautiful two-hour hike in each direction. We got to hang back and let the girls lead the way. Which was certainly for the best, considering that it was harder for them all to openly ogle Trevor if he was walking fifteen feet behind them.

"What are you laughing at?" he said, catching the look on my face. I was horrifyingly sweaty, my hair tied back with an old bandanna.

His expression was exasperated–as if he already knew what I was about to say–and it only made me laugh more. "You've got some fans," I said, gesturing ahead of us at the three girls in the back of the pack.

Though it was hard to hike while staring behind you, these three were proving that it was, in fact, not impossible. It was funny how subtle they thought they were being.

"Shut up," Trevor said, rolling his eyes. He punched me lightly on the shoulder, just as the girls turned around for the one hundredth time. Not surprisingly, they exploded into groans and raucous giggles at the mere sight of me and Trevor touching.

"I didn't know they were together, let's go back–"

"Every hot guy at this camp, like, already has a girlfriend, I'm suing–"

I snorted an unflattering laugh, then slapped a hand to my mouth. "Wow, we sure got serious fast," I teased. "I'm already your girlfriend and you haven't even taken me to dinner yet."

Trevor didn't say anything right away, and I snuck a glance at him. He was staring at me with an unexpected intensity that made my toes curl in my shoes.

I stopped walking, hit over the head with the rush of it, and so did he.

He was so tall. I had to crane my neck to see him, as close as we were now standing. As always, he smelled like salt water and mint, though part of me wondered if it was just the tiniest bit more concentrated today.

"What is it?" I asked.

He flashed his teeth, then tugged on a lock of hair that had fallen loose from my ponytail. "Just trying to decide."

"Trying to decide . . . what?" The words came out low and breathy as his finger barely grazed my cheek.

"Where I'd take you to dinner."

Heat rushed to my face. "That's–"

"Miss Greer?" Kendall's voice up ahead jarred me solidly back into the present moment, and my responsibilities. We were not on a date, unfortunately; we were chaperoning a hike for children. Whatever this was would have to wait. Trevor dropped his hand just as I took a step back from him.

"We're right behind you," I called up the path, entirely flustered, and I made myself move forward. I was certain he was smirking.

"I've made a decision," Kendall announced.

It was hours later, and we were the last two awake, except for Trevor, who'd snuck off to the beach a while ago after a few too many screams at lizard sightings. We were sitting around the makeshift campfire we'd built out of flashlights–fires were strictly forbidden this summer due to the dry conditions–and she'd stifled three yawns in the past five minutes. I'd just been about to suggest she head to her tent.

"Kendall," I said with a sigh. "Remember, we talked about this. I know you want to go home, but you're going to have to wait until the end of summer like everyone else."

"No, that's not what I meant. I've officially decided who my first-ever crush will be."

I raised my eyebrows at her, fighting a smile. "First crush *ever*? Seriously?"

"Yes, ever. The boys at my school are not smart. And they all smell bad."

I nodded somberly, accepting this astute assessment. "Fair enough. This is a big deal, then. Who is it?"

"Carter Banks. He's in Bluegill."

I scrunched my nose, attempting to scan my brain for any image of Carter Banks. I wasn't sure if I recognized his name.

"This is his first year, too," she explained.

A toad croaked from somewhere, and Kendall gave a pointed look of disgust.

"Well, tell me everything," I said, nudging her with my knee. "What do you like about him?"

Her expression was thoughtful, as usual. "We have a lot in common. We both like the same comic books and graphic novels. And he's funny. He thinks I'm funny."

I could tell, even in the dim light, that a flush was creeping up her cheeks.

"He believes me, about seeing the Phantom in the woods." She lowered her voice, conspiratorial now. "He saw it, too. Walking past his cabin."

I stilled. "He saw . . . what?"

"The same thing I did. There's someone out there, Miss Greer." She took a sip from her water bottle, some of it dribbling onto her chin. She wiped it off delicately with the napkin she still had folded in her lap from dinner, as formal as if we were at a tea party with Meghan Markle. "The Phantom."

When I didn't say anything, she looked at me. "Please don't be mad. Everyone's talking about it, not just me and Carter. Another boy in Bluegill, Jeremy Wallis, saw him, too."

I frowned. Before I could ask my next question, Kendall yawned again, the loudest yet.

"I'm tired. Good night, Miss Greer," Kendall chirped at me before disappearing into her tent, where Harper was snoring loud enough to raise the dead.

As I turned off the flashlights, I wondered how my mom would react when I told her all this. The whole thing made me uneasy, thinking about Kendall having whispered conversations with other kids, all of them working each other into a frenzy over what they'd seen—no, what they thought they'd seen.

And then I worried about just how many other campers were

having these same clandestine meetings with each other. Kendall had said *everyone's talking about it.* Was she right?

Just how quickly would all this Phantom shit get completely out of hand?

I grabbed my sweatshirt that I'd let Kendall borrow from the log we'd been sitting on, and tied it around my waist. The air was warm still, but not stifling, now that the sun was down. Setting up camp this close to the water had its advantages—there was a pleasant, if not cool breeze that rustled my hair every few minutes.

I stretched my arms over my head, thinking of sleep, but then my eyes flitted toward the beach. That's when I realized—now, it was just Trevor and me. Every anxious thought I had about the Phantom left my brain completely, and I went to find him.

He sat on the small beach, his feet in the water. The shore was a little rocky, but I didn't mind, and I dropped down next to him.

He took a pull from a flask that he must have snuck with him, and I watched his lips move.

Psychopath. Stop it.

"You brought a flask?" I asked, scrambling to talk about anything innocuous. He held it out to me, and I hesitated only a moment before accepting.

I misjudged how bad it would taste and immediately started sputtering, putting my hand over my mouth to keep quiet. "What is this?"

"You don't like it?"

"That is lethal," I said, coughing dramatically, just to make him laugh. It was dark, but I was smiling. I knew he could hear it.

A low chuckle. "I'm aware."

"Did you . . ." I trailed off, searching my brain for another topic. "So, I mean, how have you been?"

I thought he might make fun of me, my almost formal nicety, but instead he took a deep breath, like he was genuinely considering the question.

"Do you want the real answer? Or the polite one?"

"The real one," I said easily.

He nodded, as if in acceptance, and closed his eyes.

"My parents were not happy that I decided to come back this summer," he said. "Especially my dad. I don't know how much you know about him, but he's a man with . . . high expectations."

Of course I knew about Trevor's dad—his law firm was one of the most prestigious in Atlanta.

"I never really had an interest in being a lawyer. Too buttoned-up for me. My older brother, Marshall, was built for it. He'll be partner in the next few years, and he's my dad's pride and joy." He shrugged one shoulder. "Which was honestly always fine and good for me. I got to play it under the radar, you know? Marshall was valedictorian, I skated by on B's. Marshall was hardwired for success, for discipline and grit, and I just—sounds stupid, but I always knew I just wanted to be happy. Be comfortable. See the world. I've always been scared of being . . . stuck."

He took a sip from the flask, then passed it to me. "It was naive of me, but I just assumed that I'd be able to finish college and do whatever I wanted. Marshall could be the perfect, accomplished son, and I could fuck off. My dad didn't feel the same way. *He'd* assumed that I'd come to work for him after school. He wanted the package set. Had a whole plan for me and everything—law school, intern at his office in the summers. Live at home, under his thumb." He shook his head and grimaced. "Yeah, that wasn't going to happen. It was like he didn't know me at all."

There was a tension between his eyes that was foreign to me.

I didn't think I'd ever seen Trevor this serious. "We never talked about it. He didn't know how to talk to me about anything. Just had these invisible, unattainable expectations that he thought I'd just—*know.* Maybe it was partially my fault, I don't know—maybe I avoided the conversation because I knew it wouldn't end well for either of us. But God, I'd never seen him angrier than when I came home this one weekend, a few months before I graduated. I was looking at jobs on my laptop—thought maybe I'd work an outdoor shop, or the parks service—and he looked over my shoulder, and . . . he went nuclear."

Trevor took the baseball cap off his head and turned it backward, a tuft of dark hair poking out. "Told me I was throwing everything he'd built for me back in his face. Even my mom wouldn't look at me, she was so . . . disappointed. I called Marshall, asked him what I should do, and he said I had two options: Go all in, give my dad what he wanted, or be content with being a fuckup for the rest of my life."

I flinched at how callous the words were; at how, even now, it seemed like they were painful for Trevor to say. He shook his head, slow and deliberate, his eyes on somewhere far across the lake. "It was sort of funny, I guess, because that conversation had the opposite of the desired effect. Marshall had assumed I was like him, at my core: that pleasing my parents was the most important thing to me." He gave a thin, humorless smile. "But I chose option two."

"You're not a fuckup," I whispered.

He glanced at me from under his eyelashes. For the first time, I noticed how long they were. "Thank you." He said it solemnly, like he really meant it. "Most of the time, I know that. It was more that I had to accept that they'd always see me that way—and that

I'd just have to be okay with making decisions about my life, knowing that my family wouldn't understand. Like coming here for another summer. It's been two years since that happened, you know? He's still pissed. All three of them are." He shrugged. "But that's okay. I can't live my whole life for other people."

I swallowed before asking my next question, knowing it was bold. "And are you happy now?"

He let out a breath and looked up at the moon. "Sometimes."

"What would make you happy all the time?"

His mouth twitched, just barely, like he was fighting a smile. "I'll let you know when I figure it out."

I thought back on Chelsea's chiding words at the start of the summer—about how Trevor was always working some dead-end job, how he didn't care about anything real. And I felt special, sitting here with him, getting to see the truth.

I put a hand on his bare knee and squeezed. His skin was warm, and I considered pulling away, but I didn't. I wanted him to know that he wasn't alone. That I understood.

We sat in comfortable silence for several minutes. "You know," I said eventually. "Your dad and my dad should really start a club."

This earned me an eyebrow raise. "Oh yeah? What would they call it?"

I tapped a finger to my chin. "Probably the Society of Rich Assholes with No Emotional Intelligence."

"Oh, man," he said, twisting his body so he was fully facing me now, holding out the flask like an offering. "Go on, then. Tell me about the copresident."

I snorted a laugh, surprising myself. "My dad—well, it's a long story."

He made a show of looking around, checking his watch. "I think I've got the time." He nudged his knee into mine. "Tell me."

I hesitated. My relationship with my dad was strange and complicated. He was neither dead nor evil. A lot of people, I imagined, would probably call him a good person. He just didn't care about me at all.

I knew I could tell Trevor no—I opened my mouth to do just that. But he was looking at me in that same way he had during the Night Before. The same way he had when we'd gone swimming together on that final day of summer. Like I was the most interesting person he'd ever seen.

So, I took a deep breath. And I dove in.

"My parents met in college. Those were the only four years my mom ever spent away from here. Like me. My grandfather was big on education, and he insisted she go. They met in the business program, during their junior year."

There was sweat pooling on my forehead, and I wiped it away with the back of my hand. "When my mom moved back here, my dad moved with her. My grandpa got sick, and she ended up needing to take over earlier than she expected. I don't know very much about that time in her life. She doesn't really like to talk about it.

"But I do know that she and my dad got married pretty quickly—my grandpa wouldn't let them live together if they didn't.

"When I was two, my dad got this big job offer in Atlanta. A finance job. My mom was surprised, obviously. She'd told him that her life was here, would always be here. He'd known that when he'd married her. When he'd had a baby with her."

I took another sip, relished the way it burned my tongue. "He told her—he told her that he had to think about his future. As if he hadn't already started building a future here. As if he hadn't made oaths. None of that mattered anymore, apparently. It was null and void because he'd found something better." My voice broke on the word.

"So he left. My mom stayed. She told me once that he'd promised her that they'd co-parent equitably, and he'd come back as many weekends as he could to spend time with me."

I passed the flask back to Trevor. He took it wordlessly, not taking his eyes off mine. "I didn't see him again until I was six. He invited me to stay for a week, at his house in Marietta. I was so excited. But when I saw him, it was weird. I knew he was my dad—I'd seen photos—but it still felt like I was hugging a stranger."

I ran a hand through my hair. "He'd gotten married again, to a woman who worked in his office named Courtney. She was already pregnant with their first daughter, Emmaline. That night at dinner, he asked me if I was excited to have a sister. And I was confused, and I said, 'Is Mom having a baby?' He got so angry, told me no, *Courtney* is having a baby. Say you're sorry. So I did, but I didn't really know what I'd done wrong. I didn't know how my dad was already mad at me when I'd just met him.

"When I went to my room for bed, Courtney had gotten this special pillow made for me, with my name embroidered on it. But she'd spelled it wrong—*G-R-I-E-R*. When my dad came to say good night, I pointed it out. He told me to grow up. Can you believe that? He told his six-year-old daughter to grow up." I laughed, but it was bitter, hollow. I squeezed my fingers into my palms, almost hard enough to draw blood.

"After they went to sleep, I snuck downstairs and called my mom. I asked her to please come and get me. She'd barely gotten back to camp, but she told me she was on her way.

"My dad was so pissed. I remember hiding around the corner with my duffel bag, listening to him argue with my mom. The thing is, he wasn't mad because I was leaving. He was mad because of the inconvenience. He said that Courtney had already bought tickets to take me to the zoo. They'd already booked a babysitter for their Tuesday night date night."

I swallowed the boulder in my throat. "I didn't see him again until I was twelve. He had two daughters by then. He sends me birthday cards, gifts on Christmas most years. But I don't really know him. And he doesn't know me."

I almost never talked about my dad, but it had all just spilled out of me, because it hurt so bad. Because the pain lived inside of me like a disease, incurable and always gnawing at me.

"I'm so sorry about your parents. I know what it's like to feel like . . . you're not worth very much." Before I knew it, hot tears were spilling down my face, dripping onto my chin, onto the sand beneath my fingers.

Our knees were pressed against each other; we were sitting so close now. Sharing the same air. His eyes were bright, thoughtful, kind.

I felt the familiar itch to run away, to throw a blanket over myself and hide. But I stayed right where I was. So did he.

We were quiet for a while, listening to the sounds of the woods and water. Finally, Trevor reached out his hand, letting it rest lightly on my thigh. I couldn't help but gasp at the contact. Goose bumps rose on my arms, the back of my neck. He trailed his finger into the crook of my knee, and I took a deep breath. In that moment, something seemed to settle between us.

"You're worth a lot, I think," he whispered.

I bit my lip, and his mouth stretched into a smile that hit me in every one of my fingertips. I thought back to that day with Margo on the beach. The way that Trevor had looked at me, how she'd laughed. *You're such a little liar.*

Now I knew for sure, as his breath tickled my face. I had been lying.

CHAPTER THIRTEEN

THEN

Thirty-Nine Days Before the Fire

The night of the Lady's Lurch hike, someone ransacked an empty cabin in the Staff Village.

Just like Kendall had said, more kids were claiming to have seen some kind of hooded figure, sneaking past their cabins. Sheriff Ramon had searched the perimeter of Dread's Cove at my mother's insistence, but no one had any idea who it could be, or what they wanted.

No matter how many times my mom expressed the importance of taking roll before bed, of diligently doing nightly rounds, the sightings kept happening.

I knew there was no monster in the woods, but even still—something bad was happening.

When I ran back to Black Bass after breakfast one morning, needing to grab my extra beach towel before heading to the lake, all the lights were on inside. My heart rate spiked, and I thought immediately of the Phantom, even though it was midmorning. "Hello?" I called from the doorway, scared to walk all the way in.

A second later, Steph appeared from the bathroom, a towel

wrapped around her head. She looked like she was getting ready for bed, even though it was barely 9:00 a.m. Clearly, she hadn't been expecting any interruptions. We'd parted ways less than ten minutes ago—Chelsea and I were taking our girls to the lake for free swim, and she and Margo were heading out to the rec center for rock climbing. I didn't think I'd see her until at least lunch.

But here she was. After a weird moment where we gaped at each other, she laughed. "You scared me, Little G. Thought you might have been the Phantom coming to kill me."

I raised an eyebrow. I'd been thinking of the Phantom, too, but she'd said it like it was all a big joke—like this Phantom thing hadn't been making the younger kids cry when they went back to their cabins at night for the past few weeks. Even Chelsea and I, who'd grown up walking through these woods alone, had started checking over our shoulders anytime we were out past dusk.

Steph flopped down on her bed and pulled a magazine into her lap. I didn't want to be a narc, but I had to ask. "Sorry, but what are you doing in here? I thought you guys had rock wall this morning?"

Her eyes flickered up from the magazine. "I've got a migraine. I get really bad insomnia in the summertime. Something about all the light, I don't know. I didn't sleep very well, and Margo was cool with me hanging back."

"Do you need to go to the nurse? We can . . ." I tapered off when her expression changed into something more vulnerable. I had the sudden, strange premonition that she might be about to cry.

"What is it? What's wrong?" She let out a breath, then set the magazine down. She hesitated only a moment before patting the space beside her on the bed. I crossed the room and dropped down beside her.

"My dad would have been forty-six today." Her words were somehow both harsh and empty. "He died of stomach cancer. Six years ago—today. On his birthday. So, I guess I'm not really in the mood to . . . I'm not in the mood for anything."

"Oh my God, Steph, I'm so sorry," I said, my heart splintering. I never would have thought that Steph Bennett didn't live a life that was as shiny and carefree as she was. Then again, I hadn't expected Trevor to have so many issues with his dad, either. "Do you, I mean—do you want to talk about it? Tell me about him."

Both Steph and Margo had been hush-hush about their personal histories. I knew that they'd met their freshman year in the dorms at the University of Georgia and had been best friends ever since. They were both about to move to Atlanta and share an apartment in some trendy neighborhood, though Margo was going on a six-month Euro trip first. I knew that Margo loved to read and that Stephanie loved to talk. I knew their plans, their hobbies, their favorite movies (Steph's was *Legally Blonde*, Margo's was *Cruel Intentions*). But on their families, they'd been pretty mum.

Steph sighed. "Cold. Distant. We were never that close, even when I was a little kid. You know I lived with my aunt and uncle most of the time. They adopted me when I was ten. I took their last name and everything. He couldn't really handle the whole *dad* thing. I think he—"

There was a long, quiet beat where I knew she was weighing how much to tell me.

"I think he blamed me for my mother leaving." Her eyes were closed so tightly it looked painful.

I'd gathered that her mom wasn't in the picture, but for whatever reason, I'd assumed she'd died. "Your mom left? When you were a baby?"

She gave a single, slow nod, eyes still closed.

"And she's never reached out to you, or anything?"

"No." The word wasn't loud, but it was final.

There was a tear leaking out of the corner of her eye, snaking its way down the side of her face. She caught me looking and wiped it away.

"I'm sorry, I don't mean to pry–"

"It's fine," she said quietly. I could tell it wasn't. "Honestly, Little G, I don't feel like talking about it."

"Of course. I'll go, if you'd rather be alone." I felt terrible for pushing her, especially because I understood. I'd been left behind by a parent, too.

"Don't leave," she said quickly.

Since I'd met Steph, I'd yet to hear her sound this unsure. This gutted.

"Just . . . talk to me about something else. Please."

She leaned back on the bed, and I followed her lead. She'd taped a few photos on the underside of Chelsea's bunk. A couple had Margo, other girls from their sorority. Her aunt and uncle. I seized the perfect opportunity for a subject change.

"Is this Paris?" I ran my finger across one with Steph sitting at a café, next to a woman I guessed was her aunt.

"Yeah," she said wistfully. "And that one's in Amsterdam," she added, pointing to the one beside it.

"Wow," I breathed.

"My Uncle Teddy is a pilot," she explained. "He likes to bring us with him." Then she scrunched her nose at me, as if realizing something. "Wait, have you never been? We should go!"

I was both embarrassed at being caught and elated that she would so casually mention something like going on a trip together.

"Actually, I've never been out of Georgia."

Steph sat up at this, almost thumping her head on the bed frame. "Are you for real? So you've never been on a plane?"

I shifted, slightly uncomfortable now. "Never."

"But don't you, like, want to?"

I opened my mouth, then closed it again. "Do I want to what?"

"Leave."

She said it so simply, like that was something anyone could do. *Leave,* like my dad had. No care for any of the destruction left in his wake. *Leave,* like her mother had, too.

I chose my words carefully, feeling like I was on the precipice of something dangerous. Something I couldn't take back. Finally, I whispered, "Maybe. But I don't know where I'd go. My whole life is here."

"So you have thought about it," she said.

"I have," I admitted. "I've always liked the idea of Colorado."

Steph clasped my hand in hers. "So, why don't you just do it? Move to Colorado. What are you so scared of?"

"I'm not scared, it's just—complicated. I don't know anyone there, I don't know what I would even do there—"

"You are scared." Not a question, a statement. "I can see it. You're scared to admit that you want things you aren't supposed to want." Her eyes flashed. "You don't want to run this camp, do you? At least not yet. You want to build your own life. Design your own road map."

I felt completely exposed, like a deer in headlights.

Her mouth curved into a small smile. "Well, I'm your biggest supporter. If you want to leave, leave. I'll even help you figure it out." She leaned in closer, bumping her shoulder against mine. "If it isn't obvious, I have no idea what I want to do yet, either. We can make our maps together. How does that sound?"

I gave her a small nod, and she squeezed my hand, satisfied. "And–for the record–if you want to make out with Trevor, you should definitely make out with Trevor."

The grin spread wide across my face. I'd told her about the hike the second we'd gotten back, and she'd been immediately in favor of it. "I think I'm, like, obsessed with him," I whispered, and Steph threw her head back and cackled, the sound bouncing around the cabin. Outside, birds startled and flew away.

"But seriously, Little G. You can do anything you want. You've got more power than you think. And if you've got the power to do something, and you don't do it, that's worse than not having the power at all, isn't it?"

When I got to the lake a few minutes later, Chelsea was talking to Trevor. He flashed a grin when he saw me, and all of my internal organs did somersaults.

"There she is," he said. "I was starting to think you were playing hooky."

For the thousandth time in the past two days, I thought about our conversation at Lady's Lurch. The way he'd looked at me. Remembering it made the butterflies start up again.

"Sorry that took so long," I said, going for breezy. "Did I miss anything?"

Trevor waved my apology away. "No, you're all good. Chels and I were just talking about Saturday night."

My mind went completely blank as Trevor and I locked eyes for a second too long. Chelsea cleared her throat, breaking whatever spell we'd both briefly been under.

"Well, I'll get back to it," he said, nodding his head toward the dock house, and the three Brook Trout girls who were waiting with crossed arms for him to pull out kayaks.

"What was that?" Chelsea asked when he was just out of earshot.

Heat crawled up my neck. "What do you mean?"

"You're being weird. You won't even look at me." It only took another second of silence before she said, "Oh my God, you're hooking up with Trevor, aren't you?"

I huffed a startled breath, glancing toward a group of girls gathered on the shore. "I am not," I said, but the strain in my voice was clear.

"Does Wes know?"

I groaned, already frustrated by this conversation. With a strong surge of resentment, I wished I was still back at Black Bass talking to Steph instead.

Steph was excited about Trevor. She'd told me to go for it. Chelsea, however, was looking at me with disappointment, as if I were a camper she'd caught sneaking out.

I felt a sharp wave of resentment at how *straitlaced* she was. She always, always had to be responsible, and pragmatic, and—boring. I wished, more than I ever had before, that she was willing to have a little bit of fun. I thought about the Chelsea who'd come out, for a short while, at the Night Before—the girl who'd stolen champagne and taken off her dress and jumped in the water with the rest of us.

I wanted to be talking to that Chelsea right now. But I didn't know if she was even in there.

"Does he know what? You want me to ask him permission to talk to another guy? You sound insane." I hated how angry I was, but I couldn't help it. Chelsea didn't feel like my best friend; she felt like my keeper. I didn't like it at all.

"Don't be mean. I'm just saying. He's not going to like it," Chelsea said. She was speaking calmly, certainly more calmly than me, but I could hear the clear note of judgment. If there were pearls around her neck, she'd be clutching them. "I know he wants to get back together with you. You know it, too."

"Why does that matter?" I said, my voice rising involuntarily. I locked eyes with Kendall, who was reading a book on the edge of the dock with her toes barely dipped in, and her eyebrows jumped into her hairline. I forced a smile and waved at her until she went back to reading. "I don't care that he wants to get back together, because I don't. And if he's waiting around for me to change my mind, he needs to get over it."

"And you think having some fling with Trevor is the best way to help him get over it?"

"It's not a *fling*, Chels. Fine, maybe I like him, but—"

"Oh, so you're serious about this? And how's that going to work?" She put a hand on her hip, then flipped one of her braids over her shoulder. "What, are you going to follow him around to odd jobs? Live in a van, maybe? Sounds awesome."

Now she was the one being mean. I was so tired of my life, and my future, being everyone else's goddamn business.

"Listen," she said, before I could argue. "I like Trevor. I do. I understand the appeal. He's great at his job, and the kids love him. But he's leaving at the end of the summer. Then he'll be on to the next thing, the next girl. And you'll be here. Wes will be here."

Chelsea was right, but only about some of it. Trevor Townsend was not the kind of guy who liked long-term plans–he'd told me as much himself, the other night. And as much as we'd been dancing around each other, touching each other's knees on dark beaches, there was still so much I didn't know about him.

"You know he's already got another job lined up for September," she said, pulling me out of my reverie. "Wes mentioned it to me yesterday. He's working at some brewery in Atlanta for a bit, and then he'll probably hike the Appalachian Trail, or something. He's a walking question mark, Greer. He's not serious."

"Well, maybe I'm not looking for something serious. Maybe I'm just seeing what happens."

She furrowed her brow, incredulous. "Greer Olsen, just *seeing what happens*? Am I supposed to believe that?"

"Can't you just be excited for me? Steph was."

It was quiet between us for a long moment, and I found myself wishing I was anywhere but here, having this conversation.

A bird chirped from somewhere. "Acadian flycatcher," she said automatically, like the sound itself was a question on a pop quiz.

I stifled the urge to roll my eyes at her.

"You seem different lately. Not like yourself. Maybe you should, I don't know, take some space from her."

I made a face, surprised. "From Steph?"

She shrugged, looked up at the sky. "Ever since she got here, everything you've done has been to impress her. It's just a little . . . obsessive, I guess."

I closed my eyes, annoyed and embarrassed. Yes, I'd been spending a lot of time with Steph. Honestly, with all our late nights together, I'd spent far more time with her this summer than I had with Chelsea. But people are allowed to change and grow and want different things.

The girl you meet when you're a baby doesn't have to be your best friend forever.

"Honestly, you sound like the obsessed one right now. Maybe you should develop some hobbies other than caring about who I'm friends with, or who I'm dating."

Chelsea's mouth fell open in surprise. Closer now, the flycatcher chirped louder, as if it were reprimanding me for being a bitch.

Immediately, I regretted the words. Before I could even begin to formulate an apology, she spoke. "You know what, I'm getting a little hot," she said, rising brusquely. "We can talk about this later."

"Fine," I said hollowly, though she'd already walked away.

CHAPTER FOURTEEN

NOW

During the brief lull between breakfast and my mom's early-afternoon service, I knew what I needed to do.

My grandfather's memorial bench was hidden beneath a canopy of pine trees, a quarter of a mile from the closest marked path. In the summers, my mom and I used to have a standing Wednesday morning date here. We'd meet before the sun had fully burst over the top of the mountains and chat for an hour about everything and nothing. She'd bring two coffees with her in the matching *Dread's Cove* tumblers I'd gotten her for Christmas one year—always extra hot, always with extra sugar, the way we both liked it.

That summer, I'd been so busy that our mornings on the bench fell by the wayside; I was more focused on whatever was happening with Trevor, and my friendship with Steph. She'd been distracted, too, her face in a near-perpetual frown as things with the Phantom continued to escalate. Almost every Tuesday night, I found myself tracking her down after dinner, saying I didn't think I could meet her the next morning. Some days, she seemed disappointed. Others, she seemed relieved.

Now, as I made my way down the quiet trail in the woods, I wished I'd made the time. If only I'd known then what I knew now; that our days together were numbered.

The air felt thick with humidity, and my breathing grew shallow as the bench came into view. It was as pristine and clean as I'd ever seen it, and I wondered if she'd continued to come here herself as the years stretched on without me around. The plaque in dedication to Grandpa Dread looked like it had been cleaned recently, the Flannery O'Connor quote he'd loved glinting in the single streak of sunlight.

It took me a moment to work up the gumption, but, finally, I sat down. Although it was early afternoon, I'd felt the need to keep our old ritual as close to tradition as possible. The coffee in my tumbler was the kind of hot that scorched your tongue, and as I drank, the sweat pooled at my hairline.

It didn't matter. When I closed my eyes, it was almost as if she were there. It was almost as if I could hear her words in the gentle breeze: *There's just something special about the woods, don't you think? The safest place in the world.*

Back at the cabin, I forced myself to put on the dress. It was black, simple, and shapeless. A dusty old thing I'd found in the back of my closet in Atlanta, one I couldn't even remember getting, or why.

I almost never wore black. It was too sad. But I'd taken a deep breath and folded it into a careful square, gently layering it in my still-open suitcase, a few pieces down so I wouldn't have to see it. I couldn't make myself buy something new; I was trying to convince myself that if I ignored it, it might disappear.

But death doesn't go anywhere. It lingers, and it digs in.

I stood in front of the mirror, my hollow, pale face staring back at me. I looked like shit.

My room was dark, claustrophobic, and I was desperate for sunlight. Maybe that would be able to magically transform my pallid, tragic complexion. I threw open the curtains of my sliding glass doors, revealing one of my favorite views in all of Dread's Cove. But the lake was obscured by a large crack in the glass, spiderwebbing out on the right door panel.

I took a step back in surprise. It looked like someone had thrown a rock—like they were trying to break in.

But . . . no. Who would do that? Why?

I swallowed the panic that was lurching up, telling myself that, even if that was true, it hadn't worked. The door was latched, and the glass hadn't broken.

And maybe—maybe it had been something else. Something entirely innocuous. A bird. A big one, slamming into the door.

Or maybe it was an old crack. I hadn't been in this room in half a decade, after all. It was entirely possible that this had happened somewhere in the interim of construction and chaos, and my mom had never gotten around to fixing it.

But then, I couldn't help but think of that match on the counter last night. The match I'd been pretty sure I hadn't lit.

Both of these things separately felt small—practically insignificant, in the scheme of things—but as a pair . . . I felt unsettled. Unsure.

I didn't know what any of it meant. Only that it scared me.

Quickly, I closed the curtains, blocking out the broken glass. Out of sight, out of mind. Because I could not descend into a panic spiral. Not now. Not when I was minutes from saying my final goodbyes to my mother, in front of a hundred other people.

Before I left my room, I grabbed the photo of Steph and her family from my nightstand and slipped it in my pocket. For whatever reason, I wanted to keep it close.

It was quiet in the kitchen, only the dull hum of the fridge keeping me company. I was fine with that. I didn't think I could handle Margo right now, even if she was playing nice.

Just one shot, I thought, eyeing the whiskey on the countertop. For courage. Or maybe to repress the throbbing mass of dread pressing against my rib cage.

I grabbed for my phone, found the playlist I'd been building over the past two weeks, adding songs to it only when I could summon the strength–usually late at night, after a long cry.

I hadn't been able to listen to any of them yet. I'd just been slowly adding memories, as they came to me, knowing that one day, I'd be ready to listen.

The first song was stupid, one I didn't remember adding but knew all the same: "Love Shack," the B-52s.

The memory was strong, and it washed over me like I was hallucinating. Chelsea and I, ten years old, dancing to this song on the back porch, the fireflies dancing with us. My mom and Rig laughing when they found us, expecting us to be asleep. The sounds echoing across the water.

Desperately happy and content. Our strange and perfect little family.

I turned it off immediately. Silence swallowed me whole again.

For a long while, I stood at the counter, eyes on the lake out the back window. I was so lost in my own thoughts, so far away, that I didn't hear the back door sliding open.

As I opened the bottle of whiskey, I felt a hand grasp my forearm. I gasped, spinning around, the cap flying somewhere on the floor.

"Didn't mean to scare you," Wes said, his voice low and soothing. He wore black slacks and a white button-down, still untucked. Once again, his hair was a wet and matted disaster. His eyes roved over me, with that same thinly veiled worry that he'd had since my arrival.

He glanced pointedly at the whiskey. "What are you doing?"

"It's called self-soothing. Or maybe self-sabotage, I'm not really sure." I drank straight from the bottle, relishing the burn as it went down.

Wes didn't say anything, but his eyebrows knitted together.

"I'll be there soon, all right?" I said, kneeling to find the cap.

He grabbed my arm, gently pulling me back to standing. "Are you okay?"

God, I was so fucking tired of that question. *Was I okay?* No, of course not. I was nowhere close to okay. There were so many things I could have said to him. So many years and lies and memories. I could have thanked him, apologized to him, yelled at him, bared my soul.

A part of me wondered, for the thousandth time, if I'd been unfair to him back then. If I'd seen what I wanted to see: a boy who I'd grown out of, who wasn't capable of meeting me where I was. If maybe, in his own way, he had been trying to give me what he thought I wanted.

It wasn't his fault that what I wanted had changed.

Right now, with his eyes so devastatingly open, it was impossible to turn him away—it was impossible to not see him as the steadfast friend I'd known my whole life. There was so much I had to make up for. But Wes was real, he was here, and for some reason, he still cared.

"I miss her so much I want to die," I said, my voice shocking even me with its pain.

"I know," he said. "I know it's hard. But you're going to get through this."

His hand was still on my wrist. He brought it slowly to his lips and brushed my knuckles with the ghost of a kiss. It was almost brotherly. We hadn't been this close in years and years. It was both so familiar and so foreign; it made my chest ache with a feeling I couldn't name.

"She'd be so proud of you. For coming back."

I gave him a watery, haunted smile. And then I forced out the words that had been swimming around my brain for the better part of two weeks: "I'm scared she died mad at me. And that no matter what I do, I'll never get to make it up to her."

He put a gentle finger under my chin, pushed it up so I could look at him. Soft brown eyes, sun-kissed nose. "All she wanted was to have you back here. And you are now. You're honoring her in the best way you can."

I let out a shaky breath. "Sure. Yeah. Maybe you're right."

"It's been a long road, but we can only move forward. The past is the past." Those kind eyes crinkled as he gave me a small smile. "You're home now. That's all that matters."

A new rush of tears burned the backs of my eyes. "Thank you. That means a lot, Wes. I thought"—I hiccupped, then took a deep breath—"I thought you'd be mad at me, too."

He reached for me again and hugged me tightly, the stubble on his chin tickling my forehead. "I'm not mad," he whispered into my hair. "I love you, Greer. It's you and me, remember?"

I bit back a wail. How long had it been since I'd heard that? I had no idea how good it would feel. All the guilt I'd been carrying for so long—finally, a small fraction of it I had permission to release.

My throat tightened at the wave of emotions that rolled over me. "I love you, too. Thank you for—for not giving up on me."

"Never." I could tell he meant it.

The last funeral I'd been to was Steph's, five years ago. In a big sterile church outside of Atlanta. It had been awful, short, and impersonal. There had been hundreds of people there, dabbing their quiet tears with prim, gloved fingers. I'd had to run out halfway through, go to the restroom, and throw up.

That day, it had been Trevor who'd held me. Trevor, who I'd fallen for that summer; Trevor, who I'd clung to like a life raft.

But Wes was exactly who I needed right now. I wrapped my arms around his waist and held him for an exceptionally long time. I'd hurt him in so many ways, but he'd come to find me anyway.

He let me cry, big, terrible tears, and he stayed.

What did it say about me, that I let him?

CHAPTER FIFTEEN

NOW

I blacked out for most of the ceremony, and then it was over. Somewhere to my left, there was an old woman crying softly. Mourners blew noses into handkerchiefs.

Besides the reporters, I recognized almost everyone here. Generations of parents and kids, many of whom I'd been with as a counselor—even shared a cabin with.

But I didn't want to talk to any of them. I wanted to disappear. Get away from the unrelenting press of bodies and questions and tears.

Across the sea of people, I locked eyes with Kendall. Before I could lift my hand in a wave, she looked away.

So, she really did hate me. The confirmation felt like a sucker punch.

A warm hand found my lower back, and I flinched, expecting I'd have to fight off some leering reporter hoping for a photo op. But when I turned, it was only Trevor.

"Oh, it's you," I said, not sure if I was grateful or angry. "I thought—never mind."

There was a tension in his eyes that made my stomach squeeze. "Can I get you anything? Do you want to go talk for a few minutes, get away from everyone? We can–"

"No," I said, harder than I meant it. The word sliced through the air between us, and his hand twitched against my back. I stepped away from him. I didn't want him to make me feel better.

"I'm all right. Thank you for coming."

He gave me a stiff nod. "You know I wouldn't have missed it."

"Greer!" We both started at the sound of my name, always said with such unearned authority. The real cherry on top of today.

I could feel my hair frizzing from the late-morning heat, the ill-fated eyeliner melting into my eyes. They were stinging, and my lips were chapped, and my pits were drenched. I was a mess. And now, I had to deal with him.

"You should go," I said.

Trevor opened his mouth to argue, but I gave him a look that must have been desperate enough to change his mind. I watched him walk away for a moment before a clammy hand squeezed my shoulder.

"Hey, Dad," I said, giving him a smile that was more like a grimace. We both simply stared at each other for a long, painfully awkward moment; to hug or not to hug?

I didn't know what the right thing was. I couldn't even remember the last time he'd hugged me. But I threw my arms around him anyway.

His whole body tensed, for less than a second, before he put a tentative arm around my shoulder. He put his other in his jacket pocket, before not-so-subtly checking his watch.

"I'm about to head out. Lexi's got a club soccer game tomorrow, and, well . . . They have a shot at the championship."

I'd known he was coming only for the afternoon. That was all he could make it up for, he'd told me a few days ago—the first time I'd been able to get him on the phone since my mom had died. It stung, knowing that he wasn't even willing to stay for the full weekend, or bring the rest of his family. Clearly, it wasn't worth it to him: supporting me and my mother.

It never had been, though, so I shouldn't have been surprised.

"Nice job with your speech," he said, and it was quiet between us for a long beat. I could feel him groping around in his mind, searching for anything at all to say to me.

"Thanks for coming, Dad. Guess I'll see you . . . later." Maybe next year. Maybe not.

I almost turned around, away from him, to let him slink off and pat himself on the back for going out of his way to be here. But then I remembered the photo in my pocket, and I forced myself to ask.

"Hey, wait," I said, pulling it out to show him. "Do you recognize this woman?"

He squinted, taking it from me to get a closer look. "Yeah, of course. Winona, right? Winona Hayes."

Winona Hayes. I was simultaneously excited and disappointed—I'd wanted to have a spark of recognition when I finally heard the name. But there was none. "Who is she?"

My dad blew out a breath. "Gosh, haven't thought about her in a long time. She used to work here, back when I did. She was married to—Frank, right? Your mom sure was heartbroken when she left."

My eyes widened in surprise. "They were friends?"

The corner of his mouth pulled up into a small, almost wistful smile. "Oh, were they. Thick as thieves. She was your mom's best friend. She never told you about her?"

I was stunned into silence. All I could do was shake my head.

My dad looked over my shoulder, out at the lake, as if he were straining to remember something. "Her little girl was the same age as you. You two would play together while your moms would talk. The two of them sure went through a lot of wine together back then. What was her daughter's name . . ." Despite the heat, a chill crept up the back of my neck.

Steph, I thought, filling in the blank in my head. As a baby, I'd played with Steph Bennett.

"You said 'when she left.' Do you know where she went?"

My dad wiped the sweat off his brow and checked his watch once more in a way that he thought was subtle. "There were all sorts of rumors about it—no one ever had anything better to do but talk around here." He glanced around at the grievers walking by, shaking his head, as if they were the gossips in question.

"Your mom came back to the house late one night, wailing like a banshee. It was just after your first birthday party, I remember. It had been such a long day, out here in the heat, playing with you in the lake. I was exhausted." He coughed a laugh, but there was no real humor in it. "I was so mad when she flung the door open, like a bat out of hell. You were sound asleep, and I thought you'd wake up. You never were a great sleeper. She was crying so hard she could barely talk. Completely hysterical. When I finally calmed her down, she said Winona was gone. She'd hightailed it out of here."

I felt nauseous, thinking about my mother losing her best friend. A best friend I'd never known a thing about.

My dad twisted his wedding ring. "We were . . . your mom was never the same, after Winona left. It changed her." He shook his head, as if he were coming out of a trance. "Anyway."

I was grateful for the information—I was—but hearing him say anything even approaching negative about my mom made me want to spit on him.

He'd had a secret plot to leave, too, after all.

We looked at each other. The shape and color of our eyes was so similar, it was sometimes startling. In his face, I saw myself. But I mostly saw a stranger. I saw a man who didn't know a god-damn thing about me, who had never cared enough to learn.

"Is that why you took that job, then?" I asked, words spilling out of their own accord. "Because she changed?"

"Greer . . . ," he said, like he was exasperated, and ran a hand through his too-short hair. "I didn't mean to upset you. I know today is hard. Your mom was a very special woman."

"Thanks," I mumbled, the ire draining out of me, then paused before I put the old photo back in my pocket. "Does this mean anything to you?" I asked, flipping it over to show him the pencil-drawn symbol.

He closed one eye and squinted at it, and I knew immediately it was a dead end. "Not a clue."

My shoulders slumped in disappointment, though I wasn't exactly surprised. "Well, I appreciate you coming. Seriously." Even if he couldn't even stay a single night.

"Annie would be proud of you," he said, though I'm not sure either of us knew what for. But I forced myself to smile anyway, and I watched my only living parent leave me behind, again.

CHAPTER SIXTEEN

THEN

Thirty-Seven Days Before the Fire

Saturday night came slowly, and I was itching to get to the beach and see Trevor.

I'd barely had a moment alone with him since our hike, but tonight felt like it might be the night.

At bedtime, the girls had been particularly rowdy. But they'd been going and going for hours—today had been the kayak regatta on the lake, followed by a movie night out on the pavilion. Chelsea had volunteered to help Wes clean up, leaving me to solo lights-out duty. I wasn't as tough on them as Chelsea was, so it took longer than usual.

I sat at the foot of Kendall's bed while the whole cabin complained and laughed about sunburns and mosquito bites and which boys had looked at them today. By the time I started my nightly tradition of reading one chapter of *The Lion, the Witch and the Wardrobe*—because even very cool thirteen-year-olds secretly love bedtime stories—the girls grew silent. It only took a few pages before the snores started in earnest, and I snuck quietly out the door.

When I made it to the beach, I spotted Trevor talking to Steph and Margo. Steph noticed me first and called out, "*Finally, Little G!*" while waving both arms in the air, as if I'd somehow be able to miss her.

Before I'd even sat down in the empty Adirondack chair, Trevor was pulling out the same flask he'd brought on our hike, pouring some into a Solo cup.

"Cheers," he said, handing it to me. Our fingers brushed, and I smiled at him, and it was just the two of us for a long, perfect moment.

"So, anyway, Trevor," Steph drawled, a knowing laugh in her voice. "Remind me where you live in Atlanta."

"Little Five Points," he said, taking a sip from his drink.

Steph and Margo locked eyes. "You're kidding."

"Oh, God. Don't tell me that's where you two are moving. You'll burn the whole neighborhood to the ground."

Steph threw her head back in a cackle, while Margo whacked Trevor on the arm.

"I'm kidding, I'm kidding," Trevor said with a grin, rubbing at the spot where Margo had hit him. "Seriously, that's awesome."

"Where is that?" I cut in, not wanting to get left behind in the conversation. I knew it was pathetic, but with this talk about them living in such proximity, I was being crushed by a wave of jealousy.

Steph's head swiveled toward me. "Wait, have you never been before?"

"Well, I mean I've driven through the city plenty of times. And my dad lives in Marietta. So I've been there, I guess, but—"

"Not the same at all!" Steph said, slapping a hand on the arm of her chair so hard that her drink wobbled. "Well, that settles it. You have to come visit in the fall."

A giddy sort of hope raced through me. "Seriously?"

"Are you kidding? Of course. Let's plan it tomorrow when I'm more sober. You can stay with me–Margo will be in Europe still, but we'll do another trip when she's back. Right, M?"

There was the slightest moment of hesitation before Margo nodded. "Of course. It's a must." But there was no sincerity or enthusiasm in her words.

I swallowed the brief surge of unease that slithered up my esophagus.

"Okay, so, Trevor," Steph said, giving him the full weight of her attention again. "You went to UGA, right?"

He nodded and leaned back slowly, crossing his arms behind his head. On his bicep was a constellation of freckles I hadn't noticed before.

"Let me guess: Hospitality, right? You feel like a hospitality guy to me. You're so good with, like, everyone. You probably want to open some fancy hiking lodge or something."

Trevor laughed lightly, clearly bashful from the compliment. "I thought about it, for sure. But no. I was an English major." He laughed again and shrugged when Steph raised her eyebrows. "I just love books. Even more than hiking, actually."

"Wait, I didn't know that," Margo cut in, leaning forward and flipping her hair behind her shoulders. "I'm working on a novel, you know. Did you ever take Christenson's fiction class?"

For a little while, Margo and Trevor talked about books and writing and the University of Georgia, while Steph periodically interjected with outrageously overconfident opinions–she didn't read anything besides magazines, so when Margo asked Trevor his thoughts on Stephen King's *Carrie*, Steph thought they were talking about *Sex and the City*.

"She's such a bitch," she said, deadly serious. "I'll never forgive her for what she did to Aidan."

Trevor, to all of our surprise, happened to have several very strong opinions about *SATC*—a girl he'd dated freshman year had made him watch the whole series with her—which he promptly began to debate with Steph. My head swiveled between them like I was watching a tennis match, their voices steadily rising as each got slightly tipsier and more indignant.

I'd forgotten the second of weirdness with Margo, and my ribs were sore from laughter when I saw the blond shock of Wes's head coming down the path. His eyes were scanning the beach, likely for me. Chelsea was next to him, her features tense. She'd barely arrived and she already looked miserable, like she wanted to disappear.

The rush of feelings took me by surprise, but I quickly made sense of it: I was disappointed. And a little annoyed. To see my oldest friends.

Part of me felt guilty. But a larger part of me was certain that I didn't want to share tonight with them. I was simply having too much fun talking to Steph and Margo and Trevor, listening to them reminisce on college and the strange, beautiful world outside of Dread's Cove.

With a pang in my gut, I had a flash of the three of them, when they were all living in Atlanta. Meeting for drinks after work, or grabbing brunch at some cute café. Going to visit Trevor at the brewery. Him pouring them free drinks, chatting across the bar. I wanted it; I wanted to be there, too. Badly.

Because I wanted to leave Dread's Cove. Not someday, not theoretically—but at the end of this summer.

That earth-shattering realization hit me full in the face. It was no longer a maybe, the way it had been when I'd talked to Steph about it.

Leaving was what I wanted, after all.

I stood up, so quickly that I almost toppled my cup that was resting precariously on the arm of my chair. Trevor reached out easily and stilled it, looking at me with wide eyes. His cheeks were flushed and adorable.

"You're not leaving yet, are you?"

"I was just going to grab a beer."

"I'll go with you," he said. Despite the existential crisis I was currently having, I couldn't help the stupid grin that spread across my face. His hand rested featherlight on my lower back, and I reveled in the laughter I heard from Steph as we walked away.

When we got to the cooler at the edges of the party, I fished out a PBR, grateful for the shock of cold against my skin. It was terribly hot, despite the late hour, and the humidity felt like a living, breathing thing, pressed up against me on all sides. Trevor must have felt the same way, because as we stood there, he pulled off his shirt. Which of course caused my first sip to go down wrong. My hand flew to my chest in embarrassment as I sputtered.

"Baby's first drink?"

"Shut up," I said, forcing myself to take another sip to prove that I could.

"No, I get it. It's just your body rejecting shitty beer. Happens to me, too."

"PBR is the best of the shitty beers, and you know it," I said, pointing a finger at him.

"You are so woefully naive. Come with me."

"Where are we going?"

"I've got a cooler back at the cabin. We'll get you something better." He held his hand out, and I hesitated.

These past few days, the air between us had felt different. There was an electrical current between us, thrumming with hope and desire and something even deeper. But I still wasn't sure exactly what was happening, or what it meant. Maybe it was the old-school, Southern girl in me, but I wanted some admission of feelings or intentions before I just let him hold my hand in the dark. I was worried it was too good to be true.

And fine, maybe I also didn't really know what I was doing. Wes had been my first boyfriend, my only boyfriend.

So I brushed past him in the direction of his cabin. I didn't see him smile so much as sense it as he fell into step beside me.

The walk was short, but the woods grew quiet quickly, and it felt like Trevor and I were the only people in the universe.

"What are you thinking about?" he asked after a minute.

"What do you mean?"

"Your thoughts sound pretty loud."

I was glad it was dark, and we were side by side; he couldn't see the look on my face.

He'd be able to see everything. Because he was doing funny things to my brain, and my chest, which would heat whenever he'd pull himself out of the water. When his eyes would crinkle, and he would glance over at me, and I could see the amusement on his face, the warmth between us. It was distracting. It was incredible.

I was beginning to realize why it had been so easy with Wes, for so many years. He hadn't been the love of my life; he'd just been safe. I'd never needed to let him all the way in. He hadn't asked me to. Things between us were always, always comfortable, for better or for worse.

Trevor was different. I wasn't comfortable with Trevor–I was on fire.

The cabin was darker than I'd expected, not even a light left on in the hallway. He closed the door behind us, and for a tenth of a second, I could feel how alone we were.

My heart was beating so hard it was painful.

Then the light flicked on, and the spell broke. God, I needed to get a grip. Trevor wasn't even looking at me, but already heading toward the large Yeti that doubled as a table, taking up a comical amount of space in the center of the cramped room. He flipped it open, then pulled out a can and tossed it my way.

He stood up and crossed his arms, and after a moment, I realized he was waiting for me to try it. I sighed, loud and dramatic, before appeasing him.

"Well?" he asked before I'd even swallowed.

I smacked my lips, feigning deep consideration. "Tastes like a PBR."

He made a face of mock horror. "Your palate is entirely unrefined. We'll have to fix that."

I made a show of swishing it around in my mouth. "Yeah, this tastes exactly the same."

He put his hand over his heart like I'd broken it, but his eyes were sparkling.

He pulled out two more beers, opening one immediately and putting the other in his pocket. When it skimmed his stomach, he jumped, surprising himself at the shock of cold against his bare skin.

I laughed, and for a second, we were both watching each other, and the air was impossibly thick.

"What do you want to do?" Trevor said, his voice soft and thoughtful in that same way it had been outside, when he'd asked what I was thinking.

There was so much in that simple question. What *did* I want to do? With my future—with the tall, ridiculously cute boy standing in front of me.

"Can I ask you something?"

"Shoot."

I rolled back on my heels, my face warm. "What are we doing? Like, what exactly is going on here?" I gestured between the two of us.

He crossed toward me slowly, and I clocked his every movement. The heavy thud of each footstep. He stopped just in front of me, pushing the hair back behind my ears, his fingers impossibly delicate on my face. His eyes were clear, and heartbreakingly gentle. "We're getting to know each other. We've got another month to see what happens. Isn't that enough?"

He leaned forward so that his forehead rested against mine. He smelled like the lake, like sunshine and sweat and mint, and I wanted all of it. I wanted to drown in him.

And that's when I began to understand. It wasn't just about leaving; it was this feeling that I was desperate for. The thrill of the unknown. Whatever it took to feel like this—empowered, emboldened, wide-awake—I would do it.

"That's enough."

I closed my eyes, and he chuckled. I never did find out what he was laughing at, because the front door swung open, interrupting us. I spun around, my hand flying to my chest.

It was Wes, out of breath like he'd run all the way here. His eyes flickered between us more than once before finally coming to rest on me. "Your mom's looking for you. You need to come with me right now."

All the air left my lungs. "Is everyone okay?"

"I don't know yet. Two campers are missing."

CHAPTER SEVENTEEN

NOW

I was looking for the best way to make my escape when Wes's older sister, Nadine, materialized in front of me, crying into my shirt before I had a chance to register that she was at least seven months pregnant.

"This must be so hard for you," she said, keeping her hand tight on my arm. "I'm so, so sorry about Anita. She was *so young*. My parents are devastated they couldn't be here, but Dad can't travel after the surgery . . . but anyway, how are you? Are you all right? Wes told me you've been . . ." She trailed off, clearly about to out herself as having gossiped about me with her brother. "He said you've really been going through it."

Though Nadine had grown up at Dread's Cove, she was far different from Wes. No one ever assumed she'd stick around long-term: She had big plans, college and traveling and a career, not to mention wanting a husband and kids by the time she turned thirty.

She'd succeeded in all of the above, though her crowning achievement was getting married on the Dread's Cove lawn.

That had been a year and a half before the fire, back when Wes and I were still together. I remembered it vividly; he'd stood as a groomsman, absurdly cute in his blue linen suit, and he'd given me a long, heavy smile as Nadine and Luke had said their vows.

"I'm dealing with it," I said, voice hoarse.

"Let me know if you need anything, okay?"

I had no idea what she could possibly offer me, but her smile seemed genuine, so I made myself nod.

"Do you want to touch her?" She waggled her eyes in a way that was supposed to be enticing, but I had to fight hard not to cringe.

"Oh, gosh, that's okay–" I began, but she'd already pulled my hand to her bump.

"I'm due in August," she explained proudly. "We're naming her Anita, of course. Annie for short."

I gasped at this casual announcement, but she was still talking, smiling at the two of our hands feeling the baby kick. I clutched the broken *Annie* around my neck, missing my mom for the thousandth time today.

"You know, it just made me so sad, when Sawyer was born, thinking about how he might not ever get the chance to be a camper here one day. It was hard there, for a while, when they weren't sure if it would ever come together. But thank goodness for your mother. She was a powerhouse, and an angel. She really, really was."

She waved at someone over my shoulder, and I spun around, worrying she was soliciting a photographer. Nadine laughed and patted me on the arm. "Just Wes and Chelsea, scaredy cat."

I gave her a tentative smile that I was sure looked haggard, needing to get out of this conversation as quickly as possible. I liked Nadine, I did, but I couldn't force myself to be friendly and chipper right now. I was overwhelmed, overstimulated, and desperate for a cold shower and a nap.

And the longer I stayed out here, the more likely it was that I'd have to start fending off questions from reporters. I didn't trust myself not to start screaming at someone if they asked the wrong thing.

"What do you think about all that, anyway?" Nadine asked, tipping her chin in the direction of the water.

I followed her gaze to Chelsea and Wes, not understanding. "About what?"

"About the two of them? I gotta say, I was *not* expecting it. Honestly, I always assumed you and Wes would find your way back to each other–"

She stopped talking abruptly, surely due to the look on my face. "What is it?"

I didn't answer her. Instead, I looked at the pair of them again, standing at the lakeshore. Wes was up to his ankles, shoes dangling in one hand, while Chelsea stood about two feet back from him. They weren't doing anything particularly intimate; they weren't even touching. But I saw exactly what she meant, when he glanced back at her: The warmth. The comfort. A certain kind of closeness that I hadn't noticed, until now.

A closeness that I thought I'd felt between us, back in my mother's cabin. When he'd let me wrap my arms around him and whispered into my hair. *I love you, Greer.*

"It's, um, really good to see you, Nadine. I'm going to get something to drink, all right?"

Holy shit. Wes and Chelsea. Together. It made sense, in so many ways. In others, though, it was mildly horrifying. He was Wes. He had always been *my* Wes. And like Nadine had said, we'd always belonged to each other. Even if that was a hold I didn't want to have over him; a hold I didn't want him to have over me.

I was a complete hypocrite. I knew this, but it didn't stop the acid burning in my throat. I'd dumped him half a decade ago, for God's sake, then almost immediately started things up with one of our friends. I couldn't exactly be mad at him for doing the same thing to me.

My gut twisted as I thought about him leaving Chelsea's bed this morning, wiping her tears, then searching for me this afternoon, like I was the next checkbox on his to-do list. I felt the sting of humiliation and a harsh wave of betrayal that threatened to overtake me.

As I watched him grab Chelsea's hand, pull her forward into the water—saw her smile, laugh with abandon—I felt more alone than I thought possible.

Even more so now, I clung to what I'd learned from my dad. Steph may have been gone, but she was still here, too. And if there was something to be found that could help her—that could keep her close—I would find it.

I would.

The morning after my mother's funeral, I woke with a headache, as I so often did these days. A grief hangover.

Last night had passed in a strange, dreamlike blur. At some point, I must have eaten dinner. Spoken to Rig and Val. Taken a shower.

I threw some shorts and a tank top on, knowing it would be

hot and humid already, despite the early hour. As quietly as possible, I tiptoed down the stairs, listening for any signs of life.

Margo appeared in the hallway a moment later, stopping short when she saw me. I spied her old faithful tucked under her arm—*Pet Sematary* by Stephen King. I almost smiled at the memory. That summer, she'd read it cover to cover at least four times.

"I take mine black," she instructed me as I pulled out the coffee carafe, setting the book on the counter and crossing her hands delicately under her chin.

"Good for you." I turned my back on her to pull the creamer out of the fridge.

"Spicy in the mornings, aren't you? Some things never change."

"I'm not spicy," I said, fighting to sound nonchalant. "I'm also not your employee. You're more than capable of pouring your own coffee—or do some things never change for you, either?"

I looked over my shoulder at her, and the glint in her eye was so wild and so Margo that I had an overwhelming sense of déjà vu. My lip twitched; hers did, too.

"Touché, Little G," she said, reaching for the carafe.

If we were keeping score, I may have just earned a point.

I held out my own mug toward her, and she hesitated for a millisecond before pouring me a cup.

I sat down next to her at the breakfast bar. "I learned something interesting yesterday," I began.

"I knew it," she said, a clear note of triumph in her voice. I blinked at her. "They're dating, aren't they? Baby and the Chef."

"Oh, um—I mean, yeah, apparently," I said, taken aback. "But how did you know?"

She smirked at me. "I saw them all cozied up by the water

yesterday. And I mean, it was sort of inevitable, wasn't it? Especially with you not being around."

"What was inevitable?"

"Be so serious right now. She was obsessed with him that summer. Don't tell me you didn't notice."

I gaped at her. *Had* Chelsea been obsessed with Wes? I'd always thought her strange insistence that I get back together with him was just her trying to micromanage me, like she did with the campers.

I'd never once considered that there was something else there. That maybe it wasn't about me at all, but Wes.

"No," I said after a beat, feeling almost dizzy with surprise. "I guess I didn't."

Margo clicked her tongue and made like she was going to head back to her room. I grabbed her arm, stopping her.

"No, wait. That wasn't what I wanted to tell you." I took a deep breath. "I talked to my dad, and he remembers her. Steph's mom. Her name was Winona Hayes, and she was best friends with my mother."

Margo leaned closer, eyes round and wide. "What? And you'd never heard of her before?"

"No, never."

"Did he tell you anything else?"

I nodded slowly. "Just that she left, in the middle of the night. And it–well, it seemed like that was the beginning of the end, for my dad. He said that my mom was never the same after losing her."

I thought about how I'd felt in the aftermath of Steph's death. How it had changed and twisted me. And these torturous past two weeks.

I wondered if that's what it had been like, when Winona left. If my mother had just been too sad, too damaged by losing such a big piece of herself.

It hurt, knowing I'd never known anything about this person who had been so important to her. It made me feel impossibly far away from her, because now, I could never ask.

Margo tapped her nails on the countertop, lost in thought.

"What is it?"

"Well, it's obvious, isn't it?" The corner of her mouth had turned up just slightly. "Our first stop today in our official investigation of Winona Hayes: an interview with the one and only Thomas Riggins, a Dread's Cove original."

I gripped my coffee mug in both hands. "Do you really think he needs to be part of this? He's kind of dealing with a lot right now."

"He was friends with your mom back then, too, right? Which means he's gotta know Winona Hayes. He probably knows more than anyone else here. Maybe he knows where she went." She gave me a knowing look. "Or maybe he's even hiding something."

I shook my head, quickly and aggressively, needing to cut this off at the head. "No, Rig isn't *hiding* anything."

Margo didn't flinch. "Are you sure? How much do you really know about him?"

My mouth opened stupidly; I was shocked by the implication. "Excuse me? Are you . . . what are you trying to say?"

"I'm *saying* that everyone knows something. He must, too."

Thinking about watching Margo give Rig an interview—no, an interrogation—made my skin prickle with unease, but I knew she was right. If anyone here knew about my mother's mysterious ex-best friend, it would be him. "Just please—remember that he's grieving. I mean it when I say don't be an asshole to him, okay?"

"I'll play nice. Pinky promise."

She grabbed her coffee and sashayed back toward her room. "Tell him I'd like to meet this morning, after breakfast."

I leaned back on the stool, running my finger along the lip of my mug, and wondered for the umpteenth time if I was making a big mistake by trusting her.

But then I stood, downed my coffee, and went to find Rig.

We met in the new communications center, in the back room that would double as Val's office and a boardroom for when donors came to visit. It smelled like fresh paint and bleach.

Margo was sitting at the head of the table when I walked in, which surprised me. I'd gotten here fifteen minutes before the agreed upon time–nine thirty. I wanted to ease Rig into the conversation, make sure Chelsea hadn't brought a weapon.

This was going to be really fun.

"You're early," I said.

Margo cut her dark eyes to me but said nothing. She pulled the cap of a pink highlighter off with her teeth, then started aggressively underlining something on the notepad in front of her.

I hovered awkwardly in the doorway for a minute, not sure if I should sit, or intercept Rig and Chelsea outside. I really, really hadn't wanted Chelsea to come, but she'd insisted.

It had been a terrible case of wrong place, wrong time. I'd gone to knock on Rig's door, and she'd been inside with him, gripping my mom's favorite rainbow trout mug in both hands and giving me what could only be described as a death glare.

"Can I talk to you for a second?" I'd asked, trying to keep my voice quiet and casual.

He'd furrowed his eyebrows, not catching my subtext. Chelsea was still watching us.

"Come on in, ladybug," he'd said, rather than stepping outside. I'd wavered, for a second, until he'd finally caught on. "What is it?"

"It's . . ." I'd trailed off. I'd had a plan for how to approach this, yes. But when I got there, had stood in front of Rig–kind, gentle, grieving Rig–I felt unbearably wrong. Almost dirty.

But the ugly thing was that, after my conversation with Margo, I realized that I wanted to know everything there was to know about Winona Hayes and her connection to my mother.

I didn't care what it cost.

So I'd pushed through my misgivings and asked Rig if Margo could interview him. I hated myself for playing on his emotions, telling him how much I would appreciate it, insisting that Margo was the only reporter here I trusted. I leaned into the work my mother had done to get so many writers here this week, that so much of Welcome Back Weekend was built around the need for good publicity. And that the *Atlanta Times* article would likely be our crowning achievement–so we had to make sure she left pleased.

I didn't let myself think about how I was lying to his face.

I'd watched from my periphery as Chelsea's face turned pale. Rig himself had looked reluctant, perhaps even uncomfortable, but after a few seconds of painful silence, he'd nodded at me.

"Let's get it over with," he'd said gruffly.

"Dad," Chelsea had warned, so much acid in that single word.

Rig had raised his eyebrows, and she'd clamped her mouth shut. "Chelsea, leave it. We're just gonna talk. You can come, too."

I'd tried not to wince, but it had been hard.

And that was how, roughly ninety minutes later, the four of us wound up in a conference room; a motley crew if I'd ever seen one. Rig and Chelsea had shuffled in awkwardly, single file, and sat on either side of the overlong table. I closed the door, still panicking about what I should do, and finally took a seat on the one end opposite Margo.

She sat at the head of the table in the nicest chair, hands laced and assessing us all coolly, as if she were Logan Roy, with all the power and time in the world. Her face was almost a smirk, but there was an iciness in her eyes that could freeze the sun itself.

Seemed like she was definitely going to honor my request and be nice.

"Well, I guess we can go ahead and get started," she said at last, with an air of affected detachment. The clock above her head ticked ominously.

"This better not take all morning," Chelsea said, so violently that it was as if she'd been holding her jaw shut until just this very moment, when she could unleash the full weight of her anger on both of us.

Margo, to her credit, was nonplussed by the outburst. "I'm writing an article for *The Atlanta Times*. Small-town paper, you probably wouldn't have heard of it out here in the woods. Please remember, you are free to leave, if you feel uncomfortable," she said, diplomatically waving toward the door. Chelsea's face turned an unflattering shade of maroon. We were all thinking about it, of course; the way that Margo had treated Chelsea back then. Like she was gum beneath her shoe.

I knew I could step in, should step in. Instead, my eyes just ping-ponged uselessly between the two of them, praying no one would throw a punch.

"Oh, no. I'm definitely staying."

Margo smiled venomously. "Maybe if you'd just sent me a real invitation, we wouldn't have had to worry about this story at all. But alas, here we are. You've only got yourself to blame, Baby."

"Hey," Rig said, and we all looked at him. The authority in his voice was both sudden and unexpected.

"Let's everyone take a few deep breaths," Rig said. "I'm happy to answer your questions, Margo. Sounds like whatever the two of you are working on is important to Greer. And if it's important to Greer, it's important to me." He gave me a meaningful look from the other side of the table. "That's why I'm doing this."

He leaned back, lacing his calloused and sun-damaged hands in front of him. "But, girls, let's keep this conversation cordial."

His eyes landed on his daughter. "And that means you, too, Chels."

I could almost hear what Chelsea was shouting in her head, her thoughts were so loud on her face. But she only shook her head, her mouth a thin line.

After another few beats of truly excruciating silence, Margo gave the world's primmest nod and picked up her pen. She clicked a few things on her phone, and I imagined she was turning on her recording app.

"Let's get started, shall we? Please state your full government name and repeat the following phrase: *I consent to being recorded.*"

He complied.

"You grew up near here, is that right?" she asked next.

"Yes."

"Yes," Margo repeated, her voice cool. "What was your childhood like?"

Rig tilted his head to the side, and I wondered how much time they'd ever actually spent together. Clearly not much. Neither had any room for interest in the other's nuances. It would have been mildly entertaining, if I wasn't stretched as taut as a rubber band.

"Not much to tell. Grew up on Saddleback Lane, in the heart of Lavender, with my mother, father, and four brothers. I was smack in the middle. My father was a mailman, and my mother helped out at First Presbyterian, where her uncle was the pastor."

Margo's expression was pinched, but she was writing something down. I wished I'd sat next to her, just to get an idea of what she deemed important.

"And your first summer at Dread's Cove was . . . ?"

"When I was seven years old," he said. "Earliest they allowed back then."

"What was it like? Coming to Dread's Cove as a camper?"

It was the first time he smiled since he'd walked in.

"It's a pretty magical place," he said, and gestured around the bland meeting room as if that was evidence. "This is where I learned to swim, ride a horse. Now, my first couple of summers were when Dread's was coming into its own. Nowhere near as big as we've got it now." He gave a wistful sigh, caught in some old memory.

"And then, well, the summer I was eleven was when Frankie showed up here. We were thick as thieves, you know. Always getting into trouble." He gave a low chuckle.

Frankie. I'd heard Rig mention Frankie a handful of times

over the years. Usually thrown into an old story, like this one. Now, I realized with a lurch, the name held much more significance. His friend Frankie must have been Steph's dad.

Margo and I locked eyes across the table. It was brief, but I knew she'd put it together, too.

Margo was writing furiously, gripping the pen in her hand so tight that her knuckles were white. "Go on," she said.

Rig waxed poetic for a while on the more minute details of day-to-day life at the Cove in the eighties. Margo prodded him with questions now and then, but once he got going, it was perhaps the most I'd ever heard Rig talk without stopping.

"And when did you decide to forgo any higher education and stay working at the camp indefinitely?" There was a bite in her words that snapped me back into place. I sucked my teeth, hoping she'd look my way.

Her eyes flickered toward me, then away, like I was a fly she'd noticed and glanced at only out of instinct.

Rig didn't seem bothered, though I could feel the coldness radiating from Chelsea, see how she'd lowered her chin.

"I never considered doing much else, to be honest with you. I fell in love with Dread's Cove my first summer. Always had a real sense of peace here. It was more home than my own home. So when the old guy who preceded me retired, it made too much sense not to raise my hand. I may have been biting off more than I could chew, but there was a good support system here, you know. Kind of like a family. Friends can be like that sometimes."

No one could ignore the low, almost guttural sound that came out of Margo's mouth. She cleared her throat, trying to cover it up as some kind of cough. "Allergies," she said in a low monotone, and gave Rig a look that clearly meant, *You were saying?*

She almost always had such a bulletproof shell, but then it would fracture for just a moment, and we'd see a glimmer of pain, like a raw nerve, pulsing just beneath her skin.

"Everyone here felt like family to me. And I met–ah, Chelsea's mom–not long after I started, and, well. The rest is history, I guess you could say."

"And when was that?" Silence, for a long beat. "When you met Chelsea's mom?"

Rig swallowed, his Adam's apple bobbing. "Must have been fall of . . ." He trailed off, caught in another memory. "Thirty or so years ago, I guess."

"And her name was?"

I tried to catch Margo's eye, but she was still ignoring me. I could almost hear her salivating, like she was feeding off the discomfort in the room.

"Hope," came Chelsea's voice, the first she'd spoken since the interview had started. It was more of a choke than anything. My stomach lurched; Hope had died giving birth to Chelsea.

Rig only nodded, then sighed gruffly. "Then Chelsea was born, and–" He took a deep breath, not finishing his thought and not needing to. "And we've both been here ever since." He said it like he hadn't just distilled decades into one sentence.

"What was your community like here, back in the nineties? You had a lot of friends around, I'd guess?"

I found myself holding my breath, nervous, though I wasn't fully sure why.

"Sure did," Rig agreed, voice mild. He was growing wary, though; I could see the lines forming between his eyes. "This was a great place to be a kid and a young man."

Margo's pen was flying across the page, even though she had

the recorder going. "Tell me about Winona Hayes. Did you know her?"

Rig stared at Margo, unblinking for a long, pregnant moment. Maybe I was imagining it, but the room felt charged now. Awake.

"Winona Hayes?" Rig said back to her, slowly, like he'd misheard her.

Margo gave a curt nod, encouraging him to go on. "She used to work here. Tell me about her."

"Lots of people have worked here," he said mildly. "I'd have to be a real genius to remember all of 'em." But Rig was no longer meeting Margo's eye, or mine, or even Chelsea's. He was staring intently at the ceiling like it was very important that he count the tiles.

"She was a friend of my mother's," I cut in. I wanted Rig to know that this wasn't a wild-goose chase of Margo's. "My dad told me about her yesterday. He said she was married to Frankie."

Rig's eyes snapped to mine, wide and bright blue. "Sure. That sounds right."

She was Steph's mom, I wanted to say. But Rig was acting strange, and I didn't want to bring Steph into this just yet.

She'd kept her research about her mother a secret that summer. Even from Margo. Even from me. For the first time, I wondered if she may have had a genuine reason for doing so, other than her own pride.

"Well, I just have a few more questions," Margo said brusquely, clearly sensing that the tide had turned. "Let's fast-forward to the summer of the fire. What did you think about the appearance of the Phantom?"

My jaw fell open. We hadn't talked about this—she was going rogue.

Rig gripped the edge of the table with both hands, as if needing it to keep him steady. "I don't really have a lot of thoughts about it. It was some kids goofing around, playing dumb pranks to stir things up. Nothing anyone needs to worry about, especially now."

Margo leaned forward, pen poised over her notepad. "So, you're saying that the fire that killed Stephanie Bennett was a *prank*? Isn't the official story that it was a wildfire, caused by a summer storm?"

After an excruciating silence, Rig scratched at his beard. "I wasn't talking about the fire," he said carefully. "I meant all the other stuff. But yes, the fire was caused by a surge of lightning on the other side of the lake."

These were the same words that my mother had said so many times that they sounded stale, rehearsed. I almost cringed, hearing them back now.

"So, *all the other stuff*, then," Margo said, undeterred. "Like those boys who almost died, and the vandalism down by the lake. All of that was just pranks? That's your official statement?"

Rig opened his mouth, closed it, then opened it again.

Margo pushed her pen aside, all pretense of taking notes gone. "Who do you think was the Phantom of Dread's Cove? What do you think they were looking for?"

His eyes flicked to mine for a fraction of a second, looking for an out. I felt terrible, I did; but I wasn't ready for this to be done yet.

The Phantom of Dread's Cove had remained a mystery, for so many years. I needed to know what he thought. Until this moment, I hadn't realized just how badly.

"I don't know who it was, and they weren't looking for anything, far as I know," he said finally, crossing his weatherworn hands on the table. "Not really sure what you mean by that."

Margo narrowed her eyes and leaned so far forward that she was practically flush against the table. "All those break-ins and ransacked cabins? Someone skulking around the property in the middle of the night? You really think that was all random, just for fun? Surely, you must have a theory."

"For God's sake," Chelsea said.

I gripped the arms of my chair, bracing for impact.

"This is supposed to be a puff piece, isn't it? I thought you did profiles, not police work."

"Oh, that's so cute, you've been keeping track of me," Margo quipped without even glancing at her, and the tops of Chelsea's cheeks turned pink.

"Stop it," I said, slightly too loudly, and their gazes all landed on me. "Whether you like it or not, Margo is here, and she's writing this story. She's the only person I trust to do this right."

Chelsea's eyes were wild. "Are you forgetting everything she said to us? She told us that she wanted us to die. She called us *fucking murderers*. Don't you remember that?"

"The fire had barely stopped burning, tensions were high for all of us, for you, too–"

"No, no, no, that's not good enough. She's playing games. Don't you get it? Spinning her web. You're falling for it hook, line and sinker, just like you did with Steph. It's pathetic."

"Please, Chelsea," I said at the same time Margo slammed her hand hard against the table.

"Don't you *dare* talk about her, you have no idea–"

"That's enough." Rig was still sitting, his hands in a steeple in front of him. Gone was the low thrum of anxiety I was sure I'd felt from him when Winona was mentioned. Now, there was a cold undercurrent of anger. "I think this interview is over. I'll be happy to answer any follow-up questions over email once Margo returns to Atlanta. But right now, I've got a camp full of guests that I need to tend to. If you'll excuse me."

Both he and Chelsea rose swiftly from their chairs. Rig stopped in the doorway, looked back at Margo and me like he might say one more thing. After a long beat, he just patted the doorframe and left without another word.

It was deathly quiet as Margo and I watched each other from opposite ends of the table.

"What are you doing?" I asked her, trying not to sound as frustrated as I felt. "I thought we were trying to figure out what happened to Winona Hayes. What does she have to do with the Phantom, or the fire?"

"I have a process," she said, pressing a finger to her eyelashes as if to curl them. "You just said you trusted me to do this. Was that another lie?"

I blinked at her, caught off guard. "No. No, it wasn't."

"Good. Then I think we're done here." She glanced at the clock, started gathering her things. "I've got to go check in with my editor. Is there anywhere else you think we might find some information about Winona?"

I ran a hand through my hair, my fingers catching on a knot. "I mean, I can try to catch up to Rig—"

She snorted, tucking her highlighter behind her ear. "I'm not dumb, Little G. He just totally stonewalled us. No, if there's anything left here, it's going to be without his help."

"I'll ask Val, then."

She leaned forward. "No way. Val's off-limits. If her husband's got secrets, you know she's keeping them, too."

I wanted to argue. I did. But her point was valid. And that was terrifying.

As I watched her go, I pictured the Margo I'd met all those summers ago. Vicious, when she wanted to be. Sneaking up on you like a snake in the grass. Taking a bite. Refusing to let go.

She scared me, yes. But I was starting to wonder if there was anyone else here who should scare me more.

CHAPTER EIGHTEEN

THEN

Thirty-Seven Days Before the Fire

The next twelve hours were the worst of that summer. Maybe of any summer I'd ever had at Dread's Cove.

Wes filled us in as we sprinted to my mother's cabin. Apparently, a camper in Bluegill had woken up in the middle of the night, needing to pee. The two beds next to him were empty; he figured his friends must have gone to the bathroom, too. But when he got there, it was empty. He rushed to wake up his counselor, and everything had spiraled from there.

"Who is it?" I asked, though I had a sinking feeling I already knew.

"Jeremy Wallis and Carter Banks."

My vision blurred at the edges. These were Kendall's new friends. That boy she had a crush on.

The boys who told her they'd seen the Phantom, too.

To investigate, of course, we had to wake up the rest of the campers—and those fourteen-year-old boys were so loud and indignant that the entire camp was awake within minutes.

We searched every building on the property, including the

other cabins. We checked under beds, in all the nooks and crannies and hidden spaces of Dread's Cove. Between me and Chelsea, my mother and Rig and Val, I was sure we knew every last hiding place.

But they were nowhere.

Not in the rec center, not in the mess hall. Not in the dock house or on the beach. Not in the Barn.

It was like they'd vanished.

Every place we looked that we couldn't find them, Kendall's haunting words flashed through my brain: *There's someone out there, Miss Greer.*

My mother called Sheriff Ramon. But it was storming tonight, and a bit of flash flooding on the winding roads posed a problem. It might be a couple of hours before he got here. So, the group of us—me, my mother, Rig, and Chelsea—took off into the woods with flashlights to search for Jeremy and Carter.

It took all night. Every moment felt tense and uncertain. There were animals out here. Black bears, coyotes, and bobcats. Silently, I prayed that nothing had attacked them. That they were safe, whole, alive.

We walked every trail on the west side of the lake. We called their names, not that it did much help; it had started to rain in earnest, and the wind was loud and demanding. We could hardly hear each other, much less two boys lost in the woods.

That was what I told myself, to keep from shaking: *They're just lost. They haven't been taken.*

As the wind whipped up, I could feel my mom growing scared. I saw it in how she was walking, spine stiff and jaw tight. It was hard not to be. I was, too.

I realized how easy it had always been for me to take for

granted that Dread's Cove was safe. But out here in the woods, as the summer storm took hold, it all felt so precarious.

It all felt like such a show.

I thought about how in the eighties, there'd been another pair of boys who'd snuck out in the middle of the night, to hike up to the bluffs on the west side of the lake.

One of them had fallen, broken his leg, and almost died.

That was the wake-up call my grandfather needed to get strict about boundaries and curfews. When my mom took over, she buckled down even harder. The northwest corner of the lake—where the shore got rocky and too high—was deemed off-limits. All campers got the same spiel their first night: If you go out of bounds, you're on the first bus home.

But when we couldn't find them anywhere else, the bluffs were the only place left to look.

The rain got heavier as we walked. The first real downpour of the summer—we'd been desperate for any precipitation—and it had to be tonight, of all nights. Our feet squished in the mud, and we hardly spoke. Occasionally, my mom would lean toward Rig and seem to say something, but I could never make out the words.

At the base of the bluffs, Rig turned to face us. He and my mom shared a long, somber look before he gave her a single nod.

"I'll head up there and look around," he said. "We'll find them."

We waited for what felt like hours, though it was more like fifteen minutes.

Finally, as the first rays of sun peeked over the horizon, a faint glow of light spilling into the sky, Rig came around a tree followed by two fourteen-year-old boys, perfectly fine, hanging their heads.

I bit back a sob, and Chelsea grasped my clammy hand in her own.

"Oh my *God*, Jeremy," my mother said, enveloping him in a crushing hug. He was a longtime Dread's Cove kid–this was his fourth summer here, and his two older sisters had come through, as well as both of his parents.

"Mom," I said, pulling her shoulder back gently.

She complied but kept her arms tight on Jeremy's forearms. His sleep shirt was entirely soaked through, and I could see the goose bumps on his pale skin.

"What the hell were you thinking?"

Jeremy's eyes went round, and mine likely did, too. I'd never heard my mother curse at a camper before; I wondered if this was the most angry, and relieved, she'd ever been.

"We were looking for the Phantom," the second boy said. Carter. He was a head or so taller than Jeremy, standing just behind him with his arms crossed. Trying to look casual in that way middle school boys often do, though I could see just how badly his chin was quivering.

Chelsea turned her flashlight on him, and he staggered back, put a hand to his face like she was the paparazzi. He had a shock of red hair peeking out from beneath a camo baseball hat.

"There is no Phantom," I said.

"We saw him," he said, holding my gaze. He uncrossed his arms, and his rain-soaked T-shirt looked like it was chilling him fully to the bone. "He walked by Bluegill. It wasn't the first time, either." He glanced at his friend, as if hoping for backup, but Jeremy was too busy using my mom as a giant Kleenex. "We followed him into the woods. But he was fast, and we got turned around and didn't know how to get back to our cabin. So we wandered around for a while, and then it started to rain, and—yeah."

He shrugged, like it was over now and that was that, like we hadn't been run ragged all night searching for them. Like we hadn't all been silently thinking through worst-case scenarios.

"All right, let's head back and get out of the rain," my mom said, fully Anita Olsen again. Fully in her element, as the matriarch of this camp. She tilted her head left, then right, like she was working out a kink, before clapping her hands together twice in a way that meant *now*.

The rest of the day seemed to pass quickly and impossibly slowly at the same time. My mother wasted no time calling both of their parents, who lived in suburbs of Atlanta. They'd be here to pick them up in a few hours' time. The rules were clear, and they'd broken them. My mother hated nothing more than sending kids home early as a punishment, but they'd left her no choice.

The last time I saw them, both boys were openly crying in the office lobby, Carter especially. All pretense of being cool and unaffected had flown out the window. My heart cracked, for them and for Kendall, and I looked away. I was needed elsewhere.

Because in our absence, camp had descended into a state of utter chaos.

We spent all morning making the rounds to every cabin to check in, give hugs, and reassure the campers that the boys were safe and there was no monster in the woods stealing kids from their beds.

This was not the work of the Phantom because the Phantom wasn't real.

But that explanation wasn't satisfactory, especially to children who were already scared. Especially with the break-ins, and the sightings in the woods that had continued to escalate.

Even though the boys were recovered safe and sound, there was no stopping the hysteria that seemed to morph into a living, breathing thing.

I would pass kids with their heads bent together in the mess hall and hear them whisper things like, "What do you think the Phantom will do next?"

"Sorry I'm late," I said through a yawn, sliding in next to Steph and grabbing a banana. Chelsea was picking at her daily oatmeal, so much brown sugar mashed in that just looking at it gave me a toothache, and Margo was trying to get *Jane Eyre* to stay upright and balanced against her coffee mug.

"Finally, you're here," Steph said dramatically, letting her head fall against my shoulder. Her smile faltered a bit as she studied my face. "Are you okay? It's been a rough week."

I sighed as I peeled my banana. "I'll be fine. I'm just exhausted still." It had been six days since that awful night, and everything and everyone felt strangely subdued.

"Must be so terribly draining to be an heiress," Margo said, and my jaw dropped open. She didn't even take her eyes off her book.

"I'm not an *heiress*," I sputtered. "I just have a lot of responsibility."

"A lot of responsibility and a few million dollars with your name written on it." Her voice had a bite to it now. "I'm sure it's more than worth it. Work now, play later, right?"

I opened my mouth to respond, though I wasn't sure what she

wanted me to say. She was right, of course, though it made me wildly uncomfortable to talk about it in such stark terms; it was no secret that Dread's Cove belonged to my mother, that it would be passed down solely to me one day.

But it was as if I was taking a test that I'd already failed, though I didn't know where I'd gone wrong. And there was no way to check my answers, go back, and change anything. She raised her eyebrows, as if daring me to try.

I took my hair out of my ponytail and retied it, just for something to do with my hands. "I'm obviously very lucky," I said. "I didn't mean to sound ungrateful."

"No, I get it." Her lip curled into something dark. "Getting everything you want has got to be so exhausting. I'm not sure how you do it."

"Everything I want?" I repeated.

Steph was clenching her mug in both hands beside me, and Chelsea had a spoonful of oatmeal hovering in front of her mouth.

"Yeah, like a mom who actually gives a shit about you. Wonder what that's like. Clearly, it's terrible." All the laughter and mischief was gone from her eyes, replaced by something bitter, vengeful. I blinked, shocked by the turn in conversation.

"Margo," Steph and I said at the exact same time. Me, with confusion. Steph, with frustration.

Her reaction to embarrassment was not that of most people; her cheeks didn't grow red. Her chin didn't quiver. Instead, she went still as a statue, no movement at all save for her eyes flickering between the table in front of her and the ceiling for several long breaths.

There was probably only one thing on earth that would have

made the moment worse, and it was exactly what happened next.

"I'm sorry about your mom, Margo." Chelsea's voice was impossibly earnest, a glob of oatmeal at the corner of her mouth. "I didn't know that. My mom died when I was—"

Margo pushed back from the table so fast that our entire corner of the mess hall turned to look. She stood, flipped her dark sheet of hair over her shoulders, and practically snarled, "I don't care about your sob story, Chelsea. Save it for the fucking birds." She paused, cocked her head. "Or, who knows. Might work on Wes."

And with that, she was gone.

The three of us were momentarily speechless. It was Steph who finally broke the silence. "Jesus, Chelsea, I don't know what's wrong with her, she's normally—"

"You're really going to defend her?" Blotches of red were blooming on Chelsea's chest.

Steph fiddled with the strap of her tank top, more uncomfortable than I was used to seeing her. "No, I'm not defending what she said. That was out of line." She took a deep breath and then gave a warm, diplomatic smile. "Something you said must have, I don't know, like, triggered her or something. But she'll cool off and apologize. I promise."

"Oh, so it's my fault? Being nice is *triggering* for her?"

For the first time since I'd sat down, I noticed that Chelsea's eyes were bloodshot. She was as tired as I was. But there was no reason for her to take it out on Steph—it was Margo who'd snapped at her.

"You know how weird that is, right?"

"Chelsea, stop it," I said, the words landing with more of an edge than I'd intended.

When she looked at me, her nose was scrunched, her classic tell that she was trying not to cry.

"Sorry, I just meant–"

"No, I understand perfectly," she said through gritted teeth. She pushed her oatmeal from her hard, the spoon clattering onto the table. Just like Margo, she stormed away.

"And then there were two," Steph said.

It made me wince.

"Bad joke," she muttered, before taking a long sip of coffee. My eyes were still on where Chelsea had disappeared out the back door, and I wondered if I should feel guilty or annoyed. "Sorry about Margo."

"No, I'm sorry about Chelsea."

"It's fine. I probably deserved that. Honestly, I don't know what has gotten into Margo. She's been so . . . surly lately, you know? I guess maybe camp isn't really her thing, after all."

I gave Steph a wan smile, unsure of what to say to her. Because the truth was that I actually had a pretty strong idea about what had gotten into Margo. And it had nothing to do with Dread's Cove.

I'd noticed the way her eyes lingered on me a little too long when Steph told me a joke or bumped her shoulder into mine. I'd seen it last weekend, down by the lake, when Steph had suggested I come and visit them this fall. Her brief moment of hesitation had spoken volumes.

She didn't like that we were becoming such close friends.

Margo Pierce felt threatened by me.

Steph's face was wide open, and if there was a good time to mention what I'd been sensing, it was now. But God, it had been such a stressful week. I didn't want to start something that I wouldn't be able to walk back. No, I would play nice; I wouldn't rock the boat. That felt like the safest choice.

Growing up, I hadn't really had any close friends other than Chelsea and Wes. The three of us had been homeschooled with the handful of other kids who'd grown up at the Cove, which kept our circle small. I'd left for college and lived in an apartment with a few girls in my business program, but we'd never fully connected. I'd always felt a little too on the outside of things, with my famous family and weird upbringing.

I was twenty-two years old, and all my deepest friendships had been set in stone when I was barely walking.

This thing with Steph felt fragile and new. I didn't want to give her any reason to reconsider choosing me. I didn't want to be like Margo—surly, difficult, combative. No, I would be easygoing, fun Greer instead.

Steph drained the rest of her coffee and clapped her hands together. "You ready, then?"

As we got up to head to the water, I told Steph I'd just be a second and stopped briefly at the Brook Trout table to say good morning. Most of the girls were finishing up, gathering their bags, and talking about this morning's activities. "I'll see y'all down by the lake in thirty minutes, all right?"

Kendall sat by herself at the end of the table, a bowl of cereal practically untouched in front of her. My chest caved in at the sight of her.

I put a gentle hand on her shoulder and squeezed, and she jumped in surprise, even though she must have known I'd been standing behind her. "Morning," I said.

"Hi, Miss Greer," she said, craning her neck to look at me. I didn't have it in me to tell her, for the umpteenth time, that she could just call me Greer. Some of those Southern niceties were written in your DNA.

"You feeling any better?"

She grimaced before turning back to her cereal, and I knew she was trying to keep herself from crying. "Not really. I miss Carter and Jeremy. They were my only friends here."

"I'm sorry." Because what else was there to say?

I heard her take a deep breath, exhale. The other girls at the table were oblivious, talking in hushed tones about something, probably the Phantom.

"I'm your friend, Kendall. You've still got me."

She didn't look at me, but she nodded, and I saw two fat tears drip onto the table in front of her. "Thank you." Her voice was quiet, but it was thick with emotion.

I patted her softly on the head. "I've got to grab something before we head down to the lake, but finish your breakfast, okay? I'll see you in a few."

When I got outside, it wasn't Steph waiting for me but Trevor. I hadn't seen him alone like this since the other night, in his cabin, when his forehead had been pressed to mine. My fingers twitched at the memory.

"What are you doing tomorrow morning?" he asked without preamble. He wore a white T-shirt that was soaked through like he'd come out of the water and immediately put it on before toweling off.

I tilted my head, trying to make sense of his question. Tomorrow was Saturday, which meant the wake-up call came an hour later than usual, and there were no scheduled morning activities. When they finally rolled out of bed, most of the campers ended up congregating at the lake, which kept Trevor up to his elbows in work. Not that he ever complained–he thrived in the chaos.

"I hadn't made any plans."

"Perfect. Meet me at the dock at sunrise, okay?"

I opened my mouth to respond when the camp horn blared, indicating the end of breakfast and the start of the first morning session.

"Tomorrow. Sunrise," he said again as he backed away, pointing at me with each hand, his mouth curved into a smile. "I'll be waiting for you."

And despite everything–all the tension with Margo and Chelsea, my growing unease about the Phantom, my heartbreak for Kendall–I thought of nothing else the rest of the day.

CHAPTER NINETEEN

THEN

Thirty Days Before the Fire

My palms were sweating from more than the early-morning heat. As I made my way down to the dock, the sun was just peeking over the mountains on the other side of the lake.

I spotted him before he saw me; he was pulling out a paddleboard. Another was already propped against the dock house. *He needs some help getting set up for today,* I told myself for the tenth time this morning. *Wes and Rig were probably both busy, and you were the next option on the list.*

Trevor's face split into a wide smile when he saw me. His eyebrows rose when he clocked my outfit, and I flushed. Beneath a flimsy, sheer white cover-up, I wore a bright red bikini–Steph's, of course. She'd practically forced it on me when she'd woken up to me sneaking out of the cabin in an old, frayed pair of shorts and my standard black one-piece.

"Come on, Little G," she'd whispered, digging through her bag despite my whispered protests. "Do something that will stun him. I dare you."

"Hi," I breathed, forcing myself not to cross my arms. I wanted to look confident, fearless, when I was anything but.

Trevor pushed his hair back from his forehead. "Hi, yourself. You look–yeah. Hi."

We stared at each other for a moment, and it hit me like a record scratch: Trevor was nervous.

I was making him nervous.

"Did you ask me down here at the crack of dawn because you needed help with the paddleboards? I don't know if I'm the girl for the job. I don't have much arm strength."

He gave a soft laugh, the humor in it more subdued than usual. God, he really was nervous. And the more nervous he was, the more nervous I became. I felt like I was fourteen years old, wondering if Wes might ask me to dance during the Night Before.

But this wasn't Wes. This was Trevor.

"Why does this feel like you're taking me on a date?" The words were out before I could think better of them.

Trevor took a step forward and reached for me. His hand just grazed down my arm until he locked his pointer finger around my own. His skin was hot.

"Because I am."

Before I had the chance to really process that I was, in fact, going on an early-morning date with Trevor, he was moving away to set the paddleboards into the lake. "You ready?"

His question had a certain sort of gravity that made my heart skip. I nodded once, pulled my dress over my head, then descended into the water.

It was shockingly cold, and I couldn't help but gasp when I

was only halfway down the ladder. Trevor laughed from the dock, and I caught his eye, indignant.

"You don't get into the water much." Gone was the nervousness; his voice was warm and lazy now as he watched me, arms crossed against his broad chest. I could see a light sheen of sunscreen on his nose.

"It's cold in the mornings."

"Such a shame," he said, his hand going to his heart in mock sadness. "A girl who owns her very own lake doesn't even like water."

I rolled my eyes. "I *like* water. I went swimming during the Night Before, remember? And last summer, with you."

A hair's breadth of a pause before he leaned down so we were almost at eye level, and he blew out a short breath. "I remember."

I forced myself to push off into the water, dipping under once to get it over with. I climbed onto the paddleboard, putting my knees together and bracing myself before standing. When I glanced up, Trevor was already in position.

"Where are we going?"

"You'll see," he said. "Do you trust me?"

"Mostly." Something in his gaze flickered, like this was a challenge he intended to win.

"Come on."

I'd been expecting us to head back to Lady's Lurch, but instead, he led me due east, toward the sunrise. The surface of the water was glass-like, the only movement from the small ripples coming off our boards.

"Tell me about your new job," I said after a few quiet moments.

He was in front of me, and I watched the muscles in his back move as he paddled. "Just leading tours at a brewery my buddy's family owns. Nothing permanent. I'm trying to go west at some point, but, you know. We'll see."

"How far west?" I paddled up beside him, and I studied his profile as he shrugged.

"Montana, maybe. Or Colorado."

My pulse accelerated. "I love Colorado. Or the idea of it, I guess. I've never been, but I want to go. Is that where you think you'll end up long-term?"

"I haven't thought about it that far ahead. Probably not forever. There are so many things I want to do."

His eyes shifted somewhere beyond my shoulder. His face split into a grin, and he nodded his head once, daring me to look.

I turned and gaped, almost dropping my paddle. Trevor had led us to a hidden cove I'd never once seen before, in all my years living here and exploring our property. There was a sliver of white sand and wildflowers in dozens of colors, with a small cave just beyond.

It was so perfect that my eyes started to burn. "What is this place?"

"I found it my first summer here. I like to come out here sometimes on my days off. It's hard to access from any of the walking trails. It's my favorite place at Dread's Cove. I doubt if your mom knows about it."

I was sure he was right. My mother was famously awful at directions; as much time as she spent in the woods, she got disoriented almost immediately when she couldn't see camp buildings anymore. She rarely ventured to the east side of the lake.

No, this place was just Trevor's. And mine now, too.

We paddled to shore, and Trevor reached for my hand to pull me toward the cave. I laced our fingers together, and he squeezed, his thumb running back and forth over my wrist.

Inside, it was dark and warm, the ceiling just high enough that Trevor could fit. Our feet squished through the sand and shallow water. I glanced back out the entrance, and the mouth of the cave framed Lady's Lake like a painting. A slight breeze ruffled through my hair, and Trevor pushed it back behind my ear.

I wanted to speak, but my heart was in my throat.

Even in the low light, I could see his eyes. Green, with flecks of gold.

"This is so beautiful," I whispered. "Thank you for bringing me here."

There was a distinct sound somewhere out of sight—like footsteps, crashing through the water—and I spun around in surprise.

"Hello?" Trevor called, then looked back on me. He held a finger to me, as if to say, *Just a second.*

He went back the way we came, and my pulse was still thrumming wildly beneath my skin. Was someone out there?

Watching us?

I hated that I was panicking—hated that a strange noise could have my nerves stretched taut like a drum—but I made myself inhale, exhale. Trevor was already turning around, heading back to me. "Just a fish or something. Don't worry."

He reached for my hand again, and I could feel the heat of his body radiating off him. "I promise, it's just us."

Then his free hand found my waist, and he pulled me close enough that we were flush against each other. I forgot to be scared. I forgot everything. He gave me that same secret smile he'd been giving me for weeks, every time we locked eyes, and I returned it.

He leaned in, and finally, he kissed me.

It surged through every part of me. I wrapped my arms around his neck and pulled him in, rising on my toes to meet him. His hands circled my lower back, and then he spun us around, until I was pressed against the cave wall.

I ran my hands through his hair and tugged him even closer, and he breathed my name against my lips. His hand ran down the length of my bare thigh before coming back to play with the tie of my bikini, and I gasped into his mouth.

"I have wanted to kiss you for so long," he said, pulling back to look at me. His eyes were dark, his face flushed, and his hands were still tight on my hips. His breath ghosted across my face as he spoke. "Since the first summer I saw you."

My heart stuttered in my chest, and I knew he could see my surprise. These were all the things I'd imagined him saying to me, as I lay in bed at night the past few weeks. Maybe much longer. Things I didn't think could possibly be true.

"When Wes told me you guys had broken up, I know it was shitty of me, maybe—but I couldn't help it. It's like you're a magnet for me. I can't stay away from you; I can't stop thinking about you."

I thought I might combust under the weight of his stare. He leaned back in, gave me another kiss, letting his lips linger on mine for a long beat.

"Trevor—" I started, but he interrupted me.

"Hold on, just listen. Please. I have to get all of this out, okay?

I don't want you to do anything that will make things complicated. I don't want to ruin things between you and Wes. I know you were close before you got together, and I don't want to be the thing that ruins that. He's a good guy, and if you want to–if you and him might–just tell me. Tell me, and I'll stop."

"There's nothing between me and Wes. I promise. It's over." I was overwhelmed by his confession, could barely breathe, but this–I could make sure he knew this much.

His shoulders visibly untensed, and I felt the relief radiating off him. "Thank God."

I reached up and ran a hand across his stubbled chin, and he closed his eyes and pressed his forehead to mine. "So, what, then? I'm your new summer fling?"

I meant it as a joke, but his eyes flew open, and he looked more serious than I'd ever seen him. Older. He was no longer the college kid who'd shown up as a lifeguard years ago. Maybe he didn't know everything he wanted just yet, but I could see at least one thing he was certain about. It was written all over his face.

"I don't want a fling. I want you."

So much warmth coursed through me that I thought I might burst. "I want you, too. So much."

After that, we didn't say anything else for quite a while.

We stayed at the cove in our own private world as long as we could. It was my favorite morning in living memory. But, of course, it had to end eventually. Trevor and I paddled back to shore, and it felt like my entire axis had shifted.

That night, as I snuck out the door to meet up with Trevor again, Steph gave me a round of silent applause from her bed.

Her approval felt like a drug. I gave her a dramatic bow as Margo and Chelsea snored, then let the door shut silently behind me.

It was only much later when I thought back on that night, that I wondered what I may have missed. I was so focused on myself, on Trevor, how his hands felt on my waist, that I wasn't thinking about Steph at all. When I snuck back to Black Bass just before dawn, my hair matted from the tree Trevor had pushed me up against, I didn't even wonder why she wasn't in bed.

I didn't even wonder where she'd gone.

CHAPTER TWENTY

NOW

I needed some space from Margo after the interview disaster. I was sure that Chelsea was on the fast track to never speaking to me again, if she hadn't been already.

This side of camp was quiet, with most of the guests down at the lake for the midmorning regatta. I was glad to miss it, though it was unsettling to have the world seem so still. I was jumpier than I'd been since I got here, which was a feat in and of itself, because I'd hardly stopped looking over my shoulder.

Lost in my thoughts, I almost smashed right into Val on my way back to the cabin.

"Oh my God, are you okay?" I stumbled back a step, then grabbed both of her bony elbows, trying to steady her. Her dark brown eyes were round and wild.

She ran a hand over her hair, already frizzing from the late-morning swell of heat. "Been looking all over for you. Did you see it?"

"See what?"

With shaking hands, she pulled a loose cigarette out of her

shirt pocket. I resisted the urge to remind her of my mom's rule, how reckless it was to smoke out here. She patted her other pockets, then spun in a useless circle. "Shit, where's my lighter—"

"Aunt Val," I said, with more bite than I meant. "Did I see what?"

She found the lighter, and it was a whole event, lighting it and sticking the cigarette between her lips. It felt like it was minutes later when she swallowed and said, "Black Bass."

Dread pooled in my stomach. "What happened? Is everyone okay?"

"Everyone's fine," she said quickly, waving a hand around vaguely. "But someone—well, just follow me."

In silence, I trudged down the path toward Black Bass. When we came out of the clearing, I opened my mouth to ask the question, then immediately snapped my mouth shut again.

There was no missing it.

On the front of the cabin, written in red spray paint, were three awful words: *YOU WILL PAY.*

"What the fuck?" I said, rounding on her. "Val, who did this?"

For one of the first times on record, Val Riggins had no comment, no gossip to add. She could only shake her head and puff her cigarette, free hand clutching her heart.

I looked around wildly, certain that at any moment, a photographer would pop out of the woods and scream, "*Gotcha!*" But there was no one. Today's activities were centered almost exclusively around the lake, which meant that this side of camp would hopefully be deserted for the near future. But not forever.

I ran a hand through my hair, feeling almost woozy from the heat and the acrid smell of Val's cigarette. My skin was sticky with sweat.

"Okay, let's think for a moment," I said, trying to keep my voice calmer than I felt. In another life, I'd been good under pressure. I needed to channel it now. "This isn't the end of the world, but we need to get rid of this. Immediately. No one can see this, Val, you understand that, right?"

She gave me a vigorous nod, and I was struck by how strange it was, to be the voice of authority in this moment. With my fear and anxiety, there was a brief lightning rod of pride that shot down my spine before I refocused on the problem. "We need something to strip this paint. Would that be out in the maintenance shed?"

Val fidgeted with her cigarette as she considered this. "No, we keep a lot of that stuff in the Barn now. More space in there."

I closed my eyes for a fraction of a second. Not the Barn. "All right, if you'll go grab it, I'll–"

"I've gotta get back to the lake," she said, shaking her head helplessly, taking a long drag from her cigarette. "I promised Chels I'd be quick. She'll know something's up, and if she sees this, she's gonna have a complete meltdown. I'm so sorry, but you're gonna have to take this one, sweetheart."

"Fine," I ground out. It was not fine at all. Childishly, I resented the fact that Val was more concerned about protecting Chelsea's feelings than mine–yes, Chelsea was running this weekend, but it was my mom who'd died.

"Tell everyone that the cabins over here are closed for the rest of the morning for–I don't know, cleaning. Just make sure no one comes over here, okay?"

Val took her marching orders in stride, puffing once more on her cigarette before carefully tapping it out against a trash can. "Should be a table right in the front," she told me, holding a flat hand to her forehead like a makeshift visor. "All the painting stuff is right there; we've been using it the past couple of weeks for last-minute touch-ups and what not. You'll see it."

"Got it," I grumbled, and she took off back toward the beach.

I knew we were under a time crunch, but I was momentarily spellbound by the words on the wall.

When *YOU WILL PAY* had been written on the mess hall that summer, it had marked the beginning of the end. That was the day my mom decided to officially close camp early. Within hours, every camper was gone.

And that night, the fire had devoured almost everything in its path.

This is what people had pointed to, in the months after. It was the proof that people needed, being passed around blogs and Reddit and the darker corners of the internet, that Dread's Cove had been set ablaze on purpose.

That someone had wanted us to pay. So we had. Steph had, with her life.

The lettering was legible but messy. I brought the back of my knuckle to it, and pulled it away red; the paint was still wet. Whoever had done this had been here only moments ago. I turned around quickly, the hairs on my neck standing up, wondering if they were still around. If they were lying in wait, as the Phantom would have, to see my reaction.

I regretted sending Val off on her own. Splitting up felt very stupid. The sun was hot on my scalp, and I could hear the uneven beat of my heart, pressing up against my chest.

Then, somewhere in the woods behind Black Bass, a twig snapped.

I staggered back, my foot twisting as I fell from the step leading to the door. Up was down, and I was staring at the sky, blinking into the quiet. "Hello?" I yelped, not moving. I felt like an animal in a cage, nowhere to go. Slowly, I sat up, careful to not make any noise. "Is someone back there?" I called, aiming for a tone of cool authority. "This section of camp is closed right now. You can head back to the lake."

My mind flashed to the other night, Margo and I stumbling through the dark and hearing someone behind us. That sixth sense that someone was watching. And the match in the kitchen, the broken glass.

What was going on? What did they want?

There was another sound of a branch breaking, but it was farther away now. There was no way to tell if it was just a sound of the woods or a person. I had the fleeting thought of attempting to follow it, but that seemed far too reckless. Even for me.

Just behind me, leaves rustled, and I swallowed a scream. But when I looked around, it was only a squirrel, blinking at me with black eyes.

I steeled myself and stood, feeling slightly off-kilter. My ankle hurt, but I was fine. I took off toward the Barn.

It had been over a decade since we'd had horses, so the Barn had fallen into disrepair. Before the fire had damaged it even further, it had been the perfect late-night rendezvous spot for parties and hookups. We'd spent more than a few nights there that summer, drinking through our supply of cheap wine and bottom-shelf vodka before slinking back to our beds before dawn broke through, and my mom or Rig discovered our empty cabins. Over the years I'd been away, it must have turned into a space to store things that no longer had a place.

But it was well-loved, thought of fondly; eternally remembered with a capital B.

It had also been the last place Steph had been seen alive, by Margo. That was the one bit of information we'd been able to get out of her the next morning. To me, that made it feel haunted. Untouchable. It was one of the places that would often flash across my nightmares, just before the fire began. I'd been committed to steering clear of it this weekend.

The Barn was secluded, at least compared to the rest of camp. There was something off-putting about being somewhere so quiet. I felt like I was intruding on something ancient or sacred.

The door slid open with an echoing thump, and I took a single step inside. Thankfully, I saw the paint stripper almost immediately–there was a large table right by the door with all sorts of paint supplies, just like Val had promised. I let out a sigh of relief. At least one thing was going right this morning.

I grabbed it and turned back toward the door. Along the front wall, there were shelves lined with boxes, some labeled on the front and some not. But I noticed that one read *Mason Ackers*, which stirred something in the depths of my subconscious. It took me a moment, but finally I remembered. He'd been the head cook that my grandfather had hired, here before even Wes's parents, thirty or so years ago.

Curious, I pulled it out and poked my head inside. A bunch of junk; a deck of cards that looked moldy, a few water-damaged Cormac McCarthy novels, and some wrinkled, musty T-shirts. These were things he must have left behind, shoved into a box, and stuffed away—too personal to throw out but too mundane to send to his new address. Instead, they were here, waiting in cardboard purgatory for someone who'd never return for them.

The idea crashed into me like a bolt of lightning. I thought about what Margo had said—where else we might be able to look for information about Steph's mom. If this is where we kept the remnants of long-gone camp staff—what if there was a box for Winona Hayes?

I bit my lip, considering. I had to get back to Black Bass and deal with the spray paint situation. But . . . everyone *was* down at the lake, for the foreseeable future. The graffiti on the cabin was mostly blocked from view by the oak tree.

Which meant that I could afford to spend a few minutes digging through some of these old boxes. Just in case.

Some of the boxes were heavy, poorly packed, and without a clear label, so I spent a while sorting through the bottom two shelves, none of which had anything notable.

I pulled the next box from the highest shelf, and the resulting cloud of dust made my eyes burn. I dusted off the top, and sucked in a breath.

There were two haunting words scrawled in Rig's chicken scratch: *Winona Hayes.*

My instincts had been right. Margo's, too. He lied to us. When he said he didn't remember her—that wasn't true.

With shaking hands, I opened it.

A small silver jewelry box sat on the top. I lifted the lid carefully. It was one of those with a spinning ballerina, and it started shouting a song immediately. I snapped it shut, panicking, but reminded myself that I was very, very alone.

I took a deep breath and opened it again. Two small rings sat inside, and a tangled necklace that looked like an antique, tinged with age and rust. There was also a small, dainty suede bag, that had once held something special but was now empty. The velvet-lined box was beautiful and still somehow looked clean and fresh. A waft of jasmine accosted me, and I wondered if it was Winona's perfume, lingering after all this time.

It gave me a swoop of haunted sadness that was almost staggering.

I set aside the jewelry box and kept poking around. My eye was drawn to a red-and-white-striped book, larger than the others. On the front, in looping cursive, was *Hayes Family Recipes.*

Inside, there were pages and pages of meticulously written recipe cards. At least fifty, from chicken casseroles to Coca-Cola cake. From the years of use, there were grease stains and spots of flour sprinkled across the pages.

Although I knew almost nothing of Winona except for the photo we'd found in the floorboard, I'd been building a mental picture. A cold mother, an unloving partner, content to abandon her daughter. A terrible best friend, who'd left my own mom in shambles. She was useless, shallow, unkind, selfish—wasn't she?

I knew it was just a few pieces of paper bound together, but Winona felt so real to me. Once upon a time, she'd been a woman who loved to cook, who'd collected recipes over the years, who'd worked to practice and perfect them with painstaking efficiency. In my hands, I wasn't just holding a piece of Winona but a piece of Steph, too.

The woman in the photo hidden beside her bed, whom she'd never known—she was right here. Real, solid proof that she'd existed.

Stuck between two sticky pages, I found a picture. I grew

faint, clammy, and slid slowly to the ground, no mind for the dirt or dust. There was nothing on earth but this photograph.

It was me and Steph. Holding hands between our high chairs. We wore matching overalls, and our sparse baby hair was tied up in bows–Steph's was green, and mine was yellow. Behind us stood our mothers. They had their arms around each other, their cheeks smashed together, and their eyes were resting on us. Their daughters.

There was so much love–so much glowing affection–not just in the way they stood holding each other but in the way they gazed at the two of us. The heartache it gave me was indescribable.

I forced myself to turn the photo around, look away from our four matching smiles. I was dizzy and overwhelmed as I ran my hands over the well-loved book, thinking about what it all meant. Winona was not a woman who was spontaneous or aloof. Who ran off in the middle of the night for no reason. Of this, I felt sure.

And then I thought of the interview in the office this morning. Margo asking Rig what he knew about Winona and where she might have gone. Why she'd never returned to her family, her daughter. His deflections, his confusion.

I'd never known Rig to lie before, but about this, he was. None of it made any sense.

I flipped to the last page of the cookbook, and in the back folder, there was a small, unlabeled envelope.

Inside, there were two Greyhound bus tickets.

I felt a pounding in my ears, the blood rushing. These tickets had never been used–they were one-way, from Lavender to Atlanta. The date read 04/04/98.

Yesterday, my dad had told me that Winona had run away the night of my first birthday: April 4.

With a cold, awful sort of dread, a new theory took shape and held me hostage. I wondered if Margo and I had only been dancing around the truth, not quite there. I wondered if this was what Steph had been piecing together all those years ago, the real mystery she'd been trying to solve that summer.

She hadn't been trying to discover why her mom had left Dread's Cove in the middle of the night.

But why she hadn't.

CHAPTER TWENTY-ONE

NOW

I ran almost all the way back to Black Bass, even as my ankle throbbed. I held Winona's cookbook tightly to my chest, like if I loosened my grip, it would disappear.

While I waited for the paint stripper to activate and for those terrible words to begin to dissolve, I sat on the front steps. An uncomfortable heat burned at the base of my neck, as though I was being watched, but there was no way to prove it. I'd even taken a few tentative steps behind the cabin, finding nothing. The woods were less dense here, and I felt confident that if someone was still out here, I'd be able to see them.

I flipped through the cookbook again, but I couldn't find anything else. Only that unlabeled envelope, the haunting photo.

The unused bus tickets.

The confirmation that Winona's plan, whatever it was, hadn't gone the way she'd intended. Because someone was supposed to go with her.

With a last look at Black Bass—nowhere near perfect, but at

least no one was staying here—I shuffled quickly down the path toward my mother's cabin.

Margo was on the couch when I got there, her laptop in front of her, aggressively cat-eyed glasses reflecting the blue glow of the screen. Her mouth opened like she was going to make a smart-ass comment, but her face changed immediately when she saw me. I must have looked haunted.

"Jesus, what is it? What happened?"

"I don't think Steph's mom left. I think someone killed her." The words had been dancing in my head for the last hour. But this was the first time I'd said this new theory out loud. We might not be looking into a runaway mother at all—but a murder.

A murder at the hands of someone here. Someone I knew.

Margo's face was unreadable. When I'd finished the story of this afternoon, of the reprised Phantom's art project on Black Bass, and the artifacts I'd found in the Barn, she leaned her head back on the back of the couch and closed her eyes. I dropped down next to her. For a long moment, we both just sat in the silence, breathing in rhythm beside each other.

"Do you think she—" My voice sounded small and pathetic. I was sure she could feel my desperation, radiating off me in waves. "Do you think Steph knew all along? That something bad happened to her mom?"

She closed her eyes, then exhaled a long, painful-sounding breath. "The night of the fire," she began, and I fought not to gasp.

I hadn't been expecting this. We'd never talked about the fire. All I knew was what she'd told the investigators the next morning, before she'd left for good: They'd been near the Barn when the fire started, and they'd gotten separated.

It had felt too deep in the trenches to dig out over the past few days. But now, I supposed, was the time to talk about it, if there ever had been. Even though it made me feel woozy.

She was rubbing her temples, like telling this story was already draining her. "I saw her stumbling into the woods. All alone, at the edges of the party. I wanted to walk her back to the cabin and put her to bed. But when she saw me, she had this *look* on her face. I don't know how to describe it–she seemed almost manic. She told me she had to go to the Barn, right then. I followed her, because I didn't know what else to do." She shook her head, wincing.

"She said, 'We're so close. I finally figured it out.' I didn't know what she meant. But when we got there, she had a meltdown. She was inconsolable. I told her that enough was enough, that she was freaking me out. I told her to come with me, to come back to the cabin so she could sleep it off. But you know what she was like. So fucking stubborn." Her voice broke on the last word, and goose bumps prickled my arms.

I tried to remember my own conversation with Steph that night, but the memory was hazy at best. "You think it was about her mom?"

For the first time, Margo met my eye. "She wouldn't tell me what she was so worked up about. But now–now, I don't know. I think she must have found something. Something bad. God, I wish she'd told me. I could have helped her."

Her last few words were filled with so much sadness that I had to turn away and collect myself. Not for the first time, I wondered how different things would have been if they'd never come here. If we hadn't shared a cabin that summer.

If I hadn't been willing to do anything to be Steph's friend.

So many maybes, and so many questions I'd never know the answers to.

"I should have pushed her more. I could tell something was going on with her, especially those last few weeks. Something happened, and it's like she wasn't Steph anymore. She was making . . . strange decisions." She gave me a pointed look, and I tensed. "Every time I asked her what was going on, she would tell me she was *close.* And I told her, 'Let me help you. We can figure this out together, if you'll just tell me what's going on.' But she wouldn't. She shut me out, because I wouldn't let it go. Steph liked having secrets. I was so scared, though. I'd never been afraid of her before that night."

I thought back on my memories of that summer. I knew what she meant; those last few weeks, there had been something bothering her. She'd never told me what it was.

"But I wasn't just afraid of her." Her voice was low and broken, and I leaned forward to hear her. "I was afraid *for* her."

She squeezed her eyes shut, and I knew she was trying to stop herself from crying. "We were arguing when we saw it. The fire." She was whispering now, quieter than I'd ever heard her. "And then we—we split up. It was Steph's idea. She was supposed to go to your mom's cabin. To wake her up and call for help. And I ran back to the beach, to warn everyone. To make sure you and Chelsea were okay."

I tried to hide the shock, though I was sure it was naked on my face.

"I wanted to stick together. But I gave in, and I ran. I left her out there in the woods." A shuddering, tortured breath. "I left her out there to die."

The heaviness of Margo's confession fell over us like a

weighted blanket, thick and suffocating, and we were silent for a long stretch.

"I wish you'd told me," I said at last, voice like gravel. "The path between the Barn and my mother's cabin wasn't touched by the fire."

Her eyes widened.

"So if that's true–if you guys split up and she was supposed to run directly to my mom's from the Barn, then . . ." I didn't finish the sentence. I let the words hang there, between us. Unspoken but heavy.

I could see she was reliving that night, the same way that I was. The heat of the flames, licking at our backs as we ran. The horror of not knowing who was alive and who was dead. And the next morning. The terrible act of counting and not finding her. Knowing that she was the only one of us who didn't make it out. Picturing her screaming, burning alive. Utterly alone.

But now, I was having even worse thoughts. Dangerous ones.

What if Steph hadn't died in the fire at all? What if someone knew what she'd learned about her mother and killed her for it?

"You know what this means, right?" She was staring at me, eyes glassy but narrowed, almost in a challenge.

Of course I did. If someone had followed Steph, and killed her, it had to have been one of the staff.

One of us.

I nodded. "And," I said. "Someone's been . . . messing with me this weekend."

Margo cocked her head, a silent urge to go on. "Not just the graffiti. Small things. That match I found in the kitchen. It felt like–a taunt. And then, my sliding glass door in my bedroom? Looks like someone threw a rock at it, tried to break it."

"What the hell, Little G? Why didn't you tell me sooner?" She looked genuinely rattled.

"It just all seemed so circumstantial. Why would I be afraid of a match, you know? But when I saw the glass door . . ."

Margo was frowning, a canyon forming between her eyebrows. "I knew it. I knew someone was in my room," she said, more to herself than me.

"Wait, what?"

"I wasn't sure, but now I am. It smelled off, like someone had lit a cigarette, and I was sure a few things weren't where I'd left them. But nothing was missing. The weirdest thing was the note, shoved under the front door earlier."

"Note? What note?"

Her mouth was a grim line. "'*LEAVE, BITCH.*'"

A cold terror crawled up my back. "Oh my God, Margo." Something was very, very wrong.

She gave an almost embarrassed shrug, like an apology for not mentioning it. "Didn't think I needed to call in the authorities. Honestly, I figured it was Baby, trying to freak me out after my interview with her dad this morning." She pushed down a few invisible flyaways, then took a deep breath.

"Okay, we need to figure out who the Phantom is," she said. "That's our next step. Because whoever it was that summer is back. They're here, they know something, and they're trying to fuck with us so we don't figure out that—that they killed her."

She choked out the final word, and that's when I knew I had to tell her. I'd never wanted to; it felt like the final, final piece of Steph that I still had all to myself. It was selfish, in so many ways. For years, I'd told myself it was out of loyalty. Not cowardice.

But she was gone now. And if breaking my promise would

help us find the truth—would help us solve the mystery she'd been desperately trying to solve, the mystery that she died for—then it might be worth it.

"Wait a second," I said, bracing myself for the fallout that I knew was coming. Margo's eyes were round and laser-focused, searching my face my clues.

"We don't need to figure out who the Phantom was," I said, the words burning my tongue. "I already know."

CHAPTER TWENTY-TWO

THEN

Eighteen Days Before the Fire

It was just after 3:00 a.m. when I snuck back to Black Bass. The moon was high, and the woods were quiet. I knew it was a stupid decision, to be out here all by myself; the Phantom had been leveling up. Last week, they'd broken into Rig and Val's cabin in the middle of the night.

It was Val who'd heard the creak on the bottom stair. She'd jolted upright in bed at the sound. Rig slept like the dead, so though she tried to shake him awake, she eventually went to check for herself.

Before she'd had a chance to flip on a light, she realized she wasn't alone—there was someone dressed all in black, their face shrouded in darkness. She'd screamed loud enough to wake the entire camp, and they'd shoulder-checked her so hard she'd slammed against the wall. I'd seen the bruise it left on her shoulder. The noise had woken Rig, and he'd come downstairs brandishing a baseball bat to find Val hunched on the floor, crying softly in the dark.

But the Phantom was long gone.

After that, my mom and Rig amped up the rules even more. Kids were told to no longer use the restroom at night, not even with a buddy. And although my mom was adamant that we didn't scare the campers, it was hard to make them understand the danger in a way that didn't make them afraid.

But somehow, despite everything, I was genuinely happy for the first time in months. I spent my mornings and afternoons on the shores of the lake, catching Trevor's eye as much as I could. I lay awake in bed each night, waiting for the steady sounds of Chelsea's and Margo's breathing to start, before I quietly crept out to meet him.

Steph was almost always still awake when I left, armed with a magazine and a reading light, and she'd blow me a kiss as I breezed out the door. There was something addictive about her attention, and her approval. I reveled in it.

Usually, we'd sneak down to the beach for a few hours, dangle our feet in the water. Tonight, though, for the first time, we'd fallen asleep in his bed. I'd woken with a start, totally disoriented, then smiled at the memory of the night before. I'd disentangled myself from him carefully, not wanting to wake him. He'd looked so deliciously adorable, calm and snoring, that I couldn't bear to disturb him. And I couldn't spend the whole night here; not when his cabin was mere steps away from basically the entire rest of the staff. Besides, Black Bass wasn't far. It would take me less than five minutes.

The sky was bright that night, no cloud cover. I made my way through camp quietly, avoiding every leaf or stick on the path, not wanting to wake any campers. All I could think about was Trevor, how good it had felt to wake up with his arms around me.

I heard a thump, and adrenaline flooded me, my confidence

disintegrating in an instant. *Shit, I'm going to die,* I thought wildly. It was dark, I was alone, and the Phantom was out here somewhere, waiting. I thought of that faceless figure clad in all black, who'd knocked Aunt Val to the ground—who may have done even worse if Rig hadn't woken up. I was being immeasurably stupid, walking through camp by myself like this. Not only would Trevor be pissed, but my mom and Rig would be, too.

I stumbled backward, shocked at the sight of a figure falling out the window of Garrett's cabin. I heard the soft hiss of "*Fuck,*" then froze.

Because it was a voice I knew.

"Steph?" I whispered, straining to see her in the dark.

She popped up easily, as if she hadn't just tumbled out of a window. She wiped her hands on her pants as my eyes adjusted, and she came into view. "What are you doing out here?"

I noted her all-black outfit, the hood over her head with the drawstring holding it tight to her face.

Her sigh was long and dramatic, like my simple question was somehow an intrusion, taking her away from an otherwise perfect evening. "What do you want me to say?"

For a long, strange moment, we were in a standoff. She crossed her arms and huffed at the sky, as if the moon and stars had betrayed her.

"Are you— You're not— Are you the *Phantom*?"

The question felt absurd to say out loud, but she didn't laugh. Instead, she leveled me with a stare that seemed to ask, *What are you going to do about it?*

My mouth went dry as I tried to catch up to what I'd just stumbled into.

Steph Bennett—sparkly, ridiculous, and louder than anyone

I'd ever met–was the Phantom of Dread's Cove. She was the one who'd been wandering around in the dark all summer. Who Kendall had seen outside the bathroom. Who Jeremy and Carter had followed into the woods.

It didn't make any sense, and yet here she was, not denying it.

I took a small step forward, raising my hands cautiously. "What's going on? Why–"

"Relax," she said, but her voice was hard. I flinched like she'd scolded me. "You're overreacting."

I blanched as a terrible thought struck me. "You pushed Val–"

Steph's lip jutted out. "I didn't *mean* to bump into her; she snuck up on me. I had to get out of there." The irony wasn't lost on me that she was blaming *Val* for sneaking up on *her.* "It was an accident. They weren't supposed to wake up. I'm just blowing off some steam, all right? I don't have a hot boyfriend to sneak out to meet when I'm bored. And you know I have trouble sleeping."

I swallowed, the sound noisy and awkward in the dark. She crossed her arms and waited, like somehow, she was the one who'd caught me sneaking out of a window that wasn't mine.

What was I supposed to do here? Over the past few weeks, I'd morphed into someone new. A version of myself that had been lying dormant within me, for maybe my whole life. This Greer was willing to take risks, to fall asleep on the beach with a boy. To try something, anything. To think about a different kind of future.

Steph had been the one to help me find her.

I'd never felt better, or more real in my life. It was like the world had burst into color, painted in shades of hope and possibility.

If I told my mother that Steph was the Phantom, she'd be kicked out. Immediately. Margo would leave with her. It would happen so fast—by tomorrow afternoon, they'd be gone. The Smallmouth campers would once again be without counselors, and we'd all be up the creek again for the last few weeks of summer.

I'd probably never see Steph Bennett again.

Kicking her out wouldn't be a fair punishment. Because this was *just Steph.* Bubbly, warm, Taylor-Swift-dance-party-with-campers Steph. She was not some shadowy villain. She was not a vengeful spirit or poltergeist sent to do harm. No, she was harmless—or she meant to be harmless. This was all simply an unfortunate manifestation of her insomnia.

Maybe, I told myself, this was actually a good thing. Now that I knew the truth, I could keep an eye on her. Protect her from getting caught and protect the camp from . . . her.

"I told you," she said, pulling the hood off to reveal a messy ponytail. "Summers have always been hard for me. They make me think of my dad. So when I can't sleep, and my mind races, I just . . ." She shrugged. "But I'll stop. If it makes you feel better, I'll stop. Maybe I'll get into books. Margo's practically got a whole library crammed under your bed."

Though her words had a lightness to them, her gaze felt heavy. For a split second, everything between us felt like it was resting on a razor's edge.

And for the first time since I'd met her, I had the distinct sense that Steph was lying to me. She wasn't planning on stopping anything. She was expecting me to take her at her word and go along with it.

Going along with this wasn't a choice I was sure that I wanted to make. But it also didn't really feel like a choice at all.

My yawn was loud, manufactured, and felt grating to my own ears. "All right, well, I'm exhausted." I made myself bark out a short, pitiful laugh, a way to keep the mood light. "I'm going to bed. You coming?"

Steph didn't smile, exactly, but the corner of her mouth turned up. She looped an arm through mine, pulling me tightly to her side. I was sure she didn't want me to ask any more questions, so I didn't.

"We should go to the Barn this weekend, just the two of us," she whispered, breath tickling my ear. Despite myself, I was elated by her suggestion. By the promise of *just the two of us.* "Margo's been so moody lately. I need a night with no drama."

She was right. Ever since that weird morning in the mess hall, Margo had only gotten more agitated. She hadn't apologized to Chelsea, like Steph had promised. She hardly spoke to either of us. The Smallmouth girls had been avoiding her like the plague—I hadn't seen her have an actual interaction with a camper in days.

Even Steph wasn't immune to her ire. Yesterday, Margo had snapped at Steph for asking to borrow her deodorant. *That's disgusting*, she'd said without looking up from her book.

"Totally," I said. Because I was learning. I was different from Margo. I would be exactly what Steph needed me to be. A friend, yes, but also a loyal follower. A foot soldier of her cause, though I didn't know if she'd ever actually tell me what that was.

I didn't know if it even mattered, as long as I was walking beside her. As long as she was choosing me.

CHAPTER TWENTY-THREE

NOW

Margo wasn't happy when I finished my confession. She locked herself in her room, and even as I pounded on the door, I knew we wouldn't be getting anywhere else this afternoon.

The rest of the day passed slowly, as I oscillated between wanting to go back to the cabin and make her talk to me and attempting to forget that she was there.

I understood why she was angry. I'd kept a pivotal piece of that summer from her. But she'd kept things from me, too. I'd never known that Steph had supposedly run directly from the Barn to my mother's cabin that night. Maybe if I had, if we'd compared notes a long time ago, we could have put the pieces together sooner.

Maybe it wouldn't have taken us this long to realize that someone must have hurt her on purpose.

But, I reminded myself, I'd been the one who'd tried to reach out to her back then. She'd ignored me. And now, she was ignoring me again.

Our relationship felt like a scab that had healed wrong, that wouldn't stop bleeding. It hurt to pick at, but it was impossible not to. It was festering, with years' worth of rot and regret beneath it.

After the sun went down, camp was finally quiet and still. The kitchen lights were on in the mess hall when I walked in, and I moved to turn them off when someone tapped me on the shoulder.

I spun around, hand over my heart, but it was only Wes.

He smiled, wiped his hands on the ancient red apron he always wore that somehow had yet to disintegrate. I remembered when he got it for Christmas from his parents, the year we turned thirteen.

I tried to smile back, though I'm sure I looked disturbed.

"Need something to eat?" he asked, throwing a dish towel over his shoulder. "I'm just getting the scones prepped for tomorrow. But I can whip you something up if you're still hungry."

"I'm good," I said, even as my stomach growled in protest. I was so flustered and distracted, I couldn't even remember if I'd eaten dinner.

He leaned against the counter, brushing some of the flour off his nose. "Come on, I heard that. How about a sandwich? I've got some of that brioche you love. Chels was just in here, I made her one." He glanced at the door, then back to me with a slight frown. "Did you not see her when you came in? She literally just left."

I couldn't help but think about what Nadine had told me as we'd watched them hold hands in the water. God, I was so stupid. I forced out a laugh that sounded like nails scraping metal. "No, thankfully. I think she's still pissed at me. I'm guessing she told you about the whole interview thing."

His shrug was unbothered. "Yeah, she told me. But you know

how she is. A textbook overreactor. She'll be fine. Y'all will be back to normal in a few weeks, I'm sure."

I hesitated. I didn't feel like getting into it right now, telling him that I hadn't decided if I was staying. But standing here with him in the mess hall, talking about making a late-night snack, seeing the glow of the moon on the lake through the wide back windows, I wanted to agree with him. To say yes, of course I was staying.

Because who would ever leave a place like this?

"You're probably right," I said at last.

Wes grinned, pleased, and I felt that familiar tug of relief to see him again. I'd missed his optimism. It was hard for me to believe that he could stand here with me like this, as if no time had passed, and as if I hadn't hurt him, too.

He'd tried so hard, in the months after the fire, to make me feel better. To beckon me home.

While Chelsea had responded to my abrupt departure in anger, Wes had responded with patience. Kindness. Which had been so much worse. *Just let me know when you're ready to come back,* he'd texted me. *I'll be here. I'll always be here.*

He'd send me updates now and then, some laced with questions. *They're starting work on rebuilding the rec center. I don't think we need two rock walls, do you?*

He never outright asked, but I understood what he was doing: He was trying to get me to admit, one way or another, what my plans were. If my new life in the city—with Trevor—was simply a hiatus, a temporary distraction while I grieved Steph and sorted out my feelings.

Or if it was permanent. If the life we'd planned for me was no longer the plan at all.

Eventually, Wes stopped trying. He sent me his very last

message exactly one year later; one year after the fire, and Stephanie's death. It had been something official. An email, rather than text. At that point, Trevor and I had broken up a few months earlier, and I was barely functional.

I hadn't even opened it. I couldn't.

I told myself that by ignoring him, I was doing him a favor. Stomping out any last hope he may have had. Because I wasn't coming back.

My head was jumbled with too many memories as I looked at him now—the good, the bad, the years here, the years away.

"Well, I'm going to head to bed," I said abruptly. "Good luck with the scones."

"Wait," he said, putting a warm hand on my arm. His fingers were rough with calluses. I thought he might insist on making me that sandwich, or—God forbid—tell me about Chelsea. I tensed, but he only asked, "Are you sure you're safe, all by yourself with Margo?"

"What do you mean?"

"I heard about what happened to Black Bass."

Damn it, Val. It took me a moment too long to understand what he was getting at. "Wait, you think it was Margo?"

"Don't act like you forgot what she was like that morning. After the fire. Pretty sure *killers* was the nicest word she used for any of us."

He wasn't wrong, and I ground my teeth rather than admitting it out loud. "So you think she's back to . . . do what, exactly?"

"I just think you should be careful with her. You know how she can be. Always . . . angling for something. I'm sure the only reason she came this weekend was to try and sabotage things."

I studied him. "Where is this coming from?"

He scratched a spot on his neck, leaving a dusting of flour on his chin. "Margo always rubbed me the wrong way. I never understood why she even came that summer. She didn't seem to *like* anything about the Cove. I had the sense she was only here to keep tabs on Steph."

"Keep tabs?"

"Yeah, you know. Like make sure she didn't stray too far. Any time Steph showed interest in anyone besides her, it was like she went full guard dog. Maybe this is out of line, but . . ." He trailed off.

"But what, Wes?"

"She always seemed . . . dangerous. Unhinged." His Adam's apple bobbed. "She's not your friend. You should remember that. You don't really know her."

It was like Chelsea all over again yesterday morning, treating me like I was a naive child. "Okay. Got it."

The front door opened, and I jumped.

"Sorry, ladybug," Rig said sheepishly, holding up his hands. "Didn't mean to scare you."

He nodded at Wes and moved past us to the tea station. "Our stove's been acting funny. Just ran over here to grab some tea for your aunt." He grabbed a to-go cup from the stack and held it under the hot water spigot.

My jaw clenched at the images that danced across my mind—me, Val, and my mom, drinking chamomile as we looked out over the water. Something we'd done a thousand times.

Rig and I hadn't spoken much today, not since the interview. I didn't know what to say; if I should apologize or poke the bear even more. At first I'd felt bad, being dishonest with him about why we were interviewing him. But now, I didn't know how to feel.

I couldn't stop thinking of the bus tickets in the envelope. His handwriting on Winona's box.

My head swiveled at the sound of beeping, coming from somewhere deep in the kitchen. "Well, that's my cue," Wes said. "I'll see y'all tomorrow. Good night, Greer."

Wes disappeared through the swinging doors, leaving me and Rig in a much more uncomfortable position now that we were alone. He was trying to decide what to say, same as me. He made a show of swirling the tea bag in the cup, busying himself unnecessarily so that he had something to do with his hands. "Trevor was looking for you earlier. Did he find you?"

"Yep," I lied. Making things right with Wes was one thing. But Trevor—well, Trevor I planned to stay away from.

"And you're feeling all settled at the cabin, then? Need anything?"

I shook my head, about to tell him that everything was fine, but then I remembered. "No, but I was wondering about my mom's Bible. Do you have any idea where it ended up?"

He lifted an eyebrow. "It wasn't on the bedside table? I swear I left it there for you."

I shook my head.

"That's odd. All right, then, I'll have a look around. See if it ended up in the office, maybe, in the shuffle of things."

It seemed unlikely, that my mom's Bible would have accidentally made it to the other side of camp. I was already preparing myself for the worst; it was gone. I made myself smile anyway, not wanting to make Rig feel even worse. "Thank you. You're probably right."

Almost absently, my hand found my mom's necklace. "I did find this," I told him, just for something to say. "A few of the letters are missing, but I thought I might try to get them replaced at some point. I think they might have diamonds."

Rig stared at the golden chain between my fingers. "You found that where?" His voice was gruff, more intense than a moment before.

I took an involuntary step back, surprised. Rig's expression was hard and strange.

"I found it in my mom's bedside drawer," I said slowly, coolly, wanting my own words to be notably casual, in stark contrast to his. "It was the only thing in there."

Rig stood as still as a statue, eyes locked on my mother's broken name around my throat. The moment stretched out, long and painful, until he finally broke the silence. "Sorry, sorry. It just—was like looking at a ghost for a second."

And then my heart splintered for the hundredth time today. Rig had always been one of my mom's closest friends. They'd practically grown up together, meeting as kids when Rig was a camper. When Chelsea and I were preteens, we'd gone through a brief *Parent Trap* phase where we'd decided they should get married. We were close as sisters, our parents got along so well—they were both single, and had been for so long. To our still-developing brains, it made all the sense in the world.

When my mom had figured out what we'd been up to, she'd been livid. Because of that, I'd been scared, even as an adult, to ask her why she'd never tried something with Rig. Their lives were already so stitched together, it just made sense. Like Wes and I had been, before I changed my mind.

I'd always wondered, though, if it had been simply a case of the wrong timing. The way Rig was looking at the necklace between my fingers, with such a devastating sadness, now seemed like confirmation of that. I wondered if that was why I'd never seen this piece of jewelry before. If it was an artifact of what almost happened between him and my mother, once upon a time, that she'd needed to hide safely away. For both of their protection. It made something in my chest seize up, at the brokenness on his face that he was trying so hard to keep from me.

"Anyway. Let me walk you back, ladybug."

"I've got her." We both turned to see Trevor, standing in the doorway.

CHAPTER TWENTY-FOUR

NOW

"I was taking a walk by the lake and saw the light was on in here."

The stubble on Trevor's chin was a little shaggy, and I thought of the hundred times I'd reminded him I liked him better clean-shaven. He ran a hand over his face, like he could read my mind.

"No, thanks," I said, hating the stilted way I sounded. I could hear the exhaustion in my voice, the frustration bordering on hostility. There was a time when just looking at Trevor had made my blood race in my veins. I was young and naive, couldn't imagine not wanting to spend every possible second with him.

That was before he'd left me behind.

"Come on, let me walk you back. I know how much you missed me." There was a glint in his eye that I knew well.

And God help me, I laughed. A real laugh, like how I used to laugh at him. Everything was terrible and wrong and impossible—my mom was dead; Steph might have been *murdered*; I was still so mad at him; I was likely going insane—but I laughed anyway. For a moment, it was worth the indulgence. "You're an idiot."

"There she is."

"How's the cabin treating you?" Rig asked–shocking me, slightly, as I'd forgotten about his existence the moment Trevor and I had locked eyes.

"Oh, it's perfect," Trevor said, smiling so wide I could almost see his molars.

"Glad to hear it, kid." He grabbed Val's tea off the counter and put on a to-go lid. "Well, think you're taken care of, ladybug. See you both in the morning." Rig nodded at both of us before slipping out the door.

When I looked back at Trevor, he was studying me intently. I wondered what he saw on my face.

"Come on. Let's get you home."

I let him lead me outside, his hand warm on my lower back as we stepped out into the night. I tried not to think of the ways *home* had shifted beneath me over the past few years. Once, he'd felt like home to me.

As we made our way to the cabin, Dread's Cove seemed deserted. It wasn't that late, but most people had retired early after a long day on the lake; today had been the hottest day this summer so far, and the heat tended to make you sleepy.

I closed my eyes in an overlong blink, trying to conjure the last time I'd gone on a walk with Trevor. I couldn't remember.

The moon was bright, and I tried and failed not to keep glancing over at his perfect face as we walked. "I'm really sorry about your mom," he said, breaking the silence at last. "Been thinking about her a lot the past few weeks. And you, obviously."

I bit my lip so hard I thought it might bleed. "Thanks," I said. "I'm not very good at this. Grieving."

Trevor's hand barely grazed mine, and my heart rate spiked.

I couldn't tell if it was on purpose, meant to be done as a comfort, or if it was simply the result of walking too close to me. Either way, I let the space between us grow.

"It's not something you have to be good at. You can just–feel it."

An owl hooted from somewhere in the trees. It was a sound that I had once loved that now felt oddly sinister.

"Can we skip this part, please? I get it. I've got stunted emotional abilities. Trust me, it's been duly noted."

He made a frustrated sound in the back of his throat. "I never said you were emotionally stunted."

"Right. Never mind." Tears threatened to make their way to the surface, making my vision blurry. "It was a long time ago. I don't know why I said that." Except, of course, that I did.

That night, after he left my apartment for the final time, I fell asleep on the floor. I sat with my back to the front door, wanting to hear him come back the moment his hand touched the doorknob.

But he never had. I waited all night, until my stiff neck became intolerable and, long after sunrise, I crawled into bed. I didn't go to work for four days–I almost got fired. But I couldn't face it. I couldn't contemplate leaving, knowing he wouldn't be there when I returned.

"So, that's why?" Trevor said beside me, pulling me back to earth.

I frowned. "Why what?"

He gave a low, almost pained chuckle in the darkness. "Why you've been avoiding me."

"I'm not avoiding you. I've just been busy."

"Not too busy to buddy up with Margo Pierce, though."

The path we were on was mostly quiet, save for the buzz of cicadas in the grass, the soft padding of our feet on the dirt. I could see my mother's cabin up ahead, not far from us; barely peeking through the pine trees. I considered, just for a moment, if I should break into a run.

"Don't be an asshole, please. I'm too tired to argue about this."

"I'm not being an asshole," he said, impossibly gentle. "And we're not arguing. I'm stating a fact. You have been avoiding me. Every time I look at you, you look away. Every time I try to talk to you, you make up some excuse and disappear. Even right now, I can tell how badly you want me to leave you alone."

I couldn't bear to look him in the eye. I didn't want to see what was so clearly reflected there: a disappointment.

For a long minute, neither of us spoke. "So, that's it?" he asked. "We're really not going to talk about it?"

My plan with Trevor had been consistent all weekend: stay far away. Because of that, I'd established no talking points, no contingency plans. I hadn't even considered what I might do if he got me alone.

It was too much already–being here, the loss of my mom, reliving the night of the fire every time I looked around. And now, what Margo and I had discovered. We were barreling toward something terrible that I couldn't stop, didn't know how to. I couldn't handle being faced with remembering the loss of Trevor, too.

It had been Trevor who'd helped me figure out what to do with myself in the days after the fire–Trevor who'd let me stay in his apartment in Atlanta for two weeks, before helping me find a studio on the same block as him. I'd fallen in love with him in those quiet moments, when he'd played with my hair on his couch and let me watch whatever movie would help me fall asleep.

Our relationship had somehow been one of the best and hardest years of my life. Trevor was my North Star–my days started and ended with him. We made plans together, to travel the world and buy a cottage in England and snorkel in Australia and a million other ridiculous things that were both impossible and perfect. I read all of his favorite books and he tried all the shitty cocktails I invented.

Once in a while, he even talked about marrying me.

I was happy. And I was lying.

I didn't quite know how to reconcile these two truths that were so at odds with each other. On Saturday mornings, when we would go see matinee movies, or lie in the grass in the park while live music drifted over us, I really was content. I'd tell myself, *I'm fine. I've healed. What happened to Steph will not be the tragedy that defines the rest of my life.*

But at night–whenever our shifts didn't match up, and I went to sleep alone–my darkest thoughts would catch up to me. I couldn't stop picturing Steph, that night in the woods. I couldn't stop myself from imagining what her last moments might have been like. How things would have been different if I'd been able to save her. Sometimes, I'd wake up screaming, terrified to go back to my dreams.

It was Trevor who suggested we move. Start fresh somewhere. It made sense at first. It was a new life raft to cling to. As I lay in bed at night, and Steph flashed through my mind, I would force myself to think of better things, future things. The move to Boulder. A whole new life in a whole new city, with Trevor beside me. At first, it had worked.

But the more excited he got, the more uneasy I became. I couldn't tell him I was having second thoughts; I wanted to make myself get over it. And I almost did.

Until that night. The night he left for good, disappointment shining in his eyes as he closed my front door for the last time.

Beside me, Trevor sighed, and I could feel it again. That fucking disappointment. One more person who I couldn't be enough for, do enough for. A person who'd already walked away from me once.

I rounded on him, eyes wild with a rush of anger. "Jesus, what do you want me to say? Do you want me to say that I'm *empty*, still? Because I am. I lost–everything."

My breath was coming in quick bursts, but Trevor was frozen solid. We'd stopped walking in the middle of the path. "Why did you even come?"

A muscle in his jaw feathered. "I wouldn't miss your mom's funeral. I didn't mean to hurt you or make this any harder, I thought you'd want me to come–"

"I didn't. I don't."

His eyebrows rose, but he said nothing.

I screwed my eyes shut, determined not to cry. "Of course I don't want to talk to you. It hurts to even look at you. Being here with Chelsea and Wes and Margo and–God–being here with you, I feel like I'm losing my mind. Nothing is right. Nothing is how it was supposed to be. And I can't accept that, but I have to, and I have to be strong and do this for *her*–"

My voice broke on the final word, and then Trevor was there, gathering me into his arms. He smelled like he always had, like salt water and mint and summertime, and I'd missed him so much that I felt physically ill. Simultaneously, I wanted to pull away and never, ever let go.

"I'm here," he whispered into my hair, and I gurgled a sob. His arms were warm and strong in the way I remembered–could never forget. "I've got you. You don't have to do this all by yourself. You're allowed to ask for help."

"It's just so hard. I miss her so much."

"Of course you do. But you need to take care of yourself, all right?"

He put his hands on my shoulders, then pushed gently back from me, as if remembering to keep the distance between us. I fought the years-old itch to lean in, push my face into his broad chest, tell him to run away with me. That I would be ready this time, for anything. That I'd follow him anywhere.

I let it wash over me, just for a second, before I put it back in the box in the very depths of my heart. All of the ways our lives could have intertwined, could still be intertwining now. Every path between us that we almost took.

We kept going and didn't speak until we made it to the cabin. I painted a smile on my face and, for good measure, patted him stiffly on the arm. "Thanks for walking me back."

Trevor gave me a two-fingered salute before I went inside. I couldn't help but think that this time, I was the one walking away.

Margo's door creaked open as I was pulling off my shoes.

"Sorry, I didn't mean to bug you," I said, hating how small my voice sounded. "I'm heading to bed, but if you want to talk tomorrow, we can."

Margo dabbed at her cheeks, and I realized that she was crying. Like, actually crying. Real tears. Not in anger, or contempt. But in visceral, ugly, close-up sadness.

"What's wrong?"

She didn't answer me, just kept her eyes on the lake, the moon.

I took a small step closer to her, wondering if it was a trick of the light. But the glow through the window was like a spotlight on her, and there was no misinterpreting it. The tears were rolling down her face, and she was wiping them off with the backs of her hands gruffly, like she couldn't hide them fast enough.

Before I could think better of it, I wrapped my arms around her, and she started to cry in earnest. I stood stock-still, not quite believing it was real, but feeling her tears stain my shirt all the same.

"What is it? Did something happen?"

She didn't answer. She just cried.

After a few moments, she jerked back from me like she'd been electrocuted. She leaned over the kitchen counter onto her elbows, her hair falling limply in front of her face.

"How about a drink?" I offered. "Can I make you something strong? What do you like? A martini? Something pretentious, probably?"

She didn't laugh, exactly, but she snorted out a breath. "Just wine," she whispered, from beneath her shield of dark hair. "Just all of the wine you have." She took a seat at the counter.

My back stiffened when I glanced at the door to the wine cellar. I shook my head, chasing the old fear away. Besides, I was pretty sure there were a few bottles above the fridge. I pulled the cabinet open, relieved to find my mother's favorite cabernet covered with a thin film of dust.

I made myself busy, pouring me and Margo overfull glasses that were more like doubles, then pushing hers slowly across the counter like I was checking for signs of life. Finally, she lifted her head up. Her face was a war zone; there was mascara running down both of her cheeks, her lipstick smeared almost garishly.

"I met Steph the first day of sorority recruitment at UGA. Did you know that?"

I shook my head.

"I was shy back then." She waited a beat, like she was checking to see if I might challenge this. I almost did. "I was a bookworm in high school. I kept to myself. It was easier that way. My mom and I moved around a lot—she was always losing her job, needing to get a new one at a moment's notice, or skipping out on a new loser boyfriend—so at a certain point, I stopped worrying about making friends. I just had to make it to college."

She played with the edges of her napkin as the memory swallowed her whole. I sat rapt with attention, afraid to even breathe, like any noise might break the spell.

"And then on that very first day, the girls in my dorm who'd signed up for recruitment had this plan to meet in the hallway, so we could all walk over together. But I was terrible at makeup back then, and I spent hours getting ready, and I kept messing up, and by the time I walked out to meet them—well, they'd all left without me."

She smiled, not at me but at whatever she must have seen in her mind. "All of them except Steph. I'd noticed her when we were moving in. She was impossible not to notice. I remember she was wearing this gorgeous green dress, almost the exact same color as mine, and it gave me this weird surge of pride. Like I'd chosen right. She said, 'You ready?' and I actually looked behind me. But it was just us in the hallway.

"I felt stupid, but I literally pointed at myself, and I said, 'Are you talking to me?' And she laughed, put a hand on her hip. 'Of course,' she said, like that was a ridiculous question. 'Those assholes were worried about being late.' She rolled her eyes, and said, 'It's not like they're going to start without *us*.'"

Margo leaned forward, and for a second, I thought she was going to fall off the barstool. But then she sat up straight again, and I saw a fresh stream of tears roll down her face. "We were an *us*, immediately. I'd never been part of an *us* before. She didn't have to be nice to me. She could have chosen anyone. But she chose me that day, in the hallway. And then we were inseparable." She used her crumpled napkin to wipe the tears from her face.

"Is that why . . . ," I started, and she lifted her red-rimmed eyes to meet mine.

"Why you scared me so bad? I thought that was obvious." She took a sip of wine that was more like a gulp. "I clocked what you were after that very first night. You were basking in the glow of Stephanie Bennett. An instant addict. I know the feeling."

I'd long suspected as much, but the confirmation was somewhere between satisfying and heartbreaking. I swallowed. "And Chelsea?"

Margo looked at me for a long moment. "What about Chelsea?"

"Why were you so mean to her?"

She sighed, as if my questions were exasperating her. "Because Chelsea was just like me. Always second best to her perfect, shiny best friend."

My mouth popped open in what was probably an almost comical show of surprise, but I couldn't help it.

Margo grabbed her glass, twisting the stem between her fingers. "That's my deep, dark secret, I guess. You finally got it out of me. Many a therapist has tried, but there it is. I'm a jealous, vindictive bitch. Happy?"

I pulled out the other barstool to sit beside her. "If we're putting it all out there, maybe I should apologize. I wasn't trying to . . . to steal her from you. Or maybe I was. It's just that Steph was unlike anyone I've ever known. And if I hadn't met her that summer, my life–I think I would have stayed here forever. Stuck in an endless loop. I know I didn't know her very long, but for what it's worth, I miss her all the time. She changed everything for me."

Margo was quiet, and when I looked back at her, she was studying me with an uncomfortable intensity. "Why do you always do that?"

"Do what?"

"Talk about her like she wasn't real. Like she's some–character in a book. Your hero. The queen of fucking England. She's not a goddess. She's a person."

She coughed, and I tensed, knowing what she was about to say. "Was a person, I mean."

"I never said she was perfect," I said quietly. I tried to tilt my head back subtly so the tears wouldn't spill over onto my cheeks. "Even then, there were moments where I felt like she was . . . using me."

She snorted before swallowing half of her glass of wine. "Oh, because you weren't using *her* for anything. You're the real victim in all this, right?"

"I wasn't using her, I–"

"But you were." She turned to fully face me. Here was the Margo I recognized–eyes sparkling before she went in for the kill.

"All damn summer you were using her. Because she made you feel special. You just said your life wouldn't be what it is now if you'd never met her. And that's why you're so grateful. That's why you've justified everything she did. You don't miss Steph, the person. You miss what she did for you. Which is why you pushed aside all the little lies that kept piling up. You ignored how she could shapeshift, from your friend into someone you didn't know at all. Into something dark."

I was shocked into silence for a long moment; the kitchen clock ticked ominously as we stared each other down. I wanted to reach for my drink, desperately—my mouth was dry as death—but I didn't want her to see my shaking hands.

Finally, I made myself speak. "Margo, that's—"

"You don't have to explain it to me," she said as she slid to her feet, voice as casual as if we'd just been discussing going on a hike in the morning. "Because I get it, Little G. I really do. You miss how you felt when you were with her. Who she helped you become."

She grabbed her wineglass and the bottle and turned on her heel. I watched as she padded down the hallway toward her room, holding my breath when she paused at the threshold. "I get it, because sometimes—even though I hate myself for it—I wonder if that's why I miss her, too."

CHAPTER TWENTY-FIVE

THEN

Fifteen Days Before the Fire

In the days after I learned the truth about Steph, things at Dread's Cove started to really go off the rails.

One hot afternoon, two ten-year-old campers had been in the middle of the lake when their canoe started sinking. They screamed loud enough to wake the dead, and Trevor was there within minutes in his dinghy to rescue them before they capsized.

Once the girls were wrapped in towels and taken to their cabin, he and Rig went back out to recover the canoe. What they found was chilling—someone had meticulously drilled dozens of tiny holes in the bottom that were almost invisible, if you weren't looking.

Someone had wanted that canoe to sink.

My mother called me on my walkie-talkie to help them investigate, and what we found was even scarier. My whole body started to tremble.

All twelve canoes in the boathouse had been altered in a similar way.

It was intentional, calculated, and cruel. With the intent to cause real, actual harm. I told myself that surely it couldn't have been Steph–but if not her, then who? After all, she'd admitted, in a roundabout way, that she was the one who'd been sneaking around at night and breaking into cabins. The one the boys had followed into the woods, who'd scared Kendall that first night. Who'd knocked Val to the ground.

And she was the only Phantom I'd caught red-handed.

But she wasn't cruel. She liked being a counselor. Margo was indifferent, bordering on hostile to the girls in her cabin. Then again, Margo had become indifferent to everyone over the past few weeks.

Steph was kind. Not just to me, but to everyone. Yesterday, I'd watched her console Chandler Harwell, one of the quieter girls in Smallmouth. Her mother had written her a letter, saying her grandma had broken her hip and was in the hospital, and poor Chandler had fallen apart completely. It was Steph who'd let her skip breakfast, taken her on a walk through the woods. Let her pick which Taylor Swift album they'd listen to for the dance party that night. And by dinner, there was color back in Chandler's cheeks, and Steph had snuck her an extra helping of strawberry shortcake. *That* was the real Steph I knew. She cared about people. Her heart was wide open, offering free tickets, inviting everyone in.

The morning of the canoe incident, my mom called an emergency staff meeting on the back deck of the mess hall. I was a thousand miles away, stuck in my own mind. I kept playing back that night: the way Steph had acted when I'd found her. Telling me that she hadn't done anything wrong, that it was just a misunderstanding.

That she hadn't meant to hurt anyone.

This Phantom Steph was a version of her that I hadn't known existed. She was sneaky. Evasive. Aloof, in the way she'd spoken about Val, and about getting caught. It was jarring, wondering what other parts of herself she'd kept hidden from me. I didn't understand how there could be multiple Stephs, all living inside of her.

My mom and the rest of the staff were all silently staring at me when I finally snapped back to reality. "What?"

She gave me a thin smile, though I could see the concern and exhaustion etched into her forehead. I'd been so lost in my own head that I hadn't noticed how awful my mom looked. We'd spent less time with each other this summer than we ever had before; I'd been busy, with Steph and Trevor, and she'd been putting out fires left and right.

She'd never been glamorous, exactly, but she was consistent. I could count on one hand how many times over the years I'd seen my mother without her hair done, pulled back in her signature twist. I didn't think I'd ever seen her without her favorite shade of berry-pink lipstick. Or at least one necklace hanging around her neck.

Right now, she was missing all three.

"Since we'll be closing all waterfront activities until further notice, I was asking if you were all right with doubling Brook Trout's daily time in the rec center. Does that work?"

I gave her a quick nod, avoiding the heat of Chelsea's gaze from the front row. My mom's eyes lingered on me for another moment, before, thankfully, she moved on to the next item on her agenda.

After she excused all of us, I forced myself to talk to her. I hated how nervous I was, speaking to my own mother. But there was something so unsettling about seeing her like this–like she was falling apart at the seams.

"Mom," I said, and she turned around. Up close, I was even more taken aback by how haunted she looked. Her eyes were sunken, her hair frizzing from the late-morning heat.

"Hey, honey," she said, patting my cheek with the back of her hand before reaching down to pack up her bag.

"Are you okay?" I asked. "You look sick."

She gave a hollow, broken laugh. "I wish I could say I was. I'm just not sure what to do about all this. I feel like it's all spiraling out of control."

My mother was the only person actively refusing to use the term *Phantom*. She said giving them a name was giving them too much power–anytime she mentioned it, it was in the same vague way: *I don't know what to do about all this. We need to figure out who's been sneaking around in the woods.*

"I'm sorry," I whispered. "You don't deserve this."

"We'll figure it out. I promise you. I'll take care of it." Her voice cracked, and that was when I decided.

I had to tell her what I knew, even if that meant Steph would be sent home. Even if it fractured us irrevocably.

My gut was churning with guilt and shame. I couldn't believe I hadn't told her immediately. I was being selfish, unfair, and completely irresponsible. I had to end this, now. It was the right thing to do.

I squared my shoulders, took a deep breath, and forced myself to say the words. "Mom, I have to–"

"Little G?"

I whipped around at the sound of Steph's voice. She was standing with her arms crossed, her ice-blue eyes piercing into me like she could read my thoughts.

"Just a second," I said weakly, but my mom was already squeezing my arm in goodbye.

"I've gotta get down to the water, baby," she said, and I felt her slipping away, already focused on the never-ending task list in her head. "I'll see you later."

And then Steph and I were alone. I wasn't sure if I was imagining it, but a strange surge of tension seemed to crackle between us.

"Can I talk to you for a minute?"

I nodded, resisting the urge to look around for an out. We were all alone, everyone else having gone inside. Breakfast was long over, and even Wes and the rest of the kitchen staff were likely on their midmorning break.

"What's up?" I said, glancing back and forth between her and my mom's retreating form. I hated how obvious I was being. She could hear the anxiety in my voice, just as well as I could.

"Come sit with me," she said, and my feet seemed to move of their own accord. I dropped onto the bench next to her, keeping my eyes on the horizon, on the mountains beyond the lake.

"I have a proposition for you." I turned to face her, intrigued despite myself. Steph was smiling, the freckles on her face popping against her tan. "I think we should be roommates."

The gasp I let out was embarrassingly loud. "What?"

"Well, you know how Margo's going on her big Euro trip for the next six months? The girl who was going to sublet from her bailed last minute. I was totally freaking out, but then I thought about our plan for you to come visit this fall, and the idea just *came* to me. Who better to share an apartment with than my new bestie? The only thing better than you visiting is you staying."

Below us, I could hear the gentle waves crashing against the rocks. I shook my head, still trying to catch up. "You want me to move to Atlanta with you?"

"Exactly." She said it so easily, like it was the simplest thing in the world. Like it didn't come with a hundred caveats. Like it didn't change everything.

I opened my mouth, closed it again. A thousand thoughts raced through my brain as I considered this. I thought of my mom, tired and stressed and desperate for things to get better.

And I thought of two little girls, screaming in fear, afraid they were about to drown.

"Steph," I started, wringing my hands together. "Just tell me . . . this wasn't you, right?"

She cocked a brow. "What are you talking about?"

"The canoes," I said. "You didn't . . . you wouldn't . . ."

Her eyes went wide. "Oh my *God*. You don't actually think I would do something like that, do you?"

I gnawed on my lip instead of answering. The truth was, I had no idea what I thought anymore. This Steph–nice, bubbly, kind Steph? Of course not. But the Steph I'd met the other night, shifty and harsh? She certainly seemed capable.

She had a darkness in her.

When I said nothing, she reached out and grasped my hand. Hers was warm, sweaty. "I know you don't actually think that, you're just scared, so I'm going to forgive you for accusing me of attempted murder, all right? Can we go back to my brilliant idea, please?"

I nodded, still incapable of speaking. My brain felt like it was short-circuiting; I'd received far too much information in the past forty-five minutes. I needed a cold shower and a pot of coffee injected directly into my bloodstream.

"Come on, think about it. It's a perfect plan. Our lease starts a week after camp ends. It's a cute little place, two blocks from your boyfriend. So, it's a yes, right? It has to be."

Part of me wanted to press her—go back to the Phantom, the canoes, all the other weird and scary things that kept happening—but I couldn't stop my imagination from taking hold.

It had taken me a minute, but I realized the gravity of what she was offering me. If I said yes, in three weeks, I could leave Dread's Cove.

Even as the idea started to form, fill me with a sort of hopeful excitement that felt like a drug, I wondered if this was some kind of trade. My silence, for her friendship. My complicity, for the exact life I wanted—rooming with her, and living just down the street from Trevor. It was almost too perfect to believe. There would be no Chelsea, Wes, or even Margo to breathe down my neck.

I would be free. To make my own life—build my own road map, alongside Steph. Just like we'd talked about.

I wasn't stupid enough to believe it was an entirely benevolent offer. I wasn't stupid enough to think Steph didn't have an ulterior motive here. She was taking advantage of me and what she knew I wanted.

But I was stupid enough for a lot of things. I was stupid enough to swallow my guilt, ignore my trepidation, and say yes.

True to her word from the other night, Steph and I waited for Margo and Chelsea to fall asleep before sneaking off toward the Barn, just the two of us.

After I'd said yes to her offer this morning, Steph had been attached to my side all day. It had felt like the early days of summer again. Simple and easy. It had felt like the Night Before, when we'd skinny-dipped in the lake and my cheeks had ached from smiling. It had felt like lying in her bed while the other two snored, long after lights-out, watching old episodes of *Gilmore Girls* on her laptop, sharing headphones.

Once again, I felt the intoxicating power that was being friends with Steph Bennett. That being in her orbit could make you feel capable of anything.

We were just heading down the path that led toward the Barn when Steph stopped dead in her tracks. "*Shit*, we didn't bring anything to drink."

"There's probably a bottle of vodka left from last week. We'll be fine."

I wanted to move quickly, before someone heard us. With all the new curfew rules, I knew my mom and Rig were going to be less forgiving than usual if we got caught sneaking through the woods alone in the middle of the night.

"Wait, I have a brilliant idea. Isn't your mom gone tonight?"

She was. Once every month or so, my mom made the trek down into Lavender to run a few errands and visit her friend Kelly Anne. Often, she'd stay the night, like she was tonight. She'd almost talked herself out of it this afternoon, but me and Rig had convinced her to go. She desperately needed a night off. "Yeah, why?"

Steph turned to look at me, her mouth already curling into something that scared me. "Doesn't she supposedly have, like, the world's best wine cellar?"

I took a step back, disoriented by this question. Yes, my mom had converted her basement into a wine cellar; it had been her fortieth birthday gift to herself. She'd always been a collector and a connoisseur, and it had been a fun project one winter to sort through all of her bottles and get them organized. My mother was modest in most aspects of her life, save for two—jewelry and wine. And she went all out for the things she loved.

"I guess so," I allowed, already apprehensive about where this might be heading.

"We should totally raid it, then, right?" Her words were light, carefree, even; but I could see the tightness in her jaw, the tension in her forehead. She didn't want me to say no. It felt like a test.

"I . . . ," I said, trailing off. "I don't think so, Steph."

She sucked her teeth, as if this were the most annoying thing I could have said. "Why not?"

I rubbed at a spot on my chest, feeling hot. "I don't want to break into my mom's place."

"It's not breaking in. It's literally your house. What are you so scared of?"

I thought back on the other time this summer she'd floored me with that question, in such a different context: *What are you so scared of?* It had been how she'd convinced me to go for Trevor, to start considering an alternative future for myself. It had felt kind, encouraging. Now, it felt like she was throwing it back in my face. Mocking me.

"Because it's stealing." I leveled her with a stare that I wasn't sure was smart. I was walking away from the cool, chill Greer who I'd vowed to be around her. But messing with my mom was a line I didn't want to cross. "And I thought you said you were done with all of this."

The corner of her mouth lifted into a smirk. "This is totally different. We'll be together, and it's literally *your house*, Little G. If she was here, we'd just ask her and she'd say yes. No big deal."

"Steph, I don't–"

"Just one measly bottle, all right?" She was already tugging on my arm, pulling me back down the trail. "It'll be fun. We've got to *cheers* to being roomies, don't we? And that requires champagne."

My resolve wavered at the genuine excitement on her face. Maybe she wasn't mocking me at all. Maybe she really did want to celebrate the cementing of our friendship and the life we'd start building together in Atlanta.

So I bit my tongue and nodded stiffly, and Steph's face split into a wide smile. She grabbed my hand and steered me back in the other direction, toward my mom's cabin. "Let's go."

Most of my life, I had never needed to use a key. There was no use for one.

Until this summer. I felt a flicker of unease as I typed the code in the lockbox, knowing that it was a new precaution my mom had started taking.

To avoid something exactly like this. A break-in.

Inside, the lights were off, and I told Steph we should keep them that way. She winked, and I got the message: *I've done this before, remember?*

Steph moved through the cabin with a quiet, practiced grace. In everyday life, she was the loudest person I knew; her voice, her steps. You always knew she was coming. But in here, she moved like a ghost. Like a real phantom.

"It's over here," I whispered, heading to the basement door beside the kitchen. She'd stopped in front of my mom's fireplace, eyeing the collection of vases and trinkets that lined the mantel. She picked up an antique bronze lighter, passed down through my family, that my mom kept in a place of honor.

"This is actually really nice," she said, doing a 360-degree spin. "Why does your mom never have us over?"

I shrugged, uncomfortable. I thought we'd be in and out; I was starting to worry she'd change her mind, decide she wanted to drink the champagne in here instead.

She leaned over the vase of red flowers on the mantel, skimming her fingers through the petals. "What are these?"

"Flame azaleas," I said. "They're my mom's favorite."

She was flicking the lighter now, almost subconsciously. It was making me nervous; I crossed the room, pulled it gently from her hand, and slipped it into my bag. "Come on," I said. "Let's get this over with."

"You're so anxious. Relax." She was now in front of my mother's bookcase, squatting and running her fingers over the spines. "God, there's so much to look at. What if we had our toast in here?"

I started to protest, but she was already rolling her eyes. "I'm kidding, chill. All right, where's this famous wine cellar?"

I jerked my chin toward the door, my hand hovering over the doorknob. I'd been about to open it, to let her inside, but I suddenly felt the warning itch to not let her in. That she'd take her sweet time, wander around, while I sat up here like a sitting duck. I could already envision the look of disappointment on Rig's face.

"I'll get it. You stay here."

To my surprise and relief, she didn't object, just gave me a wink.

"Something pink and fizzy, ideally."

I nodded and moved quietly down the stairs.

As I groped blindly on the ceiling for the light pull, the door swung shut behind me with a *click*.

"Steph?" I said, reaching backward in the dark, wondering if she'd snuck inside with me after all. But there was no one; I was entirely alone. When my hand found the handle and pulled, nothing happened. I slammed my hands against it hard, but Steph didn't come to open it.

"Hey, the door is locked," I called, louder this time. I pressed my ear to the door, straining to hear, but it was thick and insulated. I could hear nothing from the other side; I had no way of knowing if she was a few feet away or on the other side of the cabin.

I ran my hands along the walls, failing to find anything resembling a light switch. A minute stretched by, then another.

"Steph!" I shouted. "Stephanie!" There was no light source that I could find, and I'd left my phone at Black Bass.

It was pitch-black, and I was trapped.

My heart was thumping against my rib cage as I pounded on the door, over and over. *Stupid, stupid,* I told myself. It turned into a steady, unrelenting rhythm, one that no one came to answer.

Tears welled in my eyes. Was this punishment for something? Why would Steph lock me in here—was this her idea of a joke?

After several more impossibly long minutes, it seemed clear that she wasn't coming back. I sat down on the first stair, my back pressed against the door, the cold draft from the basement on my legs, giving me goose bumps. I did everything I could not to think about mice or bugs, creatures that I couldn't see. I closed my eyes, made myself swallow a few deep breaths. I would be okay. Probably.

I couldn't be locked in here forever, could I? Surely, eventually, someone would find me.

Then all of a sudden I was falling backward, and a scream ripped through me before I had a chance to realize what was happening. The stairs hadn't given way. No, the door had opened, and Steph was standing over me.

"What the fuck are you screaming for?" she said, eyes wild. "Do you want to wake up the whole camp?"

I sat up. "You locked me in there."

Steph blinked at me. "No, I didn't. Why would I do that?"

"I don't know, the door closed, and I was yelling for you, but you didn't open it."

She poked her head around, into the doorway. "There's a crazy draft in here. It must have blown closed."

"But didn't you hear me calling for you?"

She narrowed her eyes, assessing me. "I did hear you. That's . . . why I opened it."

I felt very, very small, and very, very stupid. Because she was right. She had opened it. I couldn't have been inside long–it had just been so terrifying, feeling swallowed whole by the darkness. Slowly, I hauled myself to my feet.

"I was looking at your bedroom, so it took me a second to get back down the hallway. I didn't mean to scare you."

I opened my mouth to say something, but it was dry. Was my mind playing tricks on me? I hadn't been inside for that long, had I?

Why had it started to feel like Steph could hear me banging on the door and was choosing not to open it?

I rolled back on my heels, embarrassed and confused. Steph was looking at me like I was a stray animal she'd found in the bushes—like I might bolt, or I might bite.

"Forget the champagne," she said after a beat, slipping her hand in to mine and dragging me toward the front door. "We've got some celebrating to do."

I only hesitated for a second before acquiescing, like we both knew I would, and following her back into the dark.

CHAPTER TWENTY-SIX

NOW

I paced the kitchen for a few minutes, feeling off-kilter. I hadn't been truly alone with nothing to do in days, and it was unsettling. Logically, I knew that camp was full of people. I was not by myself in these woods.

But as I looked out onto the back porch, it felt too still. Once again, I was itching for the sounds of my apartment back in Atlanta. The shuffling of feet overhead, even in the dead of night; the sounds of music bleeding through the walls.

And now, with Margo's words echoing around my brain, I desperately needed something to drown it all out.

I felt two inches tall as I played back just how Margo had completely dressed me down. *All damn summer you were using her.* She was right. I felt like a fool, and a completely delusional asshole for ever having thought anything different.

Because Steph had made me an offer, it was true. But I'd been the one to accept it. I thought about my mother–what I put her through then by not telling her the truth–and wondered how different things could have been if I'd been honest when I'd had the chance.

I wanted to disappear entirely. I was overcome with the type of shame that seeps into your bones, crushes you into dust.

A distraction. I needed a distraction, and I needed it now. I couldn't entertain the garbage disposal that was my brain a second longer.

So I would do what I did best, when I wanted to use my hands and not my head. I dimmed the overhead lights, lit a few candles, and opened my mother's liquor cabinet. Once I found what I was looking for, I set to work. The garbage disposal grew quieter.

At Dogwood House, I was responsible for coming up with a cocktail special every couple of months. Back when I'd first started—and had basically no experience—Trevor would help me research at night, poring through recipe books and articles on mixology. Now, I didn't have to think about it as much. Some things just go together.

I reached out to the cabinet to pull out a glass and hesitated. Was I really going to sit in my mother's kitchen and get shit-faced alone, on cocktails made from her best gin?

When the strip of light under Margo's door flickered out, that was enough for me. I grabbed the sweaty shaker and stuffed it in my bag—hesitating only a second before grabbing the bottle of gin, too—and went back outside before I could think better of it.

Then I made my way to Trevor's cabin.

He was pulling a new T-shirt over his head when he answered the door. His hair was wet, and I could smell his shampoo. The scent memory was jarring; I thought of so many moments just like this, so many lifetimes ago. Showing up at his door after my shift, his crooked grins and knowing looks. Grabbing my wrist and pulling me inside, clothes on the floor before the lights were off.

But that was not how he greeted me tonight. Instead, we stared at each other for a weird moment.

"Greer?" he said at last, as if needing to confirm my existence, while he rubbed his eyes with the heel of his palm.

"Shit, were you going to bed?" I said, all traces of heady confidence evaporating. "I'm sorry, this was . . . Sorry. I'll go." I took a step backward, almost losing my footing on the step. His arm shot out, grabbing me before I ate shit on the front porch.

"No, no, don't leave," he said quickly. "I just wasn't expecting—" He squinted at the bulging bag over my shoulder and figured it all out in less than a second. My brilliant, stupid plan. "Wait, did you come over here to make me a *drink*?" There was a laugh in his eyes, and I was twenty-two again, and we were bold and in love.

I hitched the bag over my other shoulder, the bottle and the shaker clanking obnoxiously. "Well, not exactly. Yes, but no. What I mean is, I already made them. Margo and I got into an—argument, or discussion, I guess—and I wanted a distraction. I kind of went on autopilot. And then I realized I'd made enough for two, and so I just thought . . ." I shrugged, unsure how to finish.

Trevor was trying and failing to conceal an almost wolfish grin.

"But, um, you should go back to sleep. This was . . . sorry. I'm sorry. I'm being stupid. Did I say I was sorry?"

"About a hundred times, give or take." He took a step closer, cocked his head to the side. "You can come in." He lowered his voice, and I sucked in a breath. I had to crane my neck to get a good look at his face. It was easy to forget how tall he was until I was standing this close to him. "But there are rules."

"Rules?" My mouth felt like sandpaper. We used to kiss, standing just like this, before one of us said goodbye. Or decided not to say goodbye.

"Yes. Rules." There was still a smile playing across his lips, but it was smaller now. More hesitant. "If you come in, you have to swear, on every drink you've ever made, that you'll be totally honest with me. About everything. Every question I ask, you have to tell the truth. No matter what. I don't want any more platitudes or bullshit. Deal?"

I swallowed. The bottle of gin was pressing uncomfortably into my back. "And what do I get?"

Trevor raised his eyebrows. "The same. I won't lie, either."

I snorted a laugh before I could stop myself. "That's not fair. You never lie."

"Do we have a deal or not?" He crossed his arms and leaned against the doorframe, and I had the urge to slap him across the face for still being so annoyingly perfect.

After the shortest of standoffs, I squared my shoulders, snapped "Fine, we have a deal," and squeezed past him, hearing his low chuckle as he closed the door.

I set to work, using the small island as a makeshift workstation. He pulled out a stool and looked at me expectantly.

After I pulled two mason jars from the cabinet, I fussed with the shaker and the garnish and did everything I could to avoid looking at him. But I could feel his heavy gaze on me, warm and familiar.

Finally, I poured the drinks. If Trevor noticed my hand shaking, he didn't say anything. He took one sip and smiled, leaning his head back and closing his eyes like he'd never had anything better. "This is fucking good."

"Really?"

He nodded, taking another sip for good measure. "It's perfect. What's in it?"

I shrugged before taking my own sip. He was right; it was good. Cold and refreshing, like a summer at the lake. "That's a trade secret," I said, before I remembered the deal. "Fine. Gin, elderflower, cucumber, and lime." I paused, only briefly. "I've been calling it the Anita. In my head, I mean. I haven't made it for anyone else."

Trevor's expression shifted, and I cut my eyes away so fast that my neck cricked. I realized just how warm it was in here, how I felt claustrophobic and nostalgic at the same time. "Can we drink these on the porch?" I asked, and thankfully, he nodded.

We sat down at the small table as the fireflies chased each other, and for a while, we only listened to the soft sounds of the lake caressing the shore in the distance.

"So, you're still working at Dogwood House, I take it?" Trevor asked. He dipped his chin at the drink, the condensation dripping from the glass onto his hand.

I took a long sip before I answered. "For the time being. It's a good job. Pays the bills and all that. And they like me."

"And this?" He gestured vaguely to the forest, the water, but it wasn't hard to understand what he meant.

"I don't know yet." Simple. But honest.

"Fair enough. It's a big decision. I did wonder if you might have gone back to school," he mused.

I chanced a look at him, and he was leaning back in his chair now, eyes fixed on the mountains.

“You used to talk about that sometimes.”

I huffed an empty laugh. “I don’t know what I would go to school for, to be honest. If I go back to the city, I’ll probably stay at Dogwood. It’s just . . .” I trailed off, searching for the right word. “Easy.”

“Is that really what you want, though? Easy?”

He was staring at me, the casualness wiped from his face. Then I clocked it: He was clean-shaven now. The way he knew I liked him best.

I swallowed. “I don’t know what I want.”

Trevor’s hand flexed, like he might be about to reach for me, but then he curled it into a fist on the table.

“Are you still in Boulder?” My voice was strained, high-pitched.

Trevor squinted at the sky, and several seconds ticked by before he finally answered. “For the time being,” he said at last, echoing me.

It was the gin and his fresh shave that gave me the courage to ask, “Are you seeing anyone?”

This, he answered much faster. “No.”

I hated how this made molten relief course through me. The air between us seemed to crackle.

“Are you?” he countered.

“No,” I said, even more quickly than he had.

I took a serious sip of my drink, big enough that the gin burned my throat. Then I took another. “Any other questions?”

“Yeah, actually,” he said, leaning back in his chair. “I want to know what you and Margo have been scheming about. And why you’re arguing.”

My cheeks burned. "We are not *scheming*, she's been staying with me. You know how she is–she can be very, um, persuasive."

"But you're not friends."

Part of me wanted to snap at him–*How would you know who my friends are these days?* But I bit back the urge. "I'm helping her with her story. She works at the *Times*. We need a great feature."

"And Margo Pierce, the girl who called us all *fucking murderers*, is supposedly writing this 'great feature'? No strings attached?"

I hesitated, and he leaned across the table, so close that our faces were nearly touching. I could smell the gin on his lips. "Tell me what you're doing with her, Greer."

This was it. I could feel it; we were standing on the precipice of two very different outcomes. I could deflect, evade, refuse to answer. Do what I did best. And Trevor would stand, stretch, and politely tell me he was headed to bed. In two days he'd go back to Colorado, and I might never see him again.

My other option was to simply follow the terms I'd agreed to. If I kept being honest with him, I could stay. Margo had said over and over that I was a liar. Maybe that was true–but I was so tired of lying to Trevor. I would tell him as much of the truth as I could bear.

"We're trying to solve a murder." I closed my eyes. "Maybe two."

For a moment, the only sounds were the cicadas buzzing, and a soft but steady wind that had begun rippling through the trees.

"What are you talking about?"

"Let me start from the beginning. I never told anyone this. I couldn't. But–that summer–it was Steph. She was the Phantom."

I didn't look at him as I told him the whole awful story, what

I'd confided in Margo. When I finished, Trevor didn't speak for a long moment. Finally, I dared to turn back to him. Shadows danced across his face.

"Are you mad at me? For not telling you?"

"I'm not mad," he said. "Surprised, maybe. But not angry. It feels so long ago now.... Doesn't do me much good to be mad at you for something like that."

He gave a long sigh, still seemed to be considering. "And maybe I'm a little sad, too, that you didn't feel like you could tell me any of this. Maybe if you had..."

"I wish I could go back in time. To that summer. Even just the day of the fire, if I could have ... I don't know, if I could have warned her, if I hadn't..."

Trevor reached for my hand for real this time, getting far enough as to actually lace his fingers with mine, and the touch surprised me so much that I literally jumped out of my chair, and made a high-pitched sound that was somewhere between a squeal and a yelp.

"Sorry," he said quickly, stuffing his hands into his pockets. "Old habits, I guess."

"So," I continued, ignoring the way I could still feel the warmth of his fingers. "I think she may have found something–I don't know what–that put a target on her back. That made someone..."

"Start the fire?"

I only looked at him.

Trevor shook his head, his hair falling in his face. "I always thought it had to be the simplest answer. Figured it was some high school campers, showing off for each other. Even that shit down at the waterfront–just campers behaving badly. Trying to look cool, or whatever. And I always believed your mom, what she said about the fire. I remember the lightning that night. It just seemed . . . like the world's worst timing. Like your mom couldn't catch a break, you know? Rowdy campers and then a horrible act of nature."

"And what do you think now?"

"I don't know. It's a lot to process. What was her endgame? What was the point of all of it?"

"She was trying to find her mom," I whispered into the night. It wasn't an excuse, but it was all I had to cling to. Not because I thought she was perfect, as Margo had claimed, but because she was my friend. Even now, after everything, I wanted to give her the benefit of the doubt. "Margo told me that she was looking for her mom, Trevor. Her mom was *here*."

He blinked at me. "That summer?"

"No, when we were younger. I mean, when we were really young. Her parents met at Dread's Cove. She was here as a baby, like me and Chelsea. And her mother, Winona, was best friends with my mom." I shuddered at the visceral memory of finding that photo of all of us together–darkly, I wondered how soon after that she'd vanished.

"I never knew about her. My mom never told me about her best friend, and Steph didn't tell me about her mother. But she's why Steph came here. Because her mom disappeared, almost thirty years ago now, and she was trying to figure out what happened to her. We think that her mom . . . that she didn't leave of her own free will. And we're wondering if–whatever she knew, whatever secret she had that made someone angry enough to get rid of her–that Steph found that same secret. That maybe she was even killed for it." By the time I finished speaking, my voice was a shriveled thing, barely audible.

"The real truth is that . . . I don't give a shit about the story. Not really. I just want to know what happened. To both of them. And maybe that's unfair of me. Maybe that . . . maybe that's actually terrible." I felt tears start to blur the edges of my vision, but I pressed on. "But I have to believe that it's the right thing to do. I have to stop pretending that nothing fucked-up happened here, you know?"

"Damn," Trevor said at last. I pursed my lips in agreement. A few tears leaked from my eyes, and I rubbed them away gruffly with my sleeve.

"Okay, so that's that. Another topic, please."

Trevor looked like he wanted to argue with me. But I really didn't want to start openly weeping on his back porch. Not when, just for a few minutes, things almost felt okay between us. Not quite as broken as they'd felt for so long.

I made a hard pivot: "Your turn. Rig said you were looking for me earlier. Why?"

"To check on you." He seemed to be considering his next words carefully. "And because I miss you."

I huffed a breath, feeling dangerously lightheaded. It was either from Trevor, the drink, the stupid deal we'd made, or my rapidly decreasing sense of self-preservation. But the words just spilled out before I had a chance to be smart. "I've missed you every day for the past four years. Whenever I make a new drink, I always wish you were there to try it first. I don't even do our same old walking path anymore. It makes me too sad, walking it alone."

Trevor's gaze was searing as I asked, "How's that for honesty?"

I reached for my glass again, but his hand clasped mine before I could grab it.

His thumb ran its way down the back of my wrist, and I shivered involuntarily. "Go on, then. This is good. Tell me everything else you've been wanting to say to me. I can take it."

I took a labored breath, my pulse vibrating beneath my skin. "Well, your hair is way too long," I began. "You look like you're in a boy band. And not a good one."

Trevor barked a laugh, the sound loud enough that it echoed. "Fair enough. Anything else?"

This was growing dangerous, fast. But I couldn't stop. It's like I'd uncorked a shaken-up bottle, and everything was spilling over, entirely uncontrolled. "I'm so fucking *mad* at you," I said. "You didn't even tell me you were coming. For two weeks, I wondered—and then you were here, and it's just so unfair."

"What do you mean? What's unfair?" His thumb was still stroking my wrist.

"You have to know how I feel about you. How it destroyed me when you left me behind. And you come back here when my life is a complete shit show and surprise me and it's just completely fucked. You let me in your cabin for a nightcap when we both know this is stupid, very stupid, but I don't even care, because all I want to do is—"

I clapped my free hand over my mouth, but it was too late. And the worst part was, I couldn't even make myself regret it. I didn't want to take it back. There was something so terribly refreshing about telling the truth.

The humor between us evaporated even more quickly than it had arrived, and then it was just Trevor and me, holding hands on his back porch, when no one else in the world was around.

It all felt so precarious. Fragile as glass, like even one breath could shatter everything.

"I don't understand," he said slowly. "You're the one who ended things. If you still felt–still feel–"

"Wait," I choked out. "That is not what happened. You broke up with me."

We stared at each other. Finally, Trevor shook his head, slow and deliberate.

"That's not true. You told me it was over. That night, in your apartment. You were very clear that you didn't want me anymore. That I was too much."

I stood up, overcome with adrenaline, and pushed back from the table. "No, I told you I couldn't do it, Trevor. That I couldn't move away. I was drowning in so much guilt and sadness that I didn't know how to process–still don't know how to process–and I just froze. The thought of leaving Georgia was just–I couldn't stand it."

Trevor's eyes were round, his pupils blown wide. "When you said you couldn't do it, I thought . . . I thought you meant that you couldn't do *this*." He gestured between us. "That you couldn't do a relationship anymore. That you were done with me."

"No," I said. "No, no, no." I was keyed up now, replaying that awful night with entirely fresh eyes.

It had been three days before we were scheduled to leave for Boulder, and I was a mess. But it felt like he didn't even care, because he was so excited. He'd come by after his shift, and started talking through a bunch of details–hotels he'd booked for the drive, his start date in two weeks–and I'd gotten so overwhelmed that it all spilled out at once. I'd started to cry, and he'd asked me what was wrong. That was when I'd said those words that had sealed everything: *I don't think I can do this.*

He'd gone white as a ghost. "Are you serious?"

"I'm . . . not ready," I'd said, wringing my hands. "It's too much, too fast."

He'd given me a curt nod, his expression closing me out like his hard drive was shutting down. "Okay. Got it. Wow. I wasn't expecting this."

"This is a lot for me, and it's just not–it's not what I want. I'm sorry."

He squeezed his eyes shut. "I wish you'd told me you were second-guessing everything."

"Well, you didn't fucking *ask* me."

We sat frozen for a moment, both of us shocked by my outburst.

"If that's what you want, then–then I'll send you back your half of the deposit."

It had felt like all the oxygen had been sucked out of the air through a vacuum. "Hold on. Just like that? You don't even want to . . . talk about this? About us?"

"What else is there to say? If you don't want to do this, then I guess that's it, right?"

A shocking clarity had rolled over me like a tidal wave. He was going to leave for Colorado, with or without me. Move into the apartment, start the job, live the life. I was the least important part of the equation. I was disposable. Easy to leave behind.

Sitting there, my dad had flashed through my mind. How unimportant I'd been to him, all those years ago. How unimportant I was to Trevor now.

"Okay," I'd breathed, digging my fingernails so hard into the tops of my thighs that I thought I might draw blood.

"Okay," he'd said back to me. He'd looked at me for one long, heart-crushing moment, as if daring me to say anything else. "Take care of yourself, Greer." And then he was gone.

The Trevor of this present moment, who was back at Dread's Cove with me, the dregs of my gin drink in front of him, was slack-jawed and trembling.

"Holy shit," he whispered. "We fucked up."

There was a ringing in my ears. It seemed like my whole life was being unraveled and restrung in front of me. "I thought you left me."

"I thought you wanted me to."

I shut my eyes tight, felt the tears start to trickle down my face anyway. "In what universe would I have ever wanted you to leave without me? I loved you. You were the only thing. The only good thing."

Trevor rubbed a fist to his eye, and my stomach swooped, because I knew he was crying now, too. "You'd just been so sad. So detached. No matter what I tried to do, you kept pulling further and further away. And then when I suggested moving, and you agreed, I thought that I'd finally gotten through to you. That a fresh start was going to be good for you, for both of us."

He leaned forward on his elbows, knocking his drink in the process. The ice shook in the glass, the sound reverberating between us. "But then when you said you couldn't do it, that it was too much, it was like I went into free fall. I realized I'd been so stupid. You hadn't gone along with the plan because you wanted to—you'd just done it to appease me. When it came down to it, when the rubber met the road—you didn't want a future with me. Because I wasn't good enough for you."

Every word was like a bullet in my chest. "I'm so sorry. I never meant to hurt you. I had no idea that was what you thought. You were more than good enough. You were perfect. Far, far better than me." I dropped back into my chair, exhausted, letting my head fall into my hands as I began to sob.

And then he was there, scooting his chair around the table, close enough to me now that our knees were touching. His fingers ghosted along my chin, and I leaned into it. "I think about you every day. I still love you. So much."

"Don't lie." My voice was shaking. My brain was malfunctioning.

"I can't, remember? That's the rule."

My head pitched forward so that my forehead rested against his shoulder, and his free hand snaked its way up my back, resting lightly at the base of my neck.

"Please don't leave," I said into his shirt. "I can't handle you leaving again."

His breath tickled my ear as he spoke. "I won't. I'll do whatever you want. Whatever will make you feel better. Just tell me. Let me make it up to you. I'm desperate to make it up to you."

I don't know what I want, I'd said to him only a few minutes ago. That had changed.

"You can stay," he breathed, the words soft and reverent.

I shot up from my chair again, so quickly I almost stumbled, and Trevor followed my lead. He tugged at his collar, shaking his head like he was coming out of a trance, before giving me a formal nod.

"Sorry, that was out of line. I'll walk you back, just–"

"Shut up now, Trevor," I said, lacing my fingers through his. "I'm serious. Stop talking. Do not say anything else." Somewhere in the woods beyond us, a twig snapped. In the back of my mind, I wondered if someone was out there, watching. The match, and the broken window, and *LEAVE, BITCH* all flashed through my mind. But I pushed them down, because I didn't want to worry anymore. I wanted to be right here, in this singular moment. I didn't want to be scared, and I didn't want to be alone.

Trevor paused only for a second before he opened the back door, and I led him inside, down the hallway toward his room, and everything felt old and new again all at once.

CHAPTER TWENTY-SEVEN

THEN

Five Days Before the Fire

Steph claimed she'd stopped her Phantom activities, and I'd desperately wanted to believe her.

What hadn't stopped, however, was the growing hysteria that seemed to permeate every inch of Dread's Cove. My mom had been right: The lore of the Phantom really had spiraled out of control. The canoe incident had emboldened reckless campers to press their luck, and things were getting out of control.

One of the sixteen-year-old boys in Darter had posted a video of an awful prank—during dinner one night, they'd faked sick and snuck into Smallmouth. They'd put a live salamander in every single bed, then staked out in the trees waiting for the fallout. When the girls had returned and promptly erupted into bloodcurdling screams, they'd filmed the reaction, and posted it with a caption that read "Dread's Cove Phantom Lives!!"

It had gone semi-viral, and the calls and emails from concerned parents and the media had begun almost immediately. That, paired with the all-night disappearance of the Bluegill boys who'd been on a secret mission to find the Phantom, had put

Dread's Cove under a magnifying glass. Sheriff Ramon and a few of his deputies had to stake out at the camp entrance, turning news vans away.

My mom was barely keeping it together. She was hardly sleeping, instead electing to spend hours in front of her computer, obsessively scrolling the "Dread's Cove Parents" Facebook group and local newspaper sites for comments calling for her removal. One night, when she was feeling particularly low, she admitted to me that she and Rig had been weighing the pros and cons of sending everyone home early. That would be a Dread's Cove first.

With everything going on, I'd decided to wait until the summer season officially ended to tell her that I was moving to Atlanta. Maybe I was procrastinating because I was worried about how she'd react—but I also just didn't think she could handle any other stressors right now.

I'd been up late the night before, going through my mom's ever-growing inbox with her in the office, and I hadn't gotten to bed until well past midnight. This morning, sensing my exhaustion, Chelsea had offered to take the Brook Trout girls to the rec center, which left me an extra hour at the cabin before lunch. I'd been grateful, considering we hadn't exactly been on great terms the past few weeks.

I was lounging in bed, flipping through one of Steph's magazines, when Margo burst through the door. I sat bolt upright, almost hitting my head on the underside of her bed.

She gave me a single, proper nod in greeting as she crossed to the bathroom. "Forgot my sunscreen," she offered, and I heard her searching around the cluttered countertop for it.

The air in the room felt tense for a moment. We were hardly

ever around each other alone like this. Every now and then, I could feel her watching me. Assessing me. Like she was searching for cracks in my veneer, places to strike.

But that was fine, I reminded myself. Even if Margo wasn't my biggest fan, I had Steph. And while Margo was away this fall, Steph and I would fully cement our friendship. When Margo returned in six months, I was sure that the three of us would become an unshakable unit. It would be inevitable.

"Hey, Margo," I said. "I've been meaning to ask you. As far as furniture goes, what were you planning on buying?"

Margo looked up from the sink and locked eyes with me in the mirror. "What are you talking about?"

I pushed a lock of hair behind my ear as apprehension pooled in my gut. "Um, for the apartment? I already sold all my stuff from my old place, so I was just thinking that if you were going to buy a new bed, I could maybe pay to rent it from you for the fall, or . . ."

I trailed off when her expression went from confused to apoplectic. It stayed that way—utterly terrifying—for only a few seconds, but it was enough to understand that I'd made a fatal error: Margo didn't know that I was moving into the apartment while she was traveling.

Steph hadn't told her.

Margo sniffed and went back to rummaging around the countertop. After a painful few beats, she found the tube in question and flipped off the bathroom light. "That won't be necessary, Little G." Her dark brown eyes looked almost black as she spoke, and I had to work hard to keep myself from visibly shivering.

I stood slowly, holding my hands up in surrender. "Sorry, I didn't mean to—I just figured Steph would have told you—"

Her nostrils flared, and I knew that had been strike two. Another worst-possible-thing-to-say.

"Forget about it," I said, blowing out a breath.

"It's forgotten," she sang back at me, as if she wasn't looking at me like she was actively plotting my murder. She made a grand show of checking her watch. "I gotta run. Steph's waiting for me."

CHAPTER TWENTY-EIGHT

NOW

The last full day of the Welcome Back Weekend snuck up on us quickly. I'd been worried that this whole *fucked-up funeral-slash-party weekend*, as Margo had so delicately put it, would pass at a glacial pace. Instead, distracted as I'd been by our investigation and the strange case of Winona Hayes—and our growing fears that Steph, too, may have been murdered—it was a bit disconcerting to wake up and realize there were less than twenty-four hours until this fever dream ended.

I snuck back to my cabin before sunrise. I didn't want the first article about this weekend being titled "Nepo Baby Walk of Shame, Days After Mother's Funeral!" Trevor had watched me get dressed with a sleepy smile.

"Come back soon," he said by way of goodbye. I stiffened at the onslaught of memories—he always used to say that when I left his apartment—but he was already snoring again by the time I thought of something witty to say. At the foot of the bed was the T-shirt he'd been wearing last night. For whatever reason, I picked it up, buried my face in it. Then I put it on and slipped out the door.

Almost the moment my head touched my pillow, I fell back into a deep sleep. An hour or so later, I was startled awake again by the padding of Margo's feet on the hardwood floors, the fridge opening and closing as she pulled out the oat milk. Then, the sound of coffee being poured into a mug, the floor creaking again before the couch moved and she sat down.

I could imagine her pulling her laptop into her lap, her coffee balancing precariously in the space between her leg and the couch cushion. A copy of some old book on the other side of her, like a safety blanket.

"No coffee?" she asked, tilting her head at me when I entered the kitchen. "You don't get humanlike until you've had your coffee. Drink up."

It was an insult disguised as a joke, but it somehow felt like one of the most normal things she'd said to me all weekend. If she didn't want to talk about last night, that was more than fine with me.

I shrugged, checking my watch. "The mess hall will be quiet right now. Thought we might want to head that way. Everyone's on that big hike this morning, so it should be just us."

Margo's eyes lit up. "Shit. I forgot about that. Thank *God*, I want an espresso, like, yesterday." As one of the final events of this weekend, Rig and Val were leading the guests on a hike to Lady's Lurch.

"Let's go," Margo said, already slipping her feet into her sneakers.

When we got to the mess hall, it was empty. Inside, there were the remains of this morning's breakfast in the buffet line, and Margo and I picked through for the best pieces of fruit and the crispiest pieces of bacon.

We were just sitting at a table when we heard the unmistakable sound of Trevor's booming voice from the deck, just out of sight. Margo and I locked eyes for only a second before she lifted her plate and made a beeline for the door.

"Margo," I warned, crowding her from behind, but she just waved a disinterested hand at me, like I was a fly she was shooing away.

"Bingo," she said, pushing the door open. I swallowed hard, sensing danger. Whatever was about to happen wouldn't be fun for anyone. Though part of me thought I should be grateful that it had taken this long.

We rounded the corner to see Chelsea, Wes, and Trevor sitting at a picnic table. They all had near-empty plates in front of them, as if they'd been out here for a while.

I froze, and it was six summers ago. Before Steph and Margo had ever arrived; before I'd ended things with Wes, and long before I'd even thought of Trevor as a real possibility. I felt as though I'd left my body and was somewhere far above all of this, hallucinating a time when things were much simpler.

Seeing Trevor and Wes sharing a table might have been the strangest part. They'd been friendly, more so than actual friends, when Trevor and I had gotten together. Wes hadn't been excited, obviously; he wasn't rude, but he no longer threw a football on the beach with Trevor on his nights off, or took a sip from his flask when it was being passed around. So it was jarring to see them now, so clearly comfortable with each other.

Wes and Chelsea sat close enough together that their elbows touched, and I watched as Wes plucked a blueberry off her plate and she swatted him away. There was a smile on her face, strong and pronounced–she hadn't smiled at me once since I'd been back. I didn't think I'd ever seen her look the way she was looking at Wes right now.

I felt stupid for not having noticed it immediately. Of course they were together.

It took until the screen door slammed shut behind us before the three of them turned our way. It was deathly quiet on the porch for a long, painful moment until Margo said, "Can we join you?"

It was Trevor who broke the silence, like I knew he would. For a millisecond, he locked eyes with me, and everything that had happened last night flickered through my brain, rapid-fire. The drinks, the honesty game, his bed–

"Of course." He jumped up, pulled one of the Adirondack chairs from the corner of the deck to the end of the table. Margo sat down beside Trevor before I could, leaving the chair to me. It was a little too low to match with the table, and I pushed my food around in front of me, feeling like a baby in a high chair, almost sick at the smell of scrambled eggs. This was too much. I was no longer hungry.

For a long moment, we all listened to the sound of Margo, making a show of cutting her food. When her first bite was halfway to her mouth, she smiled, like she was reveling in the tension. "Don't let us interrupt you. Go ahead, finish your conversation. Like we're not even here."

Trevor fussed with the brim of his hat for a moment before glancing around at the rest of us. "No, that's all right. You been having a good weekend so far, Margo?"

Her fork clattered to her plate, and she leaned back, as if she were a snake that had been waiting to strike. "Have I been having a good weekend? Wow, what a loaded question."

She put her chin on her fist, sighing in a fake, dreamy sort of way, like she was reminiscing. "It's been so great being back here. Remembering the way my best friend died."

Chelsea gave me a pointed, withering look, like this was something I alone needed to fix. I opened my mouth to try, but Margo wasn't finished.

"What about you guys? Having fun pretending like she didn't burn alive?"

"You should leave." Chelsea spoke through clenched teeth.

Margo raised her hands up in mock innocence, her mouth curling into a sneer. "Ooh, I've got a fun game. You can go first, Baby. You said yourself that we all remember Stephanie Bennett *fondly* here. Tell me, what was your fondest memory of Steph? I'm dying to know."

Chelsea closed her eyes for a long moment. "I have nothing against Steph, Margo. I'm sorry that she's gone, and what happened to her was horrible. But this weekend isn't about you."

"Fine, then, I'll go first, if you insist." Margo's smile was jagged, cruel. "My favorite memory was–"

"Margo, please stop," I begged.

Her eyes burned into mine. "Sorry, Little G, I forgot how uncomfortable you get with the whole *truth* thing. You can go if this is too much for you."

"Don't be such a bitch, Margo," Wes said, voice low with anger and warning, at the same time that Trevor said, "Hey, don't talk to her like that."

She just laughed, the sound high-pitched and grating and not genuine at all.

"This again?" she said, gesturing between the two of them. "Why don't you two just have a duel over her and be done with it."

Kill me. Someone, please, kill me.

"I know what you're doing." Chelsea's face was beet red. She flipped her hair over her shoulder and put her hands on her hips in some sort of attempted show of dominance. "You were the Phantom, you started the fire, and now you're back to . . . to sabotage us again. I see right through you. You're completely unhinged. This is all just some sick revenge fantasy."

Her words were eerily similar to what Wes had said to me last night in the mess hall, and my spine stiffened. Margo picked up a strawberry from her plate, set it on her tongue, and chewed it slowly.

But then, her mouth curved into a triumphant smile. "Wait a second. I thought the fire was an *act of God.* It was the storm from that night. Right? How could I have started the fire? Am I God now?"

"No one knows for sure what happened that night," Chelsea said without much conviction, picking at a hangnail.

"No, no," Margo said, wagging her finger in the air. "Can't close back up that Pandora's box. So, tell me. What's the going theory, then? How did I do it?" She flipped the press badge hanging from her neck around and gave an exaggerated wink. "Off the record, of course. Between old friends."

No one spoke. The sun was hot, scorching my scalp, and I pulled at the collar of my shirt, hoping for some air flow. Beside me, Margo sniffed with impatience, her lip curling as the seconds stretched out between all of us.

Finally, Chelsea squared her shoulders. "I'm not an idiot. And we were never friends. You made sure of that. But we're not going to let you slander us. Anita deserves better."

Margo raised her hands above her head, showing her bare arms to us, then patted herself down. "No wire here. Just tell me. I have to know. What was my motive?"

"It wasn't her," I said in a croak, and only Trevor looked at me, one eyebrow raised. Wes and Chelsea were both staring at Margo, as though if they took their eyes off her even for a second, she'd burn this place down again. "We shared a bunk bed. I would have known if she was sneaking out in the middle of the night."

"Not a bad point," Margo mused, like we were discussing something banal, like last night's dessert.

"No," Chelsea said through gritted teeth. "I don't believe anything Greer says, not about the two of you."

Not about the two of you. Margo and Steph. She'd never put it in such frank terms before, but I'd long suspected as much. That summer had ruined Chelsea and me, irrevocably. Because if Chelsea cared about anything in this world, it was unwavering loyalty. *Us against them.*

After the fire, when I was more focused on Steph's death than what would become of Dread's Cove, she'd seen that as a shocking betrayal. And then I'd left altogether, moved to Atlanta, and blew all of my lifelong plans into dust. Chelsea had never looked at me with such contempt as when I'd packed up my things that morning, a few days after the fire. "You're making a mistake," she'd said, arms crossed and eyes tight with emotion. "You're abandoning your family. You're abandoning *me*."

She'd been right. And I'd done it anyway.

"I know you're the one who's been sneaking into my cabin, leaving me those notes," Chelsea continued, her voice rising. "*FUCK YOU* written on my mirror? Setting off my fire alarm in the middle of the night? Seriously? What are you, a child?"

I reared back in my chair, startled by this revelation. "Wait, someone's been sneaking into your cabin? Chelsea, what else did–"

But Margo was louder than me, and my question was drowned out. "Seriously, I'm getting bored. Tell me my motive."

"You forget that I know you, Margo," Chelsea said, practically spitting now. "I was paying attention that summer. You're not as smart or as subtle as you think you are, okay? It was obvious that you were jealous of Steph. You were mad she liked Greer more than she liked you. And because you're–you. You don't need a reason to be mean. You just are. The girls were all scared of you. Everyone was. You're a bitter, terrible person. That's why."

Wes gave a nod of agreement, while Trevor's eyebrows shot up into his hairline; my jaw dropped open in surprise. Even when Chelsea had confronted me in the past, it had never been so outright. I had never seen such brutal rage, shining bright on her face.

"That's what you think?" Margo's voice had dropped into a charged, dangerous whisper. "That I'm the bitter one? Isn't that a little rich, coming from you?" She waved a hand around. "You know this is all *Greer's*, right? You can work as hard as you fucking want, but you'll never be her. You'll never have Olsen as your last name. You can even take her scraps into your bed, if you want." Margo winked audaciously at Wes, and he and Chelsea both blanched.

"I want to point out, I did see that one coming. But I digress. None of that matters, Baby. Because when you die, there won't be a big funeral like yesterday. No one will come out of the woodwork to celebrate you and your prolific life. Absolutely no one. You're like a piece of dust, blowing in the wind. Nothing. And somewhere in that pathetic, shriveled heart of yours, you know that. Which actually makes you just about the most bitter, sad person I've ever had the displeasure of encountering."

Several things happened in rapid succession, so quickly that I could hardly keep up. Chelsea lunged at Margo from across the table. I stood up from my chair, not knowing what else to do, my own voice erupting into a hoarse scream I hardly recognized. And then Trevor was there, throwing his arm in front of me to keep me from getting closer, and Wes was pulling Chelsea away from a crumpled Margo.

"What the fuck is wrong with you?" Margo hissed, and Chelsea was crying, beating her fists against Wes's chest. Margo stood and staggered backward, and we locked eyes.

For just a moment, I was sure I saw a streak of pride. She'd finally made Chelsea Riggins break for real. It only took five years.

I had a brief flash of her words last night, her confession—*Chelsea was just like me.*

Trevor held out his hand. She hesitated, like he might be faking her out, but after his exasperated "Come on, Margo," she let him pull her up to standing.

I made to reach for my plate, but Trevor gave a brisk shake of his head, and I snapped my hand back. He nodded in the direction of the door, dismissing us. "I got it. Why don't you walk Margo back?"

He passed her off to me as if she were a child and we had

shared custody. I gave him a weak nod, hardly daring to look at Wes and Chelsea, who I could hear taking gasping breaths.

When we were safely back inside, I rounded on her. "What are you doing? Are you just playing some kind of game?"

She pushed past me, her shoulder knocking into mine. "I don't play games, Little G. I win them."

CHAPTER TWENTY-NINE

THEN

One Day Before the Fire

I passed the office one afternoon and saw my mom standing outside with Val, who had her back to me; this was how she liked to have a clandestine cigarette. She was a lifelong smoker, but smoking was prohibited at Dread's Cove, especially during a summer as dry as this one.

My mom was stubborn, but Val was possibly even worse, so they'd agreed to a strange truce over the years. Val would smoke only on the office porch, and my mom would always be there to chaperone. They usually took it as a good opportunity for a break from the roller coaster that was running a summer camp.

When my mom turned in my direction, her expression was almost hostile. It softened slightly, when she saw me, but I still stiffened—had she found out about our break-in?

With a pointed glance at Val, who snuffed out her cigarette and retreated inside without another word, she nodded me over.

She had a tumbler full of ice cubes, and she pressed one to her red forehead as she spoke. "What's going on with Stephanie?

She's been skipping meals this week. She knows that's not exactly fulfilling her counselor duties, right?"

I winced. "She hasn't been feeling well. I think she's on her period." I felt compelled to defend her, to deflect, even though I hated being dishonest with my mom. It was true that Steph had been acting strange since that night. I just didn't know why.

Every time I'd tried to bring it up since then, she'd had one of two reactions: to laugh, or to jump down my throat. "What are you so mad about? I didn't know you were trapped in there. What else can I do?" When she put it that way, I had no good answer. Of course I believed her, that it was an accident, but there was something that still sat heavy on my chest at the thought of it. Even though it felt akin to a betrayal somehow, it made me nervous, thinking about her wandering around my mom's cabin while I called out in the dark.

But I trusted her, didn't I? I had to. I mean, we were moving in together soon. It was her name on the lease—hers and Margo's. She was my ticket out of Dread's Cove. And if I didn't have her, if I didn't take this one chance—I didn't know if I'd ever make it out.

I didn't know if I was brave enough to do it alone.

"I'll talk to her," I told my mom, smile plastered on my face.

She matched mine with a smaller one, though I couldn't tell if it was real or not. I wondered just how much we were both lying to each other.

Despite her complaints to my mother, Margo had night rounds, and Chelsea had volunteered to help Wes do inventory in the kitchen, which would leave Steph and me alone for the rest of the evening.

After I dropped the girls off at their cabin and said good night to them, Trevor walked me back to Black Bass. He had plans to play poker with some of the lifeguards out in the Barn, and he kissed me before heading that way. I was both wary and excited, thinking about spending the next few hours with Steph. It had been a while since we'd had some dedicated time just for the two of us, and I hoped we could finally talk about our apartment and our plans for the fall.

Ever since the night at my mom's place, I'd been even more aware of the two-Steph phenomenon. Some nights, after I got back from seeing Trevor, she'd pat that spot next to her in bed, and I'd fall asleep with my head on her shoulder. But other nights, she'd be in her own world, the light of her laptop casting shadow across her face. I'd ask what she was up to, and she'd put a single finger to her lips like a dismissal. Or, worse, she'd snap at me, tell me to leave it alone.

I couldn't tell yet which Steph I would get tonight. It was looking like it might be the latter, the way she was bunched up against the pillows, nose buried in her journal, tongue out in concentration. "What are you working on?"

She didn't answer, just gave a thin smile that didn't reach her eyes.

"I wanted to ask you," I said, and, finally, she glanced up. "The other day, Margo seemed kind of confused that I was taking her room. Has she talked to you at all?"

Steph blinked, like she was trying to place me. For the length of a heartbeat, I convinced myself that I had hallucinated all of it. That because I'd wanted these things so badly—to be roommates with Steph, live down the street from Trevor, and have the power and freedom to build my own road map—that maybe I'd simply made it up.

But then Steph blew out a breath, rolled her eyes. "You know how dramatic she can be. I thought I told her, but I must have forgotten. Don't let it get to you, okay? She'll come around."

My face heated at this not-so-subtle admission that I'd been right: Margo wasn't a fan of me. And Steph knew it, too.

"Okay," I said, rubbing the back of my neck. Her eyes were already back on her journal, but I didn't want to lose her yet. "Well, do you want to watch a movie or something? We could–"

"Why did your dad leave your mom?"

The question was so unexpected, so strange, that it took me a beat to respond. "Sorry, what?"

She turned fully to face me, sitting crisscross on her mattress. She set her journal beside her gingerly, keeping her eyes locked on mine. "Your dad left your mom when you were a baby, right? Do you know why?"

I didn't understand. She knew exactly how my dad had messed me up. How much it still hurt, to feel like an afterthought to him.

"Why are you asking me about this?"

She leaned forward, her expression eerily calm, almost detached. "Was it because of your mom? Did she do something? Maybe she was going to leave him, and he beat her to it?"

"What are you talking about? Did my mom do something to make my shitty dad leave us?"

"It's just a question. Don't get all jumpy."

I wanted to shout at her. I wanted to remind her about the time I'd tried to learn about her mother, her backstory, and she'd shut me down completely. But her face was so relaxed that I told myself I had to be overreacting.

"I don't know," I ground out at last. "He got a job offer and decided to take it. He didn't want us. I don't think there's much more to it."

Steph nodded, like she accepted this explanation, then grabbed her journal again.

She'd rattled me with her weird questions, and I almost talked myself out of it.

But I had to ask her—I owed my mom that much. "Can I talk to you about something?"

"Sure."

"Are you . . . is everything okay?"

She scrunched her eyebrows together. "What are you talking about?"

"Well, my mom's worried about you, and I—"

She slammed the journal back down on the bed with impressive force. "You talked to your mom about me?" She spoke quietly, with a festering rage that I couldn't comprehend.

Immediately, I knew I'd messed up. "She asked me to talk to you—"

"She's too fucking scared to talk to me herself? Is that it?"

My mouth popped open. I was shocked by the force of her anger, and her clear contempt for my mom, of all people. "I wasn't trying to upset you. Like I said, we're just worried."

"You don't know me well enough to be worried about me." Keeping her eyes on me, she reached for the light switch, and we plunged into darkness. There it was again; that streak of vicious anger that would come out, seemingly out of nowhere. So hard to reconcile with the fun, kind person I'd been sharing a room with all summer.

"I don't want to fight when we're about to be roommates." I was sure I sounded pathetic, lobbing this out into the void, but it was easier to say with the lights off. All I wanted was confirmation that this wasn't built on shaky ground. That we were in this together. That I'd keep her secrets, and she knew what it would cost me.

That she wouldn't let me down.

But she didn't confirm anything. Instead, she coughed pointedly, and I heard the mattress creak as she turned to face the wall.

"You know, I'm pretty tired, actually. Let's talk about this tomorrow, all right?"

"Oh, um–okay, then. Yeah, we can talk tomorrow."

I stared at the slats above my bed for what felt like hours, trying to sift through the hidden meaning that must have been embedded in her words. Eventually I dozed off, awoken by the sound of the creaking door. My eyes flickered open immediately, trying to recognize the figure in the dark. Margo. She paused in the doorway, and I could tell she was waiting for her eyes to adjust–in here, there was no moonlight shining through.

She was waiting to see if we were still awake.

I kept my eyes shut tight, and eventually, I heard her cross the room to sit on the edge of Steph's bed.

"Stephanie," Margo whispered. I peered through barely opened lids, wondering what she was up to.

At the sound of her name, Steph sat bolt upright in bed, hand flying to her heart.

"Don't worry, it's just me," Margo whispered. "Not the Phantom."

"Jesus. What time is it?" I heard Steph feeling around, searching for her phone.

"After midnight."

"What the hell?" There was sleep in Steph's voice, and thinly veiled annoyance. "Did you just wake me up for fun?"

I didn't miss the way Margo's head swiveled toward me. I sealed my eyes shut once again, hardly daring to breathe. "I need to talk to you. I just got an email from Emory. They accepted me into that creative writing program. The new cohort starts in a month."

I feigned turning over in my sleep so they couldn't hear my gasp.

"Are you serious?" The exasperation was gone in an instant. "That's amazing, oh my God. I thought you said there was no way. I didn't even realize you'd applied."

"Dead serious. I'll tell you all about it. But listen, I'm going to need my room back. The three of us can't all live in the apartment together. It's not big enough. I'm not sharing a room again, not after doing bunk beds for two months." Her tone was forcedly light, but I could hear the real request behind the words. I knew what she wanted: me, out of the equation.

An awful cord of fear snaked its way down my spine. Steph didn't even hesitate. "Don't worry, I'll talk to her. We'll figure it out."

Everything felt as precarious as a house of cards, suddenly. The new life that I thought I was building, that we were building. I couldn't move to Atlanta if I didn't have a place to live. I'd be trapped here. I knew I would.

This was my one chance. Steph was my only chance.

My bed creaked again, and through the slits of my eyes, I could see them both glance my way. They were being careless, talking like this with me in the room, and they seemed to realize it at the same moment.

"Let's go, so she doesn't wake up," Steph whispered, then stood and pulled Margo along with her. As the door closed behind them, their words settled over me like a tarp, heavy with the weight of what I knew I might be about to lose.

I felt the sting of betrayal, hot on my face, long after they'd left. Not just from Steph, but Margo, too. She'd seen an opportunity, and she'd taken it. A predator, hunting its prey. Striking when the iron was hot.

I couldn't blame her, in the end, though, could I? It was fair play, after all, when it came to Steph.

I was more than willing to do the same.

CHAPTER THIRTY

NOW

The afternoon rolled by, more quickly than I expected. When the hikers returned, Rig needed me to help set up for the goodbye dinner. We were pulling out all the stops–the fanciest table linens, the most expensive liquor. Our last shot to impress the donors, the reporters, and leave everyone on the edge of their seats, wanting more.

I was grateful for the distraction. It would be a chance to let my mind be occupied by a constant slew of rote tasks–folding, table-setting, vacuuming, repeat. In a lot of ways, it reminded me of why I liked bartending so much; it gave my garbage disposal of a brain a chance to rest.

When I got back to the cabin hours later, I was exhausted. I took off my sweaty clothes and threw on Trevor's T-shirt that I'd worn home that morning. I fell asleep almost immediately.

The song of a bird woke me an hour or so later. The sun had shifted; it was close to twilight now. "Shit," I said, throwing myself out of bed. I needed to get myself together, get dressed for the final night. I also needed a serious caffeine intervention.

I opened my door and noticed Margo's was closed. I figured she'd been writing all afternoon, holed up in here—or maybe she'd been out exploring. Trying to dig up more on Winona Hayes.

I hesitated in front of her door, hand poised to knock and ask if I should make enough coffee for both of us. A peace offering, after the chaos of this morning's fucked-up breakfast. I could hear the low drum of the shower, signaling that she was occupied. I almost turned around, but something came over me, and I pushed the door open anyway. There was a buzzing in my ears as I stepped over the threshold, knowing that what I was doing was crossing a line. But then I took another step.

Being in here was jarring. It smelled strange, like Margo's perfume instead of my mother's favorite cookie-scented candle, and there were silk pillowcases on the bed I didn't recognize. The door to the bathroom was closed to keep the steam in, and I noticed that her phone was face up on the desk.

I thought about what Wes had said, what Chelsea had corroborated this morning. They thought Margo was dangerous. They thought she was here with the intention to cause harm—that she was the one sneaking into places she shouldn't have been, leaving crude messages.

My feet seemed to move of their own accord, and I found myself standing in front of her phone. It was locked, of course, and I considered trying a few passwords to see if I could get in.

But just as I told myself to walk away, to pretend that the thought had never struck me, the preview of a new email appeared in her inbox. From her editor.

Re: re: Story Pitch—Who killed Stephanie Bennett?

OMG sounds like you might have been right all along. G.O. is definitely hiding something. If you really think she had something to do with—

I could only read the first few lines, but it was enough to understand, with fierce certainty. It was like a bucket of ice water being poured over my head. Margo really had been lying to me all along.

Since the very beginning, she'd been here to figure out what exactly happened that night.

To pin it on *me*.

I thought about her idea in Black Bass that first night, when we found that photo–getting me to soften to her.

I thought back on our conversation this morning, with Chelsea and Trevor and Wes. The way she'd riled Chelsea up until she snapped like a rubber band. Poking and prodding and forcing our hands, waiting to see if we broke.

And I thought about last night, when I'd poured her a glass of wine while she ugly cried. I'd consoled her, damn it. Hugged her, like we really were the old friends we'd been acting like all weekend.

Here I'd been, thinking we were making new discoveries together. Doing something good.

This had never been about mutual gain. It hadn't been about making things right. This had been about her. Her plans, her games. Her revenge. On me.

Chelsea had been right; Wes had been right. I was the idiot, and I had been all along.

The shower turned off, and I heard the curtain slide open. As quietly as I could, I slipped out the door.

I waited fifteen seconds, until the bathroom door creaked. I made myself swallow the scream in my throat and arranged my face into something I hoped was neutral. Then, when I was ready, I put my fist to the door and knocked.

"Come in," came Margo's voice, and I pushed the door open again. I glanced around the room, like I was seeing it with fresh eyes. The steam had filtered into the bedroom from the shower, fogging up the mirror over the dresser, and Margo sat perched on the end of the bed, hair wrapped in a towel.

She narrowed her eyes, but it seemed to be more out of curiosity than accusation. I forced myself not to look over at her phone, where I knew it sat.

"What's up?" She grabbed a bottle of lotion from the bedside table, squirting some into her hands before beginning the ritual of running it up and down her arms.

It was so normal that I stood frozen for a beat too long; it made me imagine a different, impossible life, where we'd all been roommates in the city. Where we would burst into one another's rooms at all hours of the day and night, paint our nails on the coffee table between glasses of cheap wine.

It gave me a swoop in my stomach that was one part nostalgia, one part debilitating sadness.

She liked to say that I was a liar, a pretender. But clearly, she was the best actress here.

"I'm running over to the office for a few things. Need the printer—just some paperwork from the lawyers I have to look over. I'll see you at dinner?"

Margo nodded, the movement small and casual, and I could

see her already making a checklist in her head of what else she needed to accomplish tonight. I started to turn, but she clicked her tongue.

My hand flew to my chest, certain that I'd been caught.

But all she said was: "I've been thinking about that weird little symbol on the back of the photo. Do you have any ideas?"

I made myself shrug, going for nonchalant. "Your guess is as good as mine."

She grabbed her phone off the desk, and my cheeks warmed, despite myself. I could tell she was scrolling through her photos, to find the picture she'd taken of the symbol on the back. She squinted at the picture and turned her phone on its side, as if that might make it make sense.

"Four lines, a circle, and a square. I'm at a loss." Her eyes found mine. "No thoughts?"

I hesitated. Part of me wanted to stay, to talk to her, solve the puzzle—a larger part of me knew I was in the lion's den. As much as I wanted to find the truth, I was growing more and more afraid of what Margo might be willing to *do* with the truth.

"Sorry, but I've got to get this done before dinner, so I'll . . ." I trailed off. I gave her what I hoped was a semi-convincing smile before closing the door again.

We'd be eating later tonight, due to this afternoon's stacked activity schedule, and it was already well past twilight as I made my way to the office building. Inside, the lights were off, and I hesitated before entering my mom's office. I felt like I was violating her trust somehow, even though she was gone.

It was spooky inside; spookier than even Black Bass had been in the middle of the night. This office building was new and sterile, the faint smell of paint still in the air. The room was cramped, hardly big enough for one person, much less two. And there were no windows, which made it feel like you were working from a broom closet.

The overhead light was too bright, and I turned it off again almost immediately, letting myself be swallowed by the darkness. Instead, I flipped on the purple desk lamp, which covered the room in a warm, soft glow.

It felt entirely wrong to break into my mother's computer. But I knew what I was looking for. And I had to know if it was here, because I had to know if Margo could find it, too.

I entered in my mother's passcode—not my birthday, but my due date, as an extra line of defense, she always told me—and found a photo of the two of us staring back at me on the desktop. I was young, maybe ten years old, eating a Popsicle on the dock. She stood beside me, draping a towel over both of us, and we smiled broadly at whoever was behind the camera.

I opened her email before I could let myself cry.

While my mom was organized, she was also the owner of a multimillion-dollar operation and the daughter of a well-known state senator, so her inbox was pure chaos.

I tried a few keywords before settling on the phrase I knew would work, though it felt like the world's greatest betrayal to type out: *Cause of fire.*

There were a few hits in the results. Several were from the first round of reporters, years ago, asking for comment. The energy shifted in the next few—angry parents and citizens, criticizing her, accusing her of lying to the media, to the community.

But the one I clicked on came through about three weeks after the fire. It was from Sheriff Ramon.

There was no message in the body of the email, just an attachment. With shaking hands, I made myself open it.

The document was fifty pages long. My head went dizzy as I read the official title: "Dread's Cove Fire Review."

> On the night of July 22, 2019, a fire started on private property in the Chattahoochee National Forest. The vegetation was drier than usual, which resulted in a no-fire ordinance in the weeks preceding the event. The residents of the property alerted firefighters quickly, and the GA Fire Rescue team was dispatched over the next several hours. Due to the remote access point of the property, the evacuation was not completed until early the next . . .
>
> The same night, a thunderstorm occurred on the northern bounds of the property, however . . .
>
> Investigators have officially determined that the fire was human-caused.

I leaned back in the chair, hardly daring to breathe. I read the same few words over and over, until they were swimming on the page.

Human-caused. Not a wildfire at all.

Years and years ago, in the weeks after Steph's death, investigators had determined that the fire that ripped our world apart was started by a person.

And my mother had known.

She'd sat on this information—buried it—for five years.

For a long few minutes, I sat in utter, shocked silence. The room was stuffy and hot, but I still felt a chill creep up the back of my neck.

Her friendship and history with Winona Hayes, and now, the fire. So many secrets. Had she known about Steph, too?

What else had she been hiding from me?

There was no one else on the email chain, but I went into her *Sent* folder. She had forwarded it to just one person: Rig.

CHAPTER THIRTY-ONE

THEN

Sixteen Hours Before the Fire

YOU WILL PAY.

Those were the three awful words, written in bright, messy red spray paint, across the wide expanse of the mess hall windows. We all saw the damning message at the same time, as we came over the hill on the way to breakfast.

My hand flew to my mouth, but I couldn't hide my gasp. Ahead of me, a boy started to cry, pulling on the sleeve of his counselor. All around me, the kids began to whisper and point, their words quickly rising to a deafening storm of fear.

"Please head back to your cabins. Breakfast will be postponed until ten this morning." My mother's voice came over the camp speakers, loud but wavering.

No one argued.

I put my arms around the two girls closest to me, Kendall and Harper, spinning them around as quickly as I could. The air was charged with a nervous energy.

"Who did that?" Harper's question was quiet, her voice strained.

I painted on a smile, though I was sure they could see how fake it was. "Just someone playing a stupid joke." But it wasn't stupid, and it didn't feel like a joke.

"Greer." My mom's voice cut through the noise, and I spun. She looked more unsure of herself than I'd ever seen her. I had to physically work to make sure my jaw didn't fall open.

"Girls, go find Chelsea, all right?" Harper and Kendall nodded sharply, running to catch up with the rest of the group.

"Mom, what's going on?"

Her eyes closed, for the briefest moment. "We're sending everyone home."

My mouth dropped open. A bird chirped above me—somewhere, Chelsea was saying "Kingfisher"—but I kept my eyes firmly on my mom. She was shaking her head, defeated. She looked so, so tired, that I had to will myself not to start crying.

"Are you serious?"

"We have to. The phone's been ringing off the hook, parents saying they're coming up here to take their kids home. It makes more sense to stop things now, before anyone else gets hurt."

"It was probably just those boys from Darter, playing another prank. If we just—"

"It doesn't matter," she cut me off, an edge to her voice that she rarely used with me. "We don't have another choice. I've got a camp of five hundred children in my care, and I've lost control of the situation, all right?"

I blinked, trying to stop the tears. The guilt, metastasizing in my gut. "But we've only got a week left. Can't we stick it out?"

She was already shaking her head. "No. There was another incident last night. Someone slashed through every single life jacket in the boathouse. With a *knife,* Greer. And of course it wasn't Trevor who found it this morning but one of the girls in Catfish who was pulling out a paddleboard. She posted the photos with that damn Dread's Cove Phantom hashtag, and, well. You can imagine how that's going. So we're closing. It's already done. I emailed everyone and sent out the press release an hour ago. I was just about to call an emergency staff meeting."

All the air felt like it had been sucked out of my lungs.

"It's bad, sweetheart. I won't lie to you. I don't know what happens next. I don't know how we recover from this." My mother sighed, and it was the saddest sound in the world. She had lipstick on her teeth, bags under her eyes.

So badly, I wanted to tell her; I almost said it. *It was Steph.* I was basically shouting it in my head, willing her to hear me. Steph is the Phantom. Steph is the problem. She's to blame.

But the words died in my throat, got stuck there. Because it was so much more complicated than that now, wasn't it? Yes, it was Steph who had started everything. She'd been the one sneaking through the woods, going places she shouldn't have been. But her actions had inspired a wave of bold and dangerous behaviors that were getting worse by the day.

Because of that, Dread's Cove was no longer safe.

There was no escape hatch here. If I told my mother, what would happen next? If this summer had taught me anything, it was that I no longer knew what the hell I wanted. Yes, I was going to leave—I was moving to Atlanta. But what if, someday, I wanted to return? Would admitting this ruin that? Would it sever my last ties to the Cove, irrevocably?

Would it push my mom past her breaking point?

I couldn't do that to her. I wouldn't. She'd been through enough.

So once again, I said nothing. Even though I was desperate to. I held my tongue about Steph's secret life. I pushed it down deep, where no one could see, where no could find out the truth of how much I was willing to ignore.

CHAPTER THIRTY-TWO

NOW

It wasn't raining, exactly, but it was misting, and it gave me goose bumps as I knocked.

The front door opened, and Val stood in her bathrobe with an unlit cigarette dangling from her lips, surprise naked on her face. "Hey, baby. What is it? You look like you've seen a ghost."

Neither of us moved for a moment as her words washed heavily over both of us. Finally, she sighed. "Sorry, that wasn't my best work, was it?"

I pushed my hair back from my face, where it had started to stick from the heat. "Is Rig here?" I knew he'd likely already headed back to the mess hall—tonight's cocktail hour would be starting any minute—but I'd hoped I might be able to head him off.

"He left for dinner a while ago." She pinched her nose, gave me an unsubtle up-and-down, her eyes lingering on my old shorts and Trevor's sweat-soaked T-shirt. "Shouldn't you be getting cleaned up, too?"

I ignored this. "What about you?"

She scoffed, pulling the cigarette from her mouth and stuffing it in her pocket. "Oh, no. I'm staying right here. Rig was running me ragged all day, leading *hikes*, of all things. He and Chels have graciously allowed me to take the night off. Wasn't that kind of them?" Her lip quirked. "Uh-oh," she said. "I've got a terrible idea."

I rubbed a spot on my chest, waiting.

"Come have a drink with me. Just one measly drink, then you can go to your stuffy dinner. Come on, *please*," she added as I started to protest. Her hand was already on my wrist, pulling me into a hug.

"Jesus, I miss her so much," she whispered against my hair, and I went rigid in her arms. She only pulled me closer.

"One drink," I agreed, because what else could I say? When I pulled back, her eyes were glistening, and mine might have been, too.

Within minutes, Val had procured two wineglasses and a bottle that I recognized as her favorite chardonnay. It was already half-empty; she'd clearly started early. She ushered me out onto the back porch, then filled my glass with a much heavier pour than I needed. I wished we were sitting in the air-conditioning, but I forced myself to smile and take a sip anyway.

"You all right, sweetheart?" She drank deeply, her pink lipstick leaving a print on the edge of her glass.

I nodded, not knowing how to broach the topic. *Hey, Aunt Val, did you know that the fire was never really a wildfire at all?*

That my mom and Rig knew?

Who do they think it was?

Why did she never tell me any of this?

None of those questions came out of my mouth, though. Because from the corner of my eye, I could see the back deck of the next-door staff cabin. And I thought of the photo and the strange symbol that had been burning a hole in my pocket all weekend; the family who had lived here, all those years ago. I thought of the one person I had yet to ask about my mom's missing best friend, and how she was sitting beside me now, with a very full glass of wine and a clear desire to talk about my mother.

For a moment, I hesitated, thinking back on what Margo had said: that Val was off-limits. But I was on my own now, wasn't I? Margo was no longer my ally. She never had been.

I crossed my legs, feeling the sweat instantly pool where my knees touched. "What do you know about Winona Hayes?"

"Excuse me?"

"Winona Hayes," I repeated. "She used to live here, when I was a baby. My dad mentioned her to me at the memorial. He said that she was my mom's best friend. But I'd never heard of her, so I was wondering if you remembered her."

Val pursed her lips and fiddled uncomfortably with her gold cross necklace, as if I'd said something uncouth in polite company. "Oh, honey. That's a real sad story."

"Sad how?"

She blew out a hard breath, her cheeks stained red from the wine and the heat. The rain had stopped for the time being, but the humidity was fierce and unrelenting. "I don't know if I should. Your mother–I don't know if she'd like it."

"It's important to me," I said, feeling as desperate at I sounded. "Please, Val. Tell me."

I could see her weighing the decision as she took a drink.

Finally, she gave a small nod. Her eyes changed, and she looked off into the trees. And I could tell what she was doing—she was taking herself back, into those memories. Shifting into another time.

"Back in the day, your granddaddy had a hard time filling positions in the summer. So there was a network out there, I guess you could say—a word-of-mouth kind of thing—and we'd get drifters and hippies, all sorts of folks passing through or needing help. Sometimes just for the summer, sometimes longer. All of them always fell in love with Dread's Cove and were happy to take a job in the kitchen or wherever we needed them."

"Did Winona Hayes need help?"

She tipped her head solemnly, playing with her wedding ring now. "She showed up here on the run from a family who treated her wrong, and she was looking for a place she could feel safe. Where she could grow roots. Nothing more human than that, right? I remember when we all saw her for the first time—well, she was just beautiful. Vivacious and kind. She pulled up to the old mess hall during dinner in a rusted Chevy truck on its last legs. Probably hadn't showered in days, but somehow she looked like a movie star. Some people just have a light like that, you know? You can't put your finger on it, but you can feel it. All she had to her name was a duffel bag, her grandmother's cookbook, and a bright-eyed optimism that was contagious. Lord, everyone was under her spell immediately. Especially your mom."

My lip began to quiver, and I took a sip of wine to hide it. I gave Val a smile that I hoped was encouraging.

"That was a big summer for everyone. Your mom had just moved back and started taking over for your granddaddy, and Rig had gotten the head of operations job. Both of them were in their early twenties, and in hindsight, probably biting off more than they could chew. They were just trying to keep their heads above water. And not just because of how much work they had to do. Hope had died that January, and your daddy was–well, excuse my French, baby, but your daddy was a damn bastard. Then and now. Nowhere near able to give your mother what she needed, or what she deserved. Your mom and Rig were both heartbroken in different ways. And God, both so young with so much responsibility–I remember being in awe of them. Seeing how hard they worked, day in and day out, and how much they loved Dread's Cove, with every last part of themselves. They both were working too hard. Burning themselves out.

"But something changed when Winona got here at the start of that summer. Your mom became someone totally new. Like a butterfly emerging from a chrysalis. Becoming friends with Winona softened her edges. She gave Annie permission to feel her feelings, to experience so many of life's small joys that she had never let herself try before. Hell, once I walked in on them baking a strawberry pie together. Straight from one of Winona's cookbooks. Flour everywhere, the place was a damn mess. But they were just having the time of their life. I'd never known your mother to touch a stove before, but Winona Hayes had her trying all sorts of things. She was like a whole new person."

My stomach churned as I thought of Steph, appearing here that summer and changing everything, too. How many times I had thought that my life was so much bigger and better with her in it.

"Of course, I was a couple of years younger than Annie and Winona, and I was just a counselor that year, so I didn't spend much time with them. But I'm woman enough now to say that I was jealous."

"Jealous?"

She waved her wineglass around clumsily, sloshing a little onto her hand. She sucked it from her thumb before continuing. "Friends like that—that other-half-of-your-soul kind of friends—they don't come around too often. Then Winona fell in love with Frankie that summer and got pregnant, right around the time Annie got pregnant with you. Your sweet mother had never been happier. She had a best girlfriend to share this place with and to raise a daughter beside."

I tried to fight a shiver at her unknowing mention of Steph.

"Winona stayed here about two years. Came at the start of summer, left at the start of summer."

"If Winona had a great life here—I mean, why did she leave?" I asked, wiping the wine from the corners of my mouth. "Was everyone surprised?"

"Well, I certainly was. I remember being just plain shocked when they told me she was gone."

"They?"

"Your mama and Rig. I found the two of them talking the morning after she'd skipped town. I'd never seen Annie in such a state—crying and snotting all over everything. She took two days off. *Two.* You ever know your mother to do that?"

"Never," I choked out.

"Me either. She was absolutely beside herself. Kept saying, 'It's all my fault. She's gone because of me.'"

A chill passed through me. "Why would she say that?"

Val shrugged, slurped her chardonnay. Her glass was already close to empty. "I guess she tried to talk Winona out of it, but she couldn't. Rig told me what had happened. Apparently, Winona decided she was going to leave Frankie and the baby. Her daughter—gosh, what was her name—was just about a year old, same as you. She didn't feel cut out for motherhood, apparently. Your mom begged her to stay, said they'd figure it out together—that we were all a family here, we looked out for one another. But Winona was adamant. She'd decided she was leaving that night, plain and simple, and wouldn't be talked out of it. Guess those roots she'd wanted had grown too deep, and she panicked. So then, Rig told me, she got on a Greyhound with nothing but the clothes on her back and left her whole life behind."

The ground seemed to tilt beneath me. "Rig said she left on—on a Greyhound."

"Sure did. Said he watched her get on the bus himself. He was the one who drove her to the station in Lavender."

I didn't think my heart had ever beat so hard in my life. I ached for water, a gallon of it at least, or anything colder than this lukewarm glass of awful wine.

Val's face was as red as a tomato. She pushed her sweaty wineglass to her forehead and waved her other hand like it was a fan. "I know you got more questions, but I think I'm fixing to retire soon, sweetheart. Too hot out here for little old me." A small laugh, crossed with a hiccup. "All this wine and heat gets me feeling sleepy. Don't forget I led a hike today."

This was her polite, slightly slurred way of telling me it was time to go, but I couldn't leave just yet. I was so close to something. "Do you know if my mom ever heard anything else from Winona?"

Val leaned back and made a sound halfway between a sigh and a snort. "When I moved back, I asked her. She snapped at me, told me she didn't want to talk about her. I remember thinking, *Note to self—do* not *mention Winona Hayes.* Too sore a subject, even all these years later. That's why you surprised me just now, when you asked me about her. Feels like her name is some kind of curse around here."

"What about Rig?" I pressed. "Did he know anything?" I was leaning forward, elbows on my knees.

If Val had been more sober, she might have bristled at the raw intensity in my voice. As it stood, she just pursed her lips, let her head sway a bit.

"Well, of course I asked him, too. But he didn't know, either. Just said that wherever Winona was now, she'd made her choice that night. And that she'd have to live with the consequences for the rest of her life." Her eyelids were fluttering as she spoke. I was about to lose her to sleep.

"Val, what did he mean by that? What consequences?"

Her answer was a snore. "Aunt Val?" I tried, desperate now, but she didn't stir.

She was out cold, her wineglass dangling precariously from her hand. As gently as I could, I took it from her and set it on the table. She snored again, but didn't move. I bit my lip so hard I tasted blood.

Quietly, I crept inside, closing the screen door behind me. What did it all mean? The day after Winona disappeared, Rig had told Val that he'd driven her to the bus station himself. That he'd *seen* her get on the bus. That she'd wanted to leave, to start a whole new life from scratch again.

But that wasn't true—because I'd found the tickets. There'd been two, not just one.

And I'd found more artifacts of her life in Winona's box. All the things she'd left behind. I'd read her cookbook, seen the evidence of the love she had for Steph. Seen her perfect handwriting, her extensive annotations in the margins.

The picture of her, and my mom, and me, and Steph–the warmth and love in her eyes, shining so bright. I couldn't accept that Winona had forsaken motherhood impulsively.

I didn't know her, but she felt so close. Close like my mom had been all weekend. Close like Steph.

The front room was still. Cocktail hour had just started, so it would likely be hours before Rig returned. I moved to put my shoes on at the door, resting my hand on the banister for balance, head throbbing with the weight of it all.

The idea was stupid. I knew this. I'd had more than one stupid idea over the past few days. But this might be my only shot. I had to see what other secrets were waiting here, just out of reach. Because I wasn't just close to Winona, or my mom, or Steph right now–I was close to the truth. The closest I'd been yet.

So I let my inner Steph win out and compel me up the stairs.

CHAPTER THIRTY-THREE

THEN

An Hour Before the Fire

Evacuating five hundred kids from a summer camp in the mountains was an exhausting affair. By the time the final bus left, and Dread's Cove was quiet and still once more, all I wanted to do was sleep.

The worst part had been saying goodbye to Kendall. To my surprise, she'd sobbed into my arms, making me pinkie promise to write to her.

"Of course I will," I told her. "I swear. And if you want, you can come back next summer."

"I'll think about it," she'd sniffled into my shirt. "I'll miss you, Miss Greer."

"I'll miss you, too." I'd squeezed her hand and felt tears prick the backs of my eyes as she zigzagged her way toward the bus, her little pink suitcase bouncing on the gravel lot as she dragged it behind her.

After everyone had gone, my mother had holed herself up in her cabin, requesting no visitors. I understood. She wanted to lick her wounds in peace. Though the thought of her, staring out at the dark lake all alone, made me sick with sadness.

It was done. Over. Official. Dread's Cove was closed for the season. Tomorrow, the nonresident staff would be bussed out—including Steph, Margo, and Trevor—and we'd start the work of turning the linens, closing down the lake, resetting for fall.

Just like every year. Except I would be leaving soon, too.

That night, we'd scrabbled together a few bottles of bottom-shelf liquor and lukewarm wine, heading out to the beach for one final hurrah. It was a quiet affair; nowhere near as rowdy as usual. It was like none of us knew what to say to one another, or if we could even trust one another anymore.

With a shaky hand, I poured a healthy splash of vodka into a Solo cup. My second of the night—or third? I couldn't remember. Someone squeezed my shoulder, and I tensed before turning to see Trevor.

He put a soft hand on my face, and I leaned into it. As I snaked my arms around his neck, I locked eyes with Margo. She was twenty or so feet away, talking to Wes and Garrett, both hands on her hips. It was dark, so I couldn't be sure, but I thought her lip may have curled. In disgust.

It was gone in a fleeting second, and she even lifted her cup to mine in a sort of cheers. I gave her a small smile back. The two of us were playing a game of cat and mouse, waiting to see what would happen next. Once again, I thought about what I'd overheard between her and Steph last night, when I'd been pretending to be asleep.

I had a sneaking suspicion that she'd only told Steph about her acceptance to that Emory program to prevent me from being able to sublet her room. Steph hadn't said anything to me about it–I had to assume nothing had changed, even if it made me nervous. All I could do was stay the course, trust her. I didn't have any other choice. Besides, we'd been through enough together at this point, hadn't we?

In a week, I was moving to Atlanta with her. I was starting my new life. Not even Margo could get in the way of that.

I saw a flash of Steph's dark, glossy ponytail just inside the tree line, which surprised me. I hadn't seen her in a few hours. After dinner, she'd been practically catatonic, forgoing any late-night plans in favor of packing, telling us she planned to turn in early.

"I'll be right back," I said in Trevor's ear, untangling his arm from over my shoulders. He squeezed my hand before I walked away.

I found her sitting against a tree, holding a nearly empty bottle of pink wine by the neck. "What's up? I thought you were packing."

"I need to talk to your mom. But she wouldn't answer the door."

Up close, she looked worse for the wear. Her hair wasn't all that glossy, after all–it was wet, unbrushed, like she'd just washed it. And her eyes were glazed over. Even with as much cheap liquor as I'd consumed tonight, I could tell immediately that she'd had far more.

While we'd been out here, she must have been imbibing alone.

"She's asleep," I said. "Why? What's going on?"

"She knows the truth. I know she does."

I felt my eyes bulge, my pulse quicken. My mom knew the truth–about her? About what she'd been up to this summer?

"What are you talking about? Did she catch you–" I froze, realizing what she must have meant. "Wait. No. Was it you? Did you slash up the life jackets? Is that what you mean?"

"No," she said on a hiccup that turned into a burp, and I tried not to grimace at the sour, awful smell. "No, I didn't cut up some stupid life jackets. Calm down. I just need to talk to her. It's very, very important."

I frowned. "You're kind of freaking me out. Tell me what's going on."

She gripped my elbow, hard enough that her nails broke the skin. I tried to snatch my arm back, but her grip was tight, unyielding. I tensed as her hot breath hit my face. "Earlier this summer, I asked her a question, and she lied. She lied. Do you get what I'm saying? I have proof, okay?"

I racked my brain for what she could possibly be talking about–what kind of weeks-old lie she was referring to–but I was coming up empty. That third cup of vodka was starting to make me dizzy. "Slow down. You asked her what? If you would just tell me–"

"I can't slow down. I'm out of time. But she knows something. Your mom knows something. I found–" She clamped her mouth shut, hard enough that I heard her teeth knock against each other, and I narrowed my eyes.

She'd been snooping again, clearly. Another lie. Another thing I'd been too naive, too desperate, to accept at face value.

"You found what?"

"Never mind. It doesn't matter. But you can let me into her cabin, so I can talk to her. That's all I'm asking."

I wrenched my arm away, almost stumbling in the process. I felt the beginnings of it, simmering in my chest. Anger. "Are you actually insane? You want me to just let you into my mom's place in the middle of the night, so you can, what, accost her while she's sleeping? No. Absolutely not. Today was probably one of the worst days of her life. Haven't you done enough?"

She raised a single eyebrow. "And what exactly have I done that's so terrible? Enlighten me."

"You have a loose relationship with the truth." This was a reckless, stupid conversation to have; I knew that Steph quite literally held my new life in her hands. Everything I wanted—everything I was *so close* to getting—was once again resting on a razor's edge, and she could push me off the cliff at any time.

But she was also drunk, confused, bitter, and frankly, so was I. I'd bent over backward for her, and somehow, it still wasn't enough. So, I kept talking. "The only liar here is you. You're the one who's been sneaking out all summer. You wouldn't even have told me about it if I hadn't caught you red-handed. And now . . . you're acting all paranoid and weird, saying things about my mother, who has never been anything but nice to you."

She was looking at me utterly stone-faced, and I pushed a sweaty lock of hair behind my ear, felt the rage bubble up, faster than I could stop it.

"This is all your fault. Dread's Cove is closing because of what you did. You started all of this, and you're not even sorry about it." A single, manic laugh escaped my lips, and I clenched my fists at my sides like a pre-tantrum toddler. "If you hadn't been sneaking around, those boys wouldn't have followed you and almost died. None of this Phantom shit would have happened if you hadn't been the kindling."

I couldn't remember the last time I'd been this honest with anyone. I wasn't finished yet. "And what about us? I heard you and Margo last night. She asked you to tell me I couldn't live with you, and you said, 'I'll talk to her.' Well, you haven't." I swallowed hard. "What is it that you want to say to me? Were you going to completely fuck me over? Pretend this summer never happened, pretend that we haven't been making plans?"

For the first time since we'd started talking, her eyes seemed to actually focus on me. "Well, if I'm so terrible, then why didn't you tell on me, Little G? What have you been waiting for?"

"Because I thought we were *friends*, goddamn it. Because I care about you, and I didn't want you to leave."

"We are friends," she confirmed, and as pathetic as it sounds, I almost breathed an actual sigh of relief. "But you know what? A real friend would help me right now."

There was a prickling, at the base of my skull. A headache, caused by exhaustion and anger and exasperation and the vodka I'd ingested far too quickly.

"If you would just give me a straight answer for once, we can–"

"All I can tell you is that I need to talk to your mom, right now. That's it. So are you going to help me or not?"

"No," I breathed. "I'm not."

In our two months of being friends, I couldn't remember a time when I'd said no to something Steph had asked of me. She clearly couldn't, either. For a long moment we only stared at each other.

And then, she threw a hand over her mouth, lurched forward, and threw up in the grass at my feet.

I reached for her immediately. She pulled at my collar, then buried her face in my shirt. It only took me a moment to realize that she was sobbing.

All at once, my rage died like a candle being snuffed out.

"Let's just get you some water, and then we can go back to the cabin. And you can get some sleep. We'll talk to my mom tomorrow, okay? We'll figure this out. First thing."

"Fine. Okay." The ire was gone from her voice, too. She just sounded exhausted, like she might fall asleep any second.

"And then next week, I'll meet you in Atlanta," I said, as much a promise to myself as it was to her, and I squeezed her hand as I pulled her back to standing. She almost tripped, bringing us both down once again, but I steadied her. "I'm sorry I got mad. It's been a terrible day, but—everything's good, okay? This fall is going to be amazing. We're making our own road map, remember?"

"Our own map," she said. "A map." She said the word with reverence, then craned her neck to look behind her, out into the trees. "A fucking *map*."

"Stay here," I told her, though she no longer seemed to be listening. "I'll be right back, okay?"

It took me less than thirty seconds, I was sure of it. I barely let her out of my sight, but to dig through the cooler for a water bottle.

By the time I got back, she was gone.

CHAPTER THIRTY-FOUR

NOW

The door to Rig's office was open. A single lamp spilled warm light across the desk, and it beckoned me in. I didn't really have a plan. I was following my instincts.

Inside, the room wasn't so much messy as it was cluttered. There were bookshelves lining each wall, some far more organized than others.

I came around to his desk and froze. Because sitting there, plain as day, was my mother's Bible.

My pulse thrummed as I picked it up. I'd asked Rig about this last night. He told me he'd look around, that it might have wound up in the office. I hadn't followed up with him.

My hand found the pendant around my neck, the only thing of hers I'd managed to unearth. The necklace that had made all the color drain from his face.

I pushed away the dangerous thoughts, the ones that told me that he'd lied to me more than once. That he'd kept me away from her things on purpose.

Inside the cover was my mother's name, written in the small, blocky handwriting that I'd inherited. *Anita Jane Olsen.*

My mom had kept an almost superstitious eye on it, always keeping it in the same spot next to her bed. I flipped through it now, looking for something, though I wasn't sure what.

All I knew was that Rig had claimed he didn't know where it was. But it was here—not only in his home, but in his office.

Closing my eyes, I made myself think back on what Margo and I had discovered so far.

My mom and Steph's mom had been best friends for two years. Winona came at the start of the season, and two summers later, she was gone.

And two decades later, Steph had come here to figure out what happened to her. Whatever she'd found had gotten her killed.

I flipped through the Bible, desperate for answers, but it seemed like there was nothing else. Just a few underlined verses and dog-eared pages. Until I got to the very end.

My heart stuttered in my chest. There was a photo of my mother and Winona. In it, Winona wore a faded green Dread's Cove sweatshirt—exactly like the one she wore in the photo Margo and I had found in Black Bass. Her hair even looked the same, like it had been snapped the same day.

And on the back inside cover, there was a crude drawing of lines and shapes, which would be utterly meaningless if you didn't recognize them.

It was the same drawing that Margo and I had found scrawled on the back of the photo of Steph's family. And now, of course, I understood. So simple and obvious. It wasn't a symbol at all.

It was a map.

There was nothing to decode. These were simply directions, to an unknown destination.

I thought back on that awful night, when Steph had convinced me to break into my mother's cabin and sneak into her wine cellar. Those terrible, dark moments where I thought she'd left me alone forever. Wondering if all along she'd been playing some sort of game that I'd been too blind to see, just like Chelsea had said.

I was seeing that night in a much different way now. Steph asking me to go to the Barn with her, then deciding we had to get a bottle of wine—that we had to break into my mom's place when she wouldn't be there. Not stopping me when I'd offered to retrieve the bottle. While I'd been banging on the cellar door, calling out for help, she must have been upstairs in my mother's bedroom—not harmlessly exploring my room, like she'd claimed. No, she must have gone through her closet, her drawers. Invaded her privacy while she was miles away.

She would have found this Bible, on my mother's bedside table, where she always kept it, unless she was going on her morning jog through the woods. I could see it now, so vividly: Steph opening it, finding the map, but in the moment not understanding what it meant. Seeing the photos—one of her own family—and taking it, because she couldn't help herself. Copying the strange symbol down on the back of the picture, because that's all she had handy, and she had to move fast before I really started screaming. Then putting the photo in her pocket, a keepsake of the mother and the secret life she couldn't remember.

I thought back on what Margo had told me about the night of the fire. How frantic Steph had been. That she'd seemed crazed, barely able to string a sentence together—how she'd said, *We're so close. I finally figured it out.*

And right before that, when I'd talked to her by the beach. How distraught she was. At that time, I'd thought she'd just been drunk and belligerent. Talking nonsense, angry at the world for reasons I didn't understand.

But that wasn't right, was it? She hadn't been angry at the world. She'd been angry at my mom—she'd told me as much. Something she said that night crashed through my brain: *I asked her a question, and she lied.*

It was starting to make sense. She must have meant that she'd asked my mom about Winona Hayes. And just like Rig had lied to me, my mom had lied to Steph.

When she told me she found proof . . . this is what she'd meant. She'd found this very Bible, the photos linking my mother and hers.

And then her eyes had lit up when I'd said the word *map.*

That was when it clicked for her. That was when I'd left her alone, and she'd gone sprinting after the truth. Margo had noticed while my back had been turned, and she'd gone after her.

I ran a finger over the lines of the map, visualizing all of Dread's Cove and the surrounding forest, and a wave of understanding washed over me. The square in the center of the drawing was the Barn.

That was the central element here, what my mother had written down. And the lines, projecting out, were the two trails bisecting in the forest.

And the small square was—whatever this map was leading to. Whatever secret Steph has been determined to find.

Margo told me that when they got to the Barn, Steph had completely freaked out. It must have been because she couldn't find her copy of the map. She'd left it back in Black Bass, either by accident or on purpose. Where it had waited between the floorboards, not to be found for years and years.

Margo had been right about me the other day. When she'd said I was always pretending. This would be different. There would be no hiding. I would follow this map wherever it led.

I had to know. I had to know everything.

It was still quiet downstairs; all I could hear was my own heart, thundering wildly in my chest. I was close now. I could feel the truth, beckoning me. Waiting me out.

It seemed like Val was still asleep. For how long, I couldn't be sure. Clutching the Bible to my chest, I crept back out of the study and into the hallway. The only other room upstairs was the primary bedroom.

The door hinges screamed as I pushed it open, and I froze, waiting to hear a sleep-addled Val's call of "Rig?" up the stairs. But the quiet seconds stretched on, and, holding my breath, I stepped inside.

The lights were off, but the full moon was bright tonight, the whole room cloaked in an eerie, almost otherworldly glow.

There was a mirror over the dresser that I stopped and looked at myself in. My eyes were sunken, haunted. My cheeks were blotchy from the heat and the chardonnay that had left a saccharine taste in my mouth. I looked scared. I was scared.

Why had Rig lied to me? About Winona, about my mother?

What was he hiding? What had he done?

My hand flew to the chain around my neck. It had turned into a source of comfort these past few days. One day soon, I would find a jewelry store, and I would fix the broken *N-I-E-*

And that's when it struck me, like an anvil being dropped on my head. The realization was so strong, so visceral, that I almost staggered back.

N-I-E. The last three letters of my mother's nickname, yes.

But they were also the last three letters of *Stephanie.*

The gasp left my mouth before I could stop it. I thought of Rig's eyes on it last night, when we'd spoken in the mess hall. How I'd thought he was sad, that maybe he'd even been the one to give it to my mother, years and years ago. But what if I'd read him totally wrong?

What if it wasn't grief I'd seen on his face—but panic? Or guilt?

What if he had killed Stephanie for what she'd discovered? And—no, no, no—what role had my mother played?

Because I'd found this necklace in her room.

I felt dizzy, like I was edging near a full-blown meltdown, and closed my eyes, trying to center myself. It was an incredible violation to dig through their bedside tables, but that had been where I'd found the necklace. Some part of my brain found logic in that—maybe I'd find more secrets here. Maybe I'd find the final piece of this impossible puzzle.

In Val's table, I found only cherry hand lotion, a deck of cards, and a few matchbooks.

I crossed to the other side of the bed slowly. My mouth was dry, even as I tried to swallow the dread and fear creeping up my esophagus.

My hand was shaking as I eased open the drawer, as I prayed to every deity I could think of that I'd find nothing. That I was mistaken—that this was all anxiety playing tricks on me. Because Rig was *Rig.* He was safe. He was the closest thing to a dad I'd ever had, and I loved him. My mom was the best person I knew, the most selfless, the most altogether *good*; she would never have had a hand in something so violent. In a murder.

Not of her best friend's daughter. And not of her daughter's new best friend.

I'd almost convinced myself, as I groped around in the darkness. That it was an overreaction, that I was jumping to conclusions. That there was no way my family—who I trusted—was capable of that kind of evil.

But then my hand found something dark and solid, and I drew it to my face to take a closer look.

Just as the front door swung open downstairs, I realized I was holding a gun.

CHAPTER THIRTY-FIVE

NOW

I pressed my palm to my mouth and made myself breathe through my nose. I could hear the thump of Rig's shoes, the creak of the floorboards. "Val? You seen Greer?"

The *thing* in my hand was too heavy, too wrong. My stomach bottomed out. Downstairs, he lumbered down the hallway, and a few seconds later, the screen door slid open.

I forced myself to move, almost tripping over my own feet as I raced back out the way I came, taking the stairs two at a time, no mind for how loud I was being. I had to get out of there. I had to get away.

When I'd barely cleared the porch I heard Rig's concerned call of my name into the night, but I didn't look back. I couldn't.

I was almost to the trailhead that led toward the Barn when I realized I was still holding the gun.

The earth beneath me seemed to shift, and I threw it to the ground. I couldn't stop to think, to find a better way to get rid of it. All I knew is this thing in my hand, this awful, wretched thing, could have been what he used to kill Steph.

Maybe even what he'd used to kill Winona.

I worked my way down the winding route out on the south side of camp, stumbling through the brush like a madwoman. With shaking hands, I stood in front of the Barn, using it as the final key to all of this. Like Steph had. It wasn't hard, once I was looking at the map, to understand what I had to do.

In the northernmost corner, there was a long, winding path that spit you out at the base of the mountain. We rarely took it; a mile or so in, the terrain got rocky, too hazardous for children or casual hikers. For the most part, we kept it blocked off, with orange rope—the official Dread's Cove sign of *Off-Limits.* Near where Carter and Jeremy had been found five summers ago, on their search for the Phantom.

I moved the rope out of the way and kept going. My breath was coming hard and fast now, my pulse thundering wildly.

I wondered what Margo had already uncovered without me. *G.O. is definitely hiding something.* She was the same old Margo, keeping her cards close to the vest. Lying in wait for the perfect moment.

Then sinking her teeth in, until you bled out.

I pressed on, twigs snapping beneath my feet as the path grew more rugged and unkempt. I held the picture in front of me, letting the map guide me forward.

I was at the outskirts of camp, near the bluffs that hung over the rocky tip of the lake, when I saw it—where the directions were leading me. The path opened up to a small clearing, a field of wildflowers. It was achingly beautiful, even in the dark.

As slowly as I could, I walked through the small meadow, admiring the colors and the stillness, spotlighted by the glow of the full moon. It was a gorgeous assortment; purple lupine, and tall, swaying goldenrods.

A little ways off, at the edge of the bluffs, I noticed another, smaller patch of flowers. Even in the dark, I could tell: These ones were red.

They were flame azaleas. My mother's favorite.

It felt like a sign. Or a reckoning.

Tentatively, I walked closer. These were different from the others, I noticed. They weren't growing wild at all. Someone had planted these here. For whatever reason, I felt compelled to kneel. Like they were an altar, and I'd come to pray.

I could almost picture Steph, five years ago. I could imagine the two of us stumbling across these, her squealing in delight at this perfect, hidden garden. Her pulling one out even though I'd tell her not to, putting it behind her ear. It wasn't a real memory, but I could see it so clearly that it could have been.

I started to smile, then flinched.

Then a wave of terror, of gut-wrenching awareness, came over me, as I ran my finger across the dirt. I took in the whole scene–I took in the rectangular mound, far off the normal path.

This wasn't a garden at all. This was a grave.

I knew I shouldn't have done it, but I was so close. I could sense what was in the dirt beneath me. Who was here. Who had been waiting for decades to be found.

That awful ghost story flashed through my head, and I thought of the legend of those little girls. Desecrating graves at the edge of the woods. How they were punished for it.

But I had to know. I had to know right then—I had to know the truth.

So I started digging.

The dirt was in my hands, on my knees, under my fingernails, everywhere, all over me. It was like I was possessed.

My knuckles brushed something hard, just below the surface. I squeezed my eyes shut as I wrapped a shaking hand around it, not wanting to know, but needing to all the same. I made myself open my eyes, to see it. To be sure.

The scream left my lips before I fully even saw the white of it. Like some ancient knowing, deep within me, had already confirmed my darkest, basest fear.

I was holding a bone.

This is what my mother's map had led to—what Steph had realized that night, what she'd been desperate to show Margo, before the fire started and the world ended.

She'd wanted to show Margo where her mother was buried.

Which meant that my mother had known where Winona Hayes was all along. My mother, who was famously bad at remembering directions. She'd written down that map in her Bible—because—because—

I staggered back, feeling swallowed by the night sky, the sheer depth of this place. Until the summer of the Phantom, I'd always thought Dread's Cove was safe. I'd thought my mom was safer than anyone. But I'd been so naive. The tears streamed hot down my face, and I wiped them away, dirt stinging my eyes.

"No . . . no," I choked out, before falling to my knees again. Up was down and down was up and nothing made sense, because there was a *body*. My mother's best friend—she was buried here.

And my mom had known. She'd fucking *known.*

What had she–

"Greer."

The voice behind me was one I'd known my whole life. I thought of his quiet sadness on the phone a few weeks ago. The way I could hear him breaking apart, piece by brittle piece.

I thought I might jump out of my skin, but I made myself turn to face Rig. He rubbed a hand down the side of his face, and I watched as his fingers caught on the salt-and-pepper stubble. I was struck by how old he looked. How tired.

"What's going on? What is this?" I was still holding a piece of Winona. Gingerly, I set it down, not taking my eyes off him.

"I will tell you," he said, hands raising in a plea. "But you have to calm down. You've gotta relax, ladybug, and you have to promise to listen to me. I'll tell you everything, but you need to know– that I did this for your mom. Because I love her, and you, and Chels, and–and everything we've ever done has been to protect our girls."

I did this for your mom. The words made me recoil. I wanted to run, to call for help. But more than that, I wanted to hear what he had to say. I wanted to know what happened to Winona, and what Stephanie had discovered.

What Rig had done, and what my mother had covered up.

"I wasn't honest with you yesterday," he began. "Winona was your mom's best friend. You caught me off guard, I haven't heard her name in–it doesn't matter." His throat bobbed, and it looked painful. "She showed up here when she was twenty-two and on the run from her old life. We all wanted her to stay. She was radiant. She was special."

The hollow ache in his words sunk deep into my skin. I said nothing, could only stare at him.

"It didn't take long for her and Frankie to hit it off. And your mom, of course, she became fast friends with Winona. It was hard not to.

"Your dad, well, you know how he was. Even then, always making excuses not to be around. After their daughter was born, Frankie was busy, distracted. So we spent a lot of time together, the three of us and our girls. Over at your mom's cabin mostly, on the back porch. That first year after Hope died, I felt underwater for a long time. I hardly remember those days. But then–well, things started to shift."

I thought of what Val had told me–about Rig and my mom, spending so much time together. Leaning on each other. Needing each other. "You and my mom." I had an awful vision: Winona walking in on them, Rig and my mom doing anything to keep her quiet, and then–

The necklace felt tight around my neck, choking me. "You had an affair. Is that it?"

Rig staggered back, the whites of his eyes catching moonlight. "No, no. It wasn't me and your mom who fell in love. It was me and Winnie."

My breath hitched. He was looking at the necklace again, and then, finally, I understood.

The *N-I-E* was not for *Annie*. It was not for *Stephanie*. "You and–you were in love with *Winona*?"

He dipped his head in a slow, solemn nod, like it was taking every last bit of energy he had. "I loved her the moment I saw her."

The whole world blurred at the edges as I attempted to realign the Rig I knew–calm, collected, slow to anger–with the man who stood before me. "Then why did you kill her? Because she wouldn't leave her husband for you? How *could* you?"

"No." The word was hard, desperate. Filled with pain. "I did not kill her."

He was looking at me with such devastation that I forced myself to swallow hard, terrified of the horrible question I knew I had to ask next. "So, my mom, then? She killed her?" I could barely string together the words.

"Winona told your mother that she was planning to leave the Cove. And Annie didn't want that. Winona was her best friend. Your mom made a decision that night, and it was one she regretted for the rest of her life."

I swayed slightly, felt the life I'd always known fall away from me like an old skin.

"But why would she–why would she kill her, I don't–"

Rig's eyes snapped to mine, like he was finally hearing me. "Oh, no, ladybug. No, you–now hold on. Yes, your mother spoke to Winona that night. She told her she was leaving, and Annie couldn't have that. So she went to Frankie and told him what was going on–she told him everything. She told him about me and Winona. That we were in love, and that Winona wanted to leave."

I could hardly speak. "She sold out her best friend? Why would she do that?"

Rig choked out a sigh. "She was scared of losing her. They were close as sisters, just like you and Chels. She went to Frankie, told him everything that Winona had told her about the two of us. And Frankie, well, he didn't have a great time controlling his temper. He was a good man–he was, deep down–but he had some hard edges to him. He came and found me that night, to confront me. Anita was trailing behind him, hollering at him to stop and think for a second–just as Winona had come to tell me her plans. She wanted me to leave with her. She'd even snuck into town, bought us bus tickets. She had it all figured out. We were arguing–I told her I had commitments, a whole life here, I couldn't disappear in the dead of night. But she was tired of this place, she said, and she felt suffocated by how isolated we were out here in the woods. It had been a good thing for her, at first, but she needed more. Especially with her baby girl. Frankie had been feeling paranoid for months and months, worrying that Winona had been stepping out on him, and he was angry. And that's when he and your mom burst through the door and found the two of us talking. We were only talking, we really were but–it looked like we were conspiring. Lord, he was angry. Angrier than I'd ever seen him. It was like he changed shape completely."

His voice dropped so low, I could hardly hear him. "And then–you have to understand, I can't even– When I think of it now–it still doesn't feel real."

I was digging my nails so hard into the palms of my hands I thought they might bleed. "Tell me what happened."

He tilted his head back, eyes to the sky. As if he were finally resigning himself to the truth. "Frankie tried to punch me, and I blocked him, but then Winnie got in the middle, put her hands up between the two of us. It was total chaos for a minute, Frankie throwing his hands, her trying to stop him, your mom screaming from somewhere, me trying to get Winnie out of the way, and then–and then–she was on the ground. Not moving."

He was crying now, big, wet tears that I'd never seen from him before. He put his hands on his thighs, leaning over, like he was hyperventilating. I was sure this was the first time Rig had ever told this story. That in almost thirty years, he hadn't been able to admit it to anyone. Even himself.

"She'd hit her head, slammed it on the side of the coffee table.

She was bleeding, and it was too much, too fast, and your mom and I knew. We knew what it meant. Frankie was yelling, hollering, and there was blood everywhere, all over the floor, and God *help me*, the *blood* . . ."

He trailed off, looking helplessly at the ground. I brought a shaky hand to my chest as I let the shock of it all wash over me.

"I grabbed Frankie, held his arms down, and then . . . your mom checked Winona, she was so still—and she, she wasn't *breathing*, you have to . . ."

He fell to his knees now, and I scrambled backward, my hands in the cool dirt. "And then? And then what, Rig?"

Rig shook his head, long hair falling in front of his face, then finally met my eye. His were glistening, haunted with decades of repressed regret. "We didn't have a lot of time. Frankie was beside himself, no help at all. Couldn't string a sentence together. So we brought her all the way out here. Your mother and me. And we buried her."

"Why?" I whispered. "If it was Frankie, then why—"

"We didn't know—in the heat of it, none of us could be sure what happened. She was alive and then"—he lurched into another sob—"and then she wasn't."

"Why wouldn't you turn yourselves in?"

"We should have. Of course we should have. I still think about it, even now. But I had Chelsea. Your mom had you; she had your daddy. And Frankie had his own daughter to think about."

For the second time since he started his confession, he met my eye. "But we never forgot her, Greer. We made sure to put her somewhere where she'd be safe. Remember what Annie used to say? Nowhere safer than the woods." He gestured weakly toward the flowers. "Your mother thought about and mourned Winnie every single day of her life. So have I."

Rig was growing inconsolable now, face covered by his hands. "Believe me, please. I loved her, and I would have–"

My head was spinning. "Rig–"

"And then it was over, she was buried out here, and there was nothing we could do, was there? We all had–so, so much to lose. You have to understand."

His pitch had risen into something scary, unhinged, with the years of keeping this story locked away. It was like the dam was finally breaking.

"Rig," I said, louder this time. "Winona–Winnie–was Stephanie Bennett's mother. That's why she came here that summer. She wanted to figure out what happened to her."

Rig didn't move. He stayed frozen, and I couldn't understand the expression on his face. If it was surprise, or guilt, or regret.

"Did you kill her, too? Because she found out what you did?"

The voice wasn't mine, though. It took me a long, almost paralyzing moment to realize; it had been the very same question, dancing on my lips. The same terrible thought.

But it wasn't me. We both turned sharply, to the figure at the base of the trees, Rig's gun held high and aimed at his heart. Margo.

"Wait, stop," I said, nowhere near loud enough. Rig didn't look at me; he only raised his hands above his head, like he was surrendering. The wind howled through the woods, the beginnings of a summer storm bleeding into the night. It was too similar, an echo of the last time things had spiraled out of control.

"It was you." Margo took another, awful step, gun still high. Her eyes were blazing with a hard fury that took me back to the morning after the fire. Then, she'd left. But now–I didn't think she was going anywhere.

"Say it, for God's sake. Say that you *killed them both*."

She'd dropped into an octave that reverberated throughout my body, made my heart threaten to burst forth from my chest.

"Put the gun down, sweetheart." He spoke with a gentleness that was unexpected, inconceivable. His face was wet, either from tears or the misting rain. "Just put it down, and we'll talk all about it." Then his jaw ticked once, betraying his fear.

"I will kill you. Why shouldn't I? It was you. You killed Winona, you buried her, and Steph found out. She figured it all out, didn't she? So you set that fire. Your last-ditch effort to protect your dirty little secret. You killed them both. You're fucking *sick*."

Rig shook his head, hands shaking with undiluted fear. "No, no, I didn't, I wouldn't, I loved Winnie–I didn't *know*, please, I didn't know–"

He looked at me with an unbidden, devastating sadness, and I knew–I could see it immediately–that he was telling the truth.

He hadn't known who Steph was. Hadn't known he'd spent a whole summer with Winona's daughter. That in the very moments before she'd died, she'd been trying to find this sacred, terrible place.

"Stop lying. Just stop lying, my God," Margo said, spitting with anger.

Rig took a single step toward Margo, and acid burned my throat. "Give me the gun, Margo."

She kept it high, but I could see it shaking. Her hands looked so small; she was holding it awkwardly, as if she had no idea what to do with it. "No," she tried to snarl, but her voice cracked.

Rig took another step. I couldn't breathe, couldn't move. Could only stare. She stayed stock-still, save for the gun trembling in her outstretched hands. When he got close enough that he could reach out and touch her, he made for the gun. Slowly, carefully, as if she were a feral animal he was trying to rescue.

But when his fingers grazed it, she lurched out of his grasp, huffing and puffing like she couldn't breathe. He lunged for her, one broad arm wrapped around her tiny form, the other fumbling for the gun.

Margo turned away, clawing at him. Finally, I found my voice and screamed, the sound ripping through the air. Reflexively, Rig turned back to look at me, and everything happened in slow motion as I watched the gun in Margo's hands come down hard on the back of his head.

And then he dropped to the forest floor.

I tried to scream again, raw with panic. Nothing came out.

Margo was staring open-mouthed at the weapon in her hand, like she couldn't make sense of what she was seeing. I crawled toward Rig, brought my hand to his chest, looking for a sign that he was all right. He had a heartbeat, but he wasn't moving. At the back of his head, I felt sticky, wet blood.

Beside me, I heard the sound of Margo's ragged breaths. I couldn't stop my brain from replaying those words she'd said this morning, now laced with something far darker: *I don't play games. I win them.*

I threw my own hands up in surrender, blood streaking them from the gash on Rig's head, tears and rain staining my cheeks as the wind whipped around me. "Margo, let me call someone, please . . ."

Her lipstick was smeared, her silk dress ripped, like she'd run and stumbled through the brush. As if, just like me, the truth had hit her square in the face, and she'd had to drop everything.

She had to know for sure, what was out here. What Steph had needed her to see, in the moments before everything went up in smoke.

"He deserves to die." Her voice was corrosive. And I understood. She wanted him to suffer. To die out here. "It should hurt. Like he hurt them. Weren't you listening? He killed Winona—and then he started the fire, to kill Steph and destroy the evidence of what he'd done."

Her eyes were wild now, the monster inside her unleashed, after years and years of waiting. I knew what Margo was like when she got angry—I knew she was dangerous.

And there was nothing more dangerous than someone with nothing left to lose.

"Move out of the way, Greer. Let me finish this. Don't you want justice, finally? He's the one who did all of this. He burned this place to the ground."

I squeezed my eyes shut, bracing myself. Finally, it was time.

"No, please. Hold on." Whatever I said next would be like the final step over a cliff. No coming back.

"It wasn't him," I said, raising my gaze to meet hers.

CHAPTER THIRTY-SIX

THEN

Minutes Before the Fire

I almost turned back around, to search the beach for Steph. But then I heard her—I heard both of them, just up the trail, headed straight for the Barn.

Steph and Margo.

I was sober and panicked immediately, as I felt the weight of all the stupid, reckless things I'd said to her. How angry she'd made me.

What had I done?

Everything was going wrong, even more than it already had. I was supposed to be the easy, affable one. I was supposed to say yes to Steph, give her what she wanted. Margo was the difficult, needy friend—not me.

But I'd cracked. They'd both pushed me too far, and I'd cracked. All the pressure, all the guilt, had fallen on me like a boulder, and every dark, terrible thought had come rushing out of me like blood from a head wound.

Though they were too far away for me to make out their words, it wasn't hard to imagine their current conversation—

Steph would be telling Margo everything I'd just said. That I'd blamed her for every bad thing that had happened this summer. She was probably saying I was fucked in the head, absolutely unhinged. And Margo would be agreeing, saying *I told you she was weird.* God, they were probably already making new plans, reworking the blueprints of the next six months. Excising me completely—the bitchy, stuck-up heiress that neither of them liked all that much anyway.

Was it all over before it had even begun?

I had to fix this. That awful, nervous feeling was creeping over my skin like a spider. I could not be trapped here. I had to go after her. After both of them.

A light hand on my arm made me jump.

"Are you okay?" Chelsea's voice was so quiet, so kind, that I thought it couldn't really have been her. On her face, I saw none of the judgment or hostility I'd been expecting. Instead, she just looked tired and worried. She looked like the girl I'd known for twenty-two years.

"No," I said simply, running a hand over my face. "I'm not. Steph went with Margo—it's all falling apart."

She furrowed her brow. "What's falling apart?"

"Everything," I said, tears blurring my vision, the vodka making my lips loose. "I can't move without her, but she picked Margo, of course she picked Margo, and—"

It was all out of my mouth before I realized what I'd just admitted. After a beat of silence, I dared to look at Chelsea. Her jaw was open, and she was gaping at me, her mouth sagging like a dead fish.

"What are you talking about?"

My throat tightened. There was no going back now. She'd

find out soon enough anyway. "I'm, um—moving to Atlanta. Next week. Me and Steph are going to be roommates. Or we're supposed to be, as long as . . ." I shook my head. "I just need to do something else for a while. Something different. I think . . . I'm not sure if this is what I want. At least not forever."

The betraying words hung between us for an exceptionally long time, and I felt like I'd invoked an ancient curse by saying them out loud. That any moment, the ground would open beneath us, the locusts would appear, the true end would make itself known.

None of these things happened. Instead, Chelsea gave me a stiff nod, her cold blue eyes staring right through me. "Why didn't you tell me?"

"Because you would have told me it was stupid."

"It is stupid," she confirmed, flipping her braids back over her shoulders. "But I can't stop you from being stupid. I would rather know than . . ." She trailed off, looked up at the sky. "Be kept in the dark."

"I didn't want you to tell anyone."

Chelsea huffed a laugh, but there was no humor in it. "I'm not a narc. I wouldn't tell your mom. I'm your best friend." We both heard the real question, unspoken between us: *Aren't I?*

"It just kind of happened," I explained, eyes back on the forest, down the path I knew they were on. "Margo's going on her big trip—or she's supposed to be—and their sublet fell through. I'm getting a job at this cute little bar where Steph's friend works. And it's right down the street from Trevor's place, too."

"Wow," Chelsea breathed, somewhere between exhaustion and wonder. "An apartment, a job, a boyfriend, and a roommate. A whole new life, really." She sniffed, and I didn't want to look at her. I needed to get out of this conversation—I needed to find Steph.

"You know I love you," she said, so sentimental that I wanted to throttle her and hug her at the same time.

Instead, I stilled.

"But I want you to be sure that . . . this . . . is safe."

"Safe?" I said, before I could stop myself. It was not the adjective I'd been expecting. "Is what safe?"

"Steph." She said it simply, with no inflection, like it was the most obvious thing in the world.

"Chels, listen," I said. The urge to throttle her had amped up. "I'm sorry I didn't know how to tell you. But I can't—I don't want to do this right now, okay? I need to talk to her."

"She's dark, Greer. There's something wrong with her." She crossed her arms over herself, pausing to listen to the birds chattering over our heads. "Don't tell me you haven't noticed what she's been like the past couple of weeks. I don't trust her. She's as bad as Margo. She's just better at hiding it."

"You're jealous." It was mean, but I didn't like how close she was getting. I didn't like that she was saying exactly what I'd been afraid of. Because I knew—without a shadow of a doubt—just how dark Steph could truly be.

And I didn't care. I needed her anyway.

Chelsea gave me a look that was impossibly patient. "This isn't about jealousy. I'm trying to help you."

The sane, normal part of me believed her. It really did. But the new ugly and monstrous part of me exploded before I even knew what I was doing. "I don't need your fucking help. I need you to leave me alone and let me live my life."

Chelsea's nose twitched. "I'm not trying to start an argument with you, but she's going to hurt you–"

"Then go." The monster was speaking of its own accord. I was so fucking tired, absolutely run ragged, by her attempts to control my life. First with Wes, now with this. Even if she was right about Steph–she didn't get to decide what was best for *me*. "My life has nothing to do with you, okay?"

Chelsea brought a hand to her face like I'd slapped her. "You've changed. I don't even recognize you anymore."

She was right. I was different. I had changed. And I had nothing left to say. So, I turned toward the woods, away from her, to make sure I did what needed to be done. Before it was too late.

A cover of clouds had stolen the stars, making the walk darker than I would have liked. I could tell exactly where they were headed, when they turned right at the fork in the path. The only other thing in that direction, before the woods became too dense and wild for hiking trails, was the Barn. I could hear the two of them, fifty or so feet in front of me, talking just quietly enough that I knew they were speaking, but I couldn't make out any of the words.

I knew this path inside and out–I could walk it blindfolded. But there was still something so eerie, being out here alone. A part of me wished I'd gone to find Trevor first, but I hadn't wanted to drag him into this. He would have told me to not worry about them, to come back to the party. To figure it out tomorrow.

I didn't have tomorrow, though. I only had tonight. One final chance to seal my fate.

The thunder crackled once, violently, so hard it made me nearly jump out of my skin. I'd seen my share of summer storms in my years at the Cove, but this summer had been unseasonably dry. It hadn't rained in weeks, and the leaves were so dry they crumbled like sand beneath my feet.

But the sky didn't open up to rain. At least not yet. I was close to the Barn now, but with the wind and the storm beginning to move, I could no longer hear Steph or Margo. They were too far ahead. A twig snapped behind me, and I spun around, heart hammering.

It was so, so dark. I knew that the Phantom was somewhere ahead of me, stumbling through the brush. If anyone had the advantage tonight, it was me.

But then another twig snapped, and my chest seized. Hot, drunk panic raced through my veins, and I groped blindly in my bag for my phone, desperate for a flashlight.

It wasn't there. Dimly, I could picture it–stuck into the charger, safe back at Black Bass. The wind whipped through the trees, blowing my hair into my face, temporarily blinding me.

I reached into the depths of my bag, my hands landing on something long and rectangular. Then I remembered–my mom's lighter. I'd grabbed it from Steph the night we'd snuck into her cabin. I hadn't put it back.

I gripped it protectively, like it was my only line of defense at whatever was behind me.

"Hello?" I said to no one, spinning in a circle, trying to catch a glimpse of movement or light. Distantly, I heard a laugh–maybe a scream. I wasn't sure. The stars were hidden by the fog, and I couldn't see anything. I felt as trapped as I had in the wine cellar–unsure if I'd ever see light again.

With shaky hands, I thumbed the lighter, trying desperately to get it to strike. I held it close to my face, the heat of the flame warming my cheek. "Who's there?" I croaked, though I heard nothing, saw no one.

All at once, the sky split open in warning, and the thunder shot through my very heart. There was no time for me to think about it; no time for me to register the action before the moment had already passed me by.

No chance to plan, prepare, make things right. No way to go back in time. No choice.

It was shock. It was nature, seizing control. Maybe–in one way or another–an act of God, after all.

The lighter slipped from my hand, onto the dry, brittle earth. I closed my eyes, but not before the forest ignited at my feet.

CHAPTER THIRTY-SEVEN

NOW

It was so quiet, though I could feel it in the air; the weight of the confession, after all this time, lifted from me, swirling with the impending storm.

I glanced down at the dirt, the flowers—planted by my mother, I knew now, in some quiet repentance—tethering me to the ground, keeping me afloat. Beside me, Rig was out cold.

"I started the fire. It was all my fault, but—"

Thunder boomed throughout the forest, and Margo's sneer was vicious with hatred and a dangerous promise. She took a single step toward me—and then, her features went slack. She dropped to the earth like a lead weight, and I looked around wildly, but the woods were quiet now, and unnaturally still.

Then, I saw him. Wes, on the other side of the clearing. He'd heard our screams and come running. Relief flooded me, like nothing I'd ever felt. "Wes, thank *God*—please, get someone, get Chels, we need to call nine-one-one right now, there's something wrong with . . ."

My words tapered off when I realized he wasn't moving

toward Margo, toward any of us. It may have been the shadows playing tricks on me, but I thought he might have been smiling. My arms prickled with an unnamed fear, making me shiver.

And then I realized, what my body had sensed before my brain had caught up. He was holding a gun of his own.

"Wes?" I said again, less confident now. A new thought sliced through me, violent and without warning, like steel in my gut. "Was that–did you–did you shoot her?" When he didn't answer, I made myself ask, "Did you follow Margo out here?"

He was crossing toward me now. So slow. So unbothered. Like we had all the time in the world.

"No. I followed *you*."

His words and expression were calm. Entirely at ease. He was passing the gun back and forth between his hands like it was a football. But I was sure I could see it in his eyes–excitement. Then his mouth quirked up, and he *laughed*. He actually laughed.

He was happy. How was he happy? Wes had just shot Margo, and he was happy about it. Nothing made sense, and I felt dizzy. I had my knees in the dirt, but I reached around blindly, desperate for something to lean on.

"What's going on? What are you doing?"

Margo gasped, then went still. Tears blurred my vision, and I crawled over Winona's desecrated grave to the sound of her voice, scrabbling through the dirt.

"You're all right," came Wes's voice, much closer now, and a chill shot up my spine. "Stand up. You're just fine. Don't worry, I've got you."

All I wanted was to get to Margo, feel her pulse. I didn't know where he'd hit her–she might be dying. She might be dead.

I stood up slowly, on shaky legs, feeling the heat of Wes's gaze on the side of my face, sensing the gun hanging at his side.

He took another step, and I flinched, almost falling back again. But his focus was on Margo now, too. He pressed the toe of his shoe into her back, and I stiffened. She stayed quiet, motionless, as he walked around her slowly, like a predator assessing his prey.

After an unbearable few moments, his chin dipped in a nod. "This actually makes things much easier."

"What?" I whispered. "Makes what easier?"

"It's perfect, actually. You did great. Here's what happened: I heard you scream and ran to find you. Margo had just attacked Rig. You tried to stop her, but you couldn't. She was having some kind of breakdown. I got here just in time, and I shot her. Subdued her, so she couldn't hurt you. Makes all the sense in the world." He gave me a crooked grin. "Don't worry. I protected you then, and I will again now."

All I could hear was the steady drumbeat of my pulse, the cicadas singing.

"Then? What do you mean—from what?"

He took a step closer to me, crowding me against the tree at the very edge of the bluffs. My back bumped uncomfortably into the trunk.

"All of it. I saw you that night, in the woods. I saw you drop the lighter."

My jaw trembled, but I made myself keep my eyes on him. "You knew? Why didn't you say anything, why didn't you—"

"Didn't you read my letter?"

"What?"

Wes was so close now, I could smell the cool mint of his breath.

"My email. On the anniversary of the fire. You didn't read it?" There was a sour note of surprise laced in his words. His smile faltered.

You fucking idiot, I said in my head. Because of course I hadn't read it.

"What did it say, Wes?" I said his name on a choke.

"I told you that it didn't matter. I love you, and you love me, and that I did it all for you. That I would be here, waiting when you were ready to come back." He pulled gently on a strand of hair that had whipped across my face, tucking it back behind my ear. "They all said you wouldn't come back. But I knew. I've always known."

My stomach lurched at the touch of his fingers on my face. "What are you– Wait, you did what for me?"

"I protected you," he said again. "From her."

And that's when I understood. When the awful, bitter truth finally surged through me like lightning.

"No," I said through a sob. "No. Please."

Wes raised his hand, and I flinched, but he only put it on the tree beside my head, using it as leverage to lean closer. "I heard you talking to Chelsea that night, at the beach. I heard you tell her that you were leaving. That Steph was taking you away."

I shook my hand, frantic and claustrophobic. I could feel his hot breath burning my cheek. "She wasn't taking me away. It was my choice."

He wasn't listening. No, he was only gathering steam. "So when you took off after that bitch in the woods, I followed you. I just wanted to talk. To set you straight. She brainwashed you, manipulated you into thinking there was something better out there. But you belong here, with me."

Icy fear wrapped around me, nearly suffocating me. I had heard someone that night, behind me in the woods. A different Phantom.

That had been my fatal mistake. Believing that I had control of the problem. That it was Steph alone I needed to keep my eye on. That summer, I'd hardly thought of Wes at all. But he'd been thinking about me. *Watching* me.

"Why didn't you say anything?"

"Why didn't you?" he countered. "I saw you jump, when the lightning struck. I stumbled back, and I knew you heard me. I didn't want to scare you. But then you pulled out the lighter. I was going to warn you. But then—well, you know what happened next.

"The woods were on fire, there was smoke everywhere, and I couldn't see you at all. I called your name, but you'd disappeared, and I was about to run back to the beach to look for you. To save you. But that's when I saw her."

The darkness that flickered across Wes's face was unlike anything I'd ever seen before.

"She was stumbling around in the woods. Drunk and pathetic. That's when I had the idea. I knew what I had to do."

The tears were streaming from my face, dripping onto my shirt. I couldn't move, couldn't speak.

"She was going to ruin everything. Ruin *you*. All of our plans. Everything your family built, everything we were going to build together. But I made it fast. In the end, it really wasn't so bad. Not like it could have been. She died quickly. So quickly that she probably didn't even feel it. Nothing like dying from a fire. It was more of a mercy than anything."

And then over Wes's shoulder, I saw Margo move. Just a fraction of an inch. I forced myself to keep my eyes on him. I had to keep him talking, even if every cell in my body was demanding that I push him away and run like hell.

"But I left anyway. You didn't stop me from leaving." My breath hitched. "I'm still ruined."

A slight dip of his head, as if in agreement. "That's what you have me for, Greer. Don't you get it? You're so–naive. You're too trusting. I protected you from her, and from him, and you still left."

I blinked at him, tears clouding my vision at the corners. "What do you mean, you protected me from *him*?"

He clicked his tongue, frustrated now. "It was embarrassing, really. How obsessed you were. I couldn't believe you actually broke up with me for some loser like Trevor fucking Townsend. It was such a cliché, wasn't it? Misguided girl breaks up with the love of her life, chasing the shiny object that will only hurt her. And that's exactly what happened, isn't it? He hurt you."

"I didn't break up with you for Trevor," I said, because I was too horrified to say anything else.

"He had nothing going for him," he said, ignoring me. "I did everything I could to make you see that. He wasn't cut out for this. For you."

"What are you saying? What do you mean you . . ."

And then the realization slammed into me, so staggering my knees almost buckled. Everything strange that happened down at the waterfront that summer–the canoes, the life jackets. Steph had been insistent that it hadn't been her who'd done those things.

Back then, I didn't know what to believe. But now I understood. About that, at least, she'd been telling the truth.

"It was you? You were the one who . . . tried to drown those little girls?"

He shook his head, impatient now. "No one drowned. I was just trying to show you that he wasn't good enough for you. He sunk his claws in you, and I had to step in. Show you his true colors. He's careless, Greer. Careless with Dread's Cove, and careless with you. He never could have taken care of you the way I did. Don't you get that?"

He laughed, and it was tinged with a mania that made my stomach clench. "And then, well, when your mom decided to close early, I felt bad—really, I did. But it was for the best. Trevor would finally have to pack it up and leave, and things would go back to normal. We could finally go back to normal."

A dark cloud settled behind his eyes. "Even though I took care of everything, you left anyway." He gave me a blazing look. "But I forgive you. You came back, and that's all that matters."

Panic slithered up my spine, but I made myself hold his stare. Behind him, Margo was trying to stand, much too slowly. I groped in the dark for another question, anything to drag this out. "So then why all those messages? *YOU WILL PAY*, breaking into my cabin? *LEAVE, BITCH?* Were you just trying to fuck with me?"

He furrowed his brow, and I saw the smallest glimpse of uncertainty pass over his features. "That wasn't me. Why would I try to scare you off?" He ran a light finger over the shell of my ear, down my jaw, before resting his hand around the base of my throat. "Everything is perfect now. We can get rid of Margo. We'll say she was overwhelmed by all her feelings of being back here, that she couldn't handle the grief of remembering her friend's tragic death. She lost her mind."

For the length of a heartbeat, I actually recognized him. I thought of a hundred nights all at once, lying in the grass, planning our futures together. My head resting on his chest, his fingers laced in my hair. But it was sour now, stale. Rotten to the core.

"What about Chelsea?" I asked wildly, just to keep him talking.

"What about her?"

"I mean—aren't you guys together? Nadine said—"

He laughed, the sound low and cruel. "No. Of course not. It's always been you. And now, we can finally be together," he crooned. I couldn't stop it; I turned my head and heaved, his hot breath on my face making me nauseated. "The way it was supposed to be."

His hand moved slowly down the front of my body like a caress until he had one finger pressed into my sternum. For a moment, he didn't move. Only his eyes flickered back and forth across the words on my T-shirt: *Powell's Fly-Fishing. Boulder, CO.*

"This is his," he said, so quietly I could hardly hear him through the press of the rain. I stiffened, my back going ramrod straight. I was wearing the shirt I'd put on this morning in Trevor's room, in lieu of my own. The one I'd thrown on again without thinking after my nap.

We stared at each other for a long, awful moment. Then his hands were both around my throat again, crushing my windpipe.

I tried to push him away, but he was too strong. "I did all of this *for you*, and this is how you thank me?" The world began to go out of focus. His grip only grew tighter.

My hands were scrabbling at him, but I could feel my strength slipping away. "Please," I garbled through broken breaths. "I didn't–it's not his."

I couldn't see Margo anymore; I couldn't see anything. I just had to hope–with everything I had left–that she was there.

That she would end this.

"It's you and me," I forced out, with all the air I could manage, and he loosened his grip, just barely. But it was enough.

Something stirred in the depths, and I saw the Wes I knew for another fleeting second. It gave me the will to lift my own hand, slowly, so that he could track the motion, and raise it just enough to graze his chin.

When he leaned into my touch, I knew I had him. His hands fell away like he'd just been waiting for the magic words. For our long-lost promise, said now like an oath.

"It's you and me," I breathed again, quiet enough that he had to lean in even closer, our faces now inches apart. "It always has been. I'm so sorry. I haven't done enough to show you. But I will. Let me show you how much I love you, Wes."

He pressed his forehead to mine, both of ours sticky with rain and sweat, and I made myself finish my final performance. The best of my life. I didn't pull away, even though every part of me was screaming, *RUN. ESCAPE. DANGER.*

Instead, I pressed my lips to his, just as Margo pulled the trigger.

And then he fell.

CHAPTER THIRTY-EIGHT

NOW

It wasn't long before Trevor and Chelsea came looking.

They'd just started down the trail toward the Barn when they heard the gunshot, worried that something was wrong when none of us showed up to dinner. After that, they ran. Chelsea, back to the mess hall, to get the sheriff. Trevor, toward us. Toward me.

It was only minutes before they plowed their way down the path. The streams of light were twisting erratically through the darkness. I could just make out Sheriff Ramon's badge, illuminated by the glow of the moon, now peeking through the clouds again. The rain had finally slowed. The storm was over before it began.

"Over here," I called.

In a different world, it would have been Stephanie Bennett leading the charge tonight. Calling the shots. Her natural instincts to lead, to be listened to. Or my mother, perhaps. Anita Olsen, whose very heart lived and beat for this place. Who would have done anything for the people she cared about.

But they were both gone now, so the role fell to me. I took it in stride—the very last thing I had left to give either of them.

"You need to call in for more help," I said into the night, my voice carrying through the trees. "There's a body here."

As they exhumed Winona Hayes's body, it finally sunk in. The sinister, long-buried truth of Dread's Cove. Both Stephanie Bennett and her mother had their lives cut short, brutally and suddenly, by people they thought they could trust.

Chelsea was absolutely wild, the way she cried and moaned over her dad's limp body in the grass. Her banshee screams had echoed across the lake, even as the paramedics assured her he'd be fine, that it was only a concussion.

In the end, Margo Pierce wasn't a killer. She'd hit Rig hard enough to knock him out but not enough to do any lasting damage. He would make a full recovery, except for a nasty gash on the back of his head that would need stitches.

Rig turned himself over to the sheriff as soon as he came to. He told him that he had information on the disappearance of Winona Hayes, that he had a hand in her death, in the concealment of her body for nearly thirty years. He said he was finally ready to take responsibility.

Wes didn't turn himself over, but he didn't have to. Margo and I did it for him.

There was a pit in my stomach as I watched them both leave that night in the ambulances—Wes with police escort.

I'd always seen the similarities between them. Tonight, all I could see were the differences. Rig had made a million mistakes; his silence had eaten him away from the inside out. But his heart, his humanity, was salvageable from beneath the wreckage and ruin. I didn't know how long it would take me to be able to forgive him.

But I knew, someday, I would. And I knew that he would forgive me, too.

Wes had never been a good guy. That would haunt me, always. Knowing what he was, what he'd done, and how close we'd all been to him. Knowing that I'd slept beside him, loved him. Trusted him completely. Believed in his inherent goodness, and selflessness. All weekend, his friendship had felt like one of the only real things I had left. But even that had been a lie.

The very worst thing was knowing that my mother had kept so many secrets from me. Secrets I'd never be able to ask her about. But I'd kept my share of secrets, too; from her, and from everyone. Secrets I no longer wanted to be chained to. And secrets I no longer had to bear alone.

I'd made plenty of mistakes. I'd hurt the people I loved. Every last one. I'd been immeasurably selfish. Tonight, though, I'd finally owned up to some of them. And for the first time in so long, I was proud of myself. Proud to be an Olsen, of the legacy I was contributing to.

For the first time in years, I felt like maybe I deserved it.

I watched from a distance as they strapped Margo onto a gurney. Trevor had gone to get me a bottle of water, and I stood just at the edges of the chaos, leaning against Sheriff Ramon's cruiser.

"Miss Greer?"

I froze. I hadn't been called that in five years.

Steeling myself with a deep breath, I forced myself to look at Kendall. She looked pale and scared, but I was once again shocked by how old she'd gotten since I'd last seen her. Tonight, she was wearing a pink silk dress and gold hoops, her hair slicked back into a sleek ponytail. There were mascara streaks under her eyes like she'd been crying.

Seeing her this way made my chest ache, and my old protective senses kicked in. "Kendall, are you okay?"

We hadn't spoken all weekend. I'd assumed she hated me. I'd never fulfilled my promise–I'd never written her a single letter.

Her lip quivered, and I reached for her, wrapping my clammy hand around her wrist. It was like the dam broke then, and she leaned forward, crying onto my shoulder. She blubbered something, but I couldn't understand. Finally, I made out the two words she was repeating: *I'm sorry.*

Puzzled, I pulled back from her, keeping my hands on her shoulders so she couldn't disappear. "Why are you sorry? What happened?"

She rubbed the heel of her hand against her eye, smearing more black makeup down her face. "I should have told you. I know who's been breaking into your cabin."

I'd almost forgotten, in the chaos of the last hour, that Wes had denied the graffiti on Black Bass, sneaking into the cabin. In the moment, I hadn't had time to fully process it. But it wouldn't have made sense, would it? He hadn't been trying to push me away at all.

He wanted, more than anything, for me to stay. He'd been willing to kill for it.

I suppressed a shiver and made myself focus on Kendall. Her face was wracked with guilt. In the back of my brain, I wondered if I should be angry at her. But I was too numb to process any more surprises from the people I cared about.

"It's okay. You had every right to be mad at me. I broke my promise. I'm so, so sorry."

Confusion clouded her features. "I don't–" Her mouth popped open. "Oh my gosh, *no*, it wasn't me. I never would have done that to you. No, it was Carter Banks."

It took my brain several seconds to catch up. To place the name. "Carter Banks? Was he–"

"One of the boys who got lost in the woods," she finished for me. "He was looking for the Phantom and got stuck in the thunderstorm. Your mom sent him home the next day."

The memories came rushing back. That awful, rain-soaked night–searching in the dark, hoping beyond hope that we wouldn't find something terrible.

Not unlike tonight.

"Wait, what do you mean? He's . . ." I couldn't finish the sentence. I had no idea what had become of Carter Banks.

Kendall bit her lip. "Getting kicked out of Dread's Cove was sort of a last straw for Carter's parents. They sent him to boarding school after that. It was hell, apparently. He blamed your mom for all of it. He blamed . . . all of you, really. So, when he heard about the Cove reopening, he got a ticket, and he wanted to come here and . . . mess with you guys. See what he could get away with."

"I didn't realize you kept in contact with him all these years."

Her eyes went wide. "No, I didn't. I only came back because I was curious, like everyone. I wanted to see what you'd done with the place. That summer was hard, but–there were good memories, too. A lot of them. Thanks to you. I sat next to him the first night, at dinner. Just by coincidence." Her voice dropped into a whisper. "He had a flask with him, and he got drunk fast. Before dessert even came out. That's when he told me about his plan—he was going to try to scare you and Chelsea. Make you think that the Phantom was back."

She took a labored breath. "He's the one who broke into your cabin and spray-painted Black Bass. I wanted to tell you, but—every time I saw you, it felt like the wrong time, you were so busy with everything, and . . . I couldn't do it. I didn't want to break his confidence. Carter was a good friend to me that summer. Almost as good to me as you."

That explained the strange looks she'd given me these past few days. It wasn't anger or resentment at all. It was fear—concern. For me.

"I'm so, so sorry. I should have told you immediately. He's gone, though. He disappeared when he heard the sirens."

I threw my arms around her. "It's okay," I promised her, and it was. She only wailed in response. I held her for a long time, until she stopped crying.

We promised to stay in touch, for real this time, and I gave her one more bear hug before she went back to her cabin.

As I watched her go, Trevor slipped his warm hand into mine and squeezed. I squeezed back, and for the first time in hours, I found myself smiling. When Sheriff Ramon called me over to take my official statement, I tensed, but Trevor spoke softly into my hair. "You're strong. You're safe. You can do this."

I nodded as tears stung the back of my eyes, and he held my hand an extra second before he let me go. "Come back soon," he whispered.

"I will." This time, I would.

EPILOGUE

ONE YEAR LATER

It was the calm before the storm. The first bus of kids would arrive in exactly two hours. I stood out on the deck, squinting into the fog, and took a deep breath.

I was nervous. More than that, though, I was excited.

But there was still one thing we had left to do.

"Coffee?"

I turned to see Chelsea, who stood in the doorway with two steaming mugs.

"Bless you," I said, and she came to stand with me at the railing. For a long few minutes, we stood in contented silence, watching the sun try to break through the clouds.

"We did it," she whispered. "She'd be so happy." The words were filled with so much emotion that I could barely do more than nod at the water.

The future of Dread's Cove had been precarious for a while. Unfortunately, Rig's recovery had been longer than expected. The doctors suggested chronic stress wasn't helping and recommended he take some time off. So, for the first time in forty years,

Thomas Riggins wasn't spending the summer here. Instead, he was visiting his brothers down in South Georgia. He'd be back before his trial began, later this fall. He was being charged with manslaughter and the concealment of a body.

Chelsea had taken over for her dad immediately, and she'd flourished in the role. She'd proved herself to be who she always had been—loyal, steadfast, with an obnoxious fixation on excellence. As head of operations, those were important traits to have.

I was eternally grateful for her help and support over the past year. The media firestorm had been relentless, but somehow, we'd made it to the other side. This afternoon, we'd welcome no fewer than five hundred campers to our first summer session in six years. It still didn't feel real.

Not everyone had wanted Dread's Cove to reopen, especially after Margo Pierce's shocking tell-all account of the truth behind Steph Bennett's tragic death. And then, of course, what had nearly happened to both of us that night.

It was impressive how quickly Margo been able to put her front-page story together—most of it she'd written in the days after she was released from the hospital. Somehow, Wes hadn't hit any of her vital organs, and she'd made a quick recovery. We still talked, now and then, even though it was hard.

But I was getting much better at hard.

I glanced at Chelsea, who gripped her mug in both hands. She'd cut her hair a few months ago, the curls now short and somehow even wilder, no longer held back by the constraints of braids.

She gave me a soft, sad smile. "Are you ready, then?"

I nodded again, tears coursing down my face before I could even reach for the small container I'd set at my feet.

Today, on the one-year anniversary of her passing, we would spread my mother's ashes.

Chelsea reached for my hand and twined our fingers together. "Anita was a good mom," she said, and I began crying in earnest. "You were so lucky. You *are* so lucky. We both are. Just knowing her makes us lucky. She was the mom I never got to have, and . . ."

She trailed off, wiped her nose on the sleeve of her shirt. I pulled her in, and after only a moment's hesitation, she rested her head on my shoulder. It had taken months and months, but we'd started to tentatively rebuild our friendship as we planned the real reopening of Dread's Cove, together. I was being incredibly careful, and so was she; like if one of us hugged too tight, smiled too wide, it might shatter again.

That was okay, though. Because it felt so much better than pretending.

"I miss her," she said at last.

"I miss her, too." I thought, as I often did, of Steph and Winona. Of all the women who'd been loved and lost at Dread's Cove. How we planned to spend our lives honoring them, in whatever small and big ways we could.

We looked out over the lake for a few long moments, as a mourning dove sang from somewhere I couldn't see. Gingerly, I opened the small container.

"Today is for my mom," I said as I scattered the first handful. "And for yours."

Tears stung my eyes, and as we both took another small handful, the morning's first gust of wind whipped up across the water.

"For the women who made us." My voice cracked, but I made myself continue. "We think of you every day. We always will."

And then, together, we let them go.

Our tears dried as we held each other, and finally, finally, I let myself smile. Like Chelsea had said–*we did it.*

After a while, the door behind us creaked, and we both turned. My smile grew, and my heart leaped in the way it always still did when I saw Trevor. I knew he'd been up since dawn, preparing the waterfront for the first crop of swimmers this afternoon.

He came up behind me, putting one hand on my hip while grabbing my coffee with his other hand. I let my head fall against his chest.

Chelsea rubbed a fist to her eye and checked her watch. "Okay. Are you guys ready to do this?"

"I am," I said.

"We are," I amended.

Trevor pressed a kiss to my temple in agreement.

Slowly–inch by inch and day by day–Dread's Cove, and the people here, had begun to heal the cracks in my heart. Had made me feel worth something again.

For a long time, I had rejected myself. Everything that had made me who I was. I thought I could only live in binaries. A planner, or spontaneous. A good friend, or a bad one. Honest, or a liar.

Innocent, or guilty.

But things had softened around the edges as I'd begun to relearn who I was. I could be more than one thing. I didn't have to decide everything I was, all at once. I could change. I was changing.

I was real. I was here.

And I could stay as long as I liked.

ACKNOWLEDGMENTS

I am profoundly lucky to have so many people to thank. My life has been full to the brim with love, friendship, support, and care. Let's dive in:

Thank you to my incredible agent, Hannah Schofield. I am unbelievably grateful to have you in my corner. Your love for this book since the beginning has meant more to me than I can ever explain. Working with you is such a joy.

Thank you to my amazing editor, Lisa Bonvissuto. Your vision and support for this book have been brilliant, and I cannot overstate how lucky I am to get to work with you. I knew it was going to work out well between us when, on our very first call, you said, "What do you think about *more* romance?"

Thank you to Tara O'Connor, Anna Venckus, Anika Bates, and Emily Osborne at Berkley/PRH.

Thank you to my entire family. I am extraordinarily fortunate to be surrounded by so many people who believe in the power of reading and the importance of writing.

Thank you to my parents, Erin and David Smith, for teaching me to love books from an early age. I'll never be able to thank you enough for all the hours we spent in bookstores and all the pages you let me get in before bedtime.

Thank you to my mother-in-law, Gena Bozeman, and my father-in-law, David Bozeman. Being part of your family is a gift.

I am very confident that, somewhere in heaven, DLS and DBB are listening to live music together. We miss you down here.

Thank you to Jill, Loren, and Georgia Weeks. Thank you to Michele, Brad, Ryan, and Alex Smith.

Thank you to my grandparents Diane Murray, Michael Murray, and James Smith. I can't wait to see you again someday. Thank you to my grandmother Mary Smith, for being an early reader of this book. I love you so much, Gram.

Thank you to Ashlee Latimer, my dearest friend and writing buddy. You've been with this story–and me–since it was the very spark of an idea, and I am so grateful for your unrelenting support.

Thank you to Chandler DeJesus. You're my girl. You already know how much I love you, but I wanted to say it here, too. WIWK?

Thank you to Talia Reinhart. I can't believe we've been friends for twenty years. I know we'll still be talking about books–and hopefully living closer to each other–in another twenty. Thank goodness for that.

Okay, wow. I seriously have *so many* friends to thank and brag about. I could write pages and pages about all of you. A big thank-you and so much love to Austin Witt, Caitlin Chamberlin, Kevin Chamberlin, Grace Josey, Edwin Josey, Madison Paff, Seth Warner, David Ratliff, Lauren Irwin, Nicole Davis, Ashley Gibson, Reagan Vicary, Clark Vicary, Elle Nelson, Cheyenne Ferguson, Mitchell Pearce, McKinley Merritt, and Sally Jernigan.

Thank you to the West Coast *Summer's Never Over* hype team. Y'all are truly the coolest friends. All the love in the world to Gayle Johnson, Blake Johnson, Kate Wildeck, Tyler Wildeck, Colin McClellan, and Jenn McClellan.

Thank you to my teachers. There are so many I could list, but Ted Nakamura and Sandy O'Banion, I'm so lucky to have learned from both of you.

Thank you to all the students I ever had who let me teach you about writing. Remember when we used to write scary stories? There are few things I'm more proud of in my life than the work we did together. I hope that your lives have been beautiful. Know that I think about you often.

And finally, thank you to Bryan, my very own summer camp crush. I cry every time I try to write this. Every now and then, even words aren't quite enough, and this is one of those times. I love you, I love you, I love you. Let's do this forever.

Author photo by Marie Hilla

DARBY BOZEMAN grew up in Portland, Oregon, but she's spent the better part of her adult life in the South. She has a master's in teaching from the University of Georgia, and she taught middle school English for five years. When she's not reading or writing, she loves acting in community theater and discussing pop culture. She lives in Knoxville with her husband, Bryan, and their cat, Claude.

VISIT DARBY BOZEMAN ONLINE

DarbyBozeman.com

DarbyBoze